Praise for Anton du Beke's Sweeping Historical Sagas

'Fans of *The Crown* will adore this wonderful world of glamour, love and drama' – SANTA MONTEFIORE

'Du Beke effectively cuts the glamour and aspiration of the ballroom with the grubby, ghastly side of the war at home' – DAILY MAIL

'You don't need to be a Strictly fan to relish this lively read, its glamour, magic and colourful characters' – LUCY HELLIKER

'A beautiful wartime tale' – JUDY MURRAY

'Heart-breaking, heart-lifting and enchanting' – CAROL KIRKWOOD

'A fabulous novel from the King of the Ballroom' – WOMAN'S WEEKLY

'A compelling, Downtonesque drama with likeable characters and nasty profiteers' – SAGA MAGAZINE

Also by Anton Du Beke

One Enchanted Evening
Moonlight Over Mayfair
A Christmas to Remember
We'll Meet Again
The Ballroom Blitz
The Royal Show

ANTON DU BEKE

The PARIS AFFAIR

ORION

An Orion Paperback
This edition published in Great Britain in 2024 by Orion Fiction
an imprint of The Orion Publishing Group Ltd
Carmelite House, 50 Victoria Embankment
London EC4Y 0DZ

An Hachette UK Company

1 3 5 7 9 10 8 6 4 2

Copyright © Anton Du Beke 2023

The moral right of Anton Du Beke to be identified as
the author of this work has been asserted in accordance
with the Copyright, Designs and Patents Act of 1988.

All rights reserved. No part of this publication may be
reproduced, stored in a retrieval system, or transmitted
in any form or by any means, electronic, mechanical,
photocopying, recording, or otherwise, without the
prior permission of both the copyright owner and the
above publisher of this book.

All the characters in this book are fictitious, and any resemblance
to actual persons, living or dead, is purely coincidental.

A CIP catalogue record for this book is
available from the British Library.

ISBN (Mass Market Paperback) 978 1 3987 1013 9
ISBN (eBook) 978 1 3987 1014 6
ISBN (Audio) 978 1 3987 1015 3

Typeset at The Spartan Press Ltd,
Lymington, Hants

Printed and bound in Great Britain by Clays Ltd,
Elcograf S.p.A.

MIX
Paper from
responsible sources
FSC® C104740

www.orionbooks.co.uk

*As always, to Hannah, Henrietta, and George –
thank you for everything!*

Paris, 1926

The Englishman has danced in clubs before, but none of them quite like this.

There is a different feeling in Paris. He could tell it the moment he stepped out of the train from Calais: something elemental, almost magical in the air. There'd been a valet to receive his suitcase and a car to take him to his digs overlooking the plush Hotel Acacias, where his benefactor has been afforded a room. It was the way the air positively hummed with expectation. The way that, as soon as night-time fell, the City of Lights came alive. How the lobby of the Hotel Acacias was flooded with artistes: writers, photographers, painters and thespians, all of them rushing out to savour the nocturnal Paris air. Not for the first time in his young life, the feeling that he doesn't belong dogs the Englishman through his days. The Paris his patrons are showing him is the Paris of the Moulin Rouge; the Paris of the Folies Bergère; the Paris of Les Acacias, where his benefactor performs, and the Casino de Paris where he is himself to be entered in competition. But these places are so grand that it only serves to remind him of his own lowly upbringing – and this is something the gentleman who brought him here, the son of a French baron, could never understand.

'That's why you need to come to a place like this,' his new

companion says. A Frenchman only a little older than he is, Hugo has the guile of a dancer born to these streets. 'If you come to Paris and you only see the Moulin Rouge, you haven't really come to Paris at all. No, if you come to see the lights, you overlook entirely the *pleasures of the dark*.'

From outside, this place is just a nondescript door between a delicatessen and a cheap riverside restaurant. But Paris is a city of hidden delights, and at the bottom of the narrow stairs the club reveals itself. Even cramped, tiny places like this can pulse with the excitement of the grandest ballroom.

The music from the small orchestra is loud. The lights are low, the air full of smoke.

'What do you think?' Hugo says, as they hover on the dance floor's edge, watching bodies pressed more tightly together than in any ballroom the Englishman has ever seen. No, his eyes are not mistaken; some of the men out there are grasping their partners' buttocks. He allows himself a wry smile. He has seen men slapped for such infractions in the clubs of Soho; here, in Paris, it signifies joy.

'I don't know,' the Englishman says. 'I'm sure Georges would disapprove. He thinks I should be back at digs, resting body and mind. I'm meant to dance tomorrow.'

'You won't dance tomorrow if you don't dance *now*,' Hugo replies, his eyes sparkling as if, in their depths, can be found all the ancient wisdoms of the dancing world. 'You need to embrace tonight. Let tomorrow take care of itself.'

Perhaps the Englishman needed little persuasion after all, for he makes no further protest. Soon, Hugo has vanished into the throng – 'I'll find us partners, *mon ami*, while you find us drinks' – and the Englishman picks his way to the small bar in the corner. The frenetic pace of it tickles his senses. The sound of the singer warbling in a language he does not wholly understand makes it seem yet more exciting and new. He longs to enter the dance floor as he has rarely longed for it before.

And here comes his chance, for when Hugo reappears, trailing from his arm are two young ladies, radiating beauty and life.

'You won't believe this, *mon ami*,' Hugo begins, 'but Hannah here has danced at Les Acacias as well. The perfect partner for the night.'

The first of the girls, her face framed in pure black hair, her almond-shaped eyes wide and playful, extends her hand. Because he is in France, and must do as Georges has taught him, the Englishmen plants a single kiss upon it. 'Charmed.'

'My friend comes from London,' Hugo intervenes. 'Whitechapel, no less. He's to compete at the Casino de Paris. The Exhibition Paris. Very stately, very grand.' And Hugo performs a little box-step, perfectly executed, of course – for Hugo has entered the competitions before, and will himself step onto the dance floor at the Casino de Paris before the week is out. 'But we decided that no amount of grandeur and elegance is enough to get in the mood for dancing. No,' Hugo grins, and turns the second girl – with her golden hair and long, lithe figure – around, 'for that we needed to come to a place like this.'

The Englishman is about to ask, 'Shall we?', but suddenly realises a vital piece of the conversation has been missed. 'The introductions!' he laughs. 'Hannah, please forgive me. It is an honour to make your acquaintance. My name is Ray. Ray Cohen.'

No sooner have the words left his mouth than his friend Hugo has started rolling his eyes. 'Ray,' he says, gently chastising, 'you forget who you are.' He turns to the girls. 'My friend, here, is having something of – what shall we call it? – a *crisis of faith* in his place as a dancer. This summer, he tours the Continent in the company of none other than Georges de la Motte. Acolyte to the great dancer of our age! Yes, this devilishly handsome young man has been chosen for great things – and the wonder begins this week, at the Casino de Paris. And yet ... he still pretends he is not truly part of it.' Hugo winks at the Englishman now. 'Ray Cohen would appreciate a dance club as wild as this, but tomorrow you must step into High Society and impress them with your elegance and poise. You need a better name for this world, my friend. You need to start using the name Georges has devised for you. And so ...'

Hugo takes the Englishman's hand in one of his own. In the other, he grips the dark-haired girl.

'Hannah Lindt,' he declares, 'prepare to be taken in hold by my dear friend. Not *Ray Cohen*, but ... Raymond de Guise.'

March 1941

Chapter One

**DISPATCHES FROM THE BUCKINGHAM HOTEL!
NEW YORK TIMES, MARCH 23, 1941**

By Jackson Ford, your man in LONDON

The Buckingham Hotel was once a playground for the rich and beautiful – and so it remains! – but in Modern Times it has become much more. It is at the Buckingham Hotel that Lord James Lasseter proposed to the American heiress Annabelle White. It is at the Buckingham Hotel that King George VI hosted a coterie of Commonwealth dignitaries before the Balfour Declaration of 1926. And yet, since the Fall of France and Great Britain's glorious retreat from Dunkirk in the spring of 1940, the Buckingham Hotel has been transformed: this hotel is no less than a fortress in the heart of London, with shelters ten fathoms deep where its staff and residents endure the nightly bombardments; a place where runaway kings rub shoulders with London chambermaids, where princes from fallen realms gather in the cocktail lounges to pore over the events of their old worlds – and, most crucially of all, a bustling headquarters from which exiled governments seek to marshal the resources of their

7

homelands and, one day, restore honour, freedom and justice to a world blighted by the Nazi menace.

At the very centre of all this is the Buckingham's fêted ballroom, the Grand. For more than a decade, ever since its inception, the Grand has been known as the playground of princes. Now, on any given night, it might be possible to see the retinue of King Zog of Albania dancing with the ladies-in-waiting of the Dutch Queen Wilhelmina; to find members of Charles de Gaulle's Free French government unwinding over cocktails, before stepping onto the dance floor in the arms of one of the hotel's fine troupe of dancers. If a hotel can be said to have a beating heart, the Buckingham's is very clearly located in its ballroom – for it is the lure of the Grand that keeps the hotel's garlanded guests from being tempted to suites at the Dorchester, the Ritz, the Savoy and the Imperial. In the quest for dominance, the Buckingham has forged itself a reputation for celebrating British triumphs in all their many guises, opening its doors on special occasions not just to the esteemed in Society, but also to the refugees who have flocked to Great Britain, to the heroes of Dunkirk and veterans from every Allied nation.

Until a few short months ago, the tumultuous life of the Grand was soundtracked by the world-famous Archie Adams Orchestra. Dignified, talented Archie Adams has provided music in the Grand since long before the rise of Nazism – but, this year, that is all to change, for the esteemed bandleader has announced his retirement. Will a new bandleader ignite a new age of joy and celebration in the Grand? Or will this change in personnel, and indeed reputation, allow the Buckingham's rivals to poach their most valuable guests away?

Only time will tell. But, as Europe burns and war intensifies in the colonies of North Africa, time is one of the many things of which the residents of Great Britain – whether that be the lords and ladies of the Buckingham Hotel, or the chambermaids and kitchen porters that do their bidding – are running short.

The first flush of colour was coming to Berkeley Square. The war was eighteen months old, London pockmarked by craters where bombs had scythed out of the sky, but in Mayfair spring still brought out bright purple crocuses and banks of golden daffodils. Every guest to the Buckingham Hotel was greeted with a vista of such vivid colour that, for fleeting moments, it was possible to imagine there was no war on after all.

By the time the Rolls Royce came to a halt beneath the white colonnade of the hotel exterior, its inhabitants were already enchanted. The doorman, upon striding down the sweeping marble steps to open the car door, met two rotund figures – who, it seemed, could not believe their eyes.

'Mr Allgood,' the doorman began. 'We've been expecting you. I have orders to take you directly to Mr Knave. The Hotel Director is waiting.'

The plump black man who had been the first to step out of the car was nearly fifty years old, dressed in brown pin-stripe trousers and braces. His shirtsleeves were rolled up to the elbow – rather, the doorman thought, like the workmen beavering away on the construction site next door – and the top two buttons of his collar undone. Though the doorman had far too much sense to comment upon it, it seemed to him that the man did not, perhaps, understand the magnitude of the job he was about to undertake. Or perhaps it was simply that he wasn't yet familiar with the ideas of decorum, etiquette and grace that underpinned the Buckingham Hotel. Of course, Mr Allgood *was* American

– and this, perhaps, explained his *laissez-faire* attitude, the way he immediately started chewing on the end of a cigar as he took in the hotel's grand façade.

'Gee, this place is really something,' Max began. His accent was flavoured with all of the various corners of the United States where he'd spent his years: New Orleans and Chicago, and latterly the streets of Harlem, New York. The Buckingham had a solid reputation with the wealthier residents of New York. Indeed, one of their number – a Mr John Hastings – had become the hotel's majority shareholder only last year. 'Hey, Daisy,' he called back, 'take a look at this. Buckingham Hotel? It might as well be Buckingham Palace.'

The second figure who stepped out of the Rolls Royce was not quite as rotund as Max but bore a strikingly similar look. Well, thought the doorman, husbands and wives often grew together. Daisy Allgood stood a little taller than her husband, and was perhaps five or six years younger – placing her squarely in her mid-forties. At least she was dressed in more appropriate attire: her floral dress was a melange of springtime greens and yellows, the diamond ring on her finger was quite startling.

The doorman began to help the Rolls Royce driver unload the boot of the car, depositing various suitcases and leather bags onto the stonework beneath the colonnade, from where the concierges would soon deliver them to the waiting suite. But the moment the penultimate bag came out, Max Allgood spun round and, with his cigar still trailing from his lips, retrieved the final case himself. This, it turned out, was no suitcase full of clothes. The long black case housed the most prized possession in Max Allgood's life: his trombone, Lucille.

'Forgive me, but she'll have to come with me. I don't let her out of my sight, you see. It's bad luck.'

'Then let's go and see Mr Knave.'

Max's eyes were full of wonder as he waddled beneath the colonnade and to the white marble steps. 'This is really going to be something, ain't it?' he said to Daisy. Then, directing his attention to the trombone case, he added, 'Ain't it, Lucille? To play in a grand old place like this? To have all those eyes on you? Isn't this where Churchill comes?'

Daisy's laugh was bold and beautiful. 'I fancy Mr Churchill's got bigger things to be doing than perfecting his foxtrot, ain't he?'

At this, Max started laughing too. 'Might be a foxtrot's what the old battler needs. Free up some of those tangles in his head. Figure out a way to win this thing.'

'I can't believe we're here, Max.'

'I know,' Max said, voice dropping to a whisper now, 'but just keep your head. Let's not upset the applecart. Our luck's finally changing. Daisy, we've finally got a *home*.'

The doorman gave a loud, deliberate cough.

'I'm sorry, sir,' he announced, 'but you'll have to follow me. That's the guest entrance.'

Max and Daisy looked quizzically at each other, as if they only half-understood.

'You'll get the hang of it, sir. I'm afraid we do things a little differently in the old world. If you'll follow me, our door's just along the mews here. As a matter of fact, it hasn't long been reopened – all the devastation next door rather put a dent in our sturdy old hotel. But it's safe enough now. Come on, I'll show you myself.'

In the Hotel Director's office, Walter Knave awaited the arrival of his new bandleader with a mounting sense of unease. Under ordinary circumstances, a post as important as this might be left to the Hotel Director himself to fill – but Max Allgood came at the personal recommendation of both Archie Adams, whose retirement had created the vacancy in the ballroom, and the head of the Hotel Board, whose contacts back home spoke of Max Allgood in the same venerated tones that they spoke of Louis Armstrong, Joe 'King' Oliver and Duke Ellington himself. 'Trust me,' John Hastings had said, 'a punt on Max has got to be worth it. Archie's carried us this far, but we need someone who won't suffer by comparison. Somebody a little bit different.' At eighty-three years old, Walter Knave had long ago learned that there were certain things in life about which he did not know best. Music was one of them, and so was dance. But there were other things about which a stately, experienced Englishmen was certain to know better than any young interloper – and the norms of decorum, dignity and deference were surely prominent among them. And yet…

'The amazing thing is that he's right here, playing at clubs in Bristol,' John Hastings had continued. 'He was on the Continent when the war came. A summer residency in Paris, then touring along the Côte d'Azur. Built himself a little orchestra of musicians culled from the clubs in La Pigalle. They've all gone to war now, but Max is right here, playing his trombone for bed and board. It's an opportunity that mustn't be missed.'

Walter Knave was, of course, of a much older generation – old enough that, though he was pained to admit it, he had wondered if it was appropriate for an establishment as esteemed as the Buckingham to have its orchestra led not only by a black man, but by an *American* at that. Yes, that seemed to Walter the important thing: that a man from the New World be invited into this bastion of the old seemed *improper* somehow. There would be complaints about this – of that, he was certain. The question was how much the old tenets of elegance, etiquette and Englishness counted in an age of upheaval such as the one they had been toiling through since war began. It was true that the hotel was changed – with so many guests from the Continent now taking up permanent stations in its rooms and suites – but was it changed so much that a man of such lowly heritage might be accepted as leader of the Grand? The ballroom, of course, was the Buckingham's crown jewel. It was the thing that enticed the most valuable guests away from London's other luxury hotels. Archie's departure had given those other hotels an opening; just like generals of war, their directors would have sensed an opportunity for attack.

Such were his thoughts when a gentle tapping at his office door announced Max Allgood's appearance.

'Enter,' Walter croaked, and shuffled round to the front of his desk. It was hard not to feel like an octogenarian in moments like these. He would just have to get the cut of the man's jib, try to understand him a little (as far as an Englishman could understand an American, at any rate), and make sure they had a good, cordial relationship. First impressions were important.

'Mr Knave,' the hotel doorman began, 'might I introduce Mr Max Allgood?'

'And I'm pleased to meet ya!' Max beamed. It was remarkable how quickly a man of his girth – and questionable gait, for he seemed to be ever-so-slightly bow-legged as he bouldered into the office – could move. In moments, he was facing Walter, spitting out his cigar into the porcelain ash tray provided, and grasping the older man by the hand. Max's fist rather dwarfed Walter's own.

Walter waited until the handshake – an elaborate performance, with at least three acts – was over before he lifted his owlish, bespectacled eyes to the doorman and said, 'Thank you, John. And perhaps you can kindly ask Mrs Allgood to wait in reception?

We shan't be long. Then I can show both our new residents the Grand.'

At the suggestion that Daisy be escorted away, Max blurted out, 'Now hang on, Mr Knave. You wouldn't want me to be without my representation, would you?' Walter stared at him, as if not quite comprehending. 'Daisy's my manager, no less. Where I go, she goes. She's the best damn manager I ever had – not that that's saying much, the last lot were thieves and … *pirates*.'

Walter heaved a sigh. Times were, indeed, changing if a lady was business manager to a musician of Max Allgood's stature. But change, Walter was repeatedly being told, was the very substance of life. As a matter of fact, it was happening all around him. His new Head of Housekeeping, Nancy de Guise, was not only a married woman, but a pregnant one at that. Even more remarkably, she intended to keep her job when she became a mother, a date which was rapidly approaching.

The problem that kept him up at night was: how much *change* could his esteemed clientele really accept? The guests at luxury hotels like the Buckingham needed to be indulged and looked after; foisting change on them was not good for business.

But here he was: an Englishman working at the behest of his American director; the war upended everything.

Inviting Daisy to sit alongside Max, he began, 'Well, Mr Allgood. It seems we both have some adjusting to do. You come, of course, highly recommended. The Head of our Board's cousins happened to see you performing at this Cotton Club in New York, some years ago. It seems you made a lasting impression. And then there's Archie…'

'Oh, old Mr Adams!' Max beamed. 'Where is the old rogue? I'd like to shake that man by the hand.'

Old rogue? thought Walter. It must have been one of those strange American idioms he sometimes heard, because Archie was nothing of the sort. A more gentlemanly man could not be imagined. Inwardly, he smarted: this Max Allgood clearly hadn't grown up among men of etiquette; he would have to learn quickly, if he was to thrive in the Grand.

'I'm told that orchestras are a little like the regiments of an army. They depend upon a delicate balance of leadership and respect. The musicians in our Orchestra adore Archie Adams. They are, for want of a better word, indebted to him. He's the one who saw their talent, brought them together, and found them this inestimable home in the Grand. I'm told that, under other circumstances, the Orchestra would follow Archie wherever he went. But Mr Adams leaves us for the quiet contentment of retirement, and the lady who is to become his wife – the lady, I might point out, who ran our Housekeeping department for many long years. It stands clear, then, that the Orchestra cannot follow. They have all been promised work here for as long as it lasts, but they need new leadership.'

'And here I am,' grinned Max. 'Now, Walt, I know what you're trying to tell me—'

Again, Walter smarted. 'Please, Mr Allgood. We respect the civilities here. My name is Mr Knave.'

Max was about to blurt out an apology tinged in laughter, but Daisy – clearly a good representative – saw what was to come and intervened. 'Mr Knave, rest assured: Max has led a number of different orchestras in his time, and studied under the very best. The Creole Jazz Band back in Chicago. Cab Calloway's Orchestra. Our own various outfits, over the years. Max knows *people*. We can make this work.'

'We've got a couple of promising young musicians waiting in the wings too,' Max chipped in.

There was silence in the room, until at last, Daisy said,

'But that's for another season. Some seasons down the line, I should think.'

'One thing I must make abundantly clear,' said Walter, with a new severity in his tone. 'This is the Buckingham Hotel: the seat of exiled kings and fallen governments. I may not know music, but I know this hotel – and I take the business of its survival very seriously indeed. I need to know you can rally the musicians Mr Adams leaves behind, Mr Allgood. I need to know you can win their trust and respect – and, dare I say it, their *love* – swiftly.' He paused. 'I need to know you can behave in a way fitting to the longstanding, valuable reputation of this hotel.'

The way Max's eyes goggled hardly filled Walter with the confidence for which he was grappling – and yet, what more could he say? 'We have high hopes for you. Please don't let us down.'

'Mr Knave,' Max declared, 'I have high hopes for me as well.'

'Well, then,' said Walter. 'Follow me, and I'll show you your new home.'

As Walter made his way through the office door and into the hallway beyond, Max picked up his trombone and whispered to Daisy from the side of his mouth: 'How did that go?'

'Well, we didn't blow it yet. But we've got to keep that promise, Max. And you know, as well as I do, how it's always ended before.'

Max gave a crumpled smile. 'Darling, we're in London now. It's different here. They got *grace*.'

By now, Walter Knave was picking his way into the Buckingham's opulent reception hall, through the check-in desks and past the golden elevator cage. On the other side stood a marble archway, decorated in a florid design. Mr Knave paused in its shadow, to allow Max and Daisy time to catch up. 'Imagine them, Mr Allgood, all flocking down here. Lords and ladies, the grandest in the land – all anticipating your music. We intend to make your debut as leader in the Grand quite an occasion. The passing of the torch from one generation to the next. I'm told it will cause quite a ripple when our guests discover that Archie Adams, the pianist extraordinaire, has left his Orchestra in the hands of a trombonist.'

Mr Hastings had told him, 'That horror, that intrigue, it's just the kind of new flavour we need!' – but, even now, Walter wasn't sure. A strange sense of trepidation was coursing through him as they approached the ballroom doors.

The great mahogany doors at the end of the passageway opened at Walter's touch. Then, as he stepped aside, the Grand revealed itself, in all its glory.

Max Allgood had played in some spectacular venues before, but the opulence of the Buckingham ballroom caught him quite off-guard. He'd heard about its lavishness of course. He'd read about the constellation of shimmering chandeliers hanging above, about the sprung dance floor with its design of inter-locking walnut, mahogany and greenwood boards; about the sweeping cocktail bar, the tiered seating area – and, of course, the stage where Archie Adams' gleaming white grand piano was still in situ. Yet nothing he'd imagined quite lived up to the sight in front of him. Later, he would decide that it was because every last one of his senses – not just his vision – was suddenly being inspired. The scents of beeswax and varnish filled the air, and the music that sailed over him – though it came from a gramophone – put him immediately in mind of what the Grand might be like with an orchestra in full swing. Even the troupe of dancers who were rehearsing on the dance floor filled him with joy. At once, he was eager to begin – to take Lucille out of her case and march straight up onto stage.

'Well, Mr Allgood? What do you think?'

Together, the three of them walked down to the sweeping balustrade which ran around the edge of the dance floor. Below, the Buckingham's dancers turned as one: four couples, each keeping perfect time with the other. Mr Knave explained it was part of a piece they were rehearsing for the afternoon demonstrations – those exhibitions intended to inspire guests for the evening's entertainment to come.

'You already know what a magical place you have here, Mr Knave,' grinned Max.

'It's a . . . temple,' Daisy added, her voice breathless with wonder.

Well, at least these two interlopers seemed to understand the gravity of the moment. 'Then you must know what's at stake here. You must know what depth of authority we are vesting in you.'

Perhaps that was the first time that Max truly felt the weight of the responsibility being handed to him. Scarcely eighteen months ago, he and Daisy had been criss-crossing Europe, collecting musicians along the way, dreaming of a permanent home in some hotel, club or casino in Paris, Barcelona, Nice or Madrid. Paris had been the real dream of his life; he'd heard such stories of the clubs of the 1920s, the way they danced the java there, the jazz the American servicemen had brought with them. Even when war came down, he'd been content to ply his trade in the old Hotel Acacias and the seamier spots of La Pigalle. Indeed, that first year of war had brought some of the most memorable moments in his musical life. People reached for pleasure, when darkness was so close at hand.

But then came the fall of France.

Then the hurried dash across the country.

They'd reached the coast days before the British Expeditionary Force ended up stranded there, but the crossing into the United

Kingdom had been no less hairy for that. Of course, Max could remember the way his grandfather had spoken of war in the Americas – all of the old battlelines, the Confederates of the South facing the Unionists in the north – but he had never imagined he might be swept up in a war every bit as vicious.

After that, he was just glad to have a roof over his head, and be playing the music he loved – even if the clubs in Bristol and Cardiff weren't quite as memorable as the cellar bars of La Pigalle. His ambition of forming an orchestra had rather dwindled after Paris – or it had, until the day he was drinking a bourbon after a poorly attended New Year show and looked up to find Archie Adams standing there. 'I'd heard you made it to Blighty, old friend,' Archie had said. 'Listen, I may have something of interest for you …'

Now that he saw it with his own two eyes, he could hardly believe the generosity Archie had shown, nor the scale of the challenge with which he was faced.

The beauty of the Grand was staggering, but so too was the size of the mountain he was going to have to climb.

At least he was doing it with Lucille, he reminded himself.

And at least Daisy was here to keep him off the bourbon when things felt too tough.

'Is M–Mr Adams here?' Max stuttered.

'He's to accompany you for a cocktail at four,' Mr Knave replied. 'In the meantime, you can familiarise yourself with your new home.' Walter Knave gave a discreet cough, catching the attention of one of the younger dancers. A slip of a lad, perhaps no more than twenty years old – fleetingly, Max wondered why he hadn't yet been conscripted – darted away from his stunning, elfin partner, and skipped up the dance floor to meet them at the balustrade. 'Frank, my boy,' Walter Knave began, 'you can have the honour of escorting Mr Allgood and his good lady wife to their suite. Frank's one of our pages,' Walter explained, 'but he's forging himself quite a name here in the ballroom. Trained by Raymond de Guise, of course, before he went off to war.'

'Raymond de Guise?' Daisy ventured.

'The King of the Ballroom,' Frank said, with a twinkle in his eye. 'And ... my brother-in-law to boot. He's somewhere in Africa now. Libya, we think. But we're keeping the ballroom alive while he's gone. Mr Arbuthnot over there,' Frank indicated the tallest man on the dance floor, a titan with russet gold hair and eyes the colour of a winter sky, 'is making sure of it.' His eyes panned down. 'Is that a trombone, sir?'

'It sure is,' Max beamed, happy to be given the chance to rhapsodise about his favourite subject again. 'You won't be used to a band being led by trombone, of course, so things are going to change in the ballroom. But I promise you excitement, Frank. I promise you a little daring. I promise you—'

'Good leadership and a steady hand,' Walter intoned.

Max nodded – a little too eagerly, perhaps, for suddenly Daisy shot him a look.

'We promise you a new era,' Daisy declared.

Then Frank led them on their way.

The suite which had been afforded Max and Daisy Allgood was tucked away on the hotel's fourth storey. By the time they arrived, the hotel concierges had already deposited all of the cases and the travelling trunk from the Rolls Royce in the big bay window overlooking the square, and a young chambermaid – who introduced herself, with an awkward curtsy, as 'Annie Brogan, at your deep and faithful service!' – was busying herself by pushing two single beds up against each other, then redressing them as a double.

'I thought you'd like it better this way,' Annie said brightly.

'More space to stretch out, you see. A lot more comfortable. Look, I dug a few extra pillows out of the store cupboards too. I've plumped them all up. Now, you can't say better than that. If it's fit for a crown prince, I say, it's fit for the new bandleader of the Grand.' Only now did Annie seem to see the serrated look Frank was giving her. 'What?' she whispered. 'What did I do wrong?'

'Better set the beds back, my dear,' Daisy began, while Max plopped himself in the armchair and started taking Lucille out of her case. 'I'm afraid Max is a dreadful snorer, and I'm dreadful for wriggling. It's the secret to a long marriage, you see – and you can count on this, later in life, I promise: *separate beds*.'

Annie had started blanching white. 'I was trying to help,' she whispered. 'Oh Lord – oh *Lord*, I'm *always* doing something like this. Every time I try to help, it just comes out all wrong. Like the time Mr Ford – he's the war reporter, down on the second floor – ordered eggs for his breakfast. Well, they were just sitting there when I came in to change the towels. I thought he needed some help taking the tops off, just like I used to do for my little brothers and sisters, so I—'

Max and Daisy Allgood were looking at Annie so strangely that she quickly fell back into silence.

'I'll put the beds back,' Daisy said promptly. 'You've done a grand job, young lady, but we'll take it from here.' Daisy led Annie to the door of the suite, where Frank was waiting to escort her away. 'And you have my word: let's keep this to ourselves.'

Now that they were alone, Daisy slammed the suite door and defiantly started separating the beds all over again.

'Do you think she … suspected?' Max began, looking up from Lucille. The trombone was a glorious instrument, a 1921 Earl Williams, and by a country mile the dearest thing in Max's life.

'Suspected?' Daisy said. 'Because of a silly bed? No, Max,

you're worrying too much. That girl, lovely as she seems, doesn't have enough between her ears to wonder what's really going on here.'

Max gazed upon Berkeley Square below. 'You know, Daisy, I could get used to this. I've slept in barns. I've slept underneath sacking. But I never imagined I'd sleep in a suite meant for a prince.'

'Well, let's not waste the opportunity then,' said Daisy, clapping her hands.

'No, let's make this work.' First, there would be cocktails with Archie Adams. Then, a gathering of the orchestra's senior musicians in the little rehearsal space tucked away behind the Grand. 'Just keep the music playing,' Max went on, 'keep the ballroom swaying – and, Daisy my dear, it's the high life from here on. They say the Buckingham's impregnable – did you know that? It's built from German steel. Even a direct hit wouldn't topple the place. And … they're still dining in the restaurants here like there's no war at all. They don't ration butter and bacon for lords and ladies, do they? So we'll be safe here – *and* we'll be fed. What could be better than that?'

Max was still cradling Lucille as he threw himself back onto the bed. 'Yes,' he said, with the eagerness of a young man meeting his first illicit lover, 'I could get used to this very much.'

A pillow hit him in the face. 'Then don't mess this one up. You know musicians by instinct, Max, but I don't think you were *listening* in Mr Knave's office. He's suspicious, from the start. We don't live up to his idea of gentlemen performers. We're …'

'*Americans*,' Max wryly smiled.

Daisy slumped down beside him. 'Let's show him he's got nothing to worry about, not with us. So don't cause a ruckus. Learn to fit in. Learn to play the part.' Daisy paled. 'And on no account, Maxwell, let them know who I really am. I don't want to go back to the way it was. I can't bear the thought. I can't bear the destitution. And there's more than just us at stake here. Don't forget that.'

'Oh, how could I?' grinned Max, and brought Lucille to his lips to let out a long, mournful note.

Chapter Two

Sirens filled the night.

Frank Nettleton had hardly lifted his head out of the trapdoor when the conical beams of searchlights started criss-crossing the sky. Hotel page by profession, hotel dancer by ambition, Frank nevertheless spent four nights a week working with the civic defence: two answering telephones at the local emergency exchange, one on foot patrol with the ARP, and one on shift up here, high above the rooftops of Mayfair, on the very pinnacle of the Buckingham Hotel itself.

The concrete observation post had been sunk into the hotel roof in the summer before war was declared. Now, it was manned nightly, a succession of hotel staff scouring the city rooftops for signs of fire.

There were nights when Frank almost enjoyed the solitude up here. Beneath him, the hotel was a hive of activity. Pacts were being made, matters of state dissected and discussed; guests were waging private wars or caught up in their love affairs, while the back passages buzzed with concierges, chambermaids and porters going about their daily business – but, up here, there was only Frank Nettleton and the night.

It had been quieter of late, but if war had taught Frank anything, it was not to take anything for granted. He'd done that once: assumed that he, Frank Nettleton, would be taking the king's shilling and heading off to war, doing his bit for the country he loved. It had taken him some time to accept the Medical Board's decision that his lungs – having grown up in a Lancashire pit town, and going down the pit as a young boy – did not have the strength required by a soldier at war. But Frank took pride in what he was doing up here. Frank Nettleton: the watchman of the city. He'd called in two dozen fires from up here.

Frank ought to have known that a wild one was coming. Not long ago, every night had been hell. Now, when a few quiet nights came, you got the feeling that the enemy was preparing itself. Frank settled himself in position, lifting the binoculars from the hook to dangle them around his neck. Then he gazed around. Four partitions in the concrete walls faced north, south, east and west. There was a thin scattering of cloud cover; perhaps that was why the Luftwaffe had sallied out, seeking to catch the Royal Air Force unawares. Frank readied himself. Sometimes, he still felt the fear of these nights – but not tonight. The calm that came over him was the inner peace of a young man ready to face whatever came his way.

The sound of the sirens was joined, suddenly, by the fierce retort of ack-ack guns somewhere in the east.

Fortress London was under siege once again.

Frank put the binoculars to his eyes, scoured the city, and held his breath.

In the hotel post room, the sirens shook Billy Brogan from the sleep that was threatening to take him under. It had been some months since the song of the sirens last cast Billy back to those despairing days when he had been stranded on the beaches at Dunkirk – but, on the edge of sleep as he was, he felt himself being dragged back there, with the bombs screaming overheard and the artillery fire raining down. Now, deep in the bowels of the Buckingham Hotel – slumped over his desk in the post room, whose stewardship he'd taken over upon his return from the front – Billy tried to shake off the terror. He stood up suddenly, slamming his lame leg against the post-room table, and was hopping around, cursing under his breath – Billy might have been a twenty-two-year-old Irishman, but he was a gentleman nonetheless, and knew not to swear audibly in the fine environs of the Buckingham Hotel – when there came a knock at the door.

'Mr Ford,' Billy said, still hopping in circles as Jackson Ford appeared. Mr Ford had been staying at the hotel since Christmas, filing his reports for the *New York Times* back home. The middle-aged American was lean, chiselled and (so the chambermaids said) ravishingly good-looking, with his chestnut-brown hair styled in a permanent cowlick, chocolatey eyes and the rugged look of a man better suited to the prairies than the newspaper offices where he worked.

'Mr Ford,' Billy said. 'You ought to get to the shelters. You know the way by now.'

The cellars of the Buckingham Hotel had been excavated long before the war was finally declared. Now, though the staff shelters were necessarily more threadbare, the old hotel laundries had been transformed into secondary suites where the hotel's prized guests could – if they so chose – sit out the bombardment of the city in relative peace, comfort and security.

Mr Ford just smiled. 'I'll be heading down there now, son, but I've got a report to file first. I need it on the next telegram, direct to New York, you hear?'

Jackson had produced a bundle of papers, which he neatly

pressed into Billy's hand. 'It's quite a piece, Mr Ford,' said Billy, weighing the article in his hands.

'Just see it done, boy. The *Times* is picking up the tab, so no expense spared – do you hear?'

Billy nodded.

As Mr Ford was bowing back through the door, off to the comfort of the shelters – where waiting staff would already be congregating, with cocktails and Moët to calm the nerves – he looked back. 'Say, Brogan, I still want to interview you, you hear?'

'You know where I'll be, Mr Ford!' he beamed, with a sudden salute.

The great American saluted back. Then, whistling some merry tune, he vanished out of Billy's sight.

Billy took a deep breath, waited until Mr Ford was surely gone, and then set about his business.

Some twenty minutes after the sirens started sounding, the Buckingham Hotel was not quite deserted, but eerily quiet compared to the hour before. When the first air raids had started, the hotel had nightly become a barren wasteland – with restaurant tables abandoned, the ballroom vacated, and the reception hall an empty, echoing husk. Yet, people become attuned to almost anything – or so Billy had often observed – and, across the unfolding months, many had begun forgoing the shelters and remaining above. Consequently, as Billy reached the reception hall, he was not the only figure at large.

He picked his way across the reception hall, greeting the night manager who lingered by the check-in desks, then slipped through the stately doorways that led to the Queen Mary restaurant. The lavish restaurant had been vacated by most diners, but several groups had steadfastly refused to leave their roast partridge and Whitstable oysters, their blackberry souffles and lavish cheeses. The sight of diners left behind always gave Billy pause, for their plates represented rich pickings – and, of course, he did not want to be seen – but there was emptiness enough for him to help himself to pieces of Red Leicester, Wensleydale and Gloucestershire cheeses. The Queen Mary was one of the only places where the creamy Lancashire and Stilton cheeses – whose production had been outlawed last year – could still be found. Billy declined to slide these into his knapsack, for a theft like that might more easily be traced, but soon he had wrapped butters, bread rolls and slices of silverside beef in wax papers and filled the bag. Then, careful not to linger too long and therefore be seen, he slipped inside the kitchens themselves.

The staff shelters stood directly beneath his feet, the hollows of the hotel wine cellars now providing protection to those who toiled in the Buckingham halls, but Billy bowed instead through the kitchen doors, and hurried towards the prominent larders. The Queen Mary kitchens were like a cathedral – or perhaps 'labyrinth' was a better description, for though the kitchen was dominated by a central range and countertops fanning out around it, there were countless nooks and crannies where the pastry chefs, sous-chefs and other underlings toiled. The head chef Henri Laurent had run the kitchens at the Ritz Paris, but found his way to London some time before the fall of France. A proud, obstinate, he had been known across Paris as a man who treated his dishes better than he did his sous-chefs – and better still than his own sons, who were all off with the war.

At least Henri was not here now. Now, he tended to gravitate to the guest shelters, where he slaved over the hot-plates and miniature range that had been carefully installed down there. Canapés for princes, while the city was under attack – Henri Laurent said it would make a fine chapter in his memoirs, one day.

At least that meant the kitchen was empty – or so Billy thought. He was barrelling forward, eyes on the larder doors, when a voice piped up from the heart of the kitchen. 'Mr Brogan?' it squeaked. 'Is that you?'

Billy turned. The young man who hovered over the ranges – evidently commanded to stay at his post, while the rest flocked to the safety below – was new to the kitchens as well. So many were; one of management's principal challenges this past year was finding staff who weren't about to be conscripted, then holding on to them even as the danger in the city intensified. His name, Billy dimly recalled, was Victor – the son of an old Italian restaurateur who was currently cooking for inmates at the internment camp on the Isle of Man. With the family restaurant closed down, Victor had been desperate for work – and found it, here in the Buckingham. He was a slight young man, with the olive complexion of his Italian father and the delicate features of his English mother. In his hands hung a wooden spoon, brandished like a cudgel.

'Victor, you almost gave me a heart attack.' Surreptitiously, Billy shifted the knapsack round to his back. It was, perhaps, best that Victor didn't see it bulging with salvage from all the abandoned meals out there. 'Don't you need to get down below?'

'Monsieur Laurent said …'

Billy nodded. Then, quick as a flash, he said, 'It was Monsieur Laurent I was looking for, actually. Is he not here?'

'Why, no, Mr Brogan. He's *below*.'

'Oh, of course!' Billy declared. Then he was turning on his heel, as if to quickly depart. 'Well, that's where I'd better be as well. Stay safe up here, Victor.'

Victor was giving Billy a puzzled look as the Irishman beat a retreat.

Well, it might not be the waste receptacles in the larder tonight – but there were other places to go to scavenge. The Housekeeping Lounge was still out of bounds after the devastation of last Christmas, but in the department's new headquarters – the old Benefactor's Study, behind the reception desks – there would be soaps and lotions to load up. The chambermaids were not averse to salvaging bits from the room-service trolleys for their own breakfasts, and Billy always knew he could help himself to these bits too.

This he did, until his knapsack was bulging. Then, he ghosted back through the hotel and into the post room. Mr Ford's letter was still on the desk, waiting for a telegram to be sent. Billy would attend to it shortly, but first of all there was another call to be made.

He slid his knapsack into the cavity beneath the floorboards at his desk, repositioned the corner of carpet on top of it, and picked up the telephone receiver to make a call. 'Mr Sellers? It's Bill. Look, I'll be up tomorrow. It isn't a proper harvest, but there's plenty here. You'll find homes for it, I'm sure.'

The voice that returned down the line was breathy with thanks. 'I've had Mr and Mrs Nash in this afternoon, after a few bits. They'll be delighted, Bill. Keep up the good work, won't you? We'll get these old sods through the war yet.'

The words brought Billy the warmth he'd been lacking all evening. As he made his goodbyes, he began to wonder at all that had brought him to this place. The Buckingham Hotel was his home – it had been ever since he was a boy – but, on his return from Dunkirk, he'd been unable to see it through quite the same eyes. The rich and the entitled still fed like kings in the Queen Mary, while the rest of the world was being rationed. Rich men grew fat on spring lamb and caviar, while the poor lined up for bacon and butter.

So last year, when Billy – quite without knowing it – crossed paths with those who *bent* the rules of rationing a little, it hadn't seemed so very awful that he might play a part himself. He didn't profit from it – not like some of those he'd known, not like the man who'd first introduced him to this world. A man who now lounged in Pentonville Prison for his crimes. Billy just helped out where he could. It was, he had decided, his own little way of helping win this war.

He was still ruminating on the rights and wrongs of it – for there was no doubt he'd be in trouble, if hotel management ever found out – when the telephone on his desk started ringing. Quickly, he fumbled it to his ear.

'Post room,' he said into the receiver.

And a breathless voice burst out: 'Bill! Billy, it's me – Frank! I'm up on observation.' His voice crackled, the static coming down the line. 'It's Lambeth, Billy. Lambeth's on fire!'

It wasn't the first conflagration of the night. The docks were aflame, way out in the east; Frank could see it as a rosy glow on the horizon, the plumes of black smoke diffusing the searchlights mounted on the other side of the river. But Lambeth was so much closer. Frank fancied he could almost smell the smoke which had blossomed upon impact.

Lambeth was home.

It was where he had digs with the Brogan family – who had provided him with board ever since he'd come to London, four years before.

The moment he put the phone down, he brought the binoculars back to his eyes. His heart was thundering. Every piece of him wanted to ditch the binoculars, tumble back through the trapdoor and join Billy in the hotel below. Together, they would sally out into the storm, pick their way through the falling bombs to reach home – and make sure that Billy's family were safe in their shelters. But there was another part of him, the part comprised of honour, self-sacrifice and duty, which rooted him to the spot. Somebody needed to call them in.

But he trained his eyes on Lambeth again, watching as the fires surged.

The Brogan house was too close to the river, and consequently so close to Westminster, for it to have been hit, wasn't it? The palaces of Westminster were one of the most heavily guarded places in London. Above the Houses of Parliament, mighty barrage balloons dominated the sky. No expense had been spared in fortifying that stretch of the river.

And yet…

Parliament drew the eye of enemy bombers. To raze a place like that to the ground would be to strike a blow at the very heart of the British defiance. So, yes, Frank thought, of *course* the bombs rained there – and, of course, the bombs that went adrift might find some other place to destroy.

A place like the house he called home.

Frank's heart was still pounding when something drew his eye to Berkeley Square below. A figure had emerged from the hotel, bursting out of the narrow ribbon of darkness that was Michaelmas Mews. Now it cantered, dragging its lame leg behind it, into the night.

Billy had done what Frank was honour bound not to do: he had abandoned his post.

Alone, he was thundering into the storm.

Frank's words had made a ruin of Billy's mind, but he was practised enough to control the panic that had immediately started rising in his gorge. The Brogans owned no telephone, so there was no way he could make direct contact with his parents.

He'd barely left Berkeley Square by the time he realised he'd made a mistake. He could smell the reefs of smoke rushing over the river, surging up Regent Street as if Piccadilly itself had been turned to a ruin. This time, he really did fancy himself back at Dunkirk – only with the added frisson that he wasn't wearing a military issue helmet, he held no rifle with which he might defend himself, and had not a single companion at his side.

Piccadilly was ablaze, firefighters already working to stem the flames licking up the walls of the Trocadero. More than once, someone bellowed for Billy to hurry for shelter. An ARP warden gripped him by the arm and tried to escort him to the Underground – but Billy shook him off and bouldered on to the Haymarket.

Through the barbed wire of Trafalgar Square he came, past the anchors of the great barrage balloons strung up above the Horse Guards Parade. By the time he reached Westminster Bridge, he could see the inferno across the river.

There came a sudden screeching from above. Billy looked up, just in time to see two of the brave boys of the RAF harrying some enemy bomber back across the night sky. The air was alive with the sound of rapid gunfire. By instinct, Billy threw himself to the floor, covering his head. Now, there was no doubt in his mind. He really was back on the beaches, his face buried in sand, the earth swallowing up every scream that came out of his mouth.

Back then, he'd looked up and seen the hand of Raymond de Guise reaching back down.

Back then, he'd been part of a regiment. They'd been in hell, but at least they'd been together.

Now he was on his own.

He tried to pick himself up, but the earth started quaking, a fountain of fire erupting somewhere beyond the abbey – and, all at once, the sound of engines filled the night.

How many more nights? he wondered.

He'd listened to the radio, only this afternoon. Mr Churchill remained defiant – 'Send us your weapons,' he'd proclaimed proudly to the President of the United States, 'and we shall finish this job alone' – but, right now, Billy wasn't so sure. His little island nation had already resisted so much, but you could only resist the tide for so long.

At last, he found the strength to pick himself up. Home was calling out to him.

But he knew, before he'd even reached his street, that home wasn't here anymore.

Fires pitted the Lambeth streets. On the corner where he and his brothers used to play, a collection of ARP wardens and WVS girls had set up a makeshift camp. They called out to him as he reeled past, but Billy paid them no mind. 'Not that way, son! It's too dangerous – there's unexploded ordnance!' Still, Billy staggered on.

The smoke was so thick that he hardly knew his way. He had to turn himself around, taking stock of what was left of his surroundings, before he finally knew where he stood. In this way, by faltering fits and starts, he reached the end of Albert Yard.

But Billy could go no further. This time, it wasn't ARP wardens and WVS girls who blocked his path – for the falling bombs had already done that job. The house directly in front of him had been obliterated, raising a jagged wall across what was left of the road. Unearthed pipes sputtered out water, which rapidly turned to steam in the heat of the fires.

Beneath his feet, the bitumen was warped and melting; it stuck, like the hot tar it was, to the soles of his shoes.

No 62 was further down the Yard, in the very centre of the street. 'I need to see it,' Billy screamed out – for now the WVS girls were heaving on his arm, trying to drag him back from the edge of the devastation. 'Off me!' he thundered. 'I need to see!'

In seconds, he was clambering over the rubble, heaving himself into the stretch of ruptured road beyond.

And there was Billy's home, No 62 Albert Yard: open, like Annie's old doll's house, to the street; half of it gone, its face ripped clean off, its outer wall destroyed. Cauldrons of fire burnt in the place where Billy's family used to eat dinner. In one of the back windows, net curtains still flew.

Billy could summon no tears. It wasn't just his family home whose walls had been torn apart; it was Billy himself. No longer would he dream of Dunkirk when he hovered on the edge of sleep. Now he would dream of this moment, standing in Albert Yard, staring at the ruins of his life.

'Bill?'

He turned at the voice. One of the WVS girls was reaching for him. It took him an aeon to remember who she was: Marge Clark's girl, from the bottom of the Yard. To Billy, she looked like something from another world.

'Billy, they're at the corner. We're looking after them.' She stopped, for Billy seemed to be looking straight through her, to some indeterminate place of flame and wreckage beyond. 'The WVS set up a station, at the grocers' on George Street. They're there now. Shaken up, Billy, but they're alive.'

Billy was too floored to feel relieved. In the end, he had to be guided out of the devastated street, round the corner and to two roads further on, where the WVS had set up their wagon and the local greengrocer had allowed them the use of his shop floor for all of the neighbourhood's shattered souls. Billy found a hot tea being pressed into his hands. Then he was bowing through the greengrocers' door, looking for his family among all the soot-stained, begrimed faces peering back at him.

There they were: sitting together at the store-room doors, his father's arm around his mother as she wept upon his shoulder.

Only now did the life rush back into Billy. He'd so rarely seen his mother cry. Orla Brogan was a proud, strong woman. She'd raised eight children in a country that was not her own, built them a life and a home in London, the very heart of the world. She'd scrimped and saved so that her children never went without. She'd cooked and cleaned and tended to every grazed knee – but, more than that, she'd filled their hearts with joy, love and wonder, all of the things that could never be rationed in the world.

Billy dropped to his knees to take hold of her. Only when she'd softened against his shoulder did he reach out too, to grasp his father by the shoulder.

'Billy, what are you doing here?' his mother breathed.

'I had to, Ma,' Billy said, unable to keep the tremble from his tone. Then he started rambling, if only to fill the silence: 'Frankie saw the bombs come down. He knew it was Lambeth, Ma. But I had to know if it was you – and … and it was!' Billy's voice cracked. 'But here you are, Ma. We're alive – every one of us, alive! – and it's going to be OK.'

There was silence. Billy didn't know when it had happened, but at some point his father had become part of the hug as well.

'You do believe me, don't you? It's going to be OK. The house is still standing – or part of it, at least. We'll rebuild. We'll put everything back like it was.'

His father shook his head sadly, and gripped Billy harder than he had done since the boy was small enough to sit on his knee. 'We're alive,' he said, 'that's the thing.'

Billy's ma shuddered. 'Without a roof over our heads. The WVS girls say there's places to put us up, but …' She could say no more. 'Charity, Bill. After all these years, pulling ourselves up by our boot-straps, it's down to charity.'

'It ain't your fault, Ma. It's *them*.' Billy's rage curdled as he looked upwards, as if he might see the Stukas and Junkers of the Luftwaffe banking through the night, even through the greengrocers' roof.

The *greengrocers'*…

Billy was still. Of course, he'd set foot in a dozen different greengrocers' of late. Not just Mr Sellers off the Camden High Road, but disparate corners from there up to Willesden Green. Twice a week, he plodded between them – sometimes taking taxicabs on account of the Buckingham Hotel – to make his deliveries. He never asked for anything in return. All he wanted was the warm glow he got from knowing he was doing his bit; knowing that, on any given night, bellies might be full on account of the way he quietly bent the hotel rules.

But as Billy stood there now, contemplating his parents as paupers, wondering where they might spend their next night, where their next meals were coming from, who'd prop them up until they could stand on their own two feet again, another thought occurred. Because there was *one* person who could help them, wasn't there? He'd see to it that they wouldn't starve.

But it was the greater question – the question of hearth and home – that was preying on him now. The question of how to restore all they had lost. Of how to repay all the love, dedication and belief they'd had in him over the years.

You could take bread rolls and pâté from the Buckingham Hotel. You could take the end of a piece of bacon, bruised fruits and day-old pastries that the entitled toffs of the hotel thought were beneath them. The problem was: you couldn't salvage a roof over your head. You couldn't take bricks and mortar. What you needed for that was money, and – for all the wealth that flowed through the Buckingham Hotel – very little of it ended up in the hands of its concierges, its pages, its chambermaids and porters. All that Billy really had were his own two hands.

Then he looked up, at the shelves all around him.

The greengrocers' shelves, just like the shelves of the shops that Billy helped fill.

'It's going to be OK, Ma,' said Billy. Still holding his mother, he fixed his father with a stare. 'I give you my word.'

Billy Brogan's word was his bond. Nothing meant more to him in all of the world.

And he had just had a terrible idea.

Chapter Three

At last, some peace and quiet.

Nancy de Guise waited until the last of her chambermaids had left the Benefactors' Study, and returned to the letter on her desk.

Dear Raymond,

I scarcely know where to begin, but let me first say that I am well. I feel our baby moving almost hourly now – and I know he is almost ready to meet the world. I am sure it is a boy. At least, when I dream of him, he is a boy. In my dreams, you are here as well: the three of us, as it is meant to be. I know I shall have to wait some time before that dream becomes reality – but, my love, if there is one thing my new role as Head of Housekeeping has taught me, it is patience.

The Buckingham goes on. Reconstruction work on the old Housekeeping wing is almost complete. Mr Knave says we are to move out of the Benefactors' Study and into our new lounge before summer. By then, of course, I shall be a mother, and you a father – but I am assured that, after a short break, I am to continue my work here.

I know the girls in Housekeeping think this strange. Some dream of nothing more than finding a husband, having their babies, staying at home and playing mother. But for me it is different. I have been playing mother since I was a girl, looking after Frankie after our mother passed on – but, in all that time, I never once gave up on my own ambitions. I will fill our child's life with all the love I have, but I do not want to give up on my own world. Does that make me awful? I am sure that some would think it callous. But the world is changing. Are we not to change with it?

Nancy was glad when the door to the study opened, and Rosa – one of the chambermaids, and Frank's sweetheart to boot – hurried through, to load up her trolley from one of the temporary store cupboards erected in the corner. The letter she was writing was for Raymond, though when it would reach him, she could not hazard a guess – he was in Libya now, or had been at the last reckoning. Yet part of her knew that, in writing to Raymond, she was really sifting through the jumble of her own mind. Nancy had come to the Buckingham only five years before, a country girl looking to make her way in the city. She hadn't anticipated marriage to the Buckingham's finest ballroom dancer. She hadn't dreamed of the house in Maida Vale, the baby on the way – and, least of all, her sudden elevation to the post of Head of Housekeeping. But Nancy had long ago learned to take life as it comes. War upended everything. It had upended Nancy's life over and again.

Vivienne moved to Maida Vale last week. It was a predictably chaotic day, and I am quite certain that your mother and aunts are unhappy with the decision – which, of course, I understand; if Vivienne is no longer in Whitechapel, then they will not see as much of baby Stan. But I am certain it is the right thing for Vivienne, and I am certain it is the right thing for me and our own child. Families grow in all sorts of different directions – and, since Artie died, Vivienne has struggled alone. I am sure it will look peculiar to our neighbours, the thought of two sisters-in-law and their children making house together, but...

Nancy had time to ruminate over the next sentence, for in this moment Annie Brogan appeared and barrelled into the store cupboards – no doubt in search of a replacement for whatever crockery she'd broken, towel she'd spilt polish all over, or breakfast tray she'd somehow spoiled. The girl had a good heart, and burning ambition to do the right thing – but in 'common sense' and 'good reason', she did not always prevail.

'Annie, are you quite all right in there?'

The noises coming from the store cupboards were verging on catastrophic.

'Right as rain, Mrs de Guise! I'll be out of your hair and back to the suites in a second.'

Nancy resisted the urge to get up and help – it was right that Annie learn to sort out problems on her own. Nancy would have just preferred it if she learned this more quickly – and if, perhaps, she might have caused less mess along the way. But at least the girl was trying.

Yes, Annie Brogan was exceedingly *trying* indeed.

While the crashing went on, Nancy returned to her letter.

I must sign off now. But before I leave, there is one more piece of news. It was with much regret that we learned, several mornings ago, that Billy's family home in

Lambeth was devastated in one of the raids. By good
fortune, his parents have survived. Billy himself has been
given permission to bed down in the hotel post room –
which, as you know, is where he already spent so many
of his nights. The boy works harder than ever since he
was invalided home; I think it is how he copes. But, of
course, the tragedy at Albert Yard has meant that our
own Frank is without a home. Well, what else could I do?
Frank is now sleeping in our sitting room at Blomfield
Road. From living alone, in the space of one week, I have
gone to being matriarch of a bustling household: my
brother, my sister-in-law, my nephew, and soon to be our
child. Life does lead us on twists and turns.

Your ever loving wife,
Na—

'Mrs de Guise, I almost forgot!'

Nancy's pen stuttered as she signed her name, leaving a great
splodge of ink on the page. Startled, she looked up to discover
that Annie had burst back out of the store cupboard, her arms
laden down with fresh towels and flannels, her face peeping over
the top like a little boy snooping over the garden wall.

'Forgot, Annie?' asked Nancy, dabbing the ink from the
page.

'I was meant to bring you a message, Mrs de Guise. That is
to say – I've got a message for you. I was on my way to tell it
when my trolley turned over. I was just hurrying, Mrs de Guise.
I didn't want to let you down... but then I went and forgot to
tell it anyway, so in the end I've let you down twice.'

Nancy's reserves of patience were well-provisioned – but they did not have infinite depths. She thought back to Mrs Moffatt, the kindly woman who'd been running Housekeeping when Nancy arrived – the woman who'd borne with all of Nancy's mistakes with patience, ignored her occasional misdemeanour, and finally set her on the road to being the woman she was today. Mrs Moffatt would no doubt have been patient as a priest with Annie – but she would not have shied away from putting the girl in her place when a few firm words were needed.

This time, Nancy's patience won the day. 'The message, Annie?'

'It's Mr Knave,' Annie stammered. 'He wants to see you in his office. I'm sorry, Mrs de Guise – he said it was urgent.'

Walter Knave was a mouse of a man: quiet, unassuming and small, he was hardly the sort of character you expected to lead an establishment as grand as the Buckingham through war. Hardly like the previous director, Maynard Charles – who, if rumour was to be believed, was now ensconced in the heart of the wartime intelligence community. And yet it was Walter Knave who had shepherded the hotel through the Great War, in his first incarnation at the hotel. With his reserved demeanour and gentle tones, Nancy could hardly imagine he'd been a more dynamic, gregarious leader in his younger days – but the man must have had hidden depths, for the Hotel Board were notoriously difficult to please.

The door to the director's office was open, so Nancy rapped gently on the wood and then slipped through. Inside, Walter Knave was fussing with papers at his expansive desk. 'Ah, Mrs de Guise,' he croaked, at last, 'I was beginning to wonder if that girl of yours had understood my message. I sometimes wonder if the young speak a different language.' Walter shook his head ruefully as he stood up. Nancy could see him appraising her body as he shuffled round the desk, pulled out one of the armchairs in the office hearth, and bade her sit down. 'Well, we can't have you on your feet. Not a lady in your condition. And it's this *condition* of yours I'd rather like to speak about.' Here Walter's face flushed red.

It was interesting, Nancy thought, how men of a certain generation could not even speak the word 'pregnancy' without getting hot under the collar.

'Now, as you know, we find ourself in Interesting Times.' Walter pronounced the words with a long, lingering emphasis. 'And, as I hope you also know, we are more than pleased with the way you have conducted yourself and your department since Mrs Moffatt's departure. These haven't been easy months – not with the old Housekeeping Lounge under rubble, and of course with your husband's departure. Might I ask if you've heard from him, Mrs de Guise?'

Nancy nodded. 'Letters are so few and far between, Mr Knave. The last I heard, he was being sent into Libya.'

'A thoroughly nasty business out there, but I'm sure you're very proud. Well, Mrs de Guise, we've agreed that you shall remain Head of Housekeeping after your child has been welcomed to the world. It didn't happen in my day – but I'm like a mammoth in a tar pit – set in my ways – but I will acknowledge that progress is a good thing. I'll acknowledge, even more, that this hotel *needs* you. You've taken over stewardship of that department without a hiccough. And yet…'

'And yet, Mr Knave?'

'And yet we reach something of a critical juncture. Your baby may arrive any week now, and – as dedicated as you've been to this hotel – you will need some weeks to settle into the new rhythm of life.'

'Mr Knave, everything is in order. My sister-in-law has come to live with me. Vivienne's a mother herself. She's to look after my baby while I'm at work.'

Walter Knave repositioned his spectacles on his nose. 'There are variables in play beyond even the most diligent planner, Mrs de Guise. I don't know how to say this delicately, so perhaps you don't mind me saying it brusquely: giving birth is no easy feat; my own sister perished in the act of it, and her daughter was laid up for some weeks when it came her turn. I say it not to frighten you, but even in the best of circumstances, you are not to be present in this hotel for some weeks.' And at last Walter revealed the true purpose of this meeting. 'I need to know that things will run smoothly in your absence.'

Nancy was still reeling from Mr Knave's forthrightness in speaking of his sister's sad demise – it was not the sort of thing a young woman on the cusp of giving birth wanted to hear – so she was grateful that the Hotel Director had asked such a simple question. 'Mr Knave, I've been building to it for months. My girls are regimented. The best army major couldn't drill a better troop. Rosa and Mary-Louise are running the floors. I've written rotas for the next three months – though I intend to be at work long before then – and back-up rotas as well, in the event one of the girls falls sick or, heaven forbid, leaves us. I know I'll be out of service for a little time, but I won't be out of contact. The telephone's already installed at home. I'll be speaking to my girls every day.'

The house telephone had seemed such an indulgence, but it was John Hastings, head of the Hotel Board, who had suggested it.

'Rosa's more than capable of marshalling the girls while I'm away, Mr Knave – but she won't need to. Everybody knows their place. We're like cogs in a great machine. You have my word…'

She hadn't finished the sentence when her eyes connected with Walter Knave's, each of them having the same thought.

'Your young lady, Miss Brogan?'

Nancy gave a crumpled smile. 'A rough diamond, Mr Knave,' she replied, willing it to be true. 'As was I, once upon a time. The girl just needs a little belief. She'll be a true asset to this hotel, Mr Knave – just like her brother.'

Nancy tried not to think about Billy's inauspicious beginnings as she left the Hotel Director's office, exited the Buckingham by Michaelmas Mews, and climbed into the taxicab waiting for her. When Nancy first met Billy, he'd been a hotel page, running errands for guests – and not caring if those errands were honourable or not. But that was a long time ago. Since then, Billy had grown, taken on responsibility, left behind his rapscallion ways. She could hardly imagine him making a poor decision now.

Annie had her own journey to go on, but Nancy was quite certain she would turn out just the same: grounded and caring, looking on both princes and paupers the same, devoted to the family she had at home and the family, at the hotel, she was building around her.

But if she could just concentrate on not upending trolleys, and not chattering inanely with the guests, it would be a fine start.

As the taxicab drew up on the kerbside of Blomfield Road, Nancy felt her baby stirring in her belly. The movements were slowing down of late; that could only mean he was filling her, at last getting ready to meet the world. 'Wait until I tell your father,' she grinned, her heart filling with hope that that would be very soon.

Then she picked her way through the garden gate and up the path to the house. The blackout blinds were already in place, but Nancy didn't need to see through the windows to know that here was a home filled with light, laughter, love, even in the darkest of times. She might forever feel the emptiness of Raymond in her home, but she would not be alone. *No,* she thought – and, curling her hand around her belly, *never again.*

Nancy did not see the figure that watched her as she followed the garden path.

Frank could hear Nancy in the hallway right now, cooing over Stan as she took off her coat. Vivienne had already called out her hellos, but she was busying herself laying the table in the dining room. The brash American girl, who'd been welcomed to Raymond's family – and then widowed when Raymond's brother Artie lost his life at Dunkirk – seemed as determined to make herself a useful part of this household as Frank. Since Frank got home from the Buckingham Hotel, he'd found her scrubbing the laundry, sweeping the floors and provisioning the Anderson shelter just in case it was needed tonight. All of this, while also juggling Stan – perhaps the most tempestuous toddler Frank had ever encountered. Stan had the same wolfishness that his father used to have. He looked more like a Cohen boy with every passing day.

'Nance,' said Frank sadly, when he sensed Nancy appearing in the kitchen doorway, Stan sitting on her hip, 'I think we might end up drinking this one. Or mopping it up with a nice bit of bread … if we have any?'

Nancy opened the cupboard. Instead of bread, there was a scraping of cornflour left in the tin, which would do to thicken a gravy. There were three ration-books in this house now, and there'd be yet more supplies when the baby was born. If Frank and Nancy were clever, and always took their main meals when they were on shift at the Buckingham, there was no reason they'd have to go hungry. 'I'll fix this, Frank. You get washed up.'

Nancy was about to hand Stan to Frank when there came three sharp raps at the door.

Back in the hallway, Vivienne had emerged from the dining room. She looked as tired as Nancy felt – but she smiled when she saw Nancy. 'We're not expecting a visitor, are we?' Nancy asked.

'Not until tomorrow, when Gertie's doing the rounds.' Gertie was the midwife who would, some day soon, lead Nancy through her labour.

'Then … who?' Nancy mouthed.

The knocking at the door came again.

Nancy hurried along the hallway, casting a single glance back at Frank – who had emerged, wringing his hands on a tea towel, from the kitchen. Then, she opened the door.

The figure standing on the doorstep was not a man she had ever seen before. At six feet tall, he was nearly a head taller than Nancy. Dressed in a long black coat, his face was dusted in the beginnings of a rich, black beard. The hair on his head was just as black, though speckled with grey around his temples. Dark eyes glimmered beneath the twin thatches of his perfectly styled eyebrows.

Nancy looked up. The man was imposing, yes, but there was something strange about the way he considered her. Sometimes, a man's character shone out. This man was genial, she decided, but there was some element of desperation, of urgency, in him as well.

'Forgive me,' he said – and Nancy noted from his voice that this was a Frenchman, for his English was inflected just the same as Henri Laurent's, who had taken over the Queen Mary kitchens. 'I am looking for … are you, perhaps, Mrs de Guise?'

'I am. But you are …?'

'Then I've come to the right place,' the man gasped, and the relief seemed to gush out of him, colouring all of his features. 'Please, you must fetch Raymond. I must see him straight away.'

'Raymond?' Nancy breathed, sensing Frank and Vivienne drawing closer, one over each shoulder. 'Sir, I think you must be mistaken. Raymond's not here. Raymond's … Well, I'm not sure precisely where he is. Raymond's at war.'

The man in the doorway fell silent – until, finally, the crest-fallen look that he wore exploded in a cry of, '*Sacre bleu!*'

'Sir, is everything OK?'

The man had grown agitated now. He rocked back on his heels, craning a look at the darkening sky. Dusk was already here. Soon, would come the night – and then, if ill-fortune found them, the sirens would start.

'You don't understand. Raymond is why I have come.' He tried to find his composure, straightened himself and took a deep breath. 'Mrs de Guise, forgive my impertinence. My name is Hugo Lavigne. I am, as perhaps you know, a very old friend of Raymond's. We danced together, in Paris. We danced together in Berlin and Vienna. All of this is many years ago now. Fifteen years separate us from that wonderful summer of dance. But Raymond and I, we were as brothers – long before he was *de Guise*. And …' Hugo had to steel himself with another breath. Nancy beckoned him forward, into the light of her hallway, and there she saw how harried were his eyes, how rigidly he was holding himself. 'Raymond once said that, if ever I was in need of a friend, I should come and find him straight away. He would help me, as I once helped him. And Mrs de Guise …' Hugo drew a hand across his brow, as if to wipe away the sweat that was beading there. 'I regret very much to do this to you, but I have never been in direr need, in all of my life.'

Chapter Four

Tonight, with but an hour to go before the doors of the ball-room opened, Max Allgood stepped through the doors of the Candlelight Club and breathed in the rich scents of tobacco smoke and cognac which filled the air. A drink to steady the nerves was practically a ritual in Max's life – but tonight he needed more than that. Thank God, then, that Archie Adams was waiting in the booth by the closed terrace doors. Archie had the statesmanlike grace of an abdicating king – he'd devoted his life to steadying the nerves of all the musicians who'd performed under him; Max only hoped that, tonight, he could steady his nerves as well.

'So, your night has come,' Archie said, welcoming Max to the booth. The brandy had already been poured; evidently, this was something of a ritual for Archie as well. 'It's not fear that dogs you, Max. I daresay it isn't even really nerves. If I'm right, it's nothing more than the feeling that greets every one of my musicians when they first step into the Grand. Max,' he smiled, encouragingly, 'it's *expectation.*'

Now Max could tell why Archie had gained such a devoted following. To be a bandleader was a strange mixture of army general, beloved uncle, and creative guiding hand. It required a man to implicitly understand another's character – and Archie evidently had that talent in abundance.

Only it wasn't quite the kind of expectation Archie meant. To play in front of dukes and duchesses, men of industry and power – this might have been the antithesis of how Max had been brought up, he and Lucille making music in the less salubrious quarters of New Orleans, but the thought of playing for such garlanded gentry would never spook a solid American man. The United States was a land that had outgrown kings and queens long before Max was born. The United States did not doff its cap to men who wore crowns. In the United States – or so it was said – a pauper might become president. So no, Max was not overwhelmed with the expectation of playing for aristocrats.

'It isn't the guests, Mr Adams.' Max only found the courage to say the next words by finishing his brandy in one deep gulp. 'It's the musicians.'

Archie inclined his head, as if asking Max to go on.

'You're anxious about them taking you to heart. You're anxious about becoming their leader.'

'Leading men who owe you nothing? Somehow it don't feel right. It don't feel earned. I don't know – perhaps I'm tying myself in knots. They seem like the nicest bunch of musicians a man could hope to jive with. But … I'm not one of them, Archie. There's a missing piece.'

But that, Archie began, was what this evening was all about.

Archie had announced his retirement from the Grand soon after the hotel's last Christmas festivities – but there was a reason his final hour in the ballroom had lasted so long. 'We didn't only need to find the right man to lead the orchestra, Max. We needed to make the change of leadership smooth. There are still some weeks before I'll truly step out of the doors.

We have to pave the way. Tonight: your first night as a member of the Orchestra. The first night Lucille,' and he smiled at the trombone case, propped up at Max's side like a faithful retainer, 'plays with the rest of the orchestra. Max, once they *hear* it, there won't be any question of whether they'll respect you as leader. Your music will come together with theirs. By the time I exit the stage, the band will be yours: the Max Allgood Orchestra.'

So, Archie would pave the way for Max to glide in, while Max paved the way for Archie to glide out. There was a beautiful symmetry to it.

'The Summer Ball's to be your evening debut as bandleader,' Archie went on. 'That gives us just over two months to effect a changing of the guard.' He saw Max's bemused expression and went on, 'That's a very English saying. Take a stroll along the Horse Guards Parade one day – the changing of the King's guard, it's quite a sight to be seen.'

'You make it sound so easy, Mr Adams.' A second brandy had mysteriously appeared, courtesy of one of the Candlelight Club's silent waiters. 'But we both know it ain't like changing the wheel on a motorcar.'

'I'm afraid that's not a task I've ever attempted, Mr Allgood.'

'Well, next time you find yourself stranded in a siding off Interstate 310, with the clock tick-tick-ticking until you've got to play in some hotel lounge, you give me a call. I'm a musician at heart, but there isn't a job I haven't done somewhere along the way. No, sir, not except … well, except leading an orchestra of musicians I hardly know.' At last, Max could see the funny side of it. 'Say, I've got to ask it, seeing as how there isn't another one of *me* in the orchestra. Why'd you do it, Mr Adams? Why'd you hire a black man to take your place?'

Archie's eyes opened fractionally wider. 'I didn't, Max. I hired a musician, and a damned fine one at that.'

'There's no need for airs, Mr Adams. I'll be the only black man in the Grand tonight, won't I? Even when I played at the Prince George, back in New York, I wasn't alone. But here in Europe...'

If there was one difference between the clubs of New York and the venues he'd played in across Europe, it was race. Paris had had its share of black jazz musicians, and of course in the clubs of London and Bristol there were trumpeters and saxophonists who hailed from far-flung corners of the Commonwealth of Nations. But in esteemed English society? Somehow, Max doubted that men of his colour skin were very often seen playing for the King.

Something told Max he had made Archie feel uncomfortable. 'My father was born a slave, Mr Adams. He was eighteen years old before emancipation. The world changes slowly, when it changes at all.'

Archie said, 'Don't mistake the United States for Great Britain, Mr Allgood. We do things rather differently here.'

Max wasn't certain about that. There were still corners of London where signs were erected at the doors of public houses, cafés, public washrooms: NO IRISH. NO DOGS. NO BLACKS.

'War changes everything, Mr Allgood,' said Archie – and, draining his glass, invited Max to stand. The hour of the Orchestra's first number was rapidly approaching.

Together, they wended their way to the cocktail lounge's exit, then out onto the plush third-storey landing. Soon, they had stepped into the golden elevator cage, and an attendant in a resplendent white suit operated the controls to guide them down.

'I still marvel at the idea, Mr Adams. Here I stand, the son of a slaved man – about to play my trombone for the class of man who once owned folks like me.'

The elevator attendant's eyes darted madly, as if he didn't quite know which way he ought to look.

'The Buckingham's changed too,' said Archie, as he led Max out of the elevator. The reception hall was alive, but soon they were approaching the dressing rooms at the rear of the Grand. 'You have to understand – the war upended everything. The old world's changing. It's had to, in the face of all *this*.' Archie hovered on the precipice, about to guide Max through the dressing-room doors. 'So whatever old worries there are inside you, just know that there's a new world being born.' Archie paused. 'Are you ready?'

Archie's words had given Max some of the bravado he ought to have been feeling all along.

'Let me,' said Max, in the same second that Archie reached for the door handle.

He'd been about to go in first, to greet the other musicians without the need for Archie to re-introduce him – yet, before he could step past, Archie brought him to a halt. Some thought seemed to have occurred to the accomplished pianist, a thought he'd been holding on to in the Candlelight Club. It seemed, all of a sudden, that Archie would not let Max through those doors without giving it voice.

'Mr Allgood, it would be remiss of me not to tell you this. Remiss, even though I'm quite certain you've a loyal orchestra in there.' Archie took a breath, as if steeling himself. 'I want you to tread carefully around my percussionist, Harry Dudgeon. Harry's one of my oldest hands. He's been playing percussion with me since long before the Grand. A finer musician you're unlikely to meet. In fact, Harry's been rather wasted as a percussionist these years – he's as fine a pianist as I've ever been, and might have been off leading his own band somewhere, if only the Grand hadn't captured his heart. Harry's going to—'

'Take your place at the piano, when all's said and done,' said Max. He'd spoken about this already, with Walter Knave and John Hastings, the Head of the Board. 'I've no objection, Mr Adams. We'll need a man who knows his way up and down the piano keys.' He hoisted Lucille up. 'I could never let her go, but it's a fine thing to have a piano at the heart of a band. Harry can make it his own.'

'He would have liked to,' said Archie.

Max faltered, before saying, 'I don't like riddles, Mr Adams. I'm a plain-speaking man. I like to say things how they are.'

'When I first broke the news that I was leaving the Grand, Harry let it be known that he would love the opportunity to steer the orchestra into its future. Quite unbeknownst to me, he even made a formal petition to Mr Knave. I happen to know that Mr Knave was quite taken by the idea. He values reliability, dependability, the things he *knows* to be true. The trouble is, music thrives very differently. Music needs reinvention. It needs a little daring. Mr Hastings knew that, and so did I. That's why you're here, Mr Allgood. To provide a touch of excitement – something a little bit different, a little bit wild and free. Yes, it's the right choice, of course – but it did rather diminish poor Harry. He and I have raised a glass together since – but it is, perhaps, worth you holding in mind.'

Max said, 'He's not bitter?'

'He'll get to play piano at the heart of the Grand, just like he always dreamed. By any standard, Harry's star is rising.'

Through the doors, the voice of Marcus Arbuthnot rallying his troupe of dancers could be heard. Marcus was a man who might have forged a career treading the boards at any of London's finest playhouses; he had the air of some Shakespearean actor,

reciting a soliloquy and rousing his followers to battle: Henry
V, perhaps, as he readied his retinue for Agincourt.

'Twenty minutes until the ballroom opens,' said Archie. 'Max,
let us begin.'

Through the doors they came. The dancers – Marcus and
Karina holding court over their younger charges – were gathered
in one corner of the long, horseshoe-shaped dressing rooms,
while the musicians lounged around the practice grand piano
in the rehearsal studio beyond. It was towards them that
Archie made his way, Max walking in his wake. Max, held up
momentarily by the well-wishes of the dancers – 'A star rises
tonight, Mr Allgood!' declared Marcus Arbuthnot, with one of
his trademark theatrical flourishes – was late to the party. By
then, the musicians were already greeting Archie. And there was
Harry Dudgeon, hunkering over the piano keys – as if, thought
Max, his patience couldn't last a few short weeks; as if, in his
eagerness to take up the instrument, he had quite forgotten that
Archie was still among them.

Harry Dudgeon was an olive-skinned man; perhaps there was
some Mediterranean blood in him, for in his eyes Max fancied
he could see the sparkle of those carefree men he'd seen playing
in the beachfront restaurants of Cannes and Nice. He was, Max
thought, a little older than him – not quite Archie's age, but
certainly pushing his half-centenary. There was a warmth to
Dudgeon, thought Max; he was laughing at some ribald joke
one of the trumpeters seemed to have made. They fell silent,
awkwardly, when they caught Max looking – but that, he supposed, was only the way men fell silent at the appearance of
an outsider. After a pregnant pause, hands were being shaken,
and Max was quickly enveloped in the convivial chatter. 'It'll
be quite a crowd tonight,' Harry Dudgeon was saying. Then the
orchestra's sole cornet player chimed in, 'M. de Geer's in tonight,

and all of his ministers. There's a diplomatic dinner going on. All very hush-hush.'

M. de Geer: the elderly premier of the Netherlands, long ago overrun by the Nazis; Queen Wilhelmina's prime minister, running her government in exile from offices, suites and clubs in London town.

The chatter went on until the rehearsal room door opened and Frank Nettleton, still the scruffiest among the hotel dancers – no matter how hard Marcus was trying to polish him up – put his head round the door. 'Five minutes. It's almost time.'

It was at this point that Archie gathered the musicians. 'My friends: we come to it, at last. Not the end – but at least its beginning.' The smile he wore was genuine – for, like an old man counting out his final days, he knew that the end was in sight. 'Mr Allgood, perhaps you might like to say a few words?'

All Max could say was, 'Mr Adams, that's good of you – but tonight, I'd rather let the music do the talking.'

When he hoisted up Lucille, he realised that, quite by accident, he'd said exactly the right thing. Only a room full of true musicians could have appreciated the wisdom – and perhaps the sheer cheek – of what Max had said. One after another, they began clapping him on the back, welcoming him aboard, geeing him on. Even Harry Dudgeon was beaming when he said, 'Let her sing, Mr Allgood, let her sing!'

Then the musicians marched back towards the dressing room and the ballroom doors beyond.

'I told you they were a welcoming crowd,' said Archie, softly.

'Let's just pray the crowd out there's as welcoming.'

The hour had come. In the dressing room, the dancers were assembled. Marcus had them lined up at the doors, even Frank Nettleton suddenly verging on debonair, Mathilde Bourchier as elegant as a princess in her gown of chiffon and lace. And yet their turn had not quite come. Before the dancers waltzed out onto the ballroom floor, the orchestra must assume their positions.

Twin doors opened directly onto the dance floor. This was the moment that always moved Archie, the moment when he knew the years of his life had been well spent. Max watched as he pushed the doors apart and, lingering in their frame for just a second, listened to the silence settle in the ballroom. At once, all the conversations out there ended. Now, the only thing hanging heavy in the air was *expectation*. Archie let it wash over them. Then he strode out.

One after another, the musicians followed. In single file they came, those with instruments carrying them as proudly as the soldiers of old carried their banners into war.

Then, at last, it was Max's turn.

'Good luck, old son,' said Harry Dudgeon, who marched directly in front of him. 'Don't just let her sing, Mr Allgood, let her *soar*.'

Soaring, thought Max as he reached the door. Yes, he liked that.

In the ballroom, Archie was taking to the stage. The rest of the orchestra assembled around him. Max was the last to the stairs. As he climbed them, he tried to steady his breathing. By God, he *belonged* here. He'd been chosen. Max Allgood, who'd picked up an instrument in a detention centre and felt, suddenly, as if he'd been summoned by the Lord, was going to take his rightful place among the Orchestra that, by the Summer Ball, would bear his name.

Archie struck the first chord. Max knew this one, for he'd been forewarned. 'Moonlight on the Ganges', a classic foxtrot, one of the oldies – but played in Archie's inimitably lively style.

The applause reached a new peak when the dance floor doors opened for the second time. Out whirled the dancers, Marcus Arbuthnot and Karina Kainz turning together as the rest of the troupe fanned out behind them. And Max thought, then, that he understood why this place was so special: it wasn't just music; it was the spectacle of the night.

He brought Lucille to his lips.

He looked out into the crowd.

Which one was a lord? he wondered. Which was a man of industry, financing the war against the Germans? Which a decorated hero of that same war?

Then his heart was stilled – because, of all the unfamiliar faces in the room, his eyes had suddenly lit upon one he'd seen before, back in another time, back in another world, back in the age when the lives of Max and Daisy Allgood were very different indeed.

Could that really be Jackson Ford, that shady hack writer from the *New York Times*, propped up by the cocktail bar, with a gin rickey in his hand?

Ford seemed to have seen him too. His face had creased with confusion – but then, in an instant, recognition dawned.

Max's lips were hovering over the trombone's cup, pursed and ready to blow. He did not miss his moment, for Max had been playing all his long life – and the body remembered what to do, even when the mind had strayed. So it was that Lucille joined 'Moonlight on the Ganges' with a bright, breezy perfection, marking out Max's first moment in the Orchestra.

His music fitted so perfectly that he might have been part of the ensemble forever.

So perfectly in fact that, in the Grand Ballroom, nobody noticed that two men's minds had been set aflutter.

Nobody knew that two men's minds were scrabbling backwards in time, trying to remember where each had come across the other before.

Nobody knew that all of Max Allgood's fears about fitting in had melted clean away – and that his heart was quaking for a different reason altogether.

Chapter Five

'Mr Lavigne,' breathed Nancy, 'are you in some kind of trouble?'

Nancy wasn't certain why, but something about the man on the doorstep drew out every good feeling in her heart. Perhaps it was merely the mention of Raymond, but there was something in Hugo's eyes – both harried and yet sparkling with warmth – that called out to her. Vivienne and Frank, it seemed, were less certain. Vivienne had taken Stan in her arms protectively, but the boy himself did not seem in the least bit perturbed. He was craning his neck to watch the new visitor as he stepped into the hall.

'I did not mean it to be like this, Mrs de Guise,' Hugo purred, the agitation he'd shown a few moments before melting away now that he no longer stood on the doorstep. 'Please, you must accept my humble apologies. I had wanted to visit the Buckingham Hotel, but I thought my appearance there might be *unprofessional* for my old friend. Now I see that he has forsaken his dancing shoes and taken the king's shilling. Tell me, is my old friend all right?'

'It's been some time since we heard from him, Mr Lavigne. The postal routes to North Africa are long and infrequent.'

Hugo's eyes widened suddenly, as if he was taking in Nancy for the first time. 'But Mrs de Guise, you are ... with child!'

Nancy nodded. 'I'm but a few weeks away. Mr Lavigne, you must come in. We've hot dinner and drink and…'

'Nance,' Frank whispered, urgently, 'oughtn't we to … make sure?'

Suddenly, the sounds of a pot boiling over on the stovetop rushed up – and Vivienne, still bearing Stan in her arms, hurried off to attend to the mess.

'Frankie,' Nancy cautioned him, 'this man's our guest.' Yet, as she said the words, some element of uncertainty must have crept into her voice as well – for, when she looked back at Hugo, a chastened air had come across his face.

'Mrs de Guise, your young man is quite right to question me. A strange Frenchman, appearing alone out of the night? Ghost stories have been built on much less. So allow me to …' Out of a pocket in his coat, he quickly produced a worn, sepia-coloured notebook whose legend read REPUBLIQUE FRANÇAIS, PASSEPORT DE SERVICE. 'I'm afraid it's issued by the current Conseil d'État – traitors, every one of them – but at least it provides my *bona-fides*. I am who I say I am, Mrs de Guise. And you,' he said, eyes lifting to Frank, 'must be the young Mr Nettleton. Lord of the dance, I am told – or so it shall one day be.' Hugo had seen the way Frank's eyes goggled at the recognition and added, 'Raymond and I might not have seen much of each other since our Continental days, but I have always admired the journey of his career from afar. I have always read, with much envy, news from the Buckingham Hotel. Please,' he went on, 'I do not wish to unnerve you. I will go, but perhaps …'

At once Nancy said, 'Mr Lavigne, you came here looking for Raymond's help. Please, tell me why you came.'

Hugo had already turned away when a sudden idea occurred to him. 'Tell me, does Raymond keep old copies of *Dancing Times*?'

Nancy could not help but smile. Raymond had been a devotee of the ballroom dance publication ever since he was a young man. The first time he'd featured in its pages was, he said, one of the proudest moments of his young life.

'They're in the back room. Please, come through.'

Frank was still uncertain as Hugo followed Nancy into the second sitting room, a small study where the fire was hardly ever lit. The cabinet by the fireside was an archive of all the issues of *Dancing Times* Raymond had collected. Soon, Nancy was on her knees, lifting out piles to place them by the hearth.

'You may need to go back to the beginning, Mrs de Guise. The Exhibition Paris, 1926.'

Nancy looked up. 'That was Raymond's first appearance...'

He'd spoken of it often: the first time his name was mentioned in the hallowed pages of the publication he loved. At least this made it easy to unearth. Very quickly, she found the reportage of the Exhibition Paris, that great ballroom contest to which Raymond's mentor had taken him, the place where he truly began to believe that the ballroom could become his life.

The mention of Raymond was brief, but the coverage of the Exhibition itself dominated the magazine's centre spread. There, in grainy black-and-white, was a picture of the enormous dance floor – and, on its chequered boards, a hundred dancers. She found Raymond immediately: ten years younger than the man she'd first met. The caption beneath the photograph read CASINO DE PARIS, COMPETITORS 1926. It was certainly an indulgent, opulent venue. It looked, perhaps, *garish* compared to the old-world elegance of the Buckingham Hotel. The Casino de Paris had an air of some old emperor's court about it – and there, at its heart, stood Raymond de Guise, waiting for the world of dance to send him on a trajectory to the stars.

'There's Raymond,' said Hugo, 'and, look, Georges de la Motte…'

Raymond's mentor – and Nancy felt certain, then, that Hugo was honest and true, for how else would he know of Georges?

'And here I am,' said Hugo.

He had pointed to a lean, angular dancer standing directly behind Raymond – and, of course, there was no doubt it was Hugo. He had the same chiselled look, the same almond-shaped eyes, even the same prim posture as the Frenchman who now crouched beside Nancy. 'It was where we met. Both of us, competing in the Exhibition. We were like brothers that summer, and brothers for the summers to come. First it was Paris. Then Berlin. Vienna…' He reeled each city off as if he was an old lover, swooning over their great romance. 'Every ballroom competition across the Continent. Three wild, ecstatic years, that made us the dancers we became. Then, of course, life intervened. Raymond was summoned to the Buckingham, and we danced in Europe no longer.' Hugo looked awkward and closed the magazine. 'It suddenly feels so mercenary of me.'

'What does?' asked Frank.

'That I should come here and say this. Mrs de Guise, Mr Nettleton, I find myself lost in the world. Paris has fallen to the Nazi scourge. My country is gone, and I have escaped by the skin of my teeth. Well, better risk a midnight crossing across the sea than another night in the patrolled streets of Paris. And yet… an exile still needs to eat. He still needs a roof above his head. My pockets are empty, of money and goodwill. And I remembered, then, how Raymond had always said: I shall always think of you as a brother, Hugo; I shall always be here, when you are in need.' He smiled, sadly. 'So that is why I have come. To call in an old favour.'

Vivienne had appeared in the doorway, trailing Stan by the hand. She parted her lips, as if she was about to invite them through for the dinner, when Nancy said, 'An old favour, Mr Lavigne?'

And Hugo nodded. 'I'm afraid so. You must understand, Raymond *owes* me. Without me, he might never have become a professional ballroom dancer at all.'

There was a story in this, a story just begging to be told.

'Vivienne,' said Nancy, successfully pretending that she hadn't just winced, for the weight of the baby was beginning to play the devil with her back, 'I think there'll be one more for dinner tonight.'

One more for dinner, Nancy thought – and, instead of the wireless playing the BBC News, a story to be told: the story of her husband Raymond, in the long-ago time when he was just becoming a man.

Ray Cohen had rarely set foot outside Whitechapel, so the idea that he would be accompanying Georges de la Motte on a Continental voyage had, at first, been too much to comprehend. It had certainly been too much to comprehend for his family, and in particular his brother Artie, who – when he wasn't busy with the boys from the Prospect of Whitby, lingering round the docksides, wondering what it might be possible to pinch – had strutted around the kitchen at the Cohen family home, shoving his nose in the air and pretending to be a haughty French lord. 'Georges isn't like that,' Raymond had protested – though, of course, he was. The final, forgotten son of a minor French baronet, he had forsaken what titles and lands might have been his and embraced a life in the ballroom, but it didn't mean he'd ever forgotten his airs and graces.

It wasn't until the moment he set foot on French soil that he truly believed this was real. He'd waited for Georges in the lobby of a small Dover hotel, having taken the morning train out of London, and even then it hadn't seemed real. He'd boarded the ferry, and felt himself green around the gills – but even then it hadn't seemed real. He couldn't keep his brother's braying laughter out of his mind until the ferry arrived at port in Calais, and he followed Georges down the pier, into a strange new land.

'How do you feel, Ray?' Georges asked, as they boarded the private carriage of another train, one that would take them directly into the heart of the old world, the heart of glamour, the eye of an impassioned musical storm: Paris itself. Georges was a stately gentlemen, with near perfect English thanks to the many years he'd spent in London. Georges had first encountered a young Ray Cohen one year before, peeling him off the floor of a Brighton public house after he'd spectacularly failed to win a place at the Grand Hotel's ballroom competition. It was Georges who, convinced that Ray had talent – despite his tumultuous display in that public house – had invited him to the Kensington mansion where he was staying, to spend a succession of long, intense afternoons instructing him in various aspects of position and poise. 'You need smartening up, young man, if you're to be a ballroom dancer. There are plenty who came from lives like yours, then touched the giddy heights. It isn't just the sons of dukes who dance. But you lack precision. You lack a certain elegant air. If you can learn these things, it will carry you far …'

Ray could still hear those words. He was thinking about them now, as the train sailed towards Paris. 'Am I ready for this, Georges?'

Georges flicked back his hair. 'Ray, your time has come.

I have had you in mind all year. I always knew our journeys would bring us together again – and so they have.'

Journeys. It was a rather strange word to use, thought Ray, when he'd spent the entire year since Brighton heaving bricks and timber in the builder's yard where his father's friends all worked, while Georges was gallivanting from ballroom to ballroom, from the townhouse of one lady to the country manor of another. Ray had, at least, been frequenting the dance halls and social clubs of the East End on a Saturday night. 'I think I might have lost some of my poise across the year, Georges. I'm not the dancer you left behind.'

'Oh, but you will be, young man. I'll see to it. We've still several days before the opening salvos of the Exhibition Paris. You'll be waltzing like a prince by the time you take to the floor.'

Georges had returned to London at the behest of a Flemish princess, currently resident at the Savoy, and was glad of the opportunity it gave him to rediscover his former charge. 'I have an offer to make you, young sir,' he had said, facing Ray across the dining table at the Academy des Artistes, that private members' club where he dined each evening. 'At the end of the month, I go to Paris, for the Exhibition at the Casino de Paris. A ballroom dance competition, Raymond, quite unlike any you'll have danced in before. My dance partner Antoinette and I will be competing, but there is an open competition which dominates the first days of the event. I would like you to enter, Raymond. I believe it could be good for you.'

'Good for me, sir?' Ray hadn't quite been certain that Georges would remember him, let alone call on him for such an assignment. 'How?'

'Well, young man, do you *want* to be a dancer, or not?'

It hardly seemed possible that a man could make a career

out of dancing. It seemed even less likely that an East End lad, without any breeding, could make it in that kind of world.

'I do,' Ray had said, 'but...'

'Sometimes, young Cohen, we have to grasp the opportunities set in front of us. Here it is, right now – my gift to you. Seize it, boy! Seize it with both hands!'

Ray tried to hold on to that sentiment as the train reached Paris. He tried to hold on to it as a taxicab, expertly summoned by Georges – the sort of man to whom the world sometimes seemed to owe its deference – took them past sights of which Ray had hardly heard: the Arc de Triomphe and the Tour Eiffel, the great Gothic hulk of Notre Dame.

The Hotel Acacias was as grand an establishment as Ray had ever seen – although it seemed to be but a minor palace to Georges, who casually abandoned his cases at the bottom of the steps, then beckoned Ray to follow him through the doors. 'There's a small ballroom here, Ray, which we may use to rehearse. They know me here. They make allowances.' The idea there was a ballroom in a hotel was itself a wonder to Ray, and the idea that the hoteliers knew Georges intimately enough to offer it up for his use was more wondrous still. It was, he decided, not so dissimilar to the local publicans knowing his father – except that here, in the Hotel Acacias, it was opulence and grandeur being offered up, not just an extra half-pint of Mackeson's stout.

Ray had been allotted less palatial digs with a landlady whose rooms looked out on the hotel – but Georges was to stay right here, at the Acacias. Ray's embarrassment at being provided for so well only left him when he saw the size of the suite Georges had been allotted. Ray Cohen had never seen a four-poster bed hidden behind curtains before. It seemed quite unthinkable that any man, no matter how lordly, would need a suite three times the size of his family home.

'Rest, Ray. Tonight we dine below, and I shall introduce you to Antoinette and her consorts.'

And this he did – only, when Ray sat at the table in the plush hotel restaurant, listening to the babble of French voices around him, he felt as out of place as he supposed Georges would if fate had brought him to Whitechapel. He shook hands and smiled demurely, and poked his *escargots* around his plate, wondering why the thought of snails for supper turned his stomach when his mother's eel pie always smelt so divine, and tried to keep at bay the insidious thought that he did not belong here.

Ray slept fitfully that night, but at least that meant he was awake at dawn, just as Georges had prescribed. 'A stiff walk in the breeze along the Seine, my boy. That's what gets the blood flowing – and you'll need it flowing freely, for what's to come today.'

The Casino de Paris: it might not have been the most ostentatious sight he'd seen since he set foot in the city, but it was the one that most overawed the young Ray Cohen as he and Georges stepped out of the taxicab he'd hired and made the approach. The dance hall, with its towering cream pillars and windows of stained glass, dominated the rue de Clichy.

The auditorium was vaster than any of the ballrooms Ray had competed in, vaster still than the Brancroft Social where he had first learned to dance. An expansive dance floor was ringed by tiers of seating, while the front of the auditorium was dominated by a grand stage, now cloaked in plush, crimson curtains. Ray had often felt small in the ballroom, but rarely had he felt as diminutive as he did now.

At least Georges was acting as if he truly belonged. Ray watched, now, as he strode onto the dance floor, a giant of a man with the daintiest, most precise footwork. He seemed to be dancing with a partner made from thin air – he'd taken her in hold, bowed her backwards, then pivoted around – as he came, at last, to the two elegant ladies standing in the dance floor's heart.

In three days' time, this dance floor would be swarmed with competitors – but now there were only a few scattered groups making use of its environs. Ray supposed they had been given permission to get used to the idiosyncrasies of the auditorium, for every dance floor was different. That was a lesson Ray had had to learn the hard way – dancing in the Brancroft Social had made him feel like a prince, but the moment he danced in a grander ballroom, he was back to being a pauper again. He gazed around. Two young couples were box-stepping on the periphery of the dance floor. A dashing young Frenchman and his partner were making a mad foxtrot from one side of the hall to the other. And there, in the midst of them all, Georges was greeting the two elegant ladies by planting kisses on the air around their cheeks.

'Raymond, my boy, come, come! Come and meet your partner.'

He'd known an introduction would have to be made, but Ray had been so blown away by the scale of the Casino de Paris that he hadn't yet wondered who the two ladies might be. Now he understood: the elder lady, with the auburn hair cascading around her shoulders, was Antoinette, the grand French dame who'd been dancing with Georges since the century was born.

'Mr Cohen, I am pleased to make your acquaintance.' Antoinette's English was not as polished as Georges's, but the tone of her voice was like music itself. Ray took her hand graciously, and bowed in imitation of Georges some moments before. 'I have heard so much, Mr Cohen. Georges's diamond in the rough!'

Ray was not certain he liked the description; to be a diamond was one thing, but to come from the rough quite another.

'But young man,' Antoinette went on, still caressing his hand, 'it surely isn't my hand you're anxious to take.' And she stepped aside, revealing the younger lady standing beside her. Smaller than Antoinette, perhaps no more than a few months in age older than Raymond, she was an angel with dark eyes. Golden hair fell in a single tight braid across her shoulder. Her lips were full and red, her body – though small – statuesque. Her eyes betrayed some element of the same nervousness Ray was feeling. She seemed not to know where to look, darting glances at all the different corners of the ballroom, until at last Antoinette went on, 'Ophelia, you may introduce yourself.'

'Raymond, you may do likewise,' intoned Georges, with a broad smile. 'Antoinette has hand-selected Ophelia from her circle, Raymond. It is hoped you two have the symmetry needed to perform most artfully in a competition like this.' He took Antoinette's hand, teasing her away from Ray and Ophelia, who had started to blush. 'Of course, no dancer performs in isolation. Dance is an art that must be shared. In the ballroom, we come together. I should be nothing without Antoinette.'

'And I should be nothing without you, Georges.'

Georges smiled. Ray felt some sense of mounting panic as he watched them retreating. 'Dance on, Ray. Dance on, Ophelia. Three days separate us from this competition. In that time, you must learn how to fly.'

After that, Antoinette and Georges carried on conversing, but both had abandoned the English language for their mother tongue, and Ray had no hope of keeping up. Instead, he turned to Ophelia and said, 'To dance without music, then. We might have a finer beginning.' He shuffled forward, opening his arms as if to take her in hold. It would be a little mechanical without music, but the other couples seemed to be managing perfectly well. And all Ray really needed was not to humiliate himself.

So he took her in his arms.

He began with a little box-stepping, just so that each could get the measure of the other. The girls Ray had danced with in the clubs back home had all been very different to one another, tall and short, slender and broad, and he was not so naïve to think that they would slip together perfectly – and yet, as he warmed into the routine, leading Ophelia first into a slow waltz and then gradually upping the tempo, he started to feel as if he was wrong, that there really was a perfect dance partner after all. Ophelia seemed to fit him like a glove. Her body arced around his. The top of her head reached his chin, and her golden braid swung in the air every time they turned.

Soon, Ray had forgotten that there wasn't any music to dance to. He fancied that Ophelia was hearing the very same songs. As they burst from their silent waltz into a wonderful, breezy fox-trot, Ray could hear the stampeding sounds of Paul Whiteman's 'Stumbling' chiming in his mind. He was in absolutely no doubt that Ophelia was listening to the same rolling beat.

At last, to the sounds of Georges and Antoinette applauding, the dance came to its end. For a moment, Ray was quite discombobulated.

'How – how did it feel?' Ray asked, nervously.

Ophelia only dipped her head, her long eyelashes fluttering. 'Thank you, Ray.'

'Ophelia, come,' Antoinette called out, and soon her young charge was leaving Ray's side, to join Antoinette and Georges by the edge of the dance floor.

For a time, Ray stood alone in the centre of the ballroom. The three French dancers had their heads bowed in conversation. It was strange, but Ophelia seemed so much more animated, now, than when she first left Ray's arms. He supposed it was because she was now able to flurry forth in her own language – but something in it injured Ray all the same. It wasn't just the way eyes kept darting at him, almost as if they were inspecting him; it was the feeling he'd had, ever since he started his journey with Georges, that he was to be the outsider here, that – no matter what Georges said – he really wasn't meant for this world.

'Do you want to know what they're saying?'

The voice shook Ray out of his reverie. Turning, he discovered the handsome Frenchman, with his perfectly coiffured black hair and striking eyes, standing beside him.

'Excuse me?'

'Allow me to introduce myself.' The Frenchman's English was full of rolling Rs and strangely pronounced vowels, but his command of it seemed superb nevertheless. 'My name is Hugo, Hugo Lavigne. I see you standing here, looking so forlorn, that it near breaks this dancer's heart.' He winked; there was evidently some element of jest in what he was saying, and this put Ray at ease. 'You already know they're speaking of you. Wouldn't you like to *know?*'

Ray hesitated for a moment, before he said, 'Yes...'

Hugo grinned. 'It is like reading someone's diary, is it not? To eavesdrop on them. To *understand*. But I say – what impudence they show, to speak of you so openly, safe in the knowledge you do not understand!' Now, he narrowed his eyes, focusing on Georges, Antoinette and Ophelia, standing twenty yards away. 'It is no good. I shall have to dance,' he declared. Then, re-summoning his partner, he set off in a close waltz around the trio, dancing closer and closer with each turn until, some moments later, he broke off and returned to Ray's side. 'The good news is she thinks you are very handsome.'

'Hugo,' Ray spluttered. 'I hardly think that's what they're—'

'The bad news is, she finds you too stiff, too jumpy, too ... brash.'

'Brash?' asked Ray, flabbergasted.

'Perhaps this is not the right word. My English is, as you must feel, very uncommon. And yet ... She is uncertain of you, my friend. She is desperate to win. Well, aren't we all? And she worries that with you, she will squander her chances.'

Ray knew he ought not to feel angry with Hugo, yet he suddenly felt as fiery as his brother Artie did every time he lost money down at the dogs. 'You're lying to me.' Because it had felt *good*, hadn't it? It hadn't even mattered that there wasn't music.

'I'm sorry, English,' Hugo shrugged, 'this competition isn't for you.'

Ray's eyes had drifted back to Georges, Antoinette and Ophelia, but now he turned sharply to Hugo. Too late – the Frenchman had waltzed away with his partner again, leaving only a bitter aftertaste in the back of Ray's throat, the taste of his bile, the taste of disappointment.

Georges had detached himself from Antoinette and Ophelia – who were now taking off across the dance floor and through the doors of the Casino de Paris – and was suddenly at his side.

'Ray, my boy, I have good news and bad.'

'I don't understand, sir. It felt good to me. She felt as if she *fitted*. I thought I could even hear the music.'

Georges shook his head sadly. 'The stars did not align. You were, I think, dancing to different pieces. And yet ...'

'And yet, Georges?'

'Antoinette and I are so rarely wrong about this kind of thing. Together, we have matched many dancers. After a little time, one develops an instinct for it. Raymond, my boy, I believe you and Ophelia can go far in this competition. I can picture it – but, very simply, you were not dancing *together* today. You were dancing apart, though you hung in each other's arms.'

Georges paused, as quietly he continued to ruminate.

'Was that the *good* news, Georges?'

'Oh, heavens, no, my boy! The good news is this: Ophelia has not written you off. She became quite emotional, I'm afraid. She wants so desperately to repay the faith Antoinette has shown in her. This competition? She sees it as her big chance. But she cannot do it without a partner in whom she wholeheartedly believes.'

Ray's heart sank. 'And that isn't me.'

'Well, not *yet*. Raymond, Ophelia has agreed that you and she should try one more time. I have access to the ballroom at the Hotel Acacias. Tomorrow, at noon, we will repair there for one hour of dance. I shall arrange musicians to accompany you. By 1 p.m., Raymond, you and Ophelia will be as one. Promise me now.'

Promise? thought Ray. He didn't know if he could promise a thing anymore. He didn't, in that very moment, know if he could even dance.

'I'll do everything I can, Georges,' he said – and this seemed to satisfy the grand older man.

Once again, Ray stood alone. He was standing alone still when the dark-haired Frenchman, Hugo, waltzed back his way and said, 'Is that it, *mon frère*? Are you to forsake the Exhibition Paris after all?'

Ray was still not feeling kindly towards the dashing young man, but he knew better than to betray the true depth of his feeling. 'I'm to be given another chance,' he replied.

'Ophelia Chalfont is a prized dancer,' Hugo said, with a kind of wistful admiration. 'A beauty as well, of course. You'll want to do all you can to win her hand.'

Ray snorted, 'I wasn't aware I had to woo the girl. I only want to dance.'

'You are making a cardinal mistake, Englishman. If she is to dance with you, she will need to feel the thrill of it. The dance isn't in the body. It's in the heart.' He paused. 'And, my English friend, your mind is somewhere else.'

There was some insult brewing here; Ray could feel it. 'What do you know of it?' he snapped.

'I know what I saw, and I know what everybody else saw. I saw a nervous, scared dancer, stiffening up. I saw a dancer who was *thinking* about each step before he took it.'

'I wasn't,' said Ray, trying not to be affronted. 'I was listening to the music.'

'There was no music.'

'The music in my head...'

At this, Hugo just laughed. 'Do you know what you really need, *mon frère*?'

Ray bristled, 'I'm sure you're about to tell me.'

'What you need is: the java.'

'The java?'

'Of course, the java. You're dancing like you're on strings. You're dancing with your head. What you need is to dance with your heart – but you've forgotten how. No, don't look at me like that – I'm no better than you are. I felt the wretchedness once too – and what saved me was the wild, carefree, untutored dancing of Pigalle. The java!'

Ray just stared. 'Hugo, I truly don't know what you're talking about.'

'No, of course you don't! The plaything of Georges de la Motte would not know the *java*. And yet... the java is the dance of the people of Paris. It will get you hot. It will get you excited. It will untangle all the knots in your body and mind.'

Hugo was beaming. There was something wicked, and yet truly magnetic, about that smile.

'Well, Ray, what do you think? Before you dance the Viennese waltz with Ophelia tomorrow. What might a night of dancing wild and free do for your soul?'

Around the dining table at Blomfield Road, where the plates were almost clean of the hotpot Vivienne had served, Hugo was about go on, when the mournful song of the air raid sirens started to be heard.

At once, Vivienne swept Stan out of his chair. 'Snuff out the candles, Frank. We're going to the shelter.'

At the table, Frank leapt to his feet. He was reaching for the candles when Nancy said, 'Take Mr Lavigne to the shelter, Frank. I'll lock up here.'

'Mrs de Guise,' Hugo ventured, rising to his feet, 'are you sure?'

But of course she was. If there'd been any doubt in her mind, then it had been dispelled the moment Hugo started speaking of Raymond. By the time Nancy first met Raymond, he was already King of the Ballroom. To hear of him in the days before, when he hadn't been certain of himself, when he'd scarcely found his footing in the ballroom – let alone envisaged a life where he might dance among lords and ladies – had opened some unknown corner of her heart.

The baby turned inside her. Perhaps he too longed for his father; he too had been moved by the man his father had once been.

'Hugo, you must stay the night.' She paused. Frank was at the door, so now it was Nancy who snuffed out the candles. As soon as it was done, Frank opened the back door and, beckoning to them both, hurried off along the garden path. 'We're nothing if we don't help the people we love. I've made it my business, ever since I came to London. I don't have much family left, Hugo – only Frank, and what I've made here. Vivienne and Stan, my girls at the hotel, Raymond and our baby. There's enough that's bad in the world, so I reckon it's on us all to do what little good we can with the time we're given.' She rushed back through the house, locked and bolted the front door – and then rejoined Hugo at the back kitchen door. 'Tomorrow I'll visit Mr Knave up at the hotel. The dance troupe's strong, but there's no secret that they are always in need of talented, male dancers. Half of the ones we had were taken when the call-ups came in. So if Mr Knave and Mr Arbuthnot have the opportunity for a new dancer of your standing...' Nancy opened the back door, and shepherded Hugo into the night.

They were halfway to the Anderson shelter when Hugo said, 'Mrs de Guise, I couldn't be more grateful for what you're doing for me.'

'One good turn deserves another, Mr Lavigne.' She ushered him past, then followed him into the sanctuary of the Anderson shelter. Inside the cramped interior, dug three feet into the ground with a cylinder of corrugated steel above, Stan was already sound asleep. 'And it rather sounds as if, if you hadn't been at the Casino de Paris, I wouldn't be where I am today. It rather sounds as if, without the java, my baby wouldn't be about to be born.'

History was made out of coincidences, thought Nancy. Who was to say that, without any one thing, a hundred more might not have happened? The ripples of one act, whether of kindness or ill-will, went out into the world and touched countless lives – and there seemed no doubt that Hugo's kindness of sixteen years ago had, somehow, shaped hers.

So it was only right that the kindness be returned.

April 1941

Chapter Six

DISPATCHES FROM THE BUCKINGHAM HOTEL! NEW YORK TIMES, APRIL 17, 1941

By Jackson Ford, your man in LONDON

'The fortunes of war are fickle and changing.' So said the great Prime Minister Winston Churchill, who has been tasked by Great Britain with claiming victory in this war. But, as yet, the war has no end in sight – and, although the people of Great Britain have made accommodation with the privations they must suffer, never before have they been in more need of good news.

The calamities of war are always felt at the Buckingham Hotel. This month, a symposium of ex-patriated Greek businessmen was convened in the Queen Mary restaurant, to voice solidarity with their countrymen now besieged by the Axis Powers, when the forces of Nazi Germany joined Mussolini's Italy already laying waste to the islands, and enforced a total blockade. Goodwill and solidarity will swiftly turn to practical help with a charitable event designed to support Greek exiles in London, and to further finance rebel elements seeking freedom in the islands.

So too is the continuing Desert War in much debate. The arrival of Wehrmacht General Erwin Rommel threatens to move the shifting stalemate of the Western Desert Campaign into something more decisive – and, with Buckingham staff, from the dancing great Raymond de Guise to the saxophonist Louis Kildare, last reported in Tobruk, now under Nazi siege, much emotion is spent in the hotel halls in fear, pride, hope, and a cruel intermingling of the three.

But, if my readers will forgive the floweriness which this desperate war often inspires in a writer: hope flies ascendant. And what hope there is in the words of Winston Churchill, as his eyes turn again to the New World and all its promise. His words for President Roosevelt, the titans of American industry and all of our proud people have been simple but stark: send us your weapons, and we shall do the rest. Arm us, if you will, for the war we are fighting – for we fight it not solely on our behalf, but for all that is good and holy in the world; for the future all our children deserve.

Whether Great Britain can prevail or not may, in the final analysis, depend upon the resources her children of the New World provide – but, from the beating heart of the Buckingham Hotel, one thing is beyond doubt: there is hunger for the fight on this isolated island. There is belief it can be done. The eye of the storm may be upon them, but the King and his people refuse to blink ...

Sellers & Sons lay a little distance along the road into Kentish Town, far enough from the Buck Street market to make it a thriving little spot for locals needing bread, milk, bacon and cheese. At least, that was how it had been in the days before the war. Too often, now, the shelves of stores like these looked denuded, tins of soups and canned meat lined up in rows only one or two deep. The glass in the counter, where fresh meats and cheese were once on display, was now as blacked-out as the windows across London town. And, instead of customers idly browsing the shelves, a thin column of people lined up in and out of the shop, ration books in hand, waiting patiently to be served.

Billy had to wait too, for this was not to be a conversation any of Mr Sellers' patrons could overhear. In the end, it took half an hour. Then, certain the coast was clear, Billy slipped inside, closed the door behind him, and deftly turned Mr Sellers' signage from 'OPEN' to 'CLOSED'.

Mr Sellers stood behind the counter, considering Billy with uncertain eyes. Billy ordinarily came to Camden on a Sunday alone, and right now it was Thursday morning. He grinned sheepishly across the gloomy shop-floor and said, 'I know I'm not expected, but I needed to see you. I won't keep you long.'

Sellers shrugged his round shoulders. 'I was going to close up for a spot of lunch, now the queue's over. I'd offer you some too, Bill, but it's looking pretty bare bones back there.'

Even so, Mr Sellers opened the flap in the counter to beckon Billy through, past the rows of jars and into the store room beyond.

'The harder you try and keep it full, the faster it all goes,' Sellers said, pulling out a chair where Billy could sit. 'There's hungry people out here. There's only so far a ration of butter and bacon can take you.' He paused. 'I take it this isn't a social visit, Bill, old son? I see you've got your satchel over your shoulder. A few cans of something for the counter, is it?'

Billy smiled. 'Mr Sellers, I've been helping you for a few months now. Ever since Christmas, in fact.'

'Aye, and I'm grateful for it. You've helped a fair few old souls fill their bellies on a cold winter's night, Bill.'

Billy opened the satchel. It was the strangest sensation, for his heart had suddenly started hammering. He'd never had a guilty conscience before – not since those dreaded days of last year when he'd first been roped in to providing plunder from the Buckingham Hotel. That had been a different situation, of course – coerced into it by a genuine racketeer, one who buttered him up, caught him in his crosshairs, and trapped him in his web. It had taken all of Billy's guile to extricate himself from that trap.

Out of the satchel came a shallow glass jar of the Queen Mary signature pâté, chicken liver and cognac. Three other glass dishes contained coarser country pâtés and something Billy knew was called a 'parfait', without having any actual knowledge of what that might mean. A half-wheel of some French cheese followed, as well as a wax paper in which curls of smoked salmon were individually wrapped.

Mr Sellers had developed a curious look on his face. 'Bill, you know this isn't the sort of stuff I could shift. Food for princes just ain't the same as food for Mr and Mrs Jones, from round the block. They'd rather have an extra crust of bread than a *pâté de campagne*.' He'd screwed his eyes up, to look at the label on one of the jars.

Billy reached into the satchel. It took him all his courage to remove the last item he'd brought: a bottle of Moët et Chandon, taken directly from a Champagne bucket waiting outside a suite on the fifth storey. No doubt there'd been a complaint to management about that, but the occasional 'theft by a fellow guest' was, in Billy's experience, often written off in the hotel ledgers. Mr Knave had to account for some skulduggery and blackguards among his clientele.

'Now, Billy, what the Dickens would this be for?'

'It's for you, Mr Sellers.'

Something told him that, in uttering those few words, he'd sold a little piece of his soul. No matter – the thing to remember was *why* he was doing this. Ever since Christmas, he'd been filling the shelves of this shop – and half a dozen others like it – out of the goodness of his heart. The truth was, he'd been doing it in penance as well – for his last paymaster, Ken, the one who'd dragged him into this shadowy world in the first place, had been living lavishly off the profits he made. Billy had liked the idea that he could continue some element of Ken's work, and yet unfasten it from avarice and greed. His conscience, such as it was, became cleaner with every delivery he made; his heart became lighter each time he brought his shopkeepers bread and bacon, oranges and butter, and walked away without a penny in return.

And yet...

There his mother and father had sat, covered in the debris of the home they'd loved. There they'd clung on to each other, while he promised them he would find a way.

What good was it to help the unseen customers who came to these shops, if Billy's own parents were in dire need?

Charity, the old saying said, begins at home...

Billy tried to look Mr Sellers in the eye. Shame made his eyes dart in every direction. 'Mr Sellers, I wanted to do something nice for you – because... because I need to ask you to do something nice for me.'

For the first time, Sellers was guarded. He folded his arms across his breast, and said, 'Oh yes, Billy?'

'Mr Sellers, I've been putting myself on the line for too long. Snaffling a few bits and pieces from the Buckingham isn't what it used to be. That job's the only thing I've got – the only thing standing between me and the streets. I can't even take the king's shilling, not anymore.' And he indicated the leg which had been so badly damaged in his frenetic, thwarted first attempt at escaping Dunkirk. 'I'm falling behind. I need a little help. And… well, it's not as if *you* give the bits I bring away, is it? I reckon, if you're making a little off the danger I put myself into, well, it seems like *I* ought to as well.'

There was silence in the back room of Sellers & Sons. Mr Sellers rocked back on his chair, but never once did his eyes leave Billy. In them was such a look of disgust and disappointment that Billy thought he could hardly bear it.

'I always knew this day would come.'

Now he was on his feet. He turned away from Billy, seemingly unable to look upon him any longer. 'Even the heroes of Dunkirk get greedy, don't they, Bill?' He paused. 'You know, when you called at Christmas and said you'd pick up where Ken left off – only that you wouldn't be accepting a penny for the trouble – I thought it was too good to be true. Said to the others that there had to be a catch. There are precious few saints ever walked the Earth, but I was pretty damn sure there wasn't one in the post room at the Buckingham Hotel. But you've been a fraud all along, haven't you, Bill? You've been buttering us all up, and now you'll stick us with the cost.'

'It's not like that,' said Billy. The venom in the room had affected him more than he'd thought it might. 'I'm not looking for much. A fraction of what Ken used to charge. And it isn't forever.' He reached into the satchel and produced the last item he'd brought, a single leaf of paper onto which he'd scribbled a list of articles and corresponding costs. 'I'm going to up my deliveries, Mr Sellers. You can look to me on Wednesdays as well as Sundays from next week on. I'll have every staple on the list, but I'm afraid I can't extend credit like Ken used to do – not to start with, at any rate. The cheeses and the pâté you can keep. The Moët too. I'm not like Ken, Mr Sellers, but I did learn a few things from the old rogue. I learned to keep my customers happy.'

He limped to the store-room door, was almost slipping through, when the overwhelming desire to explain himself came over him. 'My parents have been bombed out,' Billy suddenly said. 'My father's lost his work *and* his home now. I need to help them, sir.' He turned, hoping for some flicker of empathy on Mr Sellers' face, and his heart soared when he did, indeed, see it. Sellers might have been disapproving of the game Billy was playing, but at least he *understood*. 'I've calculated a cost, you see. There are workmen in, Rod Law & Sons, reconstructing the Housekeeping wing of the hotel. They gave me a rough estimate, what it might take to rebuild at Albert Yard. Then there's the rent they're having to find now, and the food on the table, all of the things they lost in the fire. A whole life, Mr Sellers, and it needs reconstituting. So...'

'You can't reconstitute a life, boy. That's the lesson in London this year.'

'My father used to tell me: Bill, you must never look back. I think it's something he learned, coming over from Ireland. London – it's where we start again. But if my family's going to start again, they need help. That's what I'm going to do. Two thousand pounds, by my reckoning.'

'Two thousand pounds, boy, on bacon and bread?'

'I've got to start somewhere.' Billy heaved his satchel over his shoulder. 'I'm sorry, Mr Sellers. You're only my first stop today. I've got the others to tell as well.'

'Aye, well, make sure you sweet talk them like you sweet-talked me, boy. Feed them your sob story. You're not the only one in London who's up against it.'

Billy shook his head. 'We're in it together, Mr Sellers,' he said, with some genuine sadness. 'I'll get back to helping out for nothing. Just a few short months, if I can make it work. But my family deserve help, just the same as everybody else.'

Sellers followed him out onto the ill-lit shop floor, and from there to the doorway. As Billy reached out to return the sign from CLOSED to OPEN, he said, 'You're playing a dirty game, Billy.'

'I know, sir.'

'And you're not the only one.'

Billy had taken a step out onto the Kentish Town Road, but now he looked back.

'Aye,' said Sellers, 'there's a lot of bigger fish than you swimming in this sea. You think Ken was the worst of it? Now, listen to me, Bill, and listen good. The men who really run this black market aren't a kind, noble sort. I reckon you've gone pretty unnoticed until now – a few odds and sods stolen from the hotel, and none of it to turn a profit, doesn't ruffle feathers. You're not disrupting their business, see. But if you're really going to start swimming with scoundrels, you're in for a rude awakening. I'm sorry for what your family's going through, but I'd be a bad friend if I didn't tell you: take it gently, boy.'

'I'm not sure I have the time to take it gently, Mr Sellers.'

Mr Sellers shooed Billy on his way. 'It's villainy, not valour, you're about to play with – so, Brogan, I'll see you on Sunday, but mind how you go.'

Chapter Seven

The taxicab rolled past the colonnade and ground to a halt at the opening of Michaelmas Mews. The narrow lane, which ran between the Buckingham and its neighbouring townhouse, was more exposed than it used to be, for the reconstruction of the devastated townhouse had made it feel broader, lighter, more hopeful somehow. Scaffolds remained in place, but most of the work was complete. As Nancy emerged from the taxicab, with Frank following – the driver opening the door and permitting Hugo Lavigne to step out – she fancied it wouldn't be long before her girls could return to the old Housekeeping Lounge. It could never be the same as it had been, of course, but there would be some sense of homecoming about it.

Of course, there was one little complication in all of this. She curled her hand around her belly. The baby would surely be coming soon. Then, whether she was back in the old Housekeeping Lounge or not, everything would change.

The tradesman's entrance was new. The little receiving hall, where boxes and crates used to be piled up, was also new. She led Frank and Hugo past it all, until at last they crossed a cordon of rope, bedecked in gold and crimson tassels, at the bottom of the service stairs. From here, they could spy the black-and-white chequered expanse of the reception hall.

'I'm afraid I leave you here,' said Nancy, and looked at Hugo with some modicum of pride. Since he'd arrived at Blomfield Road, he'd been telling them yet more stories of himself and Raymond and their Continental tour. If he hadn't yet finished the story of that first meeting in Paris, the tantalising prospect of going out to dance the java, he'd told them of some riotous nights in Berlin, of the moment when Georges de la Motte had welcomed them both to the Vienna Opera House for its famous masquerade. Frank had arranged for Hugo to join one of the local ARP routes and, between this and several shifts at the telephone exchange, it seemed Hugo had begun to feel useful in London after all. 'Frank will take care of you, Hugo. Truth be told, Mr Knave doesn't quite understand the ballroom – but he'll see you for precisely what you are: an opportunity, to be exploited at once.'

'Just don't go stealing my place on the dance floor,' Frank joked. Living with Hugo, off and on, had been something of a masterclass for Frank, for the Frenchman had taken joy in passing on advice. On one memorable evening, Nancy had even caught Frank and Vivienne waltzing around the sitting room, with Hugo either shouting out pointers or stopping the music to rearrange their bodies. This was a sight which had brought Nancy joy on so many levels – not only for the way Frank looked at Hugo (just as he looked at Raymond), but for the simple fact that Vivienne was dancing. She'd heard Vivienne laugh. She'd seen a smile cross her face. It had been so long since Nancy had seen either of those things.

'Frank, *mon frère*,' said Hugo, 'I could no more steal your place than bring peace back to the world. But I should like to share the ballroom with you, sir. I should find some honour in that.' Hugo clicked his heel and turned back to Nancy. 'You've already done so much. Nancy, I'll find a way to thank you.'

'Use that charm on Mr Knave, Hugo. From here on in, it's up to you.'

In the earlier days of her pregnancy, Nancy had made sure to arrive at the hotel long before dawn, so that she could ensure the day began on the right note. Two months ago, however, she'd been forced to concede that the pregnancy was slowing her down. Consequently, it was Rosa who organised the girls at dawn – and, this morning, it had been Rosa who handed the girls their assignments, allocating them certain suites, certain rooms, certain halls.

Most of the girls were already streaming off when Nancy arrived. Rosa, who herself was taking charge of the prized Continental suite – home to a Yugoslav prince and his various lovers – already looked harassed. 'They've been up all night in the Grand Colonial. There's stains all over the bed linen. Wine all over the carpets. I don't want to bother Mr Knave with it, but...'

'Then don't,' said Nancy, more sharply than she'd meant to. She was fond of Rosa, but her capacity for drama sometimes needed keeping in hand. The business of a hotel was to make problems go away, not to exacerbate them. 'Mr Knave doesn't need to know how tricky it is. He just needs to know that it's done.'

'Oh, but Nance!' came the voice of Annie Brogan, who was labouring in the corner, filling up trolleys from the makeshift store. 'You should have seen the *grot* of it! Lord, my baby brother's cot was cleaner after he'd eaten my mother's—'

'Yes, that's *quite* enough, Annie.'

Nancy was trying not to grin as she gravitated towards the back of the study. Her feet had already started aching; what she wouldn't have given for the privacy of Mrs Moffatt's old office today.

'Oh, Mrs de Guise, I'm sorry!' Annie blurted out. Then, quite against Nancy's wishes, she was rushing into the cubbyhole herself, arranging Nancy's chair, puffing up whatever cushions she could find. 'Did I make you feel sick, Nance ... I mean, Mrs de Guise? Me and my big mouth, talking about the grot on that man's bedcovers ...' Annie stepped back. 'Hey, Mrs de Guise, you're *big*. Of course, you were big yesterday, and the day before that – but this morning ...' Annie's eyes near popped out of her head. 'That happened to my mother too, just before she popped.'

'How are your parents, Annie?' asked Nancy, determined to avoid the subject.

'They're bearing up. I'm sending them half my pay now. So's Billy. Dad's going on patrols, but he's looking for work. Ma's still taking in sewing. Hey, I reckon she could knit you a few bonnets. Some booties, for the baby, when it comes.' Annie furrowed her eyes, looking again at Nancy's swollen belly. 'You're going to need them soon, Mrs de Guise.'

Nancy took a breath. 'Yes, thank you, Annie.'

'Really soon, Mrs de Guise. So, anything you want, just say!'

When, at last, she was alone, Nancy reached for the paperwork on her table. A sudden twinge in her side told her she'd moved too quickly – so she took a moment, settled herself with a breath, and decided to remedy the feeling with tea. Annie had been right; she really was feeling sick.

What was the sudden sensation of unearthliness that rushed through her?

And why, suddenly, did she feel as if she needed to prowl around the walls of the Benefactor's Study, to rid herself of some unusual energy?

'Enter,' came Walter Knave's frail voice – and, with a last sparkling look at Hugo, Frank opened the door and pushed through.

The Hotel Director's office was a spartan affair, but then

Walter Knave was a spartan kind of man. To him, the ostentation and glamour of the Buckingham Hotel was but a necessity of business, for he certainly had no proclivity for the fine things in life. 'Let the lords enjoy their glamour,' he had once said, 'while I enjoy my port.' To Hugo, who had been expecting the office to be a Buckingham Hotel in miniature – with, perhaps, fittings of bronze and gold, a miniature chandelier to light up an antique mahogany desk – it was a surprise to find Walter Knave sitting in an armchair by a low-burning hearthfire, pottering his way through the selection of newspapers. Evidently, all sorts of news-sheets were delivered to the Buckingham Hotel, for Hugo quickly saw that there were a good number of languages on display.

'Our own man, Mr Ford,' Walter declared, inviting Hugo to approach. 'He's writing a column for the *New York Times*, DISPATCHES FROM THE BUCKINGHAM HOTEL, but it seems he's syndicated to the *Express* as well. A fine writer, if you excuse the American tendency to hyperbole.'

While Mr Knave was speaking, Hugo took a seat. 'You've done your duty, Mr Nettleton. I should like a private chat with Mr Lavigne, if you will.'

Frank, who'd been relishing the chance to impress Mr Knave with some ballroom talk of his own, felt his heart sink as he took his leave.

'You may wait on the door, Mr Nettleton,' Walter called out, as he slipped away. 'We shall need an escort to the Grand before long.'

After he was gone, Walter readied himself. 'I've been hearing much about you, Mr Lavigne. My Head of Housekeeping speaks very highly of you – both as a man, and as a dancer, and I happen to know she's a fine judge of both. So I'll cut straight to the crux of the matter: you are in search of a job?'

'All men need to work,' said Hugo.

'Well, then, an opportunity presents itself. But first I must ask: how is it you have come to London, Mr Lavigne?'

'Washed up,' Hugo sighed. 'Thrown out. In exile. Until very recently I had, for some time, been making my life in Vienna. There is much dance in Vienna, sir. Much, much opportunity. The Vienna Opera, of course, but … the private balls, the lessons I was giving to young brides-to-be, the masquerades. Yes, Vienna had been home for some years when the war began.'

'And then …'

'Well, then, the world changes, does it not? I turned tail and fled for my Parisian home. I am thirty-eight years of age, sir, and fitter by far than many among my countrymen of far fewer years. I knew I had something to give to the defence of France. Yet, when the battle began …' Hugo shrugged. 'My company were routed. By the end of last summer, I was back in Paris. Would you believe it, sir, but the night-life thrives in the occupied city. They dance in cellar bars. They dance in the catacombs. There is revelry to be found, if you have a mind to search it out. And if you are not inclined to deny the occupiers, sir, there is money to be made in the ballroom. Even Nazis,' he spat the word, 'like to dance.'

Walter stiffened. 'But you are not that calibre of man.'

'Indeed I am not. And soon it became very clear that I could not remain, not without corrupting my soul. And perhaps you will think me a coward – for perhaps there was some way I could have undermined the occupiers from within – but there came a night when I could take it no longer. I had heard tell of fishermen, off the port at Le Havre, who had made it their speciality to cross the channel with runaways. A deal was struck, and I spent my Christmas Day being battered about by the coastal winds, until I set ashore at Worthing.'

'And since then, sir?'

'Old lovers. Old friends. The charity of strangers. Until, one night, I remembered a pact I once made with Raymond de Guise. I believed he might help – but, of course, he is at war… so it is his wife that I owe thanks to instead.'

'She is a remarkable kind of woman,' said Walter, as if the idea had caught him off-guard somehow. 'She has stepped into a role, here, that some might think several years beyond her – and yet, despite the peculiarities of her personal situation, she serves us with aplomb.'

'She's served me too. And I should very much like to repay that debt. In endeavouring to do so, however, I would need…'

'A job.'

Hugo nodded. 'I come here with few expectations. Like many dancers, all I have is within me – a little talent, a little poise, a little belief in oneself. Nancy said you are always in need of gentleman dancers.'

'Well, the war takes away.'

'And here I am.'

'Good,' said Walter, sharply. Evidently, he'd been impressed by what he'd heard and come to some conclusion. 'Mr Nettleton, do I hear you breathing at my door?'

The door opened. There was Frank, exactly where he'd been told to be – but looking rather sheepish for it, all the same. 'Sir?' he ventured.

'Escort Mr Lavigne to the Grand, will you? Mr Arbuthnot will be waiting.' Walter paused. 'We'll talk remuneration, bed and board etc., after you've danced. I am not a dancing soul, Mr Lavigne, so I cannot presume to know what Marcus will make of you in our ballroom – but a friend of Raymond de Guise will always be a friend of this hotel. I only hope you dance as well as you speak.'

*

Annie hadn't been in the Trafalgar Suite more than five minutes before she found more 'grot'. The problem was, this time, the 'grot' belonged to Annie herself. She'd hardly set foot through the door when, tussling with the bedsheets piled up on her own trolley, she staggered backwards, upending the breakfast a concierge had already delivered. Eggs arced into the air, raining their yolks across the bedspread. Hollandaise sauce coloured the carpet. A rasher of bacon hung delicately from the handle of the vintage armoire set up against the bed. And, in Annie's heart, a silent shrieking began.

There was still time to put this right. Annie had learned, over a short and inglorious career, that it was best to rectify your own mistakes, rather than let them be discovered. This involved the destruction of all the evidence, and the delivery of a second breakfast to replace the first. In this, the only thing she really had on her side was speed. Therefore, hoiking both her own trolley and the devastated breakfast trolley together, she scrambled out of the suite, up the corridor, and crashed wildly into the service elevator.

There were manifold back ways around the hotel. Annie was yet to learn them all (which was why she often found herself in the smoking room, or the cocktail lounge, when she ought to be back in Housekeeping), but at least she knew the back way to the Queen Mary kitchens. By the time she got there, the restaurant floor was filling up.

The back way took her directly into the service area, where a squabble of waiters bedecked in white, ribbons of gold glinting at their collars, were waiting for the beautifully dressed plates to appear. Annie found herself beached among them. She'd abandoned the Housekeeping trolley by the service elevator, to be picked up later, so that left her with only the ruined breakfast trolley to navigate. By good fortune, the waiters all seemed focused on their own tasks. She was almost at the counter, when she ploughed directly into a short man – little more than a boy really, scarcely Annie's own age – with a fuzz of black hair, darker eyes, and an incredulous expression.

Not a waiter, thought Annie. This boy looked like a kitchen hand.

Annie appeared to have crashed into him with such ferocity that the wheel of the trolley had savaged his toe. He was hopping about, trying not to shout out when Annie blurted out, 'I need another breakfast, and fast.' Then, after a pregnant pause, she whimpered, 'Please?'

'I'll say you need another breakfast,' said the young man. 'What happened here?'

'It was the – the guest!' Annie blurted out. 'He took a tumble. I offered to help. Well, I know it's not in a chambermaid's duties, but I like to do what I can. He's sent me down here for a new order. There were eggs. Bacon. The whole breakfast menu, I should think. I p-promised to get it to him straight away. Faster than lightning, in fact. I've burnt the carpets, I've got here so quickly.'

The kitchen hand looked at her with an inscrutable expression. Annie had seen that expression before: it looked like Jackson Ford, the American reporter, when she'd seen him trying to work through a particularly tricksome crossword puzzle.

At last, his face broke into a wild, unbidden smile. 'You did this, didn't you?'

'It was … it was …'

'*You*,' the kitchen hand cackled. Then, casting a furtive glance back into the kitchen – where a good number of chefs were currently enslaved to the ranges, their faces as pink as the bacon they served, 'What's your name?'

'Annie,' she spluttered. Admitting this, at least, seemed safe enough.

'I'm Victor,' he said, leaning in conspiratorially. 'Look, there are enough breakfasts going out – I can snaffle you some bits. Just don't let old Laurent in there catch wind of it. He's on a crusade against waste.' Victor darted a look round. 'I'll be back in one second. Just hold tight.'

By the time Victor returned – carrying a silver platter, which he slipped deftly onto her trolley – five minutes had ticked by. Annie's mind was a whirl. Quite possibly, the guest had returned to the Trafalgar Suite already – to discover a significant smear of hollandaise on the sheepskin rug. At some point soon, that news would make its way back to Mrs de Guise. Then there'd be a dressing-down, quite possibly a dock in pay – something she could hardly allow, with everything happening to her parents – and the shame that came with it.

'I threw a couple of extra rashers in there,' said Victor, with another furtive glance over his shoulder. 'That should smooth the way for whoever your guest is.' He paused, for he'd seen the visible emotion on Annie's face. 'Hey, what's wrong?'

'N-nothing,' she stammered, for all of the pluck had drained out of her in the whirlwind of ugly thoughts. 'Just ... th-thank you, Victor.'

Victor lingered at Annie's side. 'You're new here, aren't you?'

'Hardly.' Annie choked back a laugh. 'I've been here since Christmas, and I even did some shifts before. But ...' *I keep messing up*, she wanted to say. *Everyone here's better than me.* 'I better hurry. I might not make a meal out of this one yet.'

She was trying to wrestle the trolley round, when Victor said, 'I'm new too.'

Annie looked back.

'I've been fouling up in this kitchen since day one. I shouldn't be – it's not like I haven't worked in kitchens all my life. My father had Rizzo's, over in Covent Garden. I've been his kitchen hand just about since I could walk. But something about *this* kitchen … I can't mix a batter without Henri Laurent breathing down my neck. I can't poach an egg. Can't even plate up a kipper.'

'But why are you working here at all, if you have a family restaurant?'

'*Did* have,' Victor said, with barely concealed dismay. 'My father's from Milan. *Italian*. Well, it kept the restaurant busy – all that traditional, authentic Italian fare. But as soon as the war came …' Victor shook his head. 'He's in one of the camps now. Isle of Man, the last we heard. So here I am. Just trying to scrape up a few pennies for my mother – at least, until the war comes for me as well.'

'To a camp?' Annie asked, in shock.

'To the front,' Victor said. 'They'll send me papers by year's end, I'm sure. I've just got to get the best out of it before they do. That's why I'm trying to keep Mr Laurent on side. He's new here too – came straight from the Ritz Paris, when France was lost.' Victor shrugged. 'I suppose we all feel the weight of expectation. Difference is, *I'm* not in a position to take it out on anyone else. Mr Laurent is.'

'Victor,' said Annie, 'I've really got to—'

Victor's eyes widened in shock. 'I'm holding you up, Annie. I'm sorry!'

Victor had darted one final look into the steaming kitchen. Through the gap in the service counter, Annie saw a titan of a man in chef's whites marching past, his great head – like a side of gammon, banked in tufts of white hair – thrust forward in front of the rest of his hulking form. 'I better get back to work. You don't want to hear Mr Laurent calling your name.'

And Victor did his beast impression of the stomping giant, mouthing '*Fe, fi, fo fum! I smell the blood of an Englishman!*', just as another coterie of waiters whistled past.

Annie hadn't expected to meet a likeminded soul in the thick of this calamity – but, now that Victor was gone, all her energies returned to the unfolding disaster of the Trafalgar Suite. She reached the bottom of the service stairs – and all she saw was the plush crimson carpet stretching in every direction, the bronze cage of the elevator doors, the empty expanse where her Housekeeping trolley should have been.

Annie turned left. She turned right. She scarpered down the old Housekeeping hall, right up to the edge of the new constructions – but still there was no sign. Perhaps Rosa, Mary-Louise or one of the other girls had stumbled upon it here and tidied it away.

Annie Brogan was not often given to tears, but she felt them welling inside her now.

She was about to give up when she remembered the yellow of egg yolk raining down upon the bedspread.

No, she told herself, this had to be sorted out. It had to be sorted out right now.

The Benefactors Study ought to be empty now. Mrs de Guise must have done her paperwork, then gone out into the halls to look over the girls. That gave Annie a chance: she would simply dash into the store, get a fresh load of bedding, pile it up alongside the bacon and eggs, and set this thing right, once and for all.

She burst through the doors.

Annie had been too lost in her own frenzy to hear the heavy breathing that filled the Benefactors Study.

Mrs de Guise was staggering towards the open study door,

one hand clutched to her belly, the other clawing out to close it before anyone could see.

'Mrs de Guise?' Annie gasped. 'N-Nancy?'

Mrs de Guise gazed at her with a look Annie knew well. She'd seen that strange mixture of surprise, apprehension – and the firmest resolve – on her mother's face a number of times.

'Oh,' said Annie. Then, without a second word, she dashed to close the door herself. Hang the bacon and eggs. Hang the fresh bedding, and whatever grot was still smeared across the Trafalgar Suite. Right here, directly in front of her, was a much bigger drama.

There was about to be a much bigger mess to clean up as well.

'Annie,' Nancy said, 'I need you to call this number,' and she pressed a folded leaf of paper into Annie's hand.

Annie darted a look around. There was no telephone in the Benefactors Study. With plaintive eyes, she looked to Nancy for direction.

'Annie,' she gasped, focusing on each breath, 'it's come sooner than I thought, so we have to be ready. To the audit office, girl. There's a telephone there. Call this number and ask for Mrs Gertie Hodge. She's my midwife.' A pain came over Nancy; she clung on to the rail of the room service trolley to steady herself. Thank goodness she was so lost in it, thought Annie, for she didn't seem to wonder why there was a room service trolley here at all. 'Tell them . . . tell them not to go to Maida Vale. Tell them my baby isn't to be born at home at all.' One last breath, and the colour seemed to suddenly fade from Nancy's cheeks. Here was strength, thought Annie – but she could see fear too. 'Tell them my baby's to be born in the Benefactors Study. Tell them Mrs Hodge is to come to the Buckingham Hotel at once!'

Chapter Eight

Hugo had seemed like a man of the world ever since Frank had met him. He'd danced in real palaces, waltzed across the courts of Europe, no doubt taken princesses in his arms – yet, still, his eyes opened in wonder upon seeing the Grand.

It helped, of course, that it was already populated with dancers and musicians. Marcus and Karina were working with Mathilde – their young protégée, and the elfin dancer who most regularly partnered Frank – on the dance floor, while Archie Adams and a little coterie of musicians played up on stage. There, Frank saw, was Max Allgood himself. He'd played with the orchestra on several occasions now, easing his way into the role before he took over stewardship of the Grand. He had a peculiar way of hopping as he played, thought Frank – for there he stood, trombone raised to the rafters, bouncing from foot to foot as the slide flew back and forth. Yes, thought Frank, Mr Allgood was so distinctive it would surely be the talk of the town when he finally took over the band.

'Well, Mr Lavigne?'

Hugo breathed in the scents of beeswax, polish – and the faintest hum of cognac – that filled the ballroom air. Even in the middle of the day, it felt like they had together slipped into a new, gilded world. 'One day, Frank, when this war is over, when the world's put back on its axis – and everything that's good is flourishing again – I shall take you to the Opera House in Vienna. Then, perhaps, you'll feel how I'm feeling right now.'

Frank puffed himself up. Raymond had spoken often of the palaces and courts of Europe. Frank had often dreamt about dancing in them, as if he might somehow be waltzing in Raymond's wake. Now, the idea of Vienna in a world restored to peace, a world where a man might dance instead of making war, filled his heart.

Hugo strode along the balustrade. There, at the dance floor's head, stood Daisy Allgood, Max's wife. Frank could hear her humming softly to herself, her voice sliding perfectly into the music being played up on stage. She had a sweet, soulful voice – it was said she had filled the clubs of New York – even though she was keeping it unusually quiet. There had been guest singers in the past. Sometimes, Mr Adams called in favours and the Summer or Christmas Balls welcomed seasoned stars to the stage. Perhaps, one day, Daisy's voice might rise in concert with the sounds of Max's trombone.

'You'll be wanting to get down there and dance, will you, Mr Nettleton?'

Frank liked her American twang; it made him feel as if he, Frank Nettleton, had somehow wandered onto the silver screen. 'I'm just here to introduce Mr Lavigne,' he said, though his eyes had certainly gravitated to the dance floor. Preparations were evidently afoot, in both the Orchestra and dance troupe, for the Summer Ball to come.

'Oh, don't give me *that*, Frank. I know you want to be out on the floor.'

'I'm in the demonstrations tomorrow,' said Frank, proudly. He still hoped to one day join the dance troupe as a permanent member. 'But everybody says I've got to polish up first.'

'Oh, they say that to *all* of the greats,' said Hugo. 'In fact, I remember it being said to Raymond, once upon a time.'

Quite without warning, Hugo pressed his hands onto the top of the balustrade, lifted his feet from the floor, and heaved himself bodily over the side. Landing gracefully, he flicked back his wild, black hair and smiled. 'Sometimes, the dance floor beckons, Frank. When it calls, don't be left waiting.'

Frank was astounded. Without even waiting for an introduction, Hugo had pivoted on his heel, then flurried his way across the dance floor to the place where Marcus and Karina were giving Mathilde instruction. In the same moment he arrived, Marcus had taken Mathilde in hold, ready to perform a fleet foxtrot across the ballroom floor. As a consequence, Karina stood alone.

But not for long. Hugo needed no words to introduce himself. Karina seemed to sense a startling dancer when she saw one; Hugo simply opened his arms and allowed her to slip into hold. As for Karina, it seemed the most natural thing in the world. Her eyes sparkled, she settled her palm upon his upper arm, and leant into the first step. Then they were off, turning first one way, then pivoting another, as together they charted their course around the dance floor.

They were sailing on air, thought Frank, as Max's trombone burst into a joyful frenzy that spoke more of the smoky jazz clubs of Soho than it did the magnificence of the Grand. They were dancing as if possessed by the spirit of music itself. It all looked so natural – elegant, yes, poised and pristine, but filled with verve, energy and excitement all the same.

It had all happened in a moment.

Yes, thought Frank, there was no doubt Hugo Lavigne was in the middle of securing a role in the Grand for the season to come. There would be no denying him his place, not when it already seemed he had been here for years. Frank even felt a slight flutter of nerves – for, as much as he was desperate to learn from the magnetic French dancer, he wondered, now, how he could ever compare.

'Well, well!' Daisy beamed, sidling closer to Frank. 'You've reeled in something extra special there, Frank, my boy. I think my Max ought to start watching his back – the Summer Ball's meant to be his starring moment. But I think you just delivered us a pretender to the throne ...'

As she leant across the balustrade to watch Hugo dance, a certain frisson worked through Frank – for he understood, now, that he was at the beginning of something very special, that the Grand he had known until now was about to be irrevocably changed, that this coming summer was to be the most magical of all.

If only Raymond could have seen them now ...

Annie Brogan didn't knock. She just burst through the audit manager's door, looked about in fright – and, quite ignoring the stupefied look on the middle-aged accountant's face, bouldered over to the desk, snatched up the telephone receiver and started frenziedly dialling.

'Excuse me, madam!' the audit manager exclaimed. Mr Stewson was an officious sort of man, the sort who has been middle-aged in spirit since his schooldays, and the interruption to his weekly dalliance with the Buckingham's ledger-sheets had been most unwelcome. Because he carried a certain amount of weight around his belly, he was not very quick to his feet – and, consequently, he had not started clawing for the telephone in Annie's hand before she dialled the last number. 'Get away with you!' she exclaimed, batting his hand away with the same air she used to bat away her brothers every time they tried to sneak a piece of her pudding. 'This is important business! Off, off!'

Mr Stewson was not expecting the slapped hands. He reared back, both chastened and uncertain quite *how* he'd been chastened by this impudent little chambermaid, when Annie's voice burst forth: 'Mrs Hodge? Is that Mrs Hodge? No? Well, can you fetch her?' She stopped. 'My name? Well, that's Annie, but that's not important. I mean, it's important to me, of course – if I didn't have a name, I'd be just a bit stuck in life – but it's Mrs de Guise you ought to be worried about. Yes, Mrs de Guise. *Nancy.* Yes, N-A-N-C-Y. Look, am I talking to Mrs Hodge or not? Is she going to be very long? This is a crucial business. There's a baby about to be born, right here in the Benefactors Study, and I'm ...' Annie groaned, as theatrically as anyone who ever trod the boards at the London Palladium. 'The Buckingham Hotel! I'm calling from the Buckingham Hotel!' Then she rolled her eyes at Mr Stewson. 'Honestly, some people are never quite where you want them to be, are they?'

'I was having exactly that thought myself!'

Annie's eyes goggled.

The voice was buzzing at her back down the phone. 'Just hurry,' she snapped, shaking her head with the weariness of somebody fifty years her senior. 'Mr Stewson,' she whispered, out of the side of her mouth, 'you'll have to help. Down to the Queen Mary with you. Round up some lemons, some brown sugar, probably a spot of brandy. That's what my ma used to have.' The voice on the other end of the line suddenly manifested once more. 'On another job?' Annie exclaimed. 'On another job, when Mrs de Guise's baby's about to be born? You can't be serious? Yes, I *know* it's three weeks early. Don't you think we don't know that? We've got a calendar, right there on the Housekeeping wall!' Annie's eyes flared, first at the telephone receiver – and then at Mr Stewson, who (perfectly reasonably, in his estimation) hadn't done precisely what she said. 'Yes, fetch me somebody right now. I need to …' Annie reared back suddenly. 'They've scurried off. Scurried off, when they ought to be jumping up and down to get here in an instant. Scurried off when … when you ought to be scurrying off too! Didn't I tell you about the Queen Mary?'

'Young lady, I don't know who taught you to speak like this to your betters, your *superiors*, but—'

'Superiors?' Annie baulked, quite oblivious to the dark look in Mr Stewson's eyes. Never in all his years of working at the Buckingham Hotel had he been spoken to in quite such a manner, even by the most outraged of guests. 'My *superior* is in the Benefactors Study right now, about to bring a new life into this world – and *you*, Mr Stewson, won't lift a finger to help. Well, that's *it*. That's just about *it*. Annie Brogan, it's like you always say – if you want a job doing, you better do it yourself.' Then, leaving the telephone receiver on the desk, she marched to the office door, threw it open, and took one stride into the hall. 'When that lady comes back to the phone, Mr Stewson, tell them we need their very best midwife here immediately. Don't let them go without a promise. Do you understand me?'

'Young lady, I don't think you're in any position to …'

But Annie was already walking away.

'I'll be speaking to Mr Knave about this impudence, young lady!'

Annie was halfway to the Queen Mary before she wondered if, perhaps, she'd been just a little bit too insistent, perhaps even a little obnoxious, with her demands. No matter – this was an emergency. Once Mr Stewson understood the gravity of this situation, he would surely realise he'd been too stubborn, and grovel his apologies to Mrs de Guise. That was what Annie would have done. That was the honourable thing.

She hadn't expected to be back at the Queen Mary restaurant so soon. By the look on Victor's face, he hadn't been expecting to see her either – though he seemed pleasantly surprised. 'Annie,' he almost laughed, 'you can't have … upended your trolley again?'

'I told you, that wasn't *me*. That was some silly English lord.'

Victor just gave her a knowing look.

'I need help, Victor. It's Mrs de Guise!'

As soon as Annie had explained, Victor leapt into action. Soon, he had filled a little cloth bag with brown sugar cubes, lemons and three breakfast pastries. 'These things take some time. She might need something to keep her going.'

'That's why I want brandy, Victor.'

Victor darted a look over his shoulder. By good fortune, Henri Laurent was still so invested in his consommé he hadn't yet heard her. 'I can't just take brandy…'

'It's for Mrs de Guise!'

When Victor saw the imploring look in Annie's eyes, he tumbled backwards – and, some moments later, returned with a half bottle of cooking brandy in hand. 'But bring it back. Mr Laurent knows what's going on in these kitchens. His war against…'

'Waging war against kitchen waste,' grinned Annie. 'I know. It's how we'll win the *real* war.' Then she paused. 'Victor, thank you,' she said – and, hoisting herself up, she planted a single kiss on Victor's cheek.

In a competition between Annie and Victor to see who could blush the fastest, it was difficult to identify a winner. In the end, without another word, Annie shoved the brandy into the cloth bag, scarpered out of the kitchen, round the restaurant floor, and back to the hotel reception.

Frank, she suddenly thought. Her eyes had been drawn to the marble arch that led down to the Grand Ballroom – and she happened to know that Frank was down there right now, fussing about with that French lodger he and Nancy had acquired. Well, Frank ought to know, she thought. Mrs de Guise probably wanted someone she loved pacing up and down outside the doorway, just like Raymond ought to have been if it wasn't for this blasted war. Yes, she thought, two minutes to fetch Frank wouldn't hurt. Mrs de Guise could last that long. Then it would be: brandy, midwife – and, sooner or later, a screaming child.

She started to run.

The dance had just ended when Frank looked up to see Annie canter into the ballroom. His heart froze. It wasn't that he felt responsible for Annie – he'd long ago learnt that the Brogans lived by rules of their own, responsible only for themselves – but he desperately didn't want to get her into trouble.

'Frank! Frankie!'

On the dance floor, Hugo had left Karina's arms, led Mathilde into a strident tango – still a most unusual dance for the Grand – and now, at last, he was stepping out of hold. Marcus applauded him as the music came to its end, Archie's piano and Max's trombone combining for one more riotous blast. Hugo himself bowed, first to Mathilde, then to Karina. It was as he looked up to catch Frank's eye that he saw the young red-headed girl crashing into him with all the elegance of a bullock on the dance floor. '*Sacre bleu!*' he whispered, as she lost control of her legs – the boards above the dance floor having recently been polished – and narrowly avoided crashing into Daisy and Frank.

'Frank, it's Nance! I mean, it's M-Mrs Nance! I mean … Mrs de Guise!'

'Nancy?' said Frank, stuttering forward.

'She's having the baby, Frankie, and the midwife's not here – damn her, she's on another job, of all things! – and I've got lemon and sugar and brandy and … and she's in the Benefactors Study right now! She's pacing up and down and the baby's about to—'

Frank was dumbfounded. At last, he whispered, 'But it's early. The midwife said it wouldn't be for weeks. And …'

Suddenly, his mind was somewhere else. The thought that he'd been suppressing for almost nine months was suddenly too powerful to ignore – because the reason Frank had grown up motherless, the reason he'd always looked to Nancy instead of a real mother, was because she'd perished in giving birth to him. It was an aberration, the doctors said. Sad things happen – that was the mantra by which he'd lived his life. Just a random accident of chance, Nancy had once told him; we don't have to understand it, just accept that it's real.

And he'd been able to do that, all of his life. He'd never missed his mother, because he'd never known her.

And yet … the thought of Nancy in the pains of labour right now shocked him to his core. The thought that, if fate played its cruel trick one more time, these might be the last few hours of Nancy's life …

He reached for Annie's hand. 'No midwife?' he gasped.

'I left that old fool Mr Stewson trying to sort it out – but, honestly, Frank, I don't think he knows what he's doing.'

Frank wheeled back to the dance floor – where the dancers and musicians had gathered together, sensing that something was wrong. 'Hugo, it's Nancy. She's having the baby. And … I've got to go,' he said, then turned to run.

He had crossed half the Grand, as graceless as Annie, when he realised that not only Annie, but Daisy as well, was hurrying alongside him. 'Mrs Allgood?' he uttered, as he hurtled on.

'Take me to her,' she said, in her rich, honeyed accent. 'I mayn't be a midwife, boy, but this wouldn't be the first baby I've brought into the world. I've a good pair of hands, until help arrives.'

Frank was so astounded he didn't think to question it. His mind was whirling so much that he didn't wonder what baby Mrs Allgood meant, nor even if she and Max had children of their own. He simply ploughed through the marble arch, up the hallway into the hotel reception, and past the checkout guests, scything his way through a guest's luggage as he went.

The excitement of a birth, the dawning realisation he was about to become an uncle, the all-consuming fear that his sister was about to face her most dangerous moment yet – all of it cascaded through him, until, at last, he stood outside the door of the Benefactors Study, rapped his fingers on the wood and cried out, 'Nancy! Nancy, it's me, Frank. Nancy, it's going to be OK. There's a midwife coming. And Mrs Allgood. Mrs Allgood says she can help...'

Nancy had prowled the walls of the Benefactors Study until the pain became too acute. It was coming in waves, which was exactly how the midwife had told her it would be – she just hadn't properly appreciated how high the waves could be, nor how quickly one might chase another. *Raymond*, she thought. She wished he was here now. No doubt decorum would dictate that he had to stand studiously outside the door, while she got on with the woman's work within, but it would have brought her some comfort to know he was near.

She could feel the pressure building again. Somehow, moving around seemed to keep it at bay – but this time there was no way she could stay standing. She staggered back to the armchair and had just fallen into it when she heard Frank's voice.

'Frankie?' she called out.

The door opened up. Annie Brogan was the first to march in, swinging a cloth bag in one hand and what looked like a brandy bottle in the other. 'Now, Mrs de Guise, I've got everything under control. Everything. You'll want a nice glass of this, of course.' Annie was already pouring one. 'And here's Mrs Allgood. And Frank, of course ...'

Nancy looked up. Frank stood sheepishly in the doorway, not certain if he was permitted to come within. 'It's OK, Frankie,' Nancy told him. 'I'm going to be OK.'

She knew what he was thinking. He'd been diligently trying not to say it for months. Well, it was easy to ignore some prophesied disaster when, nightly, disaster rained from above. Only, now that the moment was here, Frank's fear seemed to be finding its way inside Nancy too. It wasn't until this very moment that she truly understood how her mother might have felt in the last hour of her life.

She reached out for Frank. In faltering footsteps, he came into the room, dared to take her hand.

'What can I do, Nance? I – I want to help.'

'You're here. That's enough.' She had to wait for another wave to pass through her before she added, 'I think I might like a little spoonful of that brandy now, Annie.'

'Oh yes, Mrs de Guise. My mother swore by it. It's medicinal, don't you know?'

After Nancy had taken it, she clutched Frank's hand yet tighter. 'My girls are going to be coming back in from their rounds. They'll need to be in the store cupboards. So I'm going to need to move.'

'One of the suites?' Annie perked up. 'I could go on up, turf them out of the Continental?'

Nancy didn't care to give the suggestion the time of day.

'I was thinking… the old Housekeeping Lounge. Yes, if it has to be the Buckingham Hotel, I should like to have my baby there. And the workmen are finished, aren't they? It's nearly time for us to start using it again.'

'We can get you there, Mrs de Guise.'

After that, it was Daisy who took charge. Soon, Nancy was back on her feet and being led through the study door.

The old Housekeeping Lounge was starker than it had once been. The new walls had been whitewashed just days before, so that the smell of it was thick in the air, and the furnishings were slowly being replaced. A great table dominated the lounge itself – while, in the office that would soon be Nancy's own, a new desk, chair and three armchairs had been arranged. At Daisy's instruction, Frank and Annie set about stripping the armchairs of cushions, then arranging them on the floor so that, when the moment came, Nancy could lie down.

'I'm going to have to ask you to step outside now, Frank,' said Daisy, not unkindly.

Frank lingered. He watched as Nancy sank down to the make-shift bed, and wanted nothing more than to go to her side. 'No,' he declared, for even now the images – memory reconstructed out of the fragments his father and Nancy herself had let slip – of his mother's last hours was forcing itself upon him. Here it came, like the hag of a madman's nightmares, smothering him in hands, peeling back his eyelids so that he was forced to see. 'I'll stay,' he said. 'I'll stay with you, Nancy. I don't care about decorum. I'll …'

There was a dumbfounded silence in the room. It seemed, then, that Daisy was about to admonish Frank, to send him away with a flea in his ear. 'This is woman's work, Frank Nettleton,' she started to say – but Nancy, sensing the severity of the moment, cut her off. 'I'll be all right, Frank,' she told him – though perhaps the trembling in her tone meant she was simply burying some deeper fear. 'Just... don't go far. I might need you. And... you should be the first. If Raymond's not here, you should be the first to hold my baby.'

Frank scarcely had the words to reply. 'I'll stand on the door. I'll bring whatever you need.' Promptly, he turned to Daisy. 'Mrs Allgood, please look after her.'

When Daisy said, 'Mr Nettleton, it's the most natural thing in the world. It's what our bodies are made for,' Frank did not truly understand – but it brought him some comfort nonetheless.

Nancy watched as he slunk outside. Then, the door to the old Housekeeping Lounge closed – and suddenly it was only she and Daisy in the office, with Annie flitting about somewhere beyond. 'Annie,' she tried to call out, 'you still have duties to attend to...' But she said it with such little conviction that, when Annie did not immediately scurry off to change some duchess's bedsheets, she uttered no further complaint. Another wave was coming over her now. She lay back, arched her neck and tried to breathe like the midwife had shown her – but the best laid plans always came to nothing, and so it was now; she had clearly forgotten how to breathe.

Daisy had taken her hand. 'Now, Mrs de Guise, you and I don't know each other, but I happen to know exactly what you're feeling right now, and I happen to know it's going to pass. Now, it might pass quickly, or it might take a little time – but I'm here to *promise* you, you'll be lying here, holding your baby in your arms, before too long. And, when you do, all of this is going to be like a dream.'

Nancy wondered if it was a dream already. The way these feelings pulsed through her, it certainly felt as if she was outside her body. She was grateful for Daisy's hand. She gripped it more tightly now. 'Did you and Max have babies, back home, Mrs Allgood?'

Daisy's face seemed fuzzy, all of a sudden. It could only be another one of those waves, building in her body. Nancy closed her eyes.

'Oh, we don't need to think about that,' Daisy replied, though her voice seemed strangely far away, 'but I know what I'm doing, Mrs de Guise.'

Nancy hoped so, because here came the pain again. She would have to flow with it until the moment came when she started to push.

Raymond, she thought again, *wherever you are, you're about to become a father.*

Chapter Nine

For some hours now, the men of the Western Desert Force had been outpacing the curdling sandstorm, but not even the best of British engineering was a match for the raging elements of North Africa. Now, with the sky a roiling mass of grey and mustard-coloured clouds, the bedraggled infantry had dug in somewhere east of the airfields at Kambut. Fifty miles still divided the routed army and the relative safety of the Egyptian line – and, though most of these men would have chosen the wildness of a desert storm over the relentless march of Erwin Rommel's Afrika Korps, none of them relished the blindness and suffocation of the storm about to smother them. As he swigged from his canteen – and earned himself something of a rebuke from the fellow at his side, for supplies were fast dwindling on the road east – Lieutenant Raymond de Guise had the inalienable feeling that something was shifting in the world.

Of course, things had been shifting for months. The battles in the desert had seemed about to be won – the Italians decimated, the British confident enough to partition some of their armies to go and bolster the defence of fallen Greece – but, though it was mere weeks, that seemed so long ago. First, the defeat at El Agheila; then the devastation at Mersa el Brega. The British had known defeats before, but not like this. Half of them were still encircled in the fortress city of Tobruk. A month ago, there'd been no doubt it would remain an Allied bastion through all the war to come. Now, save for its seaward side, it stood at siege. Lieutenant de Guise and his men had been fortunate not to find themselves among the encircled.

But there were different kinds of fortune – and now, as Raymond looked at the churning sky, he knew that there were different kinds of sieges as well.

'We've got to keep going,' he said.

The other men, tumbling from their vehicles and gathering in the lee of the roadside outbuildings, looked at him askance. 'Sir, the order's come from on high. Dig in, until the road clears. We can be in Egypt within twelve hours, if they have it right. But if we keep on—'

Orders, thought Raymond savagely. He was not, as a man, happy with the idea of insubordination – and nor would he countenance it in others. That was why the sudden urgency he had to reach Cairo had to itself be smothered; that was why, when the orders started buzzing down the radio, he rallied the men to take shelter as the sky grew thick with sand.

But he could not keep his mind from racing.

He could not stop his desperation to reach the border – and the barracks, the succour, the lines of communication that lay beyond.

It wasn't until the storm had really crashed down, and the air was a miasma of desert sand, that he realised how his urgency reached far further than the need to outpace the relentless march of the Afrika Korps. Because, to Raymond de Guise, Cairo represented something else: the chance to write home; the chance to find out if he himself had been written to; the chance to find out if, at last, he had become a father.

There was a kernel of dread in him, he realised, that was more to do with this than it was to do with the advancing army, the men stranded at Tobruk, the sand half-choking his men.

In the rush of whirling grit and sand, he could almost hear Nancy's voice.

She was calling out for him.

Screaming his name.

Reaching for his hand . . .

Chapter Ten

In the Buckingham Hotel, one hour had passed.

Two hours.

Three.

By the time the fourth hour dawned, Frank's fears were near insurmountable. He had tried to close his ears to the sounds coming from the Housekeeping Lounge, but it was an impossible challenge. Every time he heard her, he wanted to reach for the door handle, before something in him seized up. What had become of Hugo, he did not know; perhaps he was still hard at work in the Grand. It seemed improbable that day-to-day life at the hotel still went on, not when a world was being forever changed behind the door at which he stood. Out there, concierges still marched to and fro; the Queen Mary was in the thick of its lunchtime service; rumour had it that Sir Stafford Cripps and Viscount Chandos – both of Mr Churchill's War Cabinet, and no doubt here to luncheon with members of the Free French government – were in one of the private dining rooms right now. Fierce debates, pertinent to the safety of the world, were being held in the Buckingham, but none of that meant a thing to Frank Nettleton.

Frank only wanted his sister to be OK.

Sometimes, Annie Brogan appeared, scurrying off on some

errand. Evidently most of these had been concocted by Daisy Allgood, simply to remove Annie from the proceedings – but one job in particular was of significant import: Annie was sent out onto Berkeley Square, searching for the midwife who had still not arrived. The hotel doctor was summoned, but he too was off on some errand – no doubt, thought Frank, tending to the grazed knee of some indulged lord – and, each time Annie reappeared, she did so sorrowfully shaking her head.

'What's going on in there?' Frank would ask.

And Annie would say, 'She needs a cuppa, Frank, and I need fresh milk to make it. Go and fetch us a silver spoon!'

Then, just as the fourth hour was growing old, Frank heard a cry quite different from the rest. There was some fresh quality about the sound Nancy was making, so much so that he thought of darting into the room again – and was stayed only when he heard Daisy saying, 'This is it, Mrs de Guise. You're in the heart of it now. Push, Nancy. Push for me, now...'

Raymond...

She'd been whispering his name like it was a mantra: something to hold on to, something to help pull her through the feelings smothering her, as deep and impenetrable as a desert sandstorm. But now she let the name go; now she breathed. It was Daisy she would have to cling on to, if this was to happen.

'I'm – I'm – *scared*,' she gasped.

'Scared, Mrs de Guise?' Daisy touched her brow. 'Oh, but so is every woman who brings forth new life. But... you mustn't be afraid, Nancy, my dear. Your baby's about to arrive.'

Her strength was fading, and all at once Nancy de Guise was eight years old again, banished to the garden outhouse while the life faded from her mother in the little room upstairs. Fleetingly, she wondered if this was how it had felt: stuck in the throes of labour, too exhausted to go on, and all her life's blood seeping away. *Raymond*, she thought, *I wish you were here*.

It wasn't dying that frightened her, she thought. It was giving life she could not nurture; it was following where her mother had gone, but without anyone to trust with her child.

'Frank,' she started to say. 'I want Frank.'

But it was too late; she didn't have the breath to give voice to the words. The exhaustion of the last four hours had built inside her. It had been two hours since she'd been able to get on top of the pain between each wave. Since then, it only grew stronger, the pressure never settling down. She grappled for Daisy's hand.

She started to push.

Was this really pain? Was that what it was? Or was it some new sensation, one her body had never felt before?

'Yes, Nancy, yes,' Daisy was saying. She was bowed at Nancy's legs, but now she reached up to touch her brow, to fix her with a look that said: *You're already doing it, my girl; anything is possible.* 'It's time, darling.'

Somewhere in the deserts of North Africa, beneath a sky besieged by sand, all the panic that had been building in Lieutenant Raymond de Guise suddenly sloughed away.

He looked up.

There, in the middle of the raging storm: a perfect circle of blue sky.

'The eye of the storm,' one of his men said, gesticulating upwards, leading the other men's eyes.

But no, thought Raymond, *this* was something else ...

No, thought Nancy, this wasn't really pain.

This was indescribable.

When Nancy heard the crying, it was like she was falling back to earth. The room, which had become such a blur, suddenly had crisp edges again. The sounds, which had seemed so far away, were suddenly impossibly close. Her body had started shaking, but with each breath she took, the strange, shivery sensation rushed away. Then she picked herself up.

The baby was in Daisy's hands, its umbilical cord dangling, grey marbled in red. Moments later, her baby was on her breast, her world changed forever.

She was a mother.

It was the most beautiful, bewildering thought.

'Mrs de Guise,' said Daisy, 'you have a baby boy.'

The moment Frank heard the crying, he reached for the door handle. This time, the compulsion to burst in could not be denied. He was still crashing through the door when Daisy called out, 'A few moments, Mr Nettleton,' with the air of an irritated schoolteacher – but Nancy was already saying, 'Frank, Frank come here, Frank come now!', so he bounded over, dropping at his sister's side.

Was this truly what a newborn child looked like? A shrivelled pink thing was wrapped in a blanket and pressed up against Nancy, who looked as if (their father's expression) she'd been dragged through a hedge backwards. The infant was mewling still, so it was some time before Nancy handed him to Frank. 'You have a nephew,' she said – and, sensing Frank's trepidation in taking hold of the baby, she sat up straighter so that they might hold him together. 'Your nephew, Frank. Your nephew... Arthur.'

'Arthur,' Frank whispered, as if in hello. 'H-hello, A-Arthur.'

The baby squirmed in response. Its puckered lips opened in another cry. Lives would be lost tonight, when the bombs came down, but right now all the privations, desperations and ugliness of the war seemed to matter not at all. For here was Arthur de Guise.

In the darkest hours of mankind, hope went on.

In the hotel post room, Billy Brogan lifted the telephone receiver. His hands always shook when he dialled a number – it was, he believed, the last vestige of his conscience, reminding him that what he was doing wasn't *right* – but this time he managed to keep control. 'Mr Greenwood,' he said, when the call was answered, 'I've got the next delivery ready. I wanted to forewarn you, because ... Yes, credit's not really an option, Mr Greenwood. I'm going to need payment when I arrive.' He paused. 'Mr Greenwood, we've been through this. If I'm to keep these deliveries up, I can't do it for nothing. But,' he checked the crate tucked underneath this feet, 'I do have some luxury soaps. They're Buckingham issued of course, stamped with the crown, so you can't put them on your shelves – but a gift for your wife, perhaps? Something for your daughters?'

After he'd put the phone down, he went to the ledger, then started filling out the columns. The trickle of money he'd started taking from the shops in Camden hadn't yet turned into a wave, but surely it wouldn't be long. The problem, it turned out, was a simple one: the demand was infinite, but Billy's avenues of supply were limited. The hotel was a vast resource, but what little he could skim away without being noticed only stretched so far.

On one side of the page was a breakdown of takings he'd made, half of it already donated to his parents so that they might be fed and warm while he reckoned with the next stage of his scheme. The single word WINTER was circled at the bottom of the page. It had seemed evident to Billy that his parents would need their home back by the time winter returned. That meant a new roof, the old house reconstructed, before November was nigh.

A house was not built by bread alone.

He was still ruminating on this problem, wondering if he should call Mr Greenwood and simply double his prices, when the door burst open.

'Bill!' Annie exclaimed, and forced a leaf of Buckingham-head notepaper into his hands. 'Well, come on, she wants it dealing with straight away!'

Billy was so busy trying to hide his ledgers that he hardly had time to ask, 'What is it?' when Annie blurted out, 'It's a boy! A boy, Bill! Nancy – I mean Mrs de Guise – has had a boy, and she's called him Arthur.' She slapped the paper in her brother's hand. 'It's a telegram, for sending right now – off to Raymond's unit, wherever they are. Nancy said you'd know what to do.'

Billy flurried out of his seat, the jubilation written all over his face. He'd known Raymond since he was a boy; he'd fought with him in France, found him on the beaches at Dunkirk, served alongside him every step of the way. That a child was born – it meant everything to him. 'I'll sort it,' he declared. 'But first I've got to see this baby for myself. Little Arthur de Guise!' It struck Billy, then, that the child was named after Artie, who'd perished at Dunkirk. A tribute like that made the heart soar. He reached for his cane and started limping towards the door. 'Onward Annie – on, on!'

By the time they reached the Housekeeping Lounge, the room was buzzing with chambermaids, all clucking and cooing to catch their first sight of the child. Billy had to sidle past Mary-Louise – who'd had so little time for him, ever since Christmas, for it was Mary-Louise's uncle who'd drawn Billy into the black market game, then been carted off to Pentonville at His Majesty's pleasure – and the rest just to catch a sight.

'Oh, Nancy,' he said, upon seeing the baby, now wrapped in towels and sleeping in her arms. 'Nancy, you did it.'

Red-cheeked, exhausted, but as happy as Billy had seen her since her wedding day, Nancy reached for his hand. 'Say hello to your Uncle Bill, Arthur.' She angled the baby so that Billy could see his every feature. 'I think he looks like Raymond.'

'One day,' said Billy, 'he'll dance like him as well.'

Moments later, a rather befuddled-looking midwife appeared, her hair tied in a grey bun, a leather bag at her side. The moment she stepped through, Annie started shaking her head dramatically. 'I'm afraid we got on quite fine, thank you,' she declared.

The midwife picked her way through, shooing chambermaids aside as she came. Then Billy watched as she took the baby from Nancy, began inspecting him closely, making sure he was as bright, breezy and healthy as he had seemed.

'Ain't it something, Bill?' said Annie – and, quite preposterously, she laid her head on his shoulder. 'It reminds me of when Conor was born. Or Gracie-May.'

'You were barely a pup yourself!'

The midwife had taken charge, at last. Even Daisy seemed to have been set aside in the chaos. Her first declaration – 'This baby seems a very healthy young man indeed!' – was met by a rapturous cheer. Her second – 'Now, all of you out!' – was met by something much closer to a groan, but at least the chambermaids seemed to take heed.

'Well, Bill,' she said, 'I suppose that's my excitement done for the—'

But when Annie looked round, Billy was nowhere to be seen. It seemed, then, that he must have left without saying goodbye.

Still, there was a day to be getting on with.

First, of course, she would need to go back to the Queen Mary. She'd promised Victor the brandy back by the lunchtime service – a promise already broken, of course – but she would return it all the same. Just to say thank you, of course. Just to say how much the brandy was valued. And *just* to plant another kiss of gratitude on his cheek, if only he let her.

Yet, when Annie looked down, she couldn't see the brandy anywhere. It was the funniest thing, but she couldn't see the box of brown sugar cubes or the three lemons they hadn't used either. The supplies she'd foraged had just vanished into thin air, just (in fact) like Billy – and, where they might possibly have gone, Annie had no idea.

May 1941

Chapter Eleven

DISPATCHES FROM THE BUCKINGHAM HOTEL!
NEW YORK TIMES, MAY 16, 1941

By Jackson Ford, your man in LONDON

Rumours abound at the Buckingham Hotel. Wander from cocktail lounge to smoking room, and it is evident that, since the Fall of France, the Buckingham Hotel has become nothing less than a seat of world government. Only three nights ago, the private dining room of the Queen Mary restaurant was formally sequestered so that Charles de Gaulle could gather the other exiled leaders of the Continent for a quiet tête-à-tête. What grave decisions were taken there? What fears were confessed and hopes rekindled? We mortal men may never know, but we can be sure that these brave men who gather at the Buckingham were brilliantly catered for as they directed the course of world events.

Life in these halls is a microcosm of all that is happening in the world beyond. Births, marriages and deaths; from the cradle to the grave, the Buckingham Hotel is host to it all. Meanwhile, the rumour of Albanian King Zog's wealth continues to titillate. King Zog – whose residence at the

Buckingham Hotel goes on, even while seeking a more permanent home on British soil – is rumoured to be paying for his stay in gold bullion, hidden somewhere in the hotel safes.

But nothing, now, is spoken about more in the Buckingham Hotel than its Summer Ball, only six weeks away. The Buckingham's Balls have always been centrepieces of London's social season, but never have they felt more vital than in these years of war. This Summer Ball provokes more gossip than ever, for it marks the arrival of the Buckingham's very own 'prince from across the waters' – none other than the trombonist and jazz supremo Max Allgood, formerly of New York City. Anticipation for Allgood's entrance to the Grand Ballroom has been stoked by several select performances over the last weeks. But tonight he is to take centre stage.

Who knows? Perhaps Mr Allgood will flourish – or perhaps he will need a little help. If so, he could do worse than call upon the help of the woman who has accompanied him to his new life at the Buckingham Hotel, a woman whose reputation in the clubs of New York was as fearsome as Max's was troubled . . .

If you know, folks, *you know*. But good luck, Mr Allgood! You can bet your bottom dollar, we'll *all* be watching . . .

The day was lengthening over Maida Vale, the sunshine of late spring giving way to summer's first blossoms. In the window of the upstairs bedroom at No. 18 Blomfield Road, Nancy cradled the three-week-old Arthur in her arms and gazed out upon the cherry blossoms below. Such things were a restorative for the soul, and in this time of war the colours only seemed more vivid.

The tea at her side was a restorative too. Frank had brought it up moments before, and now he stood in the bedroom doorway.

He seemed antsy tonight, thought Nancy, anxious whether he ought to leave. 'Frankie,' she told him, 'I'll be fine. Just go. *Go!*'

She was grinning as she dismissed him, and that was just the tonic Frank needed. It wasn't as if he'd been at her side every hour of every day since Arthur was born. There were still hotel duties to attend to, his nights at the telephone exchange, his others at the observation post high on the Buckingham roof. But those were the necessities of life; to dance seemed suddenly frivolous somehow.

But not to Nancy. 'Look, Arthur,' she told the baby, 'your uncle Frank, off to dance for the lords...'

She was dog-tired, of course, but being dog-tired somehow seemed a measure of love. And, if the bombs rained down at night – which sometimes they did – and she had to carry a screaming Arthur out to the Anderson shelter, at least she had Vivienne and Stan with her. She had received a simple telegram back from Raymond's unit, 'My love, we are complete!', with promises of a letter to follow – and, though none had yet arrived, she had taken to setting down the tiniest details of their baby's life, so that he might in some way experience it when he was home. A bundle of letters lay, half-written, on the dresser where she sat. '*Dear Raymond, today Arthur looked me in the eye and I believe I saw you...*'; '*Dearest Raymond, I am writing this as Arthur clings to my finger with the entirety of his hand. Does this, perhaps, mean your son is writing his first letter to you, using me as his instrument?*'

'Your father danced in the Grand when we first met,' Nancy said, rocking Arthur. 'He danced there, too, when he came back from the dead. Just back from Dunkirk – late, as usual, and...' It had been the moment he broke the news of his brother Artie's death. Nancy brought the moment to mind, as if to honour it – but there were other moments to honour as well. You had to memorialise the good, as well as the bad. 'Then we danced,' she said – and, as if to dispel any lingering bad feeling, she beamed at Frank. 'And you should dance too, Frank. Be the star of that ballroom tonight. When Max Allgood steps into the limelight, make sure it's rapturous. Make sure it's rapturous for Hugo as well…' He'd been given quarters at the Buckingham – in fact, the very same room Raymond had once lodged in – so Nancy had seen little of him since the baby arrived. 'Frank, we'll be fine. But this is the night Max takes over the Orchestra. It's Archie's swansong. You deserve to be there. Here, say good luck to your uncle, little one.'

Nancy placed Arthur into Frank's arms. The first time she'd done this, he'd been so uncomfortable. Now, his arms curled around his nephew like he truly belonged.

'The Grand, Frank,' said Nancy as he left. 'It's been your dream for so long. Go and live it.'

After she had watched him go, she returned to one of the letters on the dresser. *Dear Raymond, there will be dancing tonight, and it makes me recall how we first met, me risking my new world and career to catch a glimpse of the Grand. Well, let me say this now: one day we will dance there with Arthur. One day we will…*

Turn and waltz with him across the Grand's famous sprung floor.

But first – Nancy wrinkled her nose – there was a nappy that needed to be changed.

The ballroom was already open to guests, but in the Candlelight Club, by the open terrace doors, Max Allgood sat contemplating his third straight bourbon of the night. Once dusk had hardened over the square, the terrace doors would have to close, the blackouts hoisted into place. But there was still a moment to breathe in the scents of the coming summer.

At the opposite side of the table, Daisy was dressed in a blue silk ballgown. John Hastings, the head of the Hotel Board, had agreed to accompany her into the Grand tonight, to be at her side as her husband was unveiled. 'This is it, Max,' she said, with such eagerness in her eyes. 'This is the night. Six weeks until the Summer Ball, and your first big fixture before an audience. Nothing's going to be able to uproot us again.'

Max threw back the bourbon, then cast his eyes into the different corners of the Club. He could not be certain, but he thought the eyes of the other patrons kept gravitating in his direction. 'They're staring,' he whispered.

Daisy said, 'Well, darling, they'll *all* be staring in the Grand.'

Now, Daisy looked around as well. It was true that, sometimes, glances were flickering in their direction – but she liked to think it was because the hotel was alive with anticipation, not because of any slight against her and Max. But then, Max had always been neurotic. It made a man that way, when he played in the clubs of New York. In New York, it was the ne'er-do-wells, men of brute strength and money – *gangsters* – who often ran the clubs. The night belonged to them. Even in spite of the years they'd spent in Europe, Max hadn't quite shaken the feeling.

'But you can't possibly have … stage fright, Max?'

As a matter of fact, he'd suffered with it all his life, in some way or another. Daisy had coached him through several different bouts. She'd got him off the hooch too, when it was truly taking its toll. But that wasn't what was fazing him now.

Daisy's eyes darkened. 'You're thinking this orchestra won't ever learn to respect you … and all because you're black.'

Max's eyes bugged out. 'Hey, darling, you know I don't think like—'

'Then tell me. Tell me what's weighing on you.'

His eyes flashed up. At the bar sat the war reporter Jackson Ford. It was, Max had observed, his ordinary haunt. Every evening, by six o'clock, he'd be propped at the bar with his dry Martini and notebook in hand, noting down all his observations on hotel life.

'He recognised me, Daisy. I know he did.'

Daisy furrowed her eyes. 'Why, of course he did, Max. You're *Max Allgood*. The eyes of the world recognise you. That's the way it's meant to be. That's what we've been working towards, all these years.'

'It was the night I first played with Archie in the Grand. He was ... *watching*.'

Daisy rolled her eyes in exasperation, as if to refer Max to her earlier statement.

'I think I recognise him too,' Max whispered. 'From the ... Cotton Club. And after that,' he lowered his voice yet further, 'at the townhouse, by St Nicholas Park.'

It was only when he whispered those final words that Daisy betrayed any unnerved reaction. She glowered a look at Jackson Ford. 'You're sure?'

Max finished his drink. 'How can I be?' he said, with some venom. 'It's been a long time. And yet ... There's something about him. I feel his eyes on me, Daisy. And look at this ...'

He had reached under the table, and now he produced a leaf of crumpled paper filled with typewritten words. 'I went to that boy, Brogan. The one who works in the post room. He's a good soul – throw him a few bucks, and he'll happily do you an odd job. It's Billy Mr Ford goes to with his reports. They need transmitting back to New York, and Billy takes care of it for him. So ...'

'He gave you the article.'

Max shrugged. 'It's a public matter. I just got it a little early.' He paused. 'Go on. Read it, darling. Read those last lines.'

So that was what Daisy did. *Who knows? Perhaps Mr Allgood will flourish – or perhaps he will need a little help. If so, he could do worse than call upon the help of the woman who has accompanied him to his new life at the Buckingham Hotel, a woman whose reputation in the clubs of New York was as fearsome as Max's was troubled…*

When Daisy blanched, it was Max who read out loud the final line. 'If you know, folks, *you know*. But good luck Mr Allgood! You can bet your bottom dollar, we'll *all* be watching…' Then he crumpled the paper and shoved it into his pocket. 'Now do you think I'm paranoid?'

Daisy stood. 'You just have to get through the night, Max. Win the ballroom over, and they won't be able to get rid of you – no matter what Mr Jackson Ford *thinks* he knows.' Suddenly, she was bristling with anger. She took Max's hands, heaved him to his feet. 'I'm doing my part, Max. I delivered that baby, didn't I? I'm doing what I can to carve us out a place here, to make us indispensable – part of the fixtures, just like I used to be back home. But you're the only one who can truly win this for us.' She had started shaking. 'I won't be back on the streets, Max. So promise me! Win them over. Make the Orchestra, make the whole damn ballroom, yours tonight!'

Backstage at the Grand was always a tempest of activity, but in the hours before the music began, the anticipation was more intense than ever. To Frank Nettleton – who stepped through the doors to find Karina fixing Mathilde's hair, Marcus in deep conversation with Hugo – it seemed as intense as it had in the hours before last year's Christmas Ball. He scurried over to his dressing table – it still made him so proud to realise he had one for himself – and, drawing the curtain around him, started changing into his dancing clothes. Raymond had always worn a midnight blue dinner jacket to dance, and so did Frank;

it made him feel close to his brother-in-law somehow. When he was finally dressed, he drew back the curtains and picked his way over to Marcus and Hugo. No sooner had he got there, than Karina started fussing around with his hair. Frank's mousey brown mop had never quite been tamed, no matter how much pomade he applied. 'You need to be dashing, Frank. It needs to be precise.'

Frank didn't feel very dashing tonight. He only felt excited.

Hugo was excited too, though the tall, dark Frenchman had more grace than to let it show. Frank, however, could see the rapture in his eyes. By the time he finally joined them, Hugo was already bedecked in a sophisticated suit of forest green, shining black dance shoes, his black beard neatly trimmed. He'd been working with the dancers in the Grand for long afternoons – had even taken part in one of the afternoon demonstration dances – but there was nothing like the feeling of making a debut. Frank remembered his own vividly. 'How are you feeling, Mr Lavigne?'

Hugo looked down. 'Sublime, *mon frère*.'

At the apex of the dressing rooms, the doors opened directly onto the back of the dance floor. Together, Hugo and Frank opened the door a tiny fraction and peered out. The ballroom, lit up in the crystalline light of the chandeliers, was already alive. Frank saw Mr Knave consorting with the Hotel Board. King Zog was in attendance, and with him his good lady wife.

'I remember when Raymond and I danced at the Bühler's Ballhaus in Berlin. Even then, with our bodies crammed against the other dancers, I somehow knew he'd end up in a place like this.'

Frank thrilled, 'And now you're here too.'

'I've danced in wondrous places, Frank. But I've always been a ship, passing through. Just to think of somewhere like this as my *home*.' The wonder of it lit up his eyes. 'Ray's paid back that night in Paris *in spades*, as you English say.'

'You know,' said Frank, 'you never did finish that story. You never did show me the java, not like you said you—'

'Ah, but tonight is for the waltz, young Frank. Tonight, we foxtrot and quickstep with duchesses in arms. I am told there are enough French exiles in the Buckingham that we might call Berkeley Square a second Paris – a free Paris, like the Paris of old. Not an occupier in sight! So I shall dance for my country-men tonight.' He paused. 'The baby? He is well?'

'Nancy says he'll dance here one day.'

'Yes,' said Hugo, 'London shall be free, Europe restored, and Raymond's son shall dance the foxtrot. Or . . .' And here he grasped Frank by the hand, to shake it vigorously. 'You and I, Frank, we shall teach him the java.'

Frank grinned, 'You'll have to teach me first!'

At that moment, the inner doors to the dressing rooms opened and a strange hush descended. Frank and Hugo retreated from the ballroom door to discover that, behind them, Max Allgood had appeared. Marcus was leading the dancers to meet him, and Archie Adams was doing the same with the Orchestra. Soon, Max was being met with a round of applause.

'Two debuts in the Grand tonight,' said Frank, once the grandeur of the occasion had properly taken hold of him. Then, more wistfully, he added, 'It's going to be so different without Mr Adams.' His eyes gravitated to Mr Allgood again. Max was shaking hands with each of the musicians. His fingers entwined with those belonging to the percussionist Harry Dudgeon; Frank thought he saw Max freeze a little, before he moved on.

'Things always change, Frank,' said Hugo. 'Empires rise. Then they fall. Wars begin, then fade away. The music starts . . . but then it stops.'

'So what do we do, Hugo?'

'Well, Frank,' said Hugo – and Frank was certain he saw some of Raymond's old charm in the way the Frenchman held himself so proud and tall, 'we *dance*.'

It was Archie Adams who led the Orchestra out, but it was Max who would lead them back in.

The moment the musicians entered the ballroom, the low hum of chatter faded into reverential silence. Two heartbeats later, it erupted into applause. The reverence across the ballroom was real – for, settling at the piano keys, flexing his fingers as he prepared to lean into the first notes, was Archie Adams, maintaining every ounce of elegance and decorum for this valedictory performance.

His fingers rolled up down the ivories as the musicians assembled around him. Now, the applause became a tumultuous wave. Backstage, Frank and Hugo heard it. By the balustrade that ran around the sprung dance floor, Daisy Allgood felt it, bearing her upward. John Hastings, the head of the Hotel Board, gazed around and thought that never before had he seen such a wide array of the garlanded, great people of London focusing all their attention on the Grand's majestic stage.

Alone in the ballroom, Daisy gazed beyond Archie. Max had settled among the Orchestra now, Lucille in his hands. Her heart lifted even further to see the smile on his face. At least he'd found a way to enjoy the moment, to lean into it with all his heart and soul. He'd seemed so 'out of sorts', as the English said, in the Candlelight Club – and so he might, for the spectre of Jackson Ford at the bar had stymied her own soul as well.

As if the thought of the war reporter had given her some strange, sixth sense, Daisy found herself craning round to gaze, not upon the Orchestra as they launched into 'Moonlight Special', but upon the marble arch instead. The doors, which had been opening and falling shut all evening, had opened again – and through them, trailing the smoke of his cigarillo, came Jackson Ford.

The war reporter had dressed up for the night. His dinner jacket was a double-breasted velveteen affair, its forest green lapels decorated in thick black stitching. The bowtie at his neck was worn loosely, perhaps even louchely. There he stood, in the ballroom doors, a plume of grey smoke settling around his head.

Daisy had been staring at him too long. She was still staring when a fresh round of applause stirred and John Hastings gently touched her arm, directing her gaze back towards the dance floor once again.

The dance floor doors had opened for a second time. Now, in bursts of dazzling motion, the dancers fanned out to heavenly applause. First came Marcus Arbuthnot, the sun-kissed titan of dance, Karina Kainz in his arms. After that, in quick succession, came the rest of the troupe. Young Frank Nettleton had taken his partner Mathilde in his arms; they flew together, a young princeling and his princess, daintier than Marcus and Karina but with their own light fleetness of foot. Moments later, the Frenchman Hugo Lavigne burst through the doors, guiding one of the second dancers in his arms. What a fresh flavour this brought to the dance floor: the dark knight of the Grand, presenting his maiden to court. Hugo moved with decisive flourishes, as if he was born to be here. Hugo Lavigne, whose country had fallen, was showing the Grand that the light had not truly been extinguished from his world.

Daisy watched as the first dance came to its conclusion, Archie's piano summoning up a storm into which Max's trombone kept diving, then breaking free. On the dance floor, the troupe came together. As the last notes struck, they spun – in one synchronised moment of drama – out of hold, turning to the balustrade and all the waiting guests. Some of the patrons tonight had reserved dances with the troupe; immediately upon seeing her, Marcus welcomed one of the Duke of Argyll's nieces into his arms – while Mathilde accepted the hand of Rémy Toussaint, the elderly French diplomat; and Hugo Lavigne, in his first commission for the Grand, led a young Parisian beauty, the daughter of some Free French official, onto the dance floor. Within moments, the nervous Parisienne was laughing gaily in his arms. Next moment, the band had struck up with their second number – and the evening's entertainment had truly begun.

'Will you dance tonight, Mrs Allgood?' asked John Hastings. He was a short, stout man, in pin-stripes and braces; the perfect image of an industrialist – and yet the Grand was where his heart came alive. After devoting so much of his adult life to numbers, it had been the temptation of the Grand that had, four years before, encouraged him to make an investment in the Buckingham.

'I'm not against a little dance, Mr Hastings,' Daisy returned, 'if a gentleman is making me an offer?'

Hastings smiled. 'You'll find me inelegant on the dance floor, Mrs Allgood, but we Americans have got to stick together.' He stepped back. 'Shall we?'

It was then that Daisy froze. Her eyes had taken in Jackson Ford again. On the other side of the dance floor, he was propped against the balustrade, his reporter's notebook in hand, no doubt taking down observations of the night.

Perhaps it would not be wise to be seen dancing.

She flashed a look around and remembered where she was. Her husband might get away with being a black man in such environs, for his talent had carried him far; but for Daisy to be seen dancing with the head of the Hotel Board? Well, that was sure to draw attention – and, as much as she'd promised herself she would ingratiate herself with Mr Hastings, attention was the last thing she wanted.

'Perhaps a little cocktail first?'

John Hastings was only too happy to oblige.

The piano reached its peak. Archie ran his hands along the keys, rose suddenly from his piano stool and, turning to the microphone positioned alongside him, declared, 'Ladies and gentlemen, let me be the first to present, for your joy and mine, the passion, the power, the musical beauty of Mr Maximillian Allgood!'

So here it was, thought Max. The moment to which the last weeks had been building. Well, at least there was no thinking about it any longer. At least, now, he could do what he was born to do.

Lucille was at his lips. He was dancing with her, as assuredly as the troupe danced down on the ballroom floor, moving his body to her rhythms, turning his face up in exultation every time she let out one of her long, joyful bursts.

In scarcely three minutes it was over. Archie lifted his hands from the piano. The Orchestra, just as they'd rehearsed, set down their instruments so that, for a few bars, Max and Lucille could go on alone. Even the dancers below spun out of hold and stood, stock-still, like soldiers on parade. For fifteen seconds, the only sound in the ballroom came from Max and Lucille, together announcing the end of one era and the beginning of the next.

The end of the Archie Adams Orchestra, and the birth of the new.

Lucille's final note faded away. Max drew her back from his lips. Until that moment, he had been holding closed his eyes, lost in a bubble in which only he and Lucille existed.

Now, he opened them to see the entirety of the ballroom fixed upon him.

'Ladies and Gentlemen,' he said, with the rolling brogue of New York and a glimmer in his eyes, 'we'll be back in fifteen minutes. Feels good tonight, doesn't it? Well, we're just getting started!'

Later that night, when the ballroom was emptying and Max Allgood stepped into the private dining room behind the Queen Mary, the applause came not from the patrons of the Grand, but from the gathered members of the Orchestra, the dance troupe, and the various members of the Hotel Board who were already around the dining table. With Daisy on his arm, and Lucille slung in her case over his shoulder, he walked to the head of the table, where Walter Knave was waiting to receive him with an outstretched hand.

'A triumph tonight,' Mr Knave began, then turned his attention to Archie, sitting at his right hand side. 'Between the two of you, we've created something special. That, ladies and gentlemen, is a night to be remembered. An end and a beginning, all wrapped up together.'

Max could remember every detail of the night's second half: how he had stood centre stage, ducking and weaving around the Orchestra as he led them through the latter part of their set – every number given a fresh, Max Allgood twist by the introduction of his rampaging trombone. In the Grand, the dancing had seemed just a little less stately, a little more urgent than it had when the evening opened. Even lords and ladies could start feeling a little bit wilder when the music took hold of them. After the last number had reached its conclusion and the Orchestra took their bows, Hugo Lavigne had reached out for Max in the dressing rooms and said, 'Mr Allgood, I almost wanted to … *jive*.' It had been the greatest compliment Max could hear.

The meal M. Laurent had prepared was as resplendent as any they had eaten in the years before rationing and privation. Pink duck breasts sat upon potatoes with russet-gold, caramelised skins, plates steeped in the scents of honey and thyme. The table was already laid with Champagne flutes. Waiters hustled around, filling them one at a time – until, when the last drop was poured, John Hastings lifted himself from the top of the table and began.

'An occasion like this deserves to be marked with fine food and fine wine – and, in these uncertain days, perhaps it is more important than ever to raise a glass … to old friends and new.' At this moment, he turned to Archie Adams – who was sitting among his old Orchestra, the dewiness in his eyes a testament to the sanctity of the occasion. 'Mr Adams, your music will stay with us, even after you are gone.

'And Mr Allgood,' he went on, 'the new custodian of that music. We saw, tonight, how you will bring your own tastes, your own passions, your own feeling to our ballroom. What an adventure we will go on together, sir.'

The first toast of the evening was made. After that, with a few words from Walter Knave, the glasses were drained and dinner began.

Max hadn't eaten as well in all of his years – and, since landing at the Buckingham Hotel, he'd tasted some fine food indeed. Henri Laurent could recreate the tastes of those fine Parisian restaurants to perfection. Halfway along the table, Harry Dudgeon was bowed in conversation with two of his fellows – but, every few words, his eyes lifted to appraise Max. Max decided to make a special effort, and beamed at him across the silver platters. At least Harry lifted his glass in acknowledgement – but Max still couldn't help feeling as if something wasn't right. 'It ought to be a celebration for him too,' he whispered to Daisy. 'Next time we're on that stage, it'll be Harry in front of that grand piano.'

'You need to take him for cocktails, Max. Invite him to a drink.'

'Romance him a little, that's what you mean.'

Daisy almost choked on her potato. 'You're being glib. But he's your pianist, Max. Between his piano and your trombone, you drive the band. You and he need to—'

At that moment, a tiny silver spoon rang along the edge of a Champagne flute, and Archie Adams got to his feet.

Archie was a softly spoken man, a private man, a delicate man; he'd only ever truly opened his heart through the piano keys. And yet here he stood.

'Some of you already know this, but a part of me thought I'd always lead my Orchestra – until my fingers got too slow, or my ears grew too deaf. Ten years, I thought. Fifteen, if the will took hold of me. But then, last Christmas…' Even Max had heard this story, though he hadn't lived it like the rest of them. When the bombs rained down on Berkeley Square, Archie was caught in the Housekeeping Lounge with Emmeline Moffatt, the old Head of Housekeeping. There, entombed by debris, they had held on to each other and finally acknowledged that this – the two of them together – was the future they desired. Mrs Moffatt had left the hotel by new year, off to the country. Now Archie lifted his Champagne flute aloft, readying himself to follow. 'Well, last Christmas, everything changed. I am romantic enough to say that love found me, and I found it, here in the ruins of our hotel. So I am to set off on a new adventure. There will be music, I'm sure, but there will be no Grand Ballroom. To that, I entrust the very dear members of my Orchestra – and its new custodian.' Archie turned. 'To Max Allgood, the new leader of the—'

'Now, hold your horses, good sir!' Max cried out, doing his best (and truly dreadful) impression of Archie's accent. 'This night ain't about me.' His eyes flicked, of their own volition, to Harry Dudgeon, only to find that he was still sharing mute whispers with the trumpeter at his side. 'But this is *your* farewell, Mr Adams! This is *your* moment. Hey, you all,' and he began rallying the diners to raise their glasses once again. 'I've got something to say. Archie, you sure leave big shoes to fill. I've been watching you play, jamming alongside your crowd, for some weeks now – and every time I've left that stage, I've been filled with awe, sir, awe at what you do. Now, I'm honoured to be chosen to step into your shoes. But I want to make you a promise, right now, in front of these good people. I'll do you proud, Mr Adams. I'll make sure we shine. And, sure, there'll be changes in the Orchestra. Season to season, we'll grow. We might set down our instruments, but the music never stops. Every musician knows it. It's part of our hearts. But one thing's for certain – now I've seen it, we'll always stay true to the ideals you laid out here. Because those are the ideals of the Grand. The music matters. And that's the torch we'll be carrying – the one you put in our hands.'

Max was about to sink down and ask Daisy if he'd done all right, but he had no need, for around the table the applause began. First it was Mr Hastings; then it was Mr Knave; then the dancers who crowded together at the table's opposite end. But soon it was the musicians as well. Archie was raising his glass and bowing his head in thanks.

It wasn't until Max truly sat down, squeezing Daisy's hand under the table, that he realised only one man around the table hadn't joined in the applause – for there sat Harry Dudgeon, stock-still and frozen in place, his mask a brooding rictus while the dining room exploded around him.

Chapter Twelve

The Grand might have brought magic and light, chronicling the Buckingham's year with its extravagant balls, demonstrations and masquerades, but it was the Queen Mary that kept the Buckingham alive. Victor, who had spent his morning turning fat Lincolnshire sausages for breakfast, was now indentured to the lunchtime service, preparing a mountain of rhubarb stalks for the tarts Henri Laurent had prepared. As he trimmed each stalk, he stared out onto the restaurant floor. This was the lull between breakfast and lunch, but some of the tables were still occupied by those who'd let their teas and crumpets linger. Mr Knave was taking tea alone while he studied the morning newspapers, no doubt preparing himself for the luncheon to come. It was a big one. M. Laurent had made sure of that, as he barked out orders almost as soon as the breakfast service was finished. 'Mr Dalton's a regular here,' he'd thundered, meaning Mr Hugh Dalton, the Minister for Economic Welfare, who often used the hotel as a convenient spot to gather the critical figures of agriculture, industry and logistics on which his department depended. 'But the lot he's bringing won't be as familiar with the hotel, so it's our job to show them what we're worth. Don't let your little minds go wandering. This here's as much of a show as the Grand's Summer Ball.'

He'd kept the same pressure up all morning long. 'A nice rhubarb tart might end this war a few months early, if it gets the creative juices going,' he'd declared, leaning over Victor's shoulder. 'It's the Danish Freedom Council we've got coming. Some sods from lost Luxembourg. Hubert Pierlot himself! All the Low Countries, getting here today to hammer things out. If those tarts are just sweet enough, just sour enough, just the right *piquancy*, we'll be doing our bit for the war effort.'

Victor was quite certain that the exact measurements of his rhubarb batons would not tip the balance of war, yet it still made him proud to know he was cooking for men of influence. One day, if it didn't end, the war would surely come for him. Until then, he would just peel and chop, peel and chop, and make the best of every day.

'This lot needs unloading!' Henri Laurent suddenly bawled.

Across the kitchen, knives skittered clumsily out of hands – as they did each time M. Laurent's voice chimed. Victor looked up, to find the hulking chef lumbering towards him.

'W-what, chef?'

'Delivery's just sitting by the larder doors. One of you layabouts should have unloaded by now. That's precious merchandise, just sitting in crates. Can't I trust any of you?'

'Me, chef?'

'You're as good as any, boy! That rhubarb ought to have taken a jiffy. You've not got the knife skills. It's all that Italian training – just kneading pasta all day long. Well, you'll have to do better, and faster, in my kitchen.'

Victor was transfixed by the big mole whose hairs kept trembling on the top of Henri Laurent's brow, so it took another glare from the head chef until he scuttled towards the back of the Queen Mary kitchens. Here, in the alcoves by the larder, stood the crates of this morning's delivery. The manifest was on top, apparently signed by whoever had opened the kitchens this morning. As his eyes roamed its innumerable lines, Victor couldn't help thinking of that ration book at home, and how much his mother struggled. There were yet bounties in London – only not for the common man.

It would be an hour's endeavour to correctly store all this produce. Soon, Victor was dragging sacks of new potatoes into the cold storage. Trays of baby broad beans were being lined up alongside the first of the season's peas, ready to be shelled. Radishes and baby carrots, cheeses wrapped in wax, sacks of flour and eggs were being slotted into place, the pheasants and partridges hung to further mature, while the mackerel, spring chickens and ground beef all went into the great refrigerated cabinet at the larder's rear. The multitude of jarred preserves, honeys from the royal apiaries, the landslide of butter and all the endless gallons of fresh cream Victor checked off the manifest was almost sickening to see.

It was only when Victor neared the end of his task that he realised something was amiss – for, though he'd spent an hour ticking off each item as he went, there were still a good number of unmarked rows on the paper. A case of Lincolnshire sausages seemed to have passed him by. So had a dozen pounds of flour, four dozen eggs, six jars of honey and a good number of kippers. He was still puzzling over the disappearance of three small barrels of marmalade when he saw Henri Laurent bearing back down.

'Stop dallying in here, boy. They need you on pastry. Surfaces need scrubbing.'

'But sir—'

Henri Laurent glowered. 'Boy?' he intoned, with all the theatrical villainy of one of the Christmas pantomimes Victor's mother once took him to see.

Do your best, he'd told himself.

So he plucked up his courage and tried to explain to M. Laurent exactly what he'd seen.

When M. Laurent grew angry, the veins at his temple started throbbing like pulsing blue worms. 'These wholesalers are trying to rob us again. All right, lad, draw me up a list of everything they haven't delivered. I'll play hell myself. Don't those black-guards know what we're doing in here? We're feeding the free world! We're filling bellies so these government men can put the world back to rights! Rob from us, and they're only prolonging the battle.'

And he walked away in a righteous fury, leaving Victor with the curious sensation that things were not as they seemed.

The sun hung above Lambeth, lighting up the bombed-out squares, the ravine where the roads used to be. As Annie Brogan stepped off the omnibus, it felt as if she was seeing Lambeth for the first time. These streets where she'd been raised had all been jumbled up, redesigned. Like scars healing over, she thought, taking in the gangs of construction workers gathered around wagons and cranes.

It didn't help that the address she was going to wasn't the old, narrow house on Albert Yard. She'd wanted to at least see the Yard at first – but somehow she'd never quite dared; she thought it would be like staring into the sun, a damaging sight she could never unsee.

The address to which she was headed was a much smaller terrace off the Kennington Road. Eliza Hatchet had been elderly at the dawn of the Great War. Back then, she'd been too old to run the ambulances in France as she'd wanted – but, at sixty-three, there had still been a space for her in the field hospital outside Arras, where she'd spent two long years. Of course, the idea of some mission to another field hospital had been out of the question this time round. Her children had urged her to leave London, but Eliza had been obstinate in her refusal: she was going to stay, and do her bit – and, if the ARP would not have her (and they wouldn't; Eliza had tried), and the WVS deemed her a little too unsteady on her legs (they were fools; Eliza could still walk miles), well, she would find her own way of helping. That was how her house on the corner of Cleaver Square had become a *de facto* sanctuary for the dispossessed, a halfway house for the bombed-to-oblivion.

The new home of Annie's parents, William and Orla Brogan.

The house was a hubbub when Annie arrived, but Eliza was glad to see her; the wrinkled old dear always enjoyed seeing the young turn up on her doorstep. Annie's parents had taken the back bedroom. It wasn't much, certainly not compared to what they had before, but it was warm and secure. Downstairs, the living room had been given up for guests as well; Eliza kept only her own small bedroom and a corner of the kitchen for herself. 'This house used to be a whirlwind, when the nippers were small,' she'd said, 'and it's a whirlwind again.'

Eliza showed Annie into the sitting room, and there she lingered until at last her parents arrived. They looked rake thin, thought Annie. Soon, the young girl was being smothered in arms.

'Bill's running late,' she said, when at last she was free, 'but look, it isn't just Billy who can provide.' She showed them her basket. 'I went down the open air market. Splash a few pennies around and you can pick some bits up off-book. And look, some knobs of butter – that's courtesy of the Buckingham Hotel.' Annie had lifted a few off the trolleys. Well, lords and ladies thought nothing of frittering away their bread and butter. Some of the chambermaids lived entirely off left-over crusts and preserve – and felt very satisfied on it. 'I'm picking up some extra shifts now. Ever since Nance – I mean, *Mrs de Guise* – had that bairn, I've been run off my feet. The other girls say they can't keep up.'

What they'd actually said is: *Slow down, Annie, we can't keep up with the mess you're making.* But Annie, who had inherited the Brogan talent for relentless optimism, seemed to overlook this particular fact.

'And look, here …'

This time it was a little brown envelope jangling with coins. 'This fortnight's pay,' she said, ignoring her father's appalled face. 'No, Ma! I *insist*. I've got bed and board, and you – you've got …'

'You need to look after yourself too,' said Mrs Brogan.

'I don't need looking after. I'm the one doing the looking after now, Ma, and that's that. I looked after Mrs de Guise, didn't I, when she was having that baby? Now, granted, Mrs Allgood had a little something to do with that too – I never did find out if she'd been a midwife back in New York! – but I reckon I'll be in line for a bonus, maybe even a promotion, when Mrs de Guise gets back. So I'm really on top of things, Ma. *Take it.*'

The stalemate had extended into a second minute when the sitting-room door opened again, and Eliza toddled through with another broad grin. 'It's a homecoming!' she announced, and stepped back to reveal Billy.

Now they flocked to him. Soon, Billy too was having to fight back the tidal wave of affection. He emerged from the tangle of arms shouting, 'Off with you now! I'm not here for kissing and cuddles. I'm here for this.' And, having first made certain that Eliza had toddled off to her other duties in the house, he turned on his heel, levered his way back to the doorstep, and came back with his arms laden in bags.

He had just set them down when he noticed Annie had done

the same. 'Good minds think alike, don't they? Us Brogans stick together. Look, Ma, Pa – you've devoted your whole lives to us. It's time we repaid the favour. So I'm making you a promise. In fact, I'm making you a dozen.' One after another, he started lifting bits from the bag. Some of it was evidently things he'd salvaged from the Buckingham Hotel – but the Brogans were no stranger to that, for Billy had been helping them out with odds and ends ever since he took up there. A box of eggs, a tin of tea, a string of pork sausages and a punnet of green tomatoes. A cloth bag of breakfast pastries came next. 'Here's my pay packet too,' he said – and, at this, Annie piped up, 'Snap, Bill! I did the very same!' This only made Billy beam further. 'Good girl, Annie. See, these two here are going to have to accept they're not running this family anymore. Well, not for a time. I'll hand you back the reins by Christmas, Ma. Because by then you'll be back in Albert Yard, where you belong.'

Mr and Mrs Brogan shared a long, quizzical look.

'Albert Yard, Bill?' ventured Mrs Brogan. 'It's in pieces. The old house, it's gone ...'

'The structure's still standing. It's just missing a few walls. Missing a roof. Well, that's easily sorted.'

'Easily sorted for those with money, Bill,' said his father, darkly. 'You forget, we're not all like those who run the Buckingham. We don't all have gold bullion squirrelled away in a hotel safe ...'

Billy grinned. So, that rumour about King Zog had reached Lambeth as well. Or perhaps he'd been chattering about it himself – Billy had always had a problem with loose lips, ever since he was small.

'Well, I'm sorting it. See, I've been running errands again for management – just like I used to do, back when Mr Charles was in charge. If I keep it up, I reckon I can have you renting a house of your own by summer – and back at Albert Yard by Christmas.'

'Billy!' Mr Brogan exclaimed. 'You've no idea what it would cost to rebuild.'

'I do, Pa, because I've got it worked out. Those Buckingham builders have been a godsend.' As he was speaking, he reached into his bag to pull out the last item. 'Trust me – on Christmas Day, we'll be wassailing round the fire, just like in the old days. But you've got to believe!'

Annie watched as Billy's fist closed around something in the bag, then pulled it out for all to see.

In his hand was a bottle of Martell brandy, half full with rich, amber liquid. Billy hoisted it aloft like a flag, or some prize he'd been triumphant in winning. The grin on his face broadened further as he spied four glasses left on a table by the hearth. 'To toast our good news,' he declared, rushing to fill the glasses.

'Billy,' said Mrs Brogan, her voice brimming with emotion, 'I just don't know what to think.'

Nor did Mr Brogan, it seemed – for he looked stupefied as Billy pressed a glass into his hand.

But Annie did.

Annie knew exactly what to think – and she didn't like it one bit.

Because she'd seen that bottle of brandy before. As a matter of fact, she was the one who'd sweet-talked Victor into handing it over. The last time she'd seen it, it had been sitting on the trolley where she'd left it, waiting for Mrs de Guise to need a quick sip.

'Hey Billy,' she said, 'where'd you get that from?'

'Oh, perks of the trade, Annie,' he said, flashing her a grin. 'Just to warm their hearts. A promise – it's going to be a hard year, but by Christmas it'll be done.'

He had the strangest look in his eyes as he drained his glass in one swift gulp. It was almost as if, thought Annie, he had to fortify himself for some big challenge. The brandy seemed to have some magical effect on Billy, for the moment its warmth ran through him, the peculiar, almost conflicted look passed from his eyes. The moment it hit Annie's belly, her gnawing doubt was dulled too. She'd never tasted brandy before – and, if the guilt of not having returned the bottle to Victor had started to play on her, it was well and truly gone by the time Billy handed her a second glass.

'To us Brogans,' he declared, 'and the things we have to do to win this damn war!'

Chapter Thirteen

Sometimes, Nancy could sleep through the sirens – but all Arthur had to do was whimper and she was out of bed like a bullet.

Nancy hummed a little as she set about feeding Arthur. He was going to have Raymond's nose, she thought, but there was so much of her own family in him as well. What a strange thing it was, to see her dearly departed father somehow brought back to life, swaddled in cloths and lying in her arms.

Once his belly was full, Arthur was content to sleep – but Nancy dared not carry him back to the cot, so for a time they lay there together. Soon, one hour had turned into the next. When Vivienne passed by the door and asked her if she might need water, tea, any toast to sustain her depleted body, she thought nothing of saying 'Yes'. Soon, Vivienne was back at the bedside with a pot of tea and two hot buttered rounds of toast, drizzled with honey. 'I don't know what I'd do without you,' Nancy said before she took her first bite. 'Without Raymond…' Then she stalled, for of course Vivienne had already lost Stan's father.

'Artie would have been a good uncle,' Vivienne said, gazing at Arthur. 'I can imagine him, now, how it might have been – Artie, always tempting Arthur a little astray. Just a little bit, of course. Just to rile his father …'

'Raymond and Artie always did rub each other up the wrong way.'

Until those last years, thought Nancy; until those final moments, the brothers stranded together on the beaches of Dunkirk.

'Have you heard from him yet?'

Nancy shook her head. 'But no telegram from the service to say he's been killed, so …' By God, even giving voice to it was painful. There'd been no telegram to report Artie's death: only Raymond, appearing like a ghost in the ballroom, back from the dead. 'His letters will get through soon. It might be he's been writing every day.'

Vivienne squeezed her hand. 'Get some sleep. You'll be back at the Buckingham before you know it. Now's the moment to rest.'

But of course Nancy couldn't.

There was nothing else for it. Moments like these had to be seized, not squandered. That was why she left Arthur lying peacefully on the bed and went to sit at the bureau in the window, where the letter she'd started yesterday evening – replete with the tiniest, intimate details of her day spent with Arthur – was lying unfinished.

There was so much to tell, so much to set in order in her head – not least those snippets of story Hugo had continued to tell.

So, 'Dear Raymond,' she went on, 'it will sound strange, but it is almost like I am only just getting to know you now – you, as you were, in the time before we met. Hugo has opened a door into a side of you I can never see. It is almost like I am falling in love with you for a second time …'

Paris by night; a city of stars. Ray had been smarting all afternoon, ever since his meeting with Ophelia, but by the time night drew its veil over Notre Dame, some of the upset had started to leave him. He tried to think of what his father would have said, in that charmingly sly way Stanley Cohen often had, and in the end it was his father's words that buoyed him: 'You're a Cohen boy. Show those rich toffs what you're made of. And don't forget who you are!'

It would have been easy to forget who he was this evening. As the daylight paled, Ray had repaired to his digs opposite the Hotel Acacias, and there he'd stood in front of an old mirror to dress in a specially tailored suit of midnight blue. Ray had felt awkward the first time he donned a tuxedo to take to the dance floor – having grown up in the clubs of Whitechapel, it seemed an ostentation too far – but since then he had got used to the idea of elegance, of a dance being judged on so much more than footwork, posture and poise. Yet this suit, commissioned by Georges and presented to him this very night, seemed to elevate him so far above his Whitechapel beginnings that he felt undone. To don it was to transform. When he looked in the mirror, he had the bearing of some young prince. It was, he supposed, just what Georges had intended.

The night began in a little restaurant in the shadow of Notre Dame, with the gentle susurration of the Seine a beautiful background music. Sitting opposite him, and alongside Georges, was a lady of impeccable good looks, silver hair and an ageless face that belied her sixty years. The evening dress she was wearing was of simple silk, but the jewels that sparkled at her wrist, her neckline and dangling from her ears gave her a kind of ethereal beauty. Ray had heard Georges speak often of Marie Dumas, his first partner in the world of dance (and, Georges had confided in him – as gentlemen often do – his first true lover as well), but he had never thought to meet her. Evidently, she too had heard much of Ray. The moment Ray appeared, she seemed to be appraising him like Ray had seen saddlers do horses on the streets of Whitechapel.

'*Les années folles*,' she pronounced, when the waiter brought three luminous glasses of crème de cassis to cleanse their palates. 'I first heard this era of ours named as such last month, and it seems right, does it not? The crazy years. War over. A world full of survivors, and they all want to *live*?'

To Ray, it had all been a whirl. 'Not like Whitechapel,' he remarked.

'This … Whitechapel? It is London, is it not?' Marie's face darkened. 'The home of the Ripper!'

'Well, that was rather a long time—'

Marie marched on, 'I have known Paris all my life. La Belle Epoque – the happy years, before the Great War, when everything was possible. But compare those days to these, and …' She beamed. 'Paris is now a city of the world. And do you know why, young man?' She pointed a slender, scarlet-tipped finger at him and pronounced, 'The Americans! So many of them never left after the war. You can hear the jazz in the air. Ragtimitis! The Revue Nègre on the Champs-Élysées, and this business with Josephine Baker at the Folies Bergère …'

Ray had heard this story; that afternoon, Hugo had frothed with rumours of the more salacious goings-on in Paris after dark. 'Didn't she dance with … bananas?' A loincloth comprised entirely of bananas, as Hugo had described it; the image had been playing on Ray's mind all day.

'Well,' Georges interjected, 'the less said about that particular matter, the better. Ray, we must come to business. I have long hoped for you to meet Marie, for she has been instrumental in welcoming so many dancers to the ballroom world.' He made a steeple of his fingers, balanced his chin upon it, and said, 'Well, my love? What do we make of my newest ward?'

Ray had that feeling again: it was almost as if Marie was looking upon her friend's new puppy, expected to either admire him for his fine coat and pleasant disposition, or admonish him for showing his teeth.

'I see it, Georges. There is something a little bit special about this boy. The problem is – he is *still* a boy. Yes, that is quite clear to see as well. Look up, young man.'

Ray felt more like one of Georges's playthings every moment. And yet they were both looking at him with such fondness that it would have been a fool who complained.

'Yes,' said Marie, 'he has the makings of a noble bearing, but he's hardly noble by birth. This name of his. *Cohen*. It hardly speaks of old-world elegance. It is a good, solid name – but it hardly suggests a man born to the ballroom.'

Georges addressed Ray: 'There is always a little artifice in the ballroom. Sometimes, a tweak must be made to posture. Other times, a tweak to ...'

'My *name?*' Ray asked, in mounting bewilderment.

'It would not be the first time,' Marie went on. 'Not all great dancers are blessed with great parentage. So let me think.' She mused on it for some time, swirling around the last of her crème de cassis. 'It must be something that speaks of a rich, talented ancestry. Something in which elegance cannot be denied.' She paused. 'Here we have Georges de la Motte,' she smiled. 'So here we must have ...' When the name came to her, her eyes lit up. 'Raymond de Guise.'

Georges nodded, favourably. 'I knew a de Guise once. An old family, from the Carcassonne country. Yes, this would do. It conjures an air of wonder. Yes, de Guise. It rather rolls off the tongue.' Georges puffed out his breast and said, 'What do you think, Raymond?'

Ray hardly knew what to think. *Raymond de Guise*. He'd never live it down on the streets of Whitechapel. All he could hear was his father's voice. *You're a Cohen boy. Son, don't forget who you are!*

He looked into each of their eyes. *De Guise*. It didn't seem he had much of a choice – and he had to admit that there was a certain ring to it. And yet...

'Ray Cohen might not have impressed Ophelia Chalfont,' Georges declared, 'but Raymond de Guise most assuredly could. Raymond, young man, tomorrow you will dance as de Guise – and, soon, blaze your way into triumph at the Casino de Paris...'

'De Guise?' scoffed Hugo, later that night – when Ray, having shed his new suit, met him on the corner outside the Hotel Acacias. 'I suppose it has a certain ring to it. And there's a mystery in it too, is there not? It is like your English word... *disguise*. Ray Cohen dons his disguise, and becomes the dashing Raymond de Guise!' He clapped Ray on the shoulder, then started steering him down the street. 'You're a new Scarlet Pimpernel!'

There had been too many things to bewilder him tonight; this was just another one. 'Scarlet Pimper...' He shook his head. 'No, don't tell me. I'm sure it will only confuse me even more. Hugo, let's just dance.'

'We'll get you loosened up, Ray. But think of it like this – a girl like Ophelia might fall for a de Guise. She certainly wouldn't fall for a lowly Whitechapel lad.'

Ray didn't even want to think about romance. If romance

came into his life, it would be with a girl more grounded, down to earth, more *real* than the ethereal Ophelia.

'Well, you might find one of those dancing the java tonight. It's a fast waltz, Ray. A *close* waltz. Too close, sometimes. I've seen folks thrown out of the clubs for dancing just a little too personally, if you understand my meaning.'

Not for the first time, Ray got the impression that this wild, bright-eyed new friend of his was more a devil on his shoulder than an angel. The fact was, something about Hugo's wolfish smile reminded him of his brother Artie – only Artie as he might have been if he too had fallen in love with the ballroom, instead of the drinking dens of Whitechapel.

'Montmartre,' Hugo declared, as he whisked them across the river. 'Pigalle. These are the places to dance, *Raymond de Guise*; I'll show you somewhere that has the *heart*.'

Ray heard it before he could see it. The streets of Montmartre were alive with light and sound. Trumpets sailed out of the doors of a cabaret called L'Abbaye; men and women in extravagant gowns and painted faces could be seen flitting in the shadows around La Petite Chaumière; the patrons of every café spilled out onto the pavements, and from each doorway came the sound of drums, of song, of good cheer.

'Here,' announced Hugo, when they came at last to a narrow arch of brick, sandwiched between two restaurants where tables were overflowing. 'Raymond, let me introduce you to the *pleasures of the dark*.'

The music crashed over him the moment he followed Hugo through the velvet curtains and into the club itself. Directly in front of him was a heaving dance floor – and, beyond that, a stage crammed with musicians. Trumpeters kept bobbing up and down, a lone saxophonist chased a melody, a percussionist kept a steady beat – while some songstress, a black woman dressed in bright scarlet, poured out her heart in song. Meanwhile, on the dance floor, bodies were pressed against each other, more tightly than in any ballroom where Ray had ever danced. He watched as couples narrowly avoided crashing into one another, as they waltzed with barely a sliver of space between themselves, as hands caressed bodies in ways that might make a good Englishman blush.

'*That*, Ray,' said Hugo, 'is the *java*.'

A little while later, once Ray had got drinks and Hugo had been on his foray across the dance hall, searching out partners for the night, Ray felt he had finally got the measure of the dance. Hugo had staked out one of the dark, candlelit booths on the quietest side of the dance floor for them, and here they had repaired with the two girls – Miss Hannah Lindt and Miss Arielle du Pont – to ready themselves for the dancing to come. Hannah and Arielle, it transpired, had visited the same club but two nights ago, and been swept not only into the java but the tabletop dancing, the Charleston performers dancing solo and in pairs.

'Is it like this in London?' Hannah asked.

Ray had to admit it was not. There was life in London, so much life, but it did not have this timbre, this rhythm, this certain (he smiled when he remembered the phrase) *je ne sais quoi*. In London the dance halls heaved with the sighs of a generation who had survived the war – but, if there was music like this, the ragtime, the jazz, Ray had not encountered it. He had certainly never seen anybody as unique as the songstress on stage right now, her voice deep and rich, Paris by way of the Mississippi Delta.

The songstress reached a note so glorious that, across the dance floor, couples came apart and joined their hands in unbridled applause. In that moment, Hugo too leapt to his feet, coaxing Arielle up alongside him. 'This next dance is ours, mademoiselle.' With a deep (and very well-practised) bow, he took her hand. 'Ray, just follow my lead.'

Ray rolled his eyes. 'I'm sure I can find my way. It's a waltz…'

'Oh,' grinned Hannah, across the table, 'but it doesn't *feel* like a waltz.'

Hugo winked as he saw Hannah take Ray's hand – but that was the last time he gave either of them any attention, for the music had struck up again, trumpets driving the melody on at an even more frenetic pace. Soon, Hugo and Arielle had slipped in among the other dancers and begun box-stepping at some practically indecent rate around the room.

'It really isn't that frightening,' said Hannah blithely, as she and Ray moved down to the dance floor. 'It looked strange to me too. But classical training – well, it's for the stage; it isn't for real life.'

'Classical training?' asked Ray.

'Oh, my parents imagine me a ballerina,' said Hannah, with a smile. 'But even a ballerina can go wild once in a while.'

This was more natural, thought Ray as he slipped into the dance. The moment he'd taken Hannah in hold, she'd inched even closer to his body, then directed his hands lower down her frame; there was something about being in a dance hall like this, bodies pressed close together, couples wheeling past in a blur of colour and noise, that made Ray feel he belonged. He was free to just follow the music – and if, at times, it seemed that Hannah was leading ('Go faster, Raymond!' she laughed, leaning in to press her lips to his ear), that hardly mattered in a place like this. They danced until the song came to an end, danced into a second – and, by the time the third had come around, and Hugo suggested a sudden swapping of partners, Ray felt as if he understood this dance implicitly.

'Practically indecent, isn't it?' Hugo laughed, as he took Hannah from Ray's hold and Arielle slipped into Ray's arms. 'They ban the java, you know. If things get too much, the *gendarmes* come and shut it down.'

Arielle was different from Hannah – just as fine a dancer, but somehow dancing within herself, as if Ray might have been any one of the dozens of other men in the room. He was glad when he and Hugo swapped partners again, for Hannah seemed to fit his body better. Hugo seemed to notice this too, for a look like irritation seemed to pass over his face when, some songs later, Hannah declined his hand and insisted she would prefer to spend the night dancing with Ray alone. 'Just remember what I said, Ray. You don't want the *gendarmes* to come and lock you up. You've still got to dance with Ophelia.'

'Ophelia?' asked Hannah, in the lull between songs.

'I was chosen to partner her in the Exhibition Paris, but...'

'You think not?'

Ray hardly wanted to say what came next, but he spilled it all the same, 'She is on the brink of rejecting me. And my mentor...' He shrugged – he did not want to let Georges down – but there was no chance to elucidate further, for the music was starting up again.

The java was a dance of equals. It was a dance of celebration. It was a dance that consumed a man, body and soul, so that neither Hugo nor Ray knew when midnight came. It was only when the musicians grew exhausted of their frenzy, and their bandleader – a plump pianist with a permanent reef of smoke around his head – announced their last song, that anyone in the club knew they had danced all night long.

'The last dance,' said Hannah. 'Let's make it count.'

And so they did. Somewhere in that song, Ray realised that they were dancing so closely that, oftentimes, their hips were touching, their lips but a whisker away from each other, Hannah's cascade of ebony hair tumbling over his own.

The song exploded. The band were done. On the dance floor, the rapture reached a peak. Raymond looked up, to see Hannah gazing into his eyes.

Silence.

Now there was silence in the club.

It was only as the foursome followed the other patrons up the stairs that they realised dawn was already hovering on the horizon beyond the old city walls.

'So,' said Hannah. 'A most unexpected night.'

'But one to be remembered,' intervened Hugo. He took Hannah's hand, planted a kiss on it, and then, bracing Arielle by the shoulders, kissed the air on either side of her cheeks. 'My friend Ray is in Paris for some days yet. Perhaps we will all dance again.'

Hannah had been listening to Hugo, but her eyes were for Raymond alone. 'I should like that very much indeed.'

After the parting of the ways, Ray and Hugo took off along the cobbled row, heading south towards the river. 'You'll have to be fleet on your feet, *mon frère*, or Georges will know you were set loose last night.'

'He's not my gaoler,' said Ray, 'and yet...'

'He would be disappointed, were he to know you were not resting, readying your soul to impress Ophelia this morning.'

Ray stopped dead. 'Ophelia. I'd half forgotten. You wouldn't find a prim, proper girl like Ophelia dancing the java like that. Not like...'

'Hannah Lindt?'

Ray nodded.

'Have you, perhaps, fallen in love?' Hugo asked, with just a hint of a sardonic smile.

'Not in the least,' said Ray. 'Or ... I don't think so. I've never been in love, Hugo.'

'Oh, *mon frère!* I fall in love practically every day. It's just the price we must pay for being men.' He stopped. Something in this thought had not appealed to Ray. 'Something is bothering you, Ray. I, Hugo Lavigne, can see it written on you. Englishmen claim to live private lives, but Frenchmen can see the true feeling in a heart. And if it isn't love, it's ... fear.'

'No, not fear,' said Ray, verging on sadness. 'It's just ... *lack*. Lack of desire, I suppose.'

'Georges would tell you: you're a showman, Raymond. That is why he has given you this name *de Guise*. So that, when the moment comes, you can don your disguise, leave Ray Cohen – and all his worries, his fears about not fitting in – behind, and sail into the ballroom as Raymond de Guise. It's like the suit of midnight blue he gifted you. A new skin for a new name.'

But Ray thought: *You're a Cohen boy. Son, don't forget who you are!*

Hugo said, 'You don't want to be de Guise?'

'It isn't that. It's that—'

'You don't want to *feel* like de Guise. You don't mind the disguise, but you don't want it to seep into you. You don't want transformation. You don't want ... Ophelia!' Hugo had cried it out with the air of an epiphany.

Ray looked so uncomfortable his feet were almost dancing of their own volition. Uneasily, he shifted weight from foot to foot.

'There is but one solution to this malady. You already know what it is.'

Ray just breathed deeply.

'You must dance with Hannah Lindt at the Exhibition Paris.

Ophelia must be set free … and so, Ray, must you. The only question,' and here he grinned, as if posing some inscrutable riddle, 'is how to convey such an idea to Georges de la Motte.'

Nancy had been lost in that moment, chronicling Raymond's own history to him, wondering at the man she'd fallen in love with and the boy he'd once been when Arthur suddenly started squalling again on the bed.

'*Hugo tells us you looked at him dumbfounded, then, as if to say there was no way you could go against Georges, no way you could do anything but dance with Ophelia at the Casino de Paris…*'

Leaving the letter on the bureau, she returned to the bed. This time, she didn't have to feed Arthur to settle him; all he needed was her touch. 'Who knows where he is right now,' she whispered, 'but wherever he is, he'll be thinking of you.'

June 1941

Chapter Fourteen

DISPATCHES FROM THE BUCKINGHAM HOTEL!
NEW YORK TIMES, JUNE 15, 1941

By Jackson Ford, your man in LONDON

There is but one topic of conversation in the hallowed halls of the Buckingham Hotel this month: not the coming Summer Ball, which hangs on the horizon, promising a spectacle for all London Society; but the prospect of the forces of the United States finally declaring war on behalf of all the fallen nations of Europe. Last month's sinking of the US cargo steamer, the SS *Robin Moor*, has provoked hot debate among the exiled governments in London that President Roosevelt is inching closer to the support the embattled nations of Europe so badly need. Greece and Crete are now fallen to Nazi hands, Britain stands alone – and, increasingly, it is seen that the financial and moral aid of the Americas is not enough. Only men in the field will win this war.

Does the sinking of the *Robin Moor* change President Roosevelt's calculations? Rumour is that he will soon address Congress to announce that Germany must be held accountable for their actions. Foreign merchant ships in US ports have already been requisitioned, and all German and Italian assets held in the United States have been frozen. But how long before the scales tip yet further? What will it finally take for the United States to declare itself an active combatant in this war?

The gossip in the Buckingham Hotel is that it will yet take an act so egregious that it cannot be ignored before the United States commits to sacrificing its young men in defence of the free world. But what might that be, and when might it come? Is Great Britain to stand alone for the duration of this long war? And can an event like the Buckingham's fêted Summer Ball serve as enough of a distraction from the bitter reality of this age of global strife?

Archie Adams left the Buckingham Hotel on a bright summer's day, when a week of clear nights had gifted him the perfect moment to make his departure. There had been sentimentality enough in the preceding days, but on the morning of his departure there was but a pot of tea in Mr Knave's office, a White Owl cigar, and a handshake to signify all the respect he'd acquired in the last twelve years. The gold pocket-watch whose chain dangled from his breast was inscribed with the legend 'Always the Music' – which was both the name of the first recording the Archie Adams Orchestra ever made, and a promise for the future. Then he was gone, a Rolls Royce waiting to spirit him from one world into the next.

On that same morning, Max Allgood woke to a new feeling in his heart. The first moment he saw the words 'THE MAX ALLGOOD ORCHESTRA' on the plaques that adorned the dressing-room walls, it had finally felt real. Much more than this, he'd felt the change in Daisy too. She'd been holding on to a tension all spring, ever since that carriage brought them to

Berkeley Square – but now the fear that what had been given could so easily be taken away was suddenly diminished in her. He took her shopping, down to the Regent Street arcades, and when they came back to the Buckingham – Daisy with a hatbox tucked neatly under her arm – it had felt, for the first time, as if they were truly coming home.

Now, as the afternoon paled towards evening, he opened the dance floor doors and stepped into the Grand to see all the musicians waiting there – and knew that he belonged.

Now, Max stood in front of his troops and felt a burst of strange pride. In two weeks' time, the Grand would dance to his tune.

'A Summer Ball at the Buckingham Hotel is, I'm told, always a special occasion – but I've no need to tell you that,' said Max, wary that his audience had been occupying the Grand for a multitude of summers. 'You've been here. You've *made* them special. What's left to us is to show them what *rebirth* looks like.' Max had been thinking about this speech for long nights, orating snippets of it to Daisy – and always grateful when she had some suggestion that was eminently better than his own. 'I was thinking about the war,' he went on. 'How it makes you live for the moment. There's enough horror in looking back, enough uncertainty in looking to the future, that what people really want is something to spirit them away from it all.' Max's face opened in a wide, toothy smile. 'And that's what we'll do, come the Summer Ball. Spirit them off into something quite unexpected – something that'll make them feel alive. Who knows when we'll dance again?'

The chatter started among the Orchestra then. David Brody, who starred on the double bass, was already on his feet, vaulting to the top of the stage to take up his instrument. Will Jacques, who led the horns, was rallying the other brass players together.

James Heath, the second percussionist – now taking over the drums – was twirling his sticks, while Nathan Lyon (who treated his cornet every bit as reverentially as Max did Lucille) was already putting the instrument to his lips.

It was only as the Orchestra settled into their places that Max realised something was wrong. Two seats sat empty among the trumpets and trombones, and the grand white piano was attended by nobody.

'Harry's not here,' he ventured at last. 'Has anyone seen him?'

The members of the Orchestra had all assumed their positions, but their faces were suddenly stark and pale.

'I can stand in at the piano,' said Nathan, setting down his cornet. 'We can stand without the cornet for a rehearsal, can't we? But we can't the piano.'

'Where is he?' Max blurted out. Then his eyes scoured the Orchestra. 'He's not the only one. 'We're two trumpets down. Fred Wright. Gus Black. *Well?*'

Silence was like a vortex, sucking them all in. Max knew what that was a tell for: it was the classic show of a secret. He'd played enough after-hours card games in the back rooms of Chicago clubs to know when somebody was embracing silence, hoping the other player might move on.

There'd been confrontations in his orchestras before. There'd been lazy musicians, drug-addled musicians, musicians in thrall to moonshine – even (perhaps *especially*) in those strange days of Prohibition, when Max and Lucille had played in every hidden speakeasy in Chicago. All musicians, Max had come to believe, had devils in them; it was just that most of those devils were satisfied by song. So, along the way, he'd learnt how to whip a rabble into shape. He'd learnt how to barrack and cajole, how to side-line and promote, how to impose his will on a group of diffident artistes.

'You all know something,' he finally ventured. 'Gentlemen, I know this a strained time for us all. But it's a time of opportunity too ... don't you want to do something magnificent?'

That last question seemed to change the mood in the Grand. The musicians started looking at him again.

'They're rehearsing a different gig,' Will eventually blurted out, and the anger at his confession ricocheted around the band. Heads were being shaken, curses muttered, backs turned on Will. 'He deserves to know. Max is right – we're meant to be in this together.' He stood. 'Harry and a couple of the others are playing tonight – a little club in Soho called the Midnight Rooms. They just want to make a bit of money while we still can – who knows what the summer's going to bring? Who knows if there'll even *be* music by next Christmas? Maybe we'll all be playing for the joy of the Germans when they ...'

'Oh, Will!' the cornet-player, Nathan, piped up. 'That's practically sedition!'

'Well, look what happened in Paris,' Will snapped back. Archie never used to mind a spot of moonlighting, you see. Well, I suppose it's that he turned a blind eye to it. He knew it keeps a musician fresh, to play in different venues, different styles. Hotel management never understood – that's why we're all on these strict contracts – but ... It's harmless, Max. It's just a club.'

'Harmless?' said Max. *Harmless?* he thought.

'They'll be running their set right about now,' Will shrugged, to yet more groans from the other musicians. 'I suppose ... I suppose Harry's a bit put out, if you want to know the truth. He led his own band once. He reckoned he'd be inheriting once Archie went off. He just wants to feel in command, even if it's just for a night here and there. He just wants his own music.'

Max stated, simply: 'It's our first rehearsal for the Summer Ball.'

But Will just shrugged. 'I reckon they got offered a show, so they took it. It isn't any more complex than that.'

But of course it was, thought Max. Only a strong, inspiring leader could keep a group together when times got tough. Archie had had that – but, to the men in this room, Max was just some imported musician. Perhaps they respected his music, but they didn't yet respect the man.

They never would, he thought, unless he set things right – clearly and decisively.

'I'll play piano,' Max announced, laying Lucille down (and whispering his apologies to her), 'just so I can show you the songs. I'm thinking a mixture of the oldies, the best of Archie Adams, and something new, something this crowd haven't heard before, something to light up the Society Pages. Something they can really *dance* to.' Max sat down at the white grand piano. It felt, somehow, a sacrilege to be sitting here, but his fingers reached for a major chord and he leaned into the music. Perhaps going through the motions might even untangle the knot in his head – for there was no thought more dominant in him, right now, than the idea that Harry Dudgeon had done this deliberately, that he was seeking to undermine him, waiting until Archie left so that he could begin his bitter, resentful campaign.

And of course this thought only looped back to Daisy, to Jackson Ford, to the terrible idea of what might become of them if something went wrong and Max found himself ejected from the Buckingham before his stewardship had really begun.

'It's a simple turnaround in C,' Max cried out, 'but wait until you see where it leads us. I call this one "Heartache in Harlem"...'

*

The words on the poster read 'Featuring ... HARRY DUDGEON AND THE MOONLIGHTERS!'. It was then that Max was certain this wasn't just paranoia. Harry Dudgeon and the *Moonlighters*. The man was brazen enough to be taunting Max openly.

The Midnight Rooms reminded him of the dozens of little speakeasies he'd played in during the era of Prohibition. It had the air of a secret about it as he levered his way down the narrow stairs and into the deep, excavated cellar where the music was already playing. The dance floor was a throng of bodies. And there, up on the tiny stage at the head of the dance floor, crammed together like sardines in a can, were the musicians who ought to have been in the Grand earlier this evening: Harry Dudgeon on the piano, Fred Wright and Gus Black playing their trumpets at either side, while a guitarist strummed away, a double bass player perched precariously on the lip of the stage, and a drummer worked feverishly upon his kit.

The music was good, thought Max, disappointed that this was his first reaction. They were playing a fast waltz, a piece Max hadn't heard before, but certainly more urgent than any they would be able to play in the Grand.

Max took a drink and lingered at the back of the club, watching the music unfold. The man playing double bass was black, and at least this settled the nagging doubt that Harry resented being led by someone of Max's heritage.

He'd just taken his third drink in hand when the dancers reeled at some tremor moving in the earth beneath them. A bomb had fallen nearby, sending its shockwaves through Soho. Up on stage, the music faltered – but only for a moment. Max saw Harry's eyes open in surprise, but then his face resolved into a wild grin. His hands rained down on the piano keys, just as the bombs rained down from above.

The dancers had paused too, but when they saw Harry throw himself back into the music, they followed his lead. Soon, Max could see couples lifting each other into the air, feet kicking, arms wheeling, bodies pressed together and then coming apart. Harry, it seemed, had started singing; though his voice was lost in the maelstrom of the music, he had thrown his head back and seemed, to Max's eyes, to be howling along in tune.

Then the earth quaked again. The lights flickered. One of the dancers, torn out of the music, stumbled and screamed.

There was blackness in the Midnight Rooms – but only fleeting blackness, for next second the lights returned. Max's hand was shaking so violently he had spilled all of the gin he'd been drinking. Max saw the dancers cascading towards the stairs, eager to reach the street above, rather than risk being entombed down here. The club's proprietor was wading towards the stage, then clambering up to announce the evening's entertainment curtailed. 'Live to dance another night!' the portly man cried out. 'On, on, on!' Then he turned to the musicians, making his urgent apologies.

Max knew that he too ought to leave, but something had frozen him in place. Now that the music had stopped and there was so little to admire, the fire was burning inside him again. This evening, he'd rehearsed with an incomplete orchestra – and all because these three valued their own endeavours more than the Grand.

The moment Max followed them through the dressing-chamber doors, the musicians turned to face him. Harry's face was a mask. He ran his fingers through his hair, shared a look with Gus and Fred – who were suddenly embroiled in packing away their trumpets, changing their shoes – and said, 'Mr Allgood, this is most unexpected.'

'Unexpected's the half of it.' Max had a habit of chewing

his cheek when he was bursting with emotion. Right now, he chewed so hard he drew blood, and the faint taste of iron filled up his throat. 'Harry, I'm not a confrontational man. So let's talk.'

'Mr Allgood, I can see you're furious, it's written all over you – but, well, everyone's got to make a living. I know we were to rehearse this evening. Maybe I ought to have told you – but ... Archie wouldn't have minded.' He shrugged, with a nonchalance that only poured fuel onto Max's fire. 'I've got a family to feed, just like Fred and Gus. It's hard times.'

'The Summer Ball, Harry.' Then Max eyeballed the trumpeters too. 'Gus. *Fred*. It's entrusted to us. The Grand's first ball without Archie. It's meant to be the start of an era. It's meant to be a declaration. *Here we are – the Max Allgood Orchestra*. Don't you know what that means?'

Harry only shrugged. 'It's your name up there, Mr Allgood. I suppose it means a great deal to you.'

'Listen, I know you thought you were heir to the band, but ...'

'Heir to the band?' Harry gasped, in horror. '*Heir to the band?* Mr Allgood, I've slaved with the Orchestra for nearly fifteen years. Mr Allgood, it *is* my band. It's my blood and sweat and tears. It's my very heart, and ...' He'd been working himself into a fury, but suddenly that fury subsided. 'You'll get your new era, Mr Allgood. The Summer Ball will be transcendent. We'll make it sublime, all of us together. But listen to me – Archie's gone, my old pal's gone, so my loyalty to the Orchestra? Well, that's a matter of business now, because there's nothing personal in it anymore.'

Max had been spoken to like this before, but never by those in his employ. The hoodlums of Hell's Kitchen, the mobsters who ran the Underside in Harlem – even they spoke with more respect than this. Darkly, he said, 'Mr Dudgeon, you're in the Buckingham's employ. All three of you are. That isn't when it takes your fancy. That's day in, day out. I'm sworn to it. So are you.'

'Just give us some rope. Archie always did. He understood – the world isn't perfect, and now it's less perfect than ever. We've all got to live. I'll be the best damned musician in your Orchestra come the Summer Ball. And it'll be your name plastered across all those Society Pages you care so much about.'

'I'm not trying to fight with you, Harry.'

Harry muttered, 'You might have fooled me, Mr Allgood. Maybe it's *de rigueur* in New York City to throw your weight around, but it isn't that way in England.'

Max was shaking as he watched him leave. Somehow, he'd walked in here with right on his side – and yet been left behind feeling as if he was mired in everything that was wrong. 'Mr Dudgeon,' he called out, 'I'll need you at rehearsals tomorrow.'

Harry turned on the spot as he stalked across the dance floor. 'And I'll be there, Mr Allgood,' he called back, with a cheery grin. 'We're in this together, after all.'

Chapter Fifteen

The chambermaids' kitchenette, tucked away in the uppermost eaves of the Buckingham's uppermost wing, was often bustling as evening approached – for the chambermaids, having finished their shifts, had by now taken their rest, fortified themselves with afternoon tea, and found a new wave of energy with which to face the evening ahead.

Gossip, of course, was the order of the evening. Rosa had been to see Mrs de Guise's baby boy – as Frank's sweetheart, she was one of the few who'd had the honour – and had not stopped chirruping about it. Most of the other girls fully expected her to start whispering to Frank about marriage and babies of her own, and something about this brought the girls gales of laughter; Frank was like a little brother to them all, and the thought of him taking wedding vows (and all that went with it) was faintly preposterous. Meanwhile, Mary-Louise – who'd sworn off boys ever since her short-lived dalliance with Billy Brogan last winter – was keeping her own counsel in the corner of the kitchen, and Annie stood adrift in the middle of them all.

Ordinarily, Annie would have been in the thick of the gossip. But she'd found herself preoccupied of late.

'You're unusually quiet tonight,' Rosa said, when she caught Annie buttering the same slice of toast over and over, eking out what meagre butter was left in the pot. 'What is it, your parents not doing good?'

'They're doing just fine, considering,' said Annie, then committed herself greedily to the toast so that she wouldn't have to say more. 'I suppose I'm just tired.' She wasn't sure why she felt so sick, so full of trepidation. 'I think I'm due an early night. I don't want to be making any more mistakes on rounds tomorrow.'

This, at least, was not a lie. Nancy was soon due to return, and Annie had not altogether eradicated her habit of putting a pillowcase on inside out, or spilling vinegar. She smiled wanly at Rosa – who was soon too swept up in chatter to notice – and trotted out of the room.

But Annie did not slope directly into her bedroom to nurse her imagined ills. Instead, she took the attic stairs, up through the trapdoor at the very top, out into the blustery darkness of the London night.

Even at the height of summer, it could be chilly on the Buckingham rooftops. Annie ought to have wrapped herself in a shawl before venturing up – and, as soon as she saw Frank at the observation post, she thought she ought to have at least brought another slice of toast too. She forgave herself this when she saw the flask at his side, and a wax parcel that Rosa had packed. Frank would be up here until the small hours, when one of the hotel concierges was due to replace him.

She sidled into the observation post beside him.

Frank opened his flask. 'Have a drink of this, Annie. Soup from the Queen Mary. A couple of days old – and I daresay too old for those that dine there – but it's silky like cream. Do you know, I rather look forward to my nights up here sometimes. A bit of dreamtime, and nothing on the mind but...'

'The bombs?' Annie said, venturing a smile. It was her first of the evening. A few seconds with Frank could bring anyone good cheer.

'I meant the ball,' Frank grinned, in return. The truth was, immediately before Annie arrived, he'd been half-waltzing with some imaginary partner across the rooftop. 'It's coming together. Max and the Orchestra played us some of their new songs. It's going to be a bit faster, a bit livelier than they're all used to – still elegant, of course, but with a dash of extra … *flavour*.' He took a sip of the warm, nourishing soup. 'Hugo helps, of course. He's brought a new feeling to the dance floor too. I don't know, maybe it's all those stories he tells – Paris and Vienna, Berlin before the war …' Frank looked up from the bowl of soup and stared across the deep, shadowed city. 'Do you think I'll ever get the chance, Annie? To go out there, like Hugo and Raymond did? To see the world?'

'I don't think the world's in a fit state to be seen.'

That sombre thought settled over them, dispelling all of Frank's dreams of the ballrooms and palaces of Europe, until at last he said, 'You came here for something, didn't you? It wasn't to bring me that toast.'

It certainly was not; Annie had already devoured it.

'I've got a question, Frank.'

'A question?'

'I wanted to ask Rosa, but …'

'Rosa's got other things on her mind,' Frank grinned.

Annie faltered twice before she summoned up the courage to say, 'It's about a boy.'

Frank flushed red. The Brogans were practically family to him, Annie practically a little sister; to speak of romance with her made him squirm. 'Maybe Rosa *would* be better, Annie, I …'

'It's ordinary, isn't it, for a boy to ask a girl to go for a walk? He takes a shine to you and says – well, let's go picnicking in

Hyde Park, or take a walk round the zoo. But what if it's a girl who takes a shine to a boy? What if it's *that* way round?'

Frank pretended to look up at the sky, feigning some indecisiveness over whether a particular twinkling light was a star or a Stuka.

'I was thinking you ought to make it known – show him you like him, so he'll take the hint, stop you in the corridor and say "Hey, there's some nice crocuses out on Berkeley Square, let's go have a gander." But . . . times are changing, aren't they? So, well,' and she grew inordinately nervous again, 'would it be so inexcusable if a *girl* asked a *boy* to share a pot of tea?'

As she babbled, Frank's own nerves had worn off. To see Annie in such a plaintive state touched his heart. 'Who is it, Annie?'

'His name's Victor. He works in the Queen Mary.'

'And is he on shift tonight?'

'I reckon so. He'll be down there now, scrubbing plates after the dinner service. Half dead on his feet, I should think, if my mornings are anything to go by.'

'Then . . .' Frank stalled, for what wisdom did he have in matters of the heart? 'Go and see him, Annie. Stop wasting your time on rooftops looking at the stars.' He thought of Raymond, so far away; he thought of Artie, six feet under the earth outside Dunkirk. He thought of Billy, sent home from the war with a gammy leg. 'Life's got very short, Annie. We might not get the chances we thought we would.' His mind turned, fleetingly, to those ballrooms of Europe again. 'So take the ones you've got, while you still can.'

The dinner service was nearing its end when Annie scuttled through the back doors of the Queen Mary. No doubt Henri Laurent would have purpled with fury to see a chambermaid moving through his ranks of waiters – but Annie had been filled with zeal by Frank's words.

The waiters ignored her. *Haughty sods,* thought Annie. Handsome souls were picked as waiters, while the ragged scrubbed pots. But Annie didn't think Victor was ragged. No – and here she craned forward to spy him through the service portal – he was quite possibly the least ragged in the whole hotel.

'Pssst!' she called out. 'Pssst, Victor, over here!'

Victor was elbow-deep in grease and soap suds, doing battle with some titanic roasting trays, so it took a few moments before he paid Annie any attention. Then, he hurried over.

But the look on his face did not mirror the mixture of nerves and delight that coloured Annie; Victor's eyes were narrowed in a frown

'You've a nerve, coming down here again.'

At first Annie did not pick up on the evident irritation in Victor's voice. Perhaps, she thought, he'd been missing her, had expected to see her sooner. 'I've been meaning to pay a visit, only ... well, with Mrs de Guise gone, we've been run off our feet.' That much was true, but it was nerves that had kept her away too; she just didn't want to show it. 'I'd have come sooner, if I could.'

He looked at her with distaste and said, 'Well? Haven't you anything to say?'

Annie just stared, uncomprehending.

'The *brandy*, Annie. The *brandy* I sneaked out of here for you. You promised you'd bring it back. Medicinal, you said. Something to get Mrs de Guise through having her baby. It'll only be gone a couple of hours. Well, how long has it been? Weeks, Annie, *weeks!*' Victor lowered his voice. 'And Mr Laurent *knows*. He reckons one of us half-inched it, and he's *fuming*.'

'It was only a spot of brandy, Victor, I didn't...'

'It's not just a spot of brandy,' Victor retorted. 'That's exactly my point. Mr Laurent's been on the warpath all month. The wholesaler swears blind they delivered it all, but a good portion was missing – just like that brandy! – and he reckons we're all slipping up. There's too much being wasted, and too much scoffed on the job besides. Truth is, he thinks we've all been taking glugs of brandy – and, yes, everybody thinks this place is a bounty, that nothing's changed since the war, but it isn't so. Mr Laurent's docking all our wages until the wastage stops – and which one of us can afford that? Not me, that's for certain. My mother's depending on me.'

All of Annie's excitement had evaporated, rapidly being re-placed by a deep sense of shame. 'Victor, I didn't know, I got swept up in it all, Mrs de Guise and...' But then she stopped, for suddenly she was in the back room of her parents' lodgings, and Billy was producing item after item from his satchel. Last of all came the half-bottle of brandy. 'What can I do? I didn't mean to get you into trouble. It's the last thing I...'

Victor shook his head wearily. 'I *know* what waste means. My father kept a tight ship, and I learnt everything from him. Wastefulness – it's the difference between success and failure. And...'

'And what?' Annie whispered, trying to blot the image of Billy filling those brandy glasses from her mind.

'What did you come here for, Annie?'

I want to go for a walk with you, she wanted to say. *I thought we might share a pot of tea.* But her silence went on and on, until Victor's face darkened again. 'You came to *borrow* more from the kitchens, didn't you?'

'I didn't!' she gasped. 'Victor, I didn't. I've already...' She felt preposterous even saying it, but still she went on, 'I've had some toast.'

He shook his head. 'I've got to get back to work, Annie. I'll see you around.'

In the same moment that Annie fled for the service elevator, Billy was stepping out of one of the Buckingham laundry vans onto a Camden backstreet, then picking his way through the blacked-out city until he stood at the door of Sellers & Sons. A few short taps on the window in the agreed rhythm brought Mr Sellers to the door. Next moment, Billy slipped into the shop's dark interior, dragging his cases with him.

His leg was aching tonight. Perhaps he ought to have been resting it, but he had started to feel a thrill with every little advancement he made. Each delivery brought him a little closer to his destination. A few pounds here, a few pounds there; it all added up. By Christmas, he'd be able to give up this line of work, leave the Queen Mary larders alone, and sink back into the invisibility of the post room.

Mr Sellers was waiting for him, there in the dark.

'You're late,' he said, sadly.

Billy didn't stop to question why he seemed so sad. He'd come here with one task in mind. 'I'm going to need down-payment, Mr Sellers.'

He opened the suitcase, then set down the haversack from over his shoulder. There were pots of treacle here, two sides of back bacon, three dozen quail eggs and a varied assortment of cheeses, butter, sugar, cocoa and flour.

'I've got your money right here,' said Mr Sellers, and moved in shadow to the counter, where an envelope was waiting.

He was about to push it distastefully into Billy's hand when Billy stopped him. '*Down*-payment, Mr Sellers. I'll take this for tonight,' and he took hold of the envelope, pushing it into the waistband of his trousers, 'but I'll need you to start making payment in advance for what's coming next.'

Mr Sellers froze. Though Billy could hardly see his features across the ill-lit shop floor, he could sense how bitterly he recoiled. 'Payment in advance?' he snorted. 'First, you stop extending credit, and now you want … money for nothing?'

'It isn't for nothing, Mr Sellers.' Billy could feel himself growing tenser as well. The truth was, it pained him to say the words.

'I've always paid you, haven't I? I've never let you down.'

'And *I've* never let *you* down,' said Billy, focusing hard to control the tremble in his tone.

By God, it felt ugly using words like these – but, after a long, tortured silence, Mr Sellers seemed to acquiesce. Billy's heart stopped cantering when, grizzling, the older man made his way to the shop counter, slipped behind, and used a key to open up his till. Moments later, another envelope was being pressed into Billy's hand, then tucked into his belt.

'You won't regret this, Mr Sellers. You have my word.'

His heart didn't stop its wild beating until he was ten yards away from Sellers & Sons.

He was at the laundry van, fumbling the key out of his pocket, when he sensed other shadows around him. The second he got the van open, a hand had clasped his shoulder. Billy was being wrenched round and thrust against the bonnet. At first, all he could see was a single lean man, in a charcoal-grey pin-striped suit, one fist bunched around Billy's collar. Then, three other shadow men materialised from the gloom. All of a sudden, his heart was caterwauling again. His free hand went instinctively to the two envelopes tucked into his belt, but they were already being wrenched free by the man who grappled with him.

'Mr Brogan, I'm told?'

At first, Billy thought it was his assailant who was speaking. He tried to squirm backwards, the better to see his face on the midnight street, but those features were impassive, cold, uncaring – as if he'd hardly had to break a sweat to pinion Billy in place.

When the voice came again, Billy realised it came from one of the other shadow men. An older man, this one, he spoke in a calm, measured voice, removing his trilby hat as he approached.

It was difficult to make out much of his face. In the scudding light of the stars, Billy saw that he wore a thin pencil moustache and eyeglasses, which he now took off. Beneath the trilby hat, his hairline was receding – but he obviously took great care of it, for he had combed it into an extravagant curl.

'Mr Brogan, I'm so glad we've run into one another. We've been hoping to have a little chat for some time, but you always keep such unconscionable hours.' He shrugged, with a nonchalance completely at odds with the hammering of Billy's heart. 'But let's let bygones be bygones. We're here now, and that's what matters.' He breathed onto the lens in his glasses, polished it and said, 'Chisholm, if you would.'

Billy didn't have time to wonder what that might have meant. The man holding him, evidently Mr Chisholm, drove a fist deep into Billy's stomach.

Billy saw stars.

Billy retched.

Billy near fainted.

When he came to, he was still pinned against the van's bonnet – but this time the man who had first spoken was reclining near him, shaking his head as if full of sorrow. 'We represent a Mr Stockdale. Like your good-self, Mr Stockdale had an acquaintance with a man named Kenneth, a good, charitable wholesaler who used to help out shops in need. When this kind-hearted gentleman found himself in a pickle with the law, of course, somebody had to step up and help out those shops. Well, cometh the hour, cometh the man. Mr Stockdale is one of several who took up that mantle. He has, since then, been keeping up the noble endeavour.' He stopped, and inclined his head to the man named Chisholm, instructing him to angle Billy's head so that he could look Billy directly in the eye. 'Do you know what we used to call you, son? The *Do-Gooder*. Mama's boy Billy, robbing from the rich to give to the poor. And we were happy enough with that. A few croissants, some jams and butter – well, it's a drop in the ocean compared to what Mr Stockdale does. But then…'

'Let me go.' Billy choked out the words. 'And please, that's *mine*. I earned it, fair and square…'

Somehow, Billy found the strength to kick out – but it was no use; his whole body was pinned in place, Chisholm's knee braced against the old wound in his leg.

'No, Mr Brogan, this is *ours* now. It will go to Mr Stockdale, in part payment for the losses he's incurred these past weeks, while you've been impinging on his business. We'll take what goods you have in your van as well.' Billy could not see, but the other men were jimmying open his wagon to reveal the Buckingham's bounty within. He'd worked so hard, so cannily, to stockpile those supplies. He'd built a dream upon it. Now, all he could do was listen as it was ferried away. 'It's a good little racket you've got going on, Mr Brogan, to plunder your hotel. But it's going to stop now. Do you hear?'

'Stop?' gasped Billy. 'But I just needed a little more time. A few months more and…'

'Mr Brogan,' said the man in charcoal grey, 'if we see you in Camden Town again, it will be the very last time. Do I make myself clear?'

'But…'

The man shook his head, disconsolate. 'Make him see sense, Mr Chisholm.'

This time, there was more than starlight. The air burst into flame around Billy as the fists piled into him.

He lay there gasping for minutes, half-hidden by the laundry van, until he heard footsteps returning. Some instinct for self-preservation must have awoken what life was left in him, for immediately he started scrabbling for sanctuary underneath the van. Yet then hands were upon him, and a consoling, familiar voice said, 'Brogan. Oh, Billy. I did try to warn you.'

Billy blinked open his eyes. They were sticky with some residue, perhaps blood from the scrape on his forehead, so at first he wasn't certain when he said, 'Mr Sellers?'

'Come on, Bill. Let's get you cleaned up.'

At least it felt safe, to be back in Sellers & Sons. Mr Sellers took a medicinal kit from the shelf, then started cleaning the cuts that coloured Billy's skin. 'Those thugs know how to beat a man,' he said, as he attended to one graze after another. 'You're not broken, Bill, but you'll be smarting for days. Did they say who they were?'

Billy was silent.

'Stockdale's lot, I shouldn't wonder. I saw them come for you from the window. I know I ought to have come out, stood up for you – but you don't know what it's like on these streets now. I take Stockdale's produce because my customers need it, yes, but it's got to be so much more than that. If I don't take it…'

'You'll end up like me,' Billy rasped.

'Son, you don't need to be doing this. You're a bloody hero. A hero of Dunkirk. What in hell do you think you're doing, tying yourself up in this sort of a mess?'

Billy winced again. It was the bruises that were flourishing deep inside him. It was his ribs, his collar bone, the incandescent pain in his already-brutalised leg. 'It isn't for me,' he muttered.

'You've told me. Your parents were bombed out. It's admirable, you wanting to help your parents. You're a good son. But what do you think they'd say if they saw you right now, beaten and broken on their account? You've been a bloody fool. You didn't come home from the war for this. You've got a good, decent, honest job at that hotel – why'd you want to risk that?'

'I can't let them drift like they are. They don't deserve it.'

Mr Sellers wasn't yet done attending to Billy's wounds, but Billy lifted himself and limped across the shop floor. Now that the pain of the attack was receding, he felt lost, discombobulated, ruined. 'I nearly had it, Mr Sellers,' he said, brokenly. 'And now …' It would not do to sob, not in front of Mr Sellers, so he braced himself on one of the shelves and steadied his breaths.

'You've been going about it all wrong. Strutting around these shops, like you've been *advertising* yourself. You're not Ken. Ken knew what he was doing. He had a whole operation worked out. He had protection. You wouldn't have found Ken cornered like you've been. Nobody would have dared. But there you are, Billy Brogan alone, thinking you can take on the world.' Mr Sellers shook his head ruefully. 'A minnow can't take on a shark, Billy.'

'So what do I do?' breathed Billy.

'You go back to the Buckingham Hotel, you keep your head down, and you forget this ever happened.'

Billy battled back the fury. 'I won't. I *can't*. I'm not going to let them down. I just have to …' *Think*, thought Billy. *I just need to think.*

Mr Sellers was staring at him. It was strange, but Billy thought he saw some sort of defiance in the old man's eyes too. 'Billy, you're risking everything.'

'If I don't risk it, I can't win. They did so much for me. All I want is to do something for them in return. I'm not a soldier, Mr Sellers. I tried my best, I held my head up high, but I didn't have it in me, not truly. But I can help my family.' He stopped, for now he knew something had shifted in Mr Sellers' demeanour. 'Will you help?'

'No, not me,' said Mr Sellers.

'Then I'll thank you for tonight and be on my way,' snapped Billy.

He reached for the door handle, was about to turn it when Mr Sellers said, 'But I know some folks who might.'

'Oh yes?' Billy asked.

'There's a couple of lads I used to deal with. Ken had them going out to the farms, bringing back off-ration bacon, game birds, eggs, milk. A steady pair of hands they, but by my reckoning they've been out of work since Ken was thrown in the slammer. They're good boys, really, but they never had Ken's drive – they'd never start trading themselves.' Mr Sellers paused. 'They're big lads, Bill. It wouldn't have been them taking a beating tonight. So, if you fancy it ...'

Billy eyed him.

'I'm sure I could make an introduction. Something to put you in good stead. I'd need you to come good on that delivery I paid for, of course – even if Mr Stockdale really has taken my down-payment. And I'd need you to keep me out of it after that. It's just an introduction. Do you understand?'

Billy nodded. It was funny, but all the hope that had been dead two minutes before was suddenly resurgent.

'All right then, Bill,' said Mr Sellers, his tone balanced perfectly between world-weariness and resignation. 'It might take me a couple of weeks to sort this out – but if you really are going to be part of this world, if I can't change your mind, well, at least let's see you do it properly.'

July 1941

Chapter Sixteen

'*Dearest Nancy,*' read the card on the mantelpiece, '*You have always been the bravest, most capable of girls. Know that I am with you every step of the way. With love, for now and the future, Emmeline X*'.

The card had landed on the doormat the morning before. Nancy had not known how much she needed it until she read those words. The truth was, she'd been aching to hear something from Raymond for weeks, something to tell her she was making the right decision, for her and their baby, but there had only been silence from the front, and in the absence of any kind words, her mind had begun to run riot.

Then this card from Mrs Moffatt, the old Head of Housekeeping, came – along with the freshly woven blanket under which Arthur was currently sleeping – and it seemed to crack her open. Nancy prided herself on being strong for the people she loved; it uprooted her when somebody like Mrs Moffatt put her arm around her and supported her too. She'd forgotten how much she missed the older woman. Nancy hadn't known a mother since she was eight years old, but for a few years Mrs Moffatt had felt like one.

But *Raymond* ...

Dawn had not yet come to Maida Vale, but Nancy had been

awake throughout the night, variously feeding Arthur and trying not to let her mind lead her into the dark places it sometimes did. Tobruk, that ancient city on the Libyan coast, was under siege, a stalwart crew of Allied soldiers defending the fortress against the Axis horde. She was quite certain Raymond was not inside the city, but – from what little news she'd been able to garner – he was part of the forces repeatedly trying to lift the blockade. When she pictured him now, he was smeared in the sand and grit of the desert, dog-tired but defiant. She held on to that image, but sometimes her mind strayed too far – and, in her darkest moments, she saw him lying bloodied in the sand. Sometimes, she saw his face reflected in Arthur's and that old fear, that one life had been exchanged for another, blossomed inside her. And perhaps this was just the curse of all mothers: from now, until the day she died, she'd be tormented by the prospect of loss.

'He'll be all right today,' came Vivienne's voice, somewhere behind her. 'I promise you, Nancy.'

Nancy turned. Vivienne was in her dressing gown, standing in the sitting room door. The grandfather clock in the corner was inching towards 5.30 a.m. In half an hour, the girls would start appearing in the Benefactors Study for the breakfast service. She'd been gone mere weeks, and yet it felt as though an aeon had passed.

'I know,' Nancy replied, then lifted him from the cot. 'Mrs Moffatt says she and Archie have been whitewashing the walls. Sorting out the borders in the garden. They've taken a little cottage near Stow-on-the-Wold. There's a village hall where Archie plays piano…'

Vivienne smiled, then took Arthur out of Nancy's arms. 'Nancy, you're changing the subject.'

Nancy smiled wanly. Part of her thought she ought to be

energised to be marching back into the Buckingham today, but part of her felt like it was a betrayal – a betrayal of motherhood, perhaps? 'Raymond still hasn't written.'

'He'll have written half a dozen times. There's half a world of war between here and there.'

Nancy gripped her hand. 'I'll be back by teatime,' she said, fearful of going any deeper into the conversation, fearful of derailing the day before it even began. She was meant to be strong today. She was meant to lead the department. Three months ago, she hadn't doubted it was possible – but three months of motherhood irrevocably changed a woman's heart.

'Teatime or not, we'll be waiting right here,' said Vivienne. 'Trust in that – oh, and Nancy?' Vivienne smiled. 'Trust in *yourself*.'

The taxicab had been laid on by the Buckingham, so at least Nancy didn't have to worry about getting herself to work. By the time it brought her to Berkeley Square, some strange magic seemed to have come over her: the sight of the hotel prompted feelings of old, the memory of that long-gone age when she hadn't been a mother, just the Head of Housekeeping. It was, she decided, like sliding out of one set of clothes and into another – just like that suit of midnight blue that had somehow turned Ray Cohen into Raymond de Guise.

The smells of the hotel rushed over her. The sounds of footsteps echoing in the corridors. By the time she followed the weaving passageway to the service stairs, she could hear the bustle of the reception hall, where concierges, porters and pages gathered to meet the day.

Behind the service stairs, the old Housekeeping hall was no longer cordoned off. They'd timed it to perfection: Nancy's first day back was to be the first day in the old Housekeeping Lounge. A fresh beginning, then, for everyone in the department.

Nancy made some mute hellos to desk clerks as she crossed the reception hall, then picked her way towards Mr Knave's office. The man was already within, for the door had been left ajar and Nancy could see him fussing with his desk inside. Nancy gave a gentle knock, then entered.

Walter Knave crossed the room to shake her hand, just like he would any gentleman of his acquaintance, than bade her sit down. 'I'm afraid I can't offer tea. I've been without a private secretary for some months now, so I've been relying on...'

Nancy smiled, 'I'll have one of my girls bring tea, Mr Knave, as soon as I've greeted them.'

'That would be most welcome, Mrs de Guise. I'm afraid the little matter of a secretary has had to wait. The Board has dictated a freeze on the hiring of staff whose roles don't immediately impact our guests. Tea and typing has been deemed rather secondary to the cause.'

Nancy wasn't sure what to make of this. Against all the odds, war was a time of bounty for the Buckingham – but the thing she'd learned about keeping wealthy folk satisfied was that it took yet more wealth.

'Well, Mrs de Guise, there are clearly some things we must speak about before the day begins. As you'll see, we've been able to open the old Housekeeping wing. I trust you'll find it to your liking. But the most critical thing is that, though your girls have done an admirable job across the past few weeks, there's no doubt standards have slipped.'

Nancy's heart tightened. 'Standards, Mr Knave?'

'I'm sure you'll whip them into shape, but there have been instances of disaffected guests. I'm told the cleanliness of the rooms has, for the most part, been maintained – barring one rather bizarre report of a breakfast trolley being spilled – but it's the *pace* that matters. Your girls haven't kept to schedules.

Guests have returned from their lunchtime forays to find their rooms still being turned over.'

Nancy winced again. 'That's something I'll certainly have to attend to.' Even if it *was* understandable. And there was a certain sort of guest who, quite frankly, enjoyed punishing the lowliest of hotel staff. To a rich man, it could practically be a sport. 'Mr Knave, I want to say this to you clearly, so that we're not in any doubt: when I step through the hotel doors, I'm the Head of Housekeeping first and foremost. The department will march on – and, any little kinks and upsets there might have been in my absence, they'll be vanishing as of today.'

Walter Knave stood up. 'Mrs de Guise, I'm glad to hear it.'

The moment the office door fell shut behind her, Nancy let out a deep, long-lasting breath. Head of Housekeeping first? No, Nancy was a mother – and she carried it with her wherever she went.

'You just have to pretend,' she told herself. *Pretend, for as long as you need to – and, maybe, after a few days of pretending, it won't feel quite as hard.*

The restored Housekeeping wing smelt strongly of whitewash, sawdust and polish. Trolleys were neatly lined up outside the store cupboards, bed linen, fresh towels and soaps piled up on each, but Nancy sailed past them until she reached the old lounge door. This, at least, felt energising. Here, at least, she felt the pull of home. She'd stood outside these doors as a chastened chambermaid, once upon a time. Now, she pushed through them to face her first day as a working mother.

The lounge erupted in applause.

The girls had done her proud. Apparently, they had come down especially early today, for the breakfast service had already been laid, with a place at the head of the table for Nancy. In moments she was being shepherded there.

In truth, she felt weak, cut off from Arthur – and her body was beginning to feel it too. The connection between mother and child was more than just spiritual; it was physical as well. Vivienne had enough milk and powdered formula at home to keep him nourished, but Nancy's body ached to feed him.

'Girls,' she said, at last. 'This has, of course, been a most unusual few weeks – but I've just come from a meeting with Mr Knave where he has been quite clear in his appreciation for how spectacularly you've carried this department.' A little white lie never hurt anyone. 'So I have a little surprise for you today – something to set our hearts alight.' Nancy paused; the girls were rapt now, staring at her in silence. Even Annie Brogan was holding her breath. 'As you all know, the Summer Ball is but two days away. In two nights' time, all the great and good of London will convene in our ballroom, in defiance of whatever Mr Hitler sends our way. So this afternoon – after, of course, we've dispensed with our usual duties – we have been asked to help decorate the Grand.'

As one, the girls lifted themselves. Faces broke open in smiles. Hands were grasped, in anticipation of the delight to come.

'Of course, we have to earn it first. I'll be doing inspections at 2 p.m. – and I expect the highest standards. Then – and *only* then – can we go down to the Grand and bring out the bunting.'

Across the Housekeeping Lounge, chatter burst upwards. So did Annie Brogan, who – perhaps sensing she needed a proper head-start – was already haring towards the doors.

Nancy didn't care to battle with it. Instead, she waved them on their way. 'Two p.m.! And we reconvene here.' Then, with the girls streaming out of the lounge, she picked her way across the room to the office door in the corner.

Inside, the office was laid out in almost exactly the same fashion as Mrs Moffatt had had it before that fateful December night. That brought Nancy some comfort – even though the feeling of sliding into Mrs Moffatt's old chair, behind her desk, felt peculiar as well.

Whoever had arranged the office had an artist's precision. Right there, on the edge of the desk, was a little bowl of barley sugars, just like Mrs Moffatt used to have.

'Onward,' Nancy said. There were rotas to look over, a stock-take of the new store cupboards to make, a whole day of itiner-aries, inspections and other hotel business.

She tried not to think of Arthur and decided there was only one thing for it:

She embraced the day.

In the Grand Ballroom, the band struck up.

Playing to an empty room never inspired the same sense of adventure as playing to a full house, but Max Allgood thought they were getting close. From his vantage point at the head of the stage, dancing with Lucille while the band played up a riot around him – it was one of Archie's old numbers, the 'Savile Row Serenade', spiced up with a new arrangement – he watched as the dance troupe appeared, each couple announcing itself in a fantastical flourish. Marcus and Karina came, like a valiant knight with his princess lover, at the head of the troupe. In their wake came Frank, perfectly matched with Mathilde. Soon, the dance floor was full of couples dancing in perfect synchronicity, until the final couple emerged into the arena. Hugo Lavigne was holding one of the part-time dancers in his arms, but to Max's eyes they looked as if they had been partners all their lives: both visions in midnight black, each the mirror of the other. It was a good job, thought Max, that Marcus did not seem a man riven with the kind of ambitions and jealousies he'd seen in the

Orchestra – for in two nights' time, the name 'Hugo Lavigne' would be on every guest's lips.

The 'Savile Row Serenade' was reaching its climax. Max brought up Lucille, pressed his lips to her and prepared to let the music flow.

He was leaning into the song when, above the dancers' heads, he saw the doors of the Grand opening.

The look on Daisy's face unmanned him. And what was that piece of paper she was brandishing in her left hand?

When the song came to its close, Daisy was waiting.

He would have vaulted from the stage then, if only his middle-aged legs would have let him. Instead, he waddled to the stair, picked his way down, clasped Marcus's and Hugo's hands in congratulation – 'It sure is a fine, fine thing to watch you boys dance' – and finally reached Daisy.

'Just look,' she said, her voice as thunderous as her stare. Her eyes remained fixed resolutely on the stage as she pressed the paper she'd been holding into Max's hand.

'What is it?'

'Just read, Max.'

Max's eyes flashed over the page, and instantly he understood where Daisy's thunder had come from.

THE AMBERGRIS LOUNGE IS PROUD TO PRESENT…

STONE CARMICHAEL

THE EDGAR MANN ORCHESTRA

&

HARRY DUDGEON AND
THE MOONLIGHTERS

Max smarted. His gaze gravitated, like Daisy's, back to the stage. Harry was cavorting up and down the piano keys. His laughter rang out.

'He sure can play,' Max whispered, 'but I've got to tread careful, Daisy. I can't just boulder on in and change everything up.'

'You're being weak, Max.'

'Weak?' he gasped, though of course he'd expected the accusation. 'Now, Daisy, isn't it *strong*? To avoid the confrontation?' He lowered his voice. 'You're the one who said it. I *need* him on side.'

'What you *need* is to be in control of the Orchestra. If you're not in control, we're not secure here, and…'

'Oh, we're secure, Daisy. You can bet your bottom dollar on it. Give me the Summer Ball to cement it. After that, they'll *need* us in the Grand. Nothing else will do. I'm gonna lay down an expectation.'

Daisy hung her head. 'Look at the date, Max.'

'What?'

'The date on the flyer.'

Max looked down. There, at the bottom of the roster of acts, was the date of the performance:

12TH JULY 1941

'But that's…'

'*Exactly*,' said Daisy, no longer even attempting to conceal her rage. 'The date of the ball. Two nights to go.'

Max felt suddenly in freefall. The sound of the Orchestra faded away. The dancers became an indistinguishable blur. He had to focus hard on his breath to bring the Grand back into resolution. 'But they can't…'

'You know what he's doing, don't you? He spoon-fed you a load of lies that night in the Midnight Rooms. The evidence is right here, in black and white – he's a snake. He wants you to fall flat on your face.'

'It can't be,' Max insisted. 'If he doesn't turn up for the ball, his own reputation would be ruined. He'd never work again – not at the Buckingham, not ever!'

'Oh, we weren't supposed to *know*, Max. Don't be so blind.' She lowered her voice. 'He'd have told you he got waylaid. He'll wake up in two mornings with a stomach bug he just can't throw off, leave you in the lurch at the last second. Anything to get away with it, and stop you in your tracks.' She gripped Max by the arm. 'But you can't let it happen. Do you hear me? We *need* the Buckingham Hotel.' And here she took a breath, tightening her grasp, her fingernails gouging into the flesh of Max's forearm. 'Nelson *needs* the hotel.'

Max tried to draw his hand away, but Daisy was holding him fast.

'I know,' he stammered. 'I know what Nelson needs.'

'We promised him, Max. We promised we'd find a safe home, somewhere secure – and then, then we'd send for him. We'd make sure he was safe too. Well, we've only done half the job. How are we to be safe – how is *Nelson* to ever be safe? – if we're thrown out?'

Max had started shaking.

'You need to kill this, Max. You need to walk on up there and put an end to it, before *it* puts an end to us. We already got run out of one city. I don't intend to be run out of another.'

'But what do you want me to do about it?' Max's voice dropped to a whisper.

'Just deal with it,' spat Daisy, with some air of disgust threaded through the panic. 'We made a solemn promise to Nelson we'd find a home for him, wherever he went. After what he did for us, that promise is everything. It binds our souls. We let him down, we're going to hell.' She turned to march away, but before she left she uttered the five words she knew would linger with Max all day long. 'It's up to you now.'

Nancy had almost finished composing the rotas when the door of the Housekeeping Lounge flew open and, through the office wall, she heard the frenetic tumbling of footsteps. There was only one person this could be: Annie Brogan.

'Is there a problem, Annie?'

'Not a one, Mrs de Guise!' Annie declared, with the certainty of a private saluting his sergeant major. 'I'm just loading up, and then I'll be …' She looked back. 'Mrs de Guise, are you *sure* you ought to be on your feet? Look, I can make you another pot of tea. There's some shortbread. If you want,' and her eagerness was plain, 'I could go on down to the Queen Mary and rustle you up some lunch. I have a friend there, I'm sure he'd …' *Help*, she didn't say, because then she remembered the last time she'd seen Victor, and suddenly she wasn't certain if he'd help at all.

She was still standing there, flummoxed by this particular problem, when Nancy said, 'Lunch won't be necessary, but there is *one* thing you might help on. Step into the office?'

'Oh lor', Mrs de Guise, that sounds terribly ominous. *Step into my parlour, said the spider to the fly*. Like when my pa used to take one of us into the back room and give us a dressing-down.'

'Annie?' said Nancy again, hovering by the office door.

'Sorry, Mrs de Guise, I've come over all funny,' and she scuttled through.

'You're not in trouble, Annie, but there is something you might shed some light on.' There were ledger books open on Nancy's desk, filled with jottings and scribbles. Nancy drew her finger down one of the columns. 'Did everything get moved over from the temporary stores? Every last item?'

'Rosa marshalled it yesterday, Mrs de Guise. There isn't a flannel left in the Benefactors Study. They're repurposing it so the Board can use it for their get-togethers again. Very important meetings, you know. They don't want old flannels lying around.'

'No,' said Nancy, 'I imagine not. But Annie, I can't for the life of me see how these ledgers match what we have in the stores. Now, I can see everything's gone swimmingly as far as the service is concerned. And yet...' Nancy had paused, for the pained expression on Annie's face warned her to tread carefully; the girl had been trying so hard, working so feverishly, to be one of the team. 'Annie, have there been many... spillages?'

Annie almost burst out of her seat. 'Mrs de Guise, I've learned my lesson. I promise! And, yes, maybe once or twice I put a pillow-case on inside out – and yes, maybe *once or twice*, there's been a bit of egg yolk on a bedspread... but they're all one-offs, Mrs de Guise! Every last one!'

Nancy sat beside Annie and took her hand. 'The thing is, Annie, these books don't make sense. The stock in these cupboards isn't close to the stock showing in the records.'

Annie's eyes were brimming with tears. 'I haven't spilled *that* much, Mrs de Guise.'

'Soaps and salts and lotions – and, why, varnishes and polishes. It's like there's a crate of it missing – two crates, if I have it right.' She paused. 'I always knew there were going to be mistakes – and I trust you, Annie; I can't believe this much could have been wasted while I was away. These items,' and she handed Annie a list, 'must be somewhere. We aren't operating the kitchens here. We can't blame wastage on rats.'

The tears which had come so easily to Annie's eyes were not so easy to drive away – but, grateful of the reprieve, Annie soon scuttled out into the corridor, the list clenched tightly in her hand.

She was only halfway to the Benefactors Study when something dreadful occurred to her. Because she was quite certain, without having to check, that nothing had been left behind.

Annie turned on her heel. The tears were gone now. In their place was a steadfast resolve.

It took her some time to catch Victor's attention. It took her even longer to convince him to step outside. As soon as he approached, Annie seized him by the hand and hoisted him to the top of the wine cellar stairs. 'I know the brandy was my fault. I know it, and I'm sorry, OK? But there's something else, Victor, and I need to ask: are things still going missing from the larders? Are the deliveries still coming in incomplete?'

Victor's look hardened. 'Everything was fine for a week. We got to thinking it really was just a bad delivery, or that the wholesaler was cheating us out of what's ours. But then … well, everything's running scarce. Sausages there one night were suddenly gone the next.' He wiped his brow. 'We're all trying not to let Mr Laurent know. He'll butcher us if he finds out. So the under-chefs are cutting corners, serving up paltry portions, switching things around to make the menu work. Annie, it's the damnedest thing – I've been checking the deliveries *personally*. The last two came in without a thing out of place. But then …'

'Gone from the larders?'

Victor nodded. 'It's as if there's rats – only, they'd have to be the cleanest, tidiest rats ever, because there hasn't been an ounce of mess.'

'It's not rats, Victor. It's happening in Housekeeping too.' And Annie brandished the list Mrs de Guise had given her. 'I think there's a thief in the hotel. And not just someone like me or …' *My brother,* she suddenly thought – for of course Billy had taken the brandy, and of course he'd been salvaging odds and ends for their family for years. But *everybody* did that. It was one of the unspoken perks of the job. 'Victor, it's a robbery – a robbery happening right under our noses. And … and I'm sure Mrs de Guise thinks I'm responsible! She thinks I've lost things, or wasted things, or spilled it all. But it isn't so. And Mr Laurent …'

'He'd blame it on any one of us if he could,' said Victor, heavy with the same realisation. He took the list and, in doing so, his fingers touched the back of her hand. In that moment, all the anger, all the enmity that had erupted between them was swept clean away. 'So what are we going to do?'

And Annie said, 'We need to find out who it is, and stop them, before it all gets too late!'

Chapter Seventeen

DISPATCHES FROM THE BUCKINGHAM HOTEL!
NEW YORK TIMES, JULY 12, 1941

By Jackson Ford, your man in LONDON

Three weeks have now passed since news broke of Nazi Germany's unexpected gambit in the east: the betrayal of its pact with the Soviet Union, and the opening of a second front in this globe-spanning war. Dispatches indicate that the Wehrmacht are rapidly advancing toward Leningrad and Moscow, but here at the Buckingham Hotel the war is going to have to wait. As I, your roving reporter, write these words, every concierge, porter, manager – and guest – at the hotel has his eyes trained on but one thing: the Grand Ballroom, whose doors will open for the Summer Ball this very night. Let us pray that no bombs rain upon the hotel because this evening all of High Society – exiled government leaders, ministers of the Crown, Royalty from home and abroad, and the men whose daily decisions direct the passage of this war – will be dancing to the music of Max Allgood and his Orchestra, in the arms of the Buckingham's troupe of world-renowned dancers...

It had taken every ounce of Max's willpower not to confront Harry, Gus and Fred with the flyer from the Ambergris Lounge. Through two further sessions he'd rehearsed, allowing the dancers to luxuriate in their new music, trying to settle his nerves by drawing the very best out of Lucille. He was quite certain it had upset his equilibrium, for he could hear it in the music – but at least Marcus and his troupe of dancers didn't seem to notice. The opening number he'd choreographed, introducing Hugo to the troupe with a quickstep whose passion rose to a wild, unbridled pitch, was going to turn every head in the room.

If Harry really was trying to sabotage the Orchestra, then Max wanted to see it with his own eyes. He wanted to know there could be no deflections, no insistence that a mistake was being made. Daisy thought she held it in the palm of her hand when she presented Max with that flyer, but Max wanted *more*. That was why, in the paling afternoon light, he stood at the doors of the Ambergris Lounge, waiting for its doors to open. The flyer said that the show began at 7 p.m. If he had to forsake Lucille and sit at the piano himself, that was what he would do.

But first he had to see.

The doors of the Ambergris Lounge were already opening up, so Max joined the punters flowing through the doors. With a Martini in hand, he surveyed the establishment. It was certainly more refined than the Midnight Rooms, its dance floor more expansive, with an elevated area on either side where patrons could gather at tables. The acoustics would be better in here as well.

Patrons were rapidly filling the tables. Max marched towards one, sank into the seat… and waited.

As 7 p.m. approached, the lights dimmed across the lounge. Moments after that, the twin chandeliers above the dance floor

– evidently electricity – started glittering, then turning slowly on the spot so that they spilled their light like a shower of stars.

On stage, the doors opened.

The musicians filed out.

The dance floor was rapt. So, too, was Max Allgood. For, up on stage, there was no sign of Harry Dudgeon. No sign of Fred Wright or Gus Black. A debonair gentleman dressed entirely in black stepped up to the microphone, his band assembling behind him, and declared in a rich honeyed voice that he, Mr Stone Carmichael, was honoured to make their acquaintance.

His voice, when he began to sing, was the voice of a baritone angel. Max admired it very much – there was something so peculiarly stately and *English* about it; he would have gone down a storm in New York – but he had no time to stop and consider its cadences, for inside he was broiling. Gripping the Martini glass so fiercely it might easily have cracked, he forced his way through the throng to the bar and caught the bartender's attention. 'I thought it was Harry Dudgeon tonight?' he called out. 'Harry Dudgeon and the Moonlighters?'

'Oh,' the barman said, with a sparkling smile that spoke of his great admiration for this particular group, 'but they're the top of the bill, sir. The governor's got them on at the close of the night, to carry us on into morning if the sirens allow. They're the ticket right now, sir, the absolute ticket!' He waved a hand airily at the dancers already throwing themselves into Stone Carmichael's set. 'This lot are going to *love* them!'

Billy hadn't felt right in days, and coming back to the streets of Camden only intensified that feeling. This time, he left the van at some distance from the high road and limped the long way round. The gloaming was settling over Camden town, but there were yet enough folks in the streets to give him some confidence

Mr Stockdale or his associates would give him a wide berth. He only wished it would stop his heart from hammering as he made his way to Sellers & Sons.

Stealing from the hotel to support his family was one thing – but stealing from the hotel, only for those ill-gotten gains to go to some filthy profiteer, well, that was quite another. Billy had always known he was wading in the mire, but at least, until now, he'd been doing it with his head held high. Now, somehow, he just felt low.

He'd had to rouse himself to come today. The fact was, he'd been on the verge of giving up altogether – of accepting the hand of fate and telling his parents he'd been wrong, that he wasn't really going to be able to help them after all. In the end, it was the thought of letting Mr Sellers down that had driven him back to the Queen Mary larders, back to the stores in the Benefactors Study, back to the Candlelight Club (whose manager, Ramon, would soon discover was short three bottles of St Lucia rum). Mr Sellers had picked him up off the cold stone Camden ground, attended to his every wound and promised to help him with an introduction to associates of old.

Well, tonight Billy could make good on that deal. It wouldn't get him any closer to rebuilding his parents' lives, but it might ease his conscience – if only a little.

At Sellers & Sons, he knocked on the glass in the old rhythm and waited until the door opened up.

'You look like you've healed up nicely, Bill,' said Mr Sellers. 'That lip's still a bit of a mess, mark you.'

'It isn't so sore, Mr Sellers.' He'd told folk at the hotel that he'd been bashed by a car during the blackout; much worse happened if you strayed too far at night. 'I can make it all straight tonight. I've got the goods back at the van.'

'I'm glad to hear it.' Mr Sellers clapped him on the shoulder, half in acknowledgement and half to guide him through the gap in the counter. 'Come on now, the lads are waiting.'

Billy hadn't realised he'd be so nervous. Part of him wanted to turn tail and flee, to pretend this enterprise had never even started – but the other part knew there was no stopping it now.

The two men waiting inside the room were little older than Billy, farmhands by the look of them. Billy took them for twin brothers, for their look was eerily similar, both with bulbous noses, jug-like ears and mops of unruly curls. Both were *big* as well, with broad shoulders and square heads, the look of a country ale house about them.

The first lumbered up to shake Billy's hand.

'Billy, meet Rod and Dirk Ankers. They're the lads I was telling you about.'

Rod, apparently, was the slightly more cumbersome fellow. He shook Billy's hand too, though at least he managed not to crush it like his brother Dirk had done. When each said hello, Billy was surprised to hear how softly spoken they were. Men who looked like this ought to have had great booming voices, riddled with expletives. To Billy's ear, these two looked like ogres but sounded like choir boys.

'We heard you been in a spot of bother,' Rod said, in a voice so cheery it cut through all of Billy's torment. 'It's not a nice business, this. There's a few rough sods about.'

'So Mr Sellers reckons you could use a couple of lads like us,' Dirk chipped in, in a voice just as fey. 'Truth is, we've been looking for something to keep us occupied since Ken went inside. We like to help folks where we can.'

Help folks, thought Billy. Yes, that was the idea. It got horribly complex, sometimes, when you tried to *help folks* – but at least you could set out with a good intention.

'I'm not a profiteer,' Billy said. 'My family got bombed out and ...'

'Oh, we don't need to know that,' said Rod, and punched Billy playfully around the shoulder. 'It's better it's just a job to us. We work on the apiaries in Bucks, so it's a busy time of year for us – what with pollinating fields and moving bees to flower and such – but it's hard to make ends meet, and we got families too. Ken used to look after us. We were thinking you'd do the same.'

Billy took a deep breath. 'I've got a line of goods coming out of the hotel where I work. It's protection I'm after. Someone to make deliveries, someone to run collections so I can stay off the streets. It won't be forever. This summer. Into the autumn, perhaps. Get my family back on their feet, then get on with our lives. But I can't be making deliveries myself, not anymore.

'And if there's bits you can bring in from the farms, eggs and vegetables, extra meat – well, that's all to the good.'

There was a momentary silence in the room. 'The lads know about Stockdale and his boys,' said Mr Sellers. 'They knew him, back when he was working for Ken.'

'Oh, he won't give us any bother. Not if he knows what's good for him. These hands,' and Rod grinned at them, 'haven't just wrung pheasants' necks, if you know what I mean.'

'I don't want any trouble,' Billy said, suddenly panicked. 'I'll take a beating, but I won't dish one out.'

'You won't have to,' Rod grinned.

'Cool heads,' said Mr Sellers, who had seen the way the Ankers boys were teasing Billy, even if Billy himself had not. 'There'll be no need for blows, not if these two are making deliveries for you.' He rubbed his hands together. 'But my part in this stops now, OK? I'll take your produce, of course, but don't go binding me up in the enterprise of it. I don't mean to end up in a Pentonville cell like Ken.'

'None of us do,' said Billy. 'And that's why we'll get this done, and get on with our lives. Just gather enough to rebuild at Albert Yard. I'm going to do this, and then it's going to end.' By now, Billy had warmed to his theme. 'You'll want paying, of course.'

'Well, we don't work for nothing,' the Ankers boys chuckled.

'I'll pay you right now,' he said. 'Consider it a... *down-payment*.'

Now that the Ankers boys were with him, Billy felt more confident about bringing the van to Mr Sellers' doors. There, the Ankers boys helped him unload the crates that would soon fill the shop shelves. Of course, Mr Sellers had no need of the pâté and vermouth Billy had hidden at the bottom of the crates, so that went directly into the Ankers' hands. 'A gift, for the time being. If this is how you want paying, I can do it. If it's a cut of the takings, well...' Billy had to hold his nerve, for to give too much away was to slow his enterprise down, to leave his parents in the lurch even longer, to put himself in peril for too lengthy a time. 'Look, it's my living I'm putting on the line. If you boys are bringing in produce from the farms, that's all to the good. We'll work a payment out. But this is *my* route, you understand? I'm paying you to make this go smoothly. I'm paying you for protection.'

'I reckon there's a couple of girls back home who'd be pretty impressed if you could get us a bottle of Champagne,' said Dirk, elbowing Rod conspiratorially.

Billy looked at them. Then he extended his hand. He'd come here tonight full of trepidation, as if the bruises of his beating were suddenly growing darker, all across his skin. He hadn't quite expected to end the night with this strange wind filling his sails, his hopes resurgent. 'Gentlemen, let's see how this goes, but I think we might just about be in business.'

*

The taxicab disgorged Max on the corner of Berkeley Square. From there, he and Lucille hurried through the marble colonnade, up the sweeping white steps – and directly through the revolving brass door, without a care in the world as to whether he ought to have been using the tradesman's entrance or not. He was quite sure the doorman had hallooed at him as he ran, but Max didn't break stride. From there, he crashed into the dressing rooms.

Along one side of the dressing rooms, the dance troupe gathered, arms around each other as Marcus gave them one of his long, theatrical spiels. 'Now is the moment to show what grandeur means!' were the only words Max heard, for at once his attention was drawn to the other side of the dressing rooms, where the Orchestra were lounging in their dinner jackets. As one, their eyes turned on Max. They seemed to be studying him like he was some intruder, and of course he probably looked a true wretch, streaming with sweat and out of breath as he was. Then, as everything came into focus, he saw that there was a deep relief etched into their faces. David Brody even hurried over and made as if he might lift Max up. 'Mr Allgood, where have you been? We thought…' He looked back, alarmed, at the rest of the Orchestra. 'We thought something must have happened. That there'd been an accident, or…'

Max clapped David on the shoulder; at least some members of his Orchestra cared about what happened tonight. He was about to make some sop of an explanation, when suddenly he saw Harry, Gus and Fred in the middle of the crowd. Tightly packed together, they were, and glaring at him with what amounted to *amusement* in their eyes.

Max didn't need David to lift him up then. He strode forward, Lucille swinging at his side, and the moment he met the

Orchestra, he whipped the Ambergris flyer out of his dinner-jacket pocket. Daisy had been right all along; he ought to have just had it out with them. 'What's the meaning of this?' he demanded, his voice sonorous and booming.

The dressing room fell silent. Even the dancers turned over their shoulders, Marcus's rallying speech petering into silence. 'HARRY DUDGEON AND THE MOONLIGHTERS, at the Ambergris Lounge? *Tonight*, of all nights?'

Harry looked at Gus and Fred. With a puzzled expression, almost insouciant, he chewed the end of his cigarette and said, 'What's the problem, Max? We talked about this. It's just a little off-piste gig. Something to keep my children fed. You know how it is…'

'It's the Summer Ball, you dog!' Max bawled. 'There are lords out there. The Hotel Board. Prime ministers and queens. We're to put on our show for them – *my first big show*. And there you are, with your eye on some other prize! There you stand, all three of you, itching to go and make an extra shilling?'

Harry said, 'It's an after-hours show, Max. We'll—'

'You'll call me *Mr Allgood* in front of my Orchestra, Harry.'

Now all the eyes which had been fixed on them were suddenly cast away. Out of the horde of dancers, Marcus emerged, softly saying, 'I say, chaps, we've a full ballroom out there. There's no guarantee they can't hear…' but soon Max was speaking over him, and even the great Marcus Arbuthnot knew not where to look.

'I don't care what you think of me, Harry. I'm old enough and ugly enough to know you can't please all the people all the time. You don't know a thing about me. But know this: hate me all you like, resent me all you want, and I'll take it; but the second it threatens my Orchestra, is the second we'll come to blows.'

Harry looked left at Fred; he looked right at Gus. Then he looked blankly, straight ahead. 'I'm here, aren't I?'

'With your mind somewhere else,' said Max, and finally he screwed up the Ambergris flyer. 'We've been given the world,' he declared, taking in all of the Orchestra for the first time. 'And *you*,' Max shook his head in despair, 'want to throw it away for a few extra pennies, and a moment of glory all for yourself.'

Max took Lucille from her case and, in the horrified silence of the dressing room, strode to the ballroom doors. There, at the hanging curtains, he paused. 'I'm new here,' he said, less frenzied now, 'but I didn't come to upend your lives. The dance troupe changes too, doesn't it? Hugo has slipped in among them, found his place. Well, that's what we must do too. Harry, Gus, Fred – we're meant to be as one. There might come a night when all a crowd wants to hear is the sound of a lone cornet, playing in the spotlight. *But it is not tonight!*'

Then there came silence again. It lingered, like an unwanted guest.

In the end, it was Marcus who broke it. 'They're waiting,' he ventured, inclining his head to the ballroom doors. 'They're ready. The question is – are *we*?'

And Max, fired up by all the words that had coursed out of him, given strength by letting it all erupt, looked back at his Orchestra and said, 'Tonight's the night. The new Orchestra can be the talk of the town, or it can be the limp follow-up act to what went before. That decision isn't for me to take – we all have to take it together.' He straightened his lapels, caressed Lucille, and declared, 'It's time to decide.'

In the Grand Ballroom, Walter Knave looked up through his golden eyeglasses and thought: *In my day, spectacle meant a brandy pudding set on fire at the end of the Christmas feast. Now, we have all this.*

Thank goodness Mrs de Guise had returned on the eve of

the ball, for she'd rallied her girls to decorate the Grand in the most enthralling manner. The Grand Ballroom itself seemed to be in blossom. The bunting strung across the vaulted ceiling displayed not only the Union flag, but the French tricolore and the flags of every Low Country whose governments now flitted in and out of the hotel. Bouquets of bright, beautiful flowers stood at the heart of every table. Candles glittered, filling the air with the scents of honey and thyme. Yes, for a room cloaked in blackout blinds to have the feel of a summer's meadow was quite the thing.

At his side, John Hastings stood proudly with Daisy Allgood. The bandleader's wife was in a dress of golden satin; it shimmered in the candlelight, so that it looked to be constantly rippling as she moved.

'Well, Mrs Allgood,' John Hastings declared. 'Here they come.'

The first to appear through the dance floor doors was Max Allgood. Daisy straightened herself at his appearance; her pride in her husband radiated outwards, like the light of the candles scattered around.

'He's come a long way from New York, hasn't he?' John Hastings said, raising his hands in applause.

'Mr Hastings,' beamed Daisy, 'you don't know the half of it.'

Max had taken to the stage. There he stood, bearing Lucille aloft, proud as an army's figurehead as the Orchestra assembled around him. Daisy's heart near skipped a beat when she saw Harry Dudgeon settling at the piano, his two turncoat friends taking seats among the other musicians – but her pride only grew; it could only mean Max had marched down to the Ambergris tonight and beat them into submission.

'Listen to this, Mr Hastings.' Daisy had seen Max lift Lucille to his lips. '*Listen to this.*'

Lucille began to sing. Somehow, Max was making her imitate

the sound of the air-raid sirens which dogged each London night.

But then, instead of panic, there was joy. The band struck up, Harry Dudgeon started pounding at the piano keys, a strident bassline kicked in from the double bass – and a riotous number began.

Here was the Max Allgood Orchestra.

And *here* came the dancers...

Frank launched into the quickstep, Mathilde in his arms. Together they turned through the parting doors, cantering in time with the music until they reached the heart of the dance floor. There, having hung frozen in time for some seconds – if only to soak up the wonder of the guests gazing down – they spun back into the dance, sailing along the line of the stage as the next couple emerged.

Frank caught sight of them in the corner of his eye. Hugo was a wonder in black, the most handsome shadow to ever grace the ballroom. There was nothing studied about the way he danced; it seemed to Frank that it required no concentration at all: no focus, only feeling. He was long and lithe, and every movement flowed by instinct. When he and his partner froze in the heart of the dance floor, the wonder in the guests above was more palpable than ever. Stuffy old ministers and retired colonels put down their drinks to watch. Walter Knave inched closer to the balustrade, as if that officious old relic of an era before the Buckingham opened its ballroom had finally seen not just the monetary worth, but the pure magic, of the Grand.

Then they danced on.

Soon, Hugo was sailing past Frank and Mathilde. For one fleeting moment, Frank's eyes locked with his. Hugo straightened himself; Frank puffed out his chest in return. '*C'est magnifique,*'

Hugo mouthed, and from that moment on Frank too was sailing on air, Mathilde light as a feather in his arms.

It seemed mere moments later that the first number came to its end.

Now was the moment the guests had been waiting for. The most eager of them were already crowding the balustrade, waiting for the dancers. On the dance floor, the couples came apart, opening their arms to the hotel's esteemed guests. Marcus was already taking some enchanted minister's wife in his arms. Karina was destined for one of the visiting barons. Frank himself was being hailed by one of that year's debutantes – but it was Hugo to whom the eyes of the ballroom were truly being drawn. Soon, he would permit one of the representatives of M. de Gaulle's cabinet-in-exile to slide into his arms. Frank felt certain the night would belong to him and all the varied members of the Free French gathering tonight. Hugo would dance with his fellow runaways from now until the very last song. He seemed born to it.

In fact, thought Frank, it was hard to believe that his coming here had been an accident at all.

The second number was a riot. The third (or so they would have said back in New Orleans) *raised hell*. Lords and ladies, it turned out, could dance every bit as passionately as the clubgoers at the Cotton Club, or that little place in the Bowery where Max had debuted so many of his songs. Sometimes, he lost himself in watching the dancers gliding back and forth; sometimes, he closed his eyes and let Lucille do her thing; sometimes, he turned at an oblique angle so that, instead of gazing out over the ballroom, he could see the Orchestra. It was all coming together, he thought. There was Harry, bent over the piano like the maestro he was, bringing fire to every song. Even when the first act came to its end and they segued into an intermission with a slower number, there was some fresh energy about it. Max gazed out over the audience and picked out Daisy in the crowd. 'You're doing it,' she seemed to be saying. 'It's your Orchestra now. We're here to stay. The sky's the limit…'

And perhaps Max might have felt the full power of it too, if only he hadn't, at that precise moment, looked over Daisy's head – and seen the war reporter, Jackson Ford, jawing with some English debutante on the edge of the dance floor.

He'd quite forgotten about that particular snake.

At least the intermission passed without incident. Drinks were flowing out in the Grand, the sirens had not yet sung, and the dancers – heady with the triumph of their first performances – were toasting the night with Champagne in their own corner of the dressing room. For Max's part, he recuperated with a large Scotch while the musicians sparked up cigars. At some point, Daisy must have appeared – for Max came from some reverie to discover her sitting beside him, her head on his shoulder, asking him, 'What happened at the Ambergris tonight?' to which Max could only say, 'The right thing happened, that's what. We ain't nothing without the Grand.'

'That's a sure thing, honey.'

'I'll have you singing up there real soon, Daisy, you just see if I don't.'

Finally, the last number of the night was upon them. Down below, Hugo Lavigne had taken his third Free French minister's wife in hold. Marcus, meanwhile, rallied the other dancers to the cause. Frank was leading some old dowager through the dance, while Mathilde had been promised to a gentleman whose girth made any traditional hold near impossible. Even so, both would make their partners feel as if they were King and Queen of the ballroom – for such was the duty of a hotel dancer.

The music reached its final movement. Just as in the very first number of the evening, the other instruments faded away, leaving piano and trombone to go on alone. It would be the signature of the Max Allgood Orchestra, for now and evermore.

Max pressed his lips to Lucille, for the last, triumphant note. Then, he opened his eyes, threw his arms open wide, and took in the adulation of the ballroom.

The trombone had stopped singing, but somehow the piano went on.

The applause which had erupted suddenly petered out, in strange fits and starts; beyond every expectation in the ballroom, the music had continued.

Max looked over his shoulder, only to find half the Orchestra discombobulated as well. Harry Dudgeon was still pounding away at the piano keys.

The rest of the Orchestra sat dumbly, not knowing what they should do.

Just as the night was coming to its rapturous end, Harry Dudgeon had started playing one of his own numbers.

It was when Gus and Fred joined in that the rest of the Orchestra seemed to follow. And yet here he stood, the one musician among the orchestra – *his* Orchestra, he had to remind himself – who wasn't playing. He put Lucille to his lips and started to play.

The dancers seemed to be sucked into the moment too. The song was fast; this demanded a quickstep. In seconds, new partnerships had been formed; next second, the first steps were being taken. Then, just as had happened up on stage, the dance took on a life of its own. For three more minutes of sheer, unadulterated joy, the Grand Ballroom danced its way into summer.

The music ended. This time, the applause – even wilder, even more unparalleled than before – went on. The dancers came apart, the musicians got to their feet – and as they all flocked, one after another, back into the dressing rooms, the guests in the ballroom continued to cheer. If this was the sound of summer, they seemed to be saying, then let it go on forever.

Max was the last to leave the ballroom. Already, Champagne corks were being popped.

Alone among them, Max's face was dour. His knuckles had whitened where he held on to Lucille.

And there was Harry, laughing among the other musicians, raising a glass of Champagne to his lips.

Max smashed it out of his hold.

'Dudgeon, what in God's good name was *that*?'

Harry had a look of incomprehension on his face, but certainly it was feigned – for it did not reach as high as his eyes. 'It's called "One More Time". Listen, Max, I didn't mean it. I was just *feeling* the music and before I knew it...' He shrugged. 'It was only one song, Max. You don't mind, do you?'

He reached out as if to shake Max's hand.

'Come on, Mr Allgood!' Fred Wright chirped. 'They *loved* it. We put on a damn fine show, that's what I say. You wanted the Summer Ball to be remembered – well, they'll remember every last song.'

Gravity had sucked him into the song out in the ballroom. Now, it drew his hand into Harry's own.

The moment he grasped it, Harry drew him inches nearer and, dropping his voice to a low whisper, said, 'Don't you ever disrespect me in front of the Orchestra again, Mr Allgood. I've been playing with these boys for years. *Don't you ever raise your voice at me again.*'

Then Harry let go of his hand and, cheerily, reached for another glass of Champagne.

Harry raised his glass. 'To a triumph of a Summer Ball! To the Max Allgood Orchestra!' Then he grinned, and – with a sly look at Gus and Fred – glugged back his drink. 'To a long summer night!'

Midnight, and at the Ambergris Lounge, Harry Dudgeon and the Moonlighters were swinging their way through their set. The dancers, reinvigorated by the appearance of the band, had been turning and weaving all night. Those who had seen the band before remarked they had rarely seen them play with such passion. Something must have fired them up tonight, the bar manager said.

After the set was done, and the dancers were returning to the night – thankful for another evening without sirens, one more unblemished night on this Earth – one figure lingered behind. As the Ambergris Lounge emptied, this particular figure nursed the final Martini of the night, waiting for the band to emerge from their dressing room.

When they did, he sidled up and extended his hand.

'I know you,' said Harry Dudgeon. 'You're a guest at the Buckingham.'

'The name's Ford,' said the man with the Martini, in a drawling American accent. 'Jackson Ford.'

'The reporter,' Harry said. 'Yes, I've read those pieces of yours. Dispatches from the Buckingham Hotel. Very droll.' Harry paused, for suddenly it occurred to him that something was wrong. 'You were there, in the Grand Ballroom tonight…'

'I was,' Ford replied, 'and I saw your little stunt. Rubbed Mr Allgood up the wrong way, of course, but I'm minded to believe that's what you wanted. And, as a matter of fact, that's why I'm standing here right now.'

Harry was intrigued. 'Oh yes, Mr Ford?'

'I have a little history with Mr Allgood. A little history, too, with that lovely creature he's living with at the hotel. I thought it might be interesting to share it. If I'm right, and your real ambition is… leadership of the Grand?'

Harry hardened. Through gritted teeth he said, 'That orchestra was promised to me. I've been its heir for years.'

'So, then, you were robbed.'

'We were.'

'Well, I should very much like to give you that opportunity again.' Ford smiled and said, 'For a price, of course.'

August 1941

Chapter Eighteen

Something in Nancy felt foolish writing again, but to stop writing would make her feel more foolish still. 'If Raymond was missing in action, you'd have been told,' Vivienne had told her, late at night as, together, they tried to settle the children. 'So keep writing. One day, he'll bring those letters back home with him. And what a chronicle of Arthur's first years that will be ...'

A chronicle of Arthur's first years. Yes, that was something to cling on to – and that was exactly what she was clinging on to today when, coming off shift at the Buckingham Hotel, she wended her way down to the hotel post room and pushed through the door.

Nancy never knocked. Billy was, perhaps, her oldest friend at the Buckingham Hotel – he'd stood on the beaches of Dunkirk at Raymond's side, so he was virtually family now – so she thought nothing of slipping through uninvited. Today, however, Billy near jumped out of his skin. The telephone receiver that had been pressed to his face burst out of his hands; he fumbled to catch it, before crashing it back into its cradle.

'S-sorry Nance,' he stuttered, 'j-just a laundry delivery. I'm organising the vans, but ...' He shrugged, with a strange world-weariness. 'Deliveries every day. When it rains, it pours.'

'Is everything all right, Billy?'

She'd seen that look on Billy's face before; once upon a time, Billy Brogan had been no stranger to a spot of trouble. Some people had a knack for it.

'I'm just run off my feet, Nance, and ...'

'Worried about your parents?'

'They're keeping their heads above water,' said Billy; then, more darkly, he added, 'but heads above water is still half-drowning. I just want them to be all right.'

She crossed the post room to take his hand. 'And they will be.'

Billy started again. In a second, he had swept away all the various papers piled up on his desk, scrabbling them into drawers as if they mustn't be seen. Nancy was still looking at him curiously when he stammered, 'W-was there something y-you needed, Nance? Another letter for Raymond?'

She handed it over. 'Still nothing back,' she said – and it was clear to Billy that the real thing she had come for was some spiritual support. 'I keep writing to him, just so he'll know about Arthur, but ...'

'You've got to hold on. Just like my folks do. Hold on, and believe something good's coming. Letters I sent to my ma ended up blacked out and late by weeks – so just imagine what getting word out of Africa's going to be like. He'll come home, and he'll meet Arthur – and then,' Billy winked, 'then you can *finally* get some rest.'

There'd be little chance for resting this evening, for tonight Hugo was due to visit.

Nancy had seen little of Hugo around the hotel, though Frank was so enthusiastic about their time in the ballroom that she felt she'd seen every last foxtrot and waltz. That was where she found him now, working with Marcus and Karina on some new opening number – perhaps their attention was already turning towards the Buckingham's next great engagement, that year's

Christmas Ball. Such was the pattern of life in a luxury hotel: summer had not yet faded into memory before preparations for winter began.

It was a joy to watch the dancers rehearse, to see them pivot and turn, then discuss the finer aspects of their elegance and poise – but it gave Nancy a strange emptiness as well, for in another age it would have been Raymond lording it over the dance floor.

It was good fortune, then, that Hugo was already sashaying over – and, with their arms threaded together, they wended their way back through the hotel.

The taxicab was waiting. 'I don't know what I'd do without the Buckingham providing my taxicabs. I'm … missing him, Hugo.'

'Raymond is a strong man. A clever man. But the one thing he has, that sets him apart from all the rest, is *luck*, Madame de Guise. I knew it from the moment I met him. Some men, whether born to the gutter or the stars, are smiled on from above. What do you English call it? *Lady Luck.*'

'I hope so,' said Nancy, 'but you mistake me. I meant – I miss Arthur. I miss him every hour of the day. It's in my body. I can feel it.'

'Ah, but the body is enslaved to the mind, Madame de Guise. All dancers know it. The body loses its way if the mind is ill at ease. The trick of every professional dancer is in learning techniques that can mask the unbalance. Perhaps you must do the same.'

Nancy grinned. 'I'm not sure the same rules apply in Housekeeping. But you have Raymond's way with words, Hugo. Raymond sees life like a dance – every person with their place in it; a technique to fall back on, in every moment.'

Hugo let out a shrill laugh. 'Oh, but he wasn't always like that, madam. Once upon a time …'

The sun was burning, bright and pure, above the river Seine – and all of Paris seemed to have turned out to absorb its beauty.

Just as well – because, after last night, Raymond's head was pounding, his body felt sluggish, and to walk through Paris made it seem like he was walking through a dream.

'What you need is coffee,' Hugo had said, and – like in so many things – he had the right of it. Coffee, cheeses and a baton of rustic bread had enlivened Raymond by the time he returned to the Hotel Acacias. Georges, Antoinette and Ophelia were, it seemed, already waiting in the ballroom – but, deciding that a few moments freshening up was worth a little tardiness, he hurried to his quarters, preened in front of the mirror until he looked vaguely presentable, and only then made his appearance.

'Mr de Guise,' Georges began, letting the new name roll around his lips, 'there you are, my boy. Ready to dance?'

Ray stood, stock-still. The last time he'd seen her, Ophelia's features had been bunched up, painted with a blatant disregard. Now, dressed in a simple ivory gown, she looked as if she wanted to *try*. Perhaps Antoinette had counselled – perhaps even *cautioned*? – her. Whatever it was, it made the thing he'd come here to do so much harder.

'We'll start with a simple waltz,' Georges intoned, his eyes sparkling with expectation. 'The stars will align today, young ones. This is the moment when everything comes together.'

Or the moment it all falls apart, thought Ray. He had to remember the look of epiphany on Hugo's face when he'd come up with the idea so that he could find the courage to say, 'Georges, might I have a quiet word?'

Georges arched a single eyebrow in enquiry. 'Ray, you've come to dance.'

'I know,' Ray said, 'but... one moment, Georges, please?'

His mentor followed him to the corner of the dance floor, distant enough that they would not be overheard.

'Georges, I'm not sure how best to approach this, but...'

'It is better, Raymond, to spit out poison than keep it in.'

Ray almost smiled; Georges's wisdom held great value to him, but there were occasions when the elder Frenchman – on rendering those pearls in English – rather lost his way.

'I've found a girl I'd like to dance with in the Exhibition, but it isn't Ophelia.'

'Not... Ophelia?' breathed Georges, with the most bewildered air. 'Raymond, I'm not sure I am fully understanding. I brought Ophelia here today so that you can get a stronger feel for each other. Feeling is all in dance...'

'Yes,' said Ray, suddenly finding his courage, 'feeling is *all*. And I just wasn't feeling the connection with Ophelia. But with Hannah...'

'Hannah?' asked Georges, his bewilderment nearly turning to affront.

'Miss Lindt, she's a dancer I met yesterday evening. A Berliner, come to Paris to visit her cousin Arielle. She's competed before, Georges – Bühler's Ballhaus, and in Vienna and...'

'Am I to understand, Ray, that you spent last night dancing in *clubs*, instead of in rest and relaxation?'

There was no eliding this particular truth. Ray said, 'But I found her, and she fits me, Georges. We danced all night.'

'And is that *all* you did?'

Ray took a step back. 'It was just dancing, Georges, but it felt right – and... and I should like to dance with her at the Casino de Paris. I think it more natural. I think we suit each other.'

'Raymond,' said Georges, and for the first time his fey voice had deepened, a note of authority permeating his tone, 'I'm sensing some lack of trust between us … we had an understanding.' He paused. 'Raymond. Mr de Guise.'

Ray tensed, though only a little; he still wasn't certain if the name would ever suit him.

'You must trust to my judgement. I would never steer you badly. I hope you know that. I have come to see you as something of a … son.' Georges paused. 'I want you to get the best from your talent, Raymond. To do that, you need the most refined and elegant partners. Ophelia is from a strong aristocratic line. Just the sort of partner you'll need if you're to truly sharpen yourself up …'

Ray had been about to nod in agreement – but these last words stopped him. A new conviction coursed out of him as he said, 'But that's exactly the point! Ophelia's like you, Georges. She's born to the ballroom. But Hannah? Hannah's like … me, I suppose. She's a dance hall girl. When I was dancing with Ophelia, I was so focused on not making a mistake, so focused on impressing her, so focused on *my feet*, that I didn't lean in. But with Hannah … well, I didn't have to think. I didn't have to second-guess the dance. I just,' and here Ray shrugged, 'danced'.

'Just watch us dance, Georges. *Please*. If you watch us dance and you can't see what I'm talking about – well, I'll … I'll take your judgement, and I won't breathe a word of it, ever again.' He paused. 'I just need … I need someone who feels like *me*.'

Georges looked up. The shock seemed to have faded from his face, to be replaced by a wry concern. Over the top of Ray's head, he considered Antoinette and Ophelia. 'You must dance with Ophelia first,' he said, sagely. 'I'll meet your condition, Ray, but it must be today. Whoever becomes your partner, there is much work to do before the Exhibition.'

*

Two hours passed before Hannah Lindt arrived at the Hotel Acacias. By then, Ophelia was already gone. The half hour Raymond had spent in her company – running through their waltzes and quicksteps, the foxtrot Antoinette was convinced would show the judges at the Exhibition exactly what potential these two young dancers had – had left him exhausted, but at least since then he'd been able to get some rest. By the time Hugo delivered Hannah to the hotel door, he felt as if he might even do the dance justice.

'You need a glass of wine, *mon frère*,' remarked Hugo. 'One glass restores the equilibrium, I promise.'

'Coffee and water has been just fine,' Ray said. 'Hugo, there's a chance he'll let me. He took some convincing, but...'

Hugo braced him by the shoulder. 'Dance the Viennese waltz with Hannah, Raymond, but in your heart hold the *java*.'

Hannah was waiting alone in the ballroom, but – aware of her surroundings as she was – she sensed it when Ray appeared. When she turned to face him, he saw her for the first time in the light – and realised what a beauty Hugo had picked out. Her hair was as black as his, shimmering as if she had spent hours in preparation. By the light in her almond-shaped eyes, the rich colour of velveteen chocolate, nobody could have guessed that she too had spent the night dancing in that tiny, cramped dance hall.

'Ray, I hardly know what to think. When Hugo sent that message, asking if I would dance with you...'

Ray opened his lips to reply, but it was Georges's voice that rang out. 'It was most unexpected,' he pronounced, and both Hannah and Ray looked round to see that he was striding out across the dance floor as imperiously as some colossus of old.

'Miss Lindt, I presume?' he said when he finally drew near; then he took her hand and planted his lips upon it.

'I'm not a presumptuous man, Miss Lindt. I'm a fair and decent one. I will be looking at technique today, but not technique alone. Poise, posture, confidence and beauty – these are the qualities, among others, that they judge in the Exhibition Paris. I didn't come to Paris this season to fail. My boy Raymond here is on the journey of his lifetime. I should be very happy to discover you, Miss Lindt, are to be a part of it. But I am very clear about what the ballroom needs. I'll be fair, but I'll be honest, even if, perhaps, that feels brutal. Do you understand?'

Ray was anxious that Hannah might have taken some offence at Georges's plain speaking, but the opposite was clearly true. By the tone of her voice, she seemed to have appreciated it. 'I trust you to spare me the competition if I'm not up to standard, Monsieur.'

'Then it's settled,' Georges pronounced – and, with a great sweep, made to vacate the dance floor. Moments later, the sounds of a gramophone filled the ballroom floor. 'Shall we begin?'

This was it, thought Ray. *This* was the moment.

The only way to achieve it was to shut down the mind, and let the heart take over.

He took Hannah in hold.

'I'll follow where you go,' Hannah whispered to him.

'Just dance like we danced last night,' said Ray.

The waltz started slowly – but, somewhere along the way, Raymond quite forgot that he was being studied. That was when he and Hannah really took flight. He let the music build in him, sailed with Hannah from one side of the dance floor to another, turned her and sailed on, carried there by the steady beat in the song. Soon, his body had taken over. He lifted Hannah from the ground and together they turned on the spot – and, when he brought her back to earth, it was as if another tide took hold of them, urging them onward. When the tempo increased, so too did the dance grow in stature. They came apart, then back together; Raymond let her fly freely, only to spiral around her, take her smoothly in hold, and dance ever on.

The song lasted three minutes, but in Ray's heart one century had ticked into another.

There came silence.

A true gentleman, Ray released Hannah from hold and presented her as the star of the dance.

Only now did he dare to look up. There stood Georges, the bewildered expression back on his features. It had to be a good thing, thought Ray. That bewilderment could only be his surprise at how fluidly the couple had danced.

'Well, Georges?' he dared to venture. 'What do you think?'

Georges grinned. 'I think, now, we need to … foxtrot.'

The taxicab had already turned onto Blomfield Road, and now it ground to a halt in front of Nancy's house. As Hugo helped Nancy onto the kerb, he said, 'The foxtrot was just as sublime, of course. Then the quickstep too. I believe, by the end, Ray was feeling so giddy that he almost asked to show Georges the java, right there and then – but a better head prevailed.'

'So, in the end, he did dance with Hannah.'

Together, they came through the garden gate. Darkness had not yet fallen over Maida Vale, so the blackout curtains were not in place. Through the window, Nancy saw Vivienne dashing from sitting room to kitchen, Stan sitting happily at her waist.

'Of course, there were other things Georges needed assurances on first.'

'Other things?' asked Nancy.

'*Mais oui*,' Hugo said, with a shrug. 'Of course, he needed to know if it was love Raymond felt for Miss Lindt. Love clouds the mind of a dancer. Georges knew that too well.'

Nancy hadn't expected her heart to be gripped with such icy coldness. Her hand was still hovering over the door handle – and, though she was desperate to take Arthur in her arms, something made her stop. 'And was it?' she whispered. 'Love, I mean. Was Raymond in love with Hannah?'

'No, Madame de Guise,' said Hugo, with an air of sadness about him. 'No, he was not. I'm afraid the particular fool who fell in love with Hannah Lindt is standing in front of you. But that,' he went on, 'is a story for another day. A story that takes place long after the Exhibition at the Casino de Paris.'

'You, Hugo?' whispered Nancy. 'In love with Hannah Lindt?'

'I am a Frenchman. It is our privilege, and curse, to fall in love many times in our lives.'

Nancy's fingers still hovered over the door handle, but next moment it opened – and there, standing in the frame, stood Vivienne.

Hugo looked her up and down. For a moment, Vivienne held his stare.

To fall in love many times…

The words echoed in Nancy's mind. Perhaps they would have echoed even longer if she hadn't heard Arthur shouting out from the sitting room beyond. 'Vivienne,' she said as she hurried past, 'it's so good to be home.' Moments later, her son was in her arms, the daily stresses of the Buckingham Hotel were fading fast – and, when she stepped back into the hallway, cradling Arthur to her breast, it was to discover Vivienne helping Hugo out of his coat, telling him that dinner would be served very soon, that she would take him through to the kitchen and pour him a glass of something warm.

Strange, but that sudden flutter of discomfort about Raymond and Hannah Lindt had vanished – and, in its place, was an altogether different kind of flutter. A flutter of potential.

To fall in love many times, she thought. All across the world, right now, there were people trying to answer the same question: when one love came an end, was it possible to start again?

Until that moment, it had never entered Nancy's head that Vivienne might be asking the same question as well.

Chapter Nineteen

The Queen Mary kitchens were a tumult tonight, as so often they were. Out on the restaurant floor, guests dined without giving a second thought to the industry going on behind the kitchen doors. This, M. Laurent always said, was the true aim of a hotel kitchen: to serve up platters of beauty and indulgence as if they were simply magicked out of the air. 'Lords don't need to know the blood, sweat and tears. They just want to be indulged. If the way to a man's heart is through his stomach, the way to the Buckingham's prosperity is through *us*.'

Prosperity, thought Victor. It was one of the words M. Laurent called on most of all: prosperity, efficiency, taste. But this didn't look like prosperity today. In fact, it hadn't looked like *prosperity* in weeks – and Victor wasn't sure how much longer he could keep it under wraps.

His shift wasn't yet done. There was still much clean-down and pot scrubbing to be done – but the sight of the larders had ignited something in him. Not just the indignation that came every time he went through the manifest, ticking off item after item and realising exactly what was gone – but some sense of epiphany too. A realisation he could not ignore. It rushed through him like a secret revealed.

There was only one person he could speak to about this.

He only hoped she might still want to hear.

Victor had never ventured into the depths of the hotel before. It was a kitchen hand's duty to remain in the kitchen, sequestered there like a prisoner in his cell, thinking of nothing but chopped chives, skinned onions, and grime-encrusted roasting trays all day long. Consequently, as far as Victor was concerned, the Buckingham Hotel began with the pot wash and ended with the service counter.

It felt fairly transgressive, therefore, when he left by the kitchen door, scurried round Berkeley Square, and slipped along Michaelmas Mews. At least, by re-entering through the tradesman's door, he wouldn't be spotted by Mr Knave sneaking across the reception hall. This way, he might even get to his destination unmolested.

It only occurred to him upon reaching the bottom of the service stairs that he ought to have taken off his apron first. Without it, he might have been mistaken for any old hotel page – but, smeared in kitchen grease, he looked like exactly what he was: an insolent young whelp, playing truant from M. Laurent's kitchen.

Thankfully, it turned out that the Buckingham Hotel was actually comprised of two separate buildings, each woven in intricate ways around the other: the first, a lavish world of deep crimson carpets, brass rails and golden fixtures, through which the guests all passed; and the second, a secret world of darker, less cared-for passages and rooms, all hidden away behind locked doors. It was this second world that Victor picked his way through, first up one storey and then into another, until at last he entered the crooked hallway where the chambermaids lived.

There were framed photographs on the walls, a rich smell of tea and toast in the air, and music was playing in the kitchenette at the very end of the corridor.

Victor had been eager to come up here, but now a little trepidation entered his body. He had to talk himself into approaching the kitchenette, then compel himself to knock on the door.

A gaggle of chambermaids looked at him as one.

And there was Annie, her face smeared with whatever preserve she'd been spreading on her toast.

'I need to talk to Annie,' Victor declared.

'*Annie?*' Rosa squawked, in delight. '*Annie*, you've got a gentleman caller!'

Annie's face had been too stuffed full of toast and greengage preserve to answer immediately. She spluttered out '*Now?*' as she tried to swallow it down – and Victor nodded meekly. 'But maybe not here,' he said, a remark which only made things worse.

Both Victor and Annie were flushed red when they gathered in the corridor, near the very top of the service stairs. Rosa had marshalled the other girls to crowd the doors of the kitchenette, hoping to eavesdrop on something rather titillating.

But it was no confession of love Victor had come here to make. 'It's still going on. It's been going on for weeks. It's only that – well, he's changed up his method. He isn't taking things straight from the orders anymore – he's waiting until there's an order been received, then stripping the larder of everything that's been left over. Then, one of the boys comes in, unloads the new order – and the larder looks full again. He's clever, Annie. He's a fox. He's got it all worked out. Strings of sausages and big pieces of back bacon. Fresh fruits and veggies. There's a box of kippers gone this week, and half the mutton we'd had left. Mr Laurent's going to blame it on us, Annie.' And here Victor's voice began to fray apart as all the fear he'd been trying to suppress found a new outlet. 'I can't get by without my wage, Annie. If it's me on the chopping block, my mother and I...'

Annie knew how that felt. She thought, suddenly, of her own parents.

'It's in Housekeeping as well,' she whispered, her mind racing ahead. 'Mary-Louise was in a dark mood today – couldn't find any of the soaps and lotions we'd had in, only last week. Mrs de Guise is having to put in an extra order. Victor, she thinks she's going mad – she told us all she must have made a mistake in the orders, all on account of how exhausted she is. Well, she's just about dead on her feet, up with the baby all night and still running the department – and the last thing she wants is to give Mr Knave a reason to think it isn't working. He might just send her packing, tell her she's a mother and she ought to be at home. But ...' Annie paused, taking stock with a deep breath. 'I don't believe, for one second, that Nancy made a mistake. I reckon somebody's taking advantage.'

'But *who*?'

'It's got to be someone who knows the hotel like the back of their hand.'

'Somebody who knows the routines of the place,' Victor added. 'And Annie, *that's* why I came. Our orders come in, regular as clockwork, on a Monday and Thursday. That's what gets us through the week. If I'm right, our boy's in the larders, just as regularly, every Sunday and Wednesday night. That way, the larders get filled up again – and nobody clocks what he's doing.' Victor took Annie's hand. Thank goodness the girls clamouring at the kitchenette doors didn't notice, for surely they would have set up a hullabaloo. 'Annie, do you know what day it is?'

'It's ... Wednesday,' Annie breathed.

Already she seemed to understand, but Victor found the courage to draw her a little nearer as he said, 'Tonight's our chance. We can find out who this is and stop it, once and for all – stop it before Mr Laurent blames the whole lot of us; stop it, before we're all out on our ear.'

'Stop it,' Annie gasped, 'before anyone blames Mrs de Guise for being too tired.' She stopped suddenly, for the true measure of what Victor was suggesting had only just dawned on her. 'We'd have to camp out, *tonight*, down there in the kitchens. Catch him in the act.'

Victor nodded. 'It's why I came. Annie, I don't want to do it alone.' He took another breath. 'I'm a little frightened – but, if we were to do it together…'

Her hand tightened on his. 'It's exactly what we'll do. And tomorrow morning, we'll go to Mr Knave and tell him exactly what we know. We'll be champions, Victor.'

'Let's do it,' she declared. 'You and me, Victor. Let's do it *together*.'

The sound of titillation flurried up the hall.

Yes, thought Annie, the girls really had caught some of what they were saying after all.

In the hotel post room, Billy slammed down the telephone receiver, then hurried to the door. At least, now, he was certain that nobody was approaching. With the door locked behind him, he dimmed the lights and, returning to his desk, pulled the ledger from his bottom drawer.

In this book, Billy described every facet of his scheme.

Perhaps it was foolish to keep a record so detailed, but it was the only way Billy could order his mind. Tucked into the front cover of the ledger was a paper slip bearing the legend of THOMAS LAW & SONS, BUILDING CONTRACTORS, a breakdown of all the costs involved in reconstructing the old house at Albert Yard. It was useful to see it every day, for it reminded Billy what he was doing this for, reinforced that there was goodness behind all the deceit.

And what deceit it was...

The beating from Stockdale's boys had faded from Billy's body, though sometimes it still lingered in his mind. Since that day, however, things had been looking *rosy*. Produce from the larders, soaps and lotions from the Housekeeping stores; Billy went everywhere without suspicion, filling his sack with plunder whenever the moment arose. Here it all was, in carefully scripted columns and lines. It was important to keep a record of it, not only because it made him see how far he'd come, but because one day he'd be able to look back and know exactly what he owed the Buckingham Hotel. He meant to one day make it all good again – and, though he hadn't exactly reckoned with *how*, the simple fact that he'd made the promise buoyed him. There was a moral ledger to be kept as well.

It was the Ankers boys that made the difference. Now that Billy wasn't having to make deliveries himself, he could concentrate his efforts on acquiring goods – and that was where his true talent lay. Of course, Dirk and Rod needed paying – and, though Billy was happy to share some of his proceeds with them, every penny that went to the brothers was a penny he couldn't add to his ledger, another penny away from restoring all his family had lost. That was why he had taken to paying them in the occasional bottle of brandy and port, the occasional crystal decanter or silk robe. Those goods didn't have value in the shops Billy was stocking – but they helped to keep the Ankers boys happy, and it was on the Ankers that Billy had to depend. A bottle of wine was more than enough recompense for them, too, to start bringing an extra side of bacon, a brace of pheasants, from the farms where they kept their beehives.

And so, by small steps and small deals, something reliable had been made.

He reached for the telephone. Then, with another furtive glance at the door, he dialled a number.

'Hullo?' came a gruff voice down the line.

'Hello,' Billy replied, 'is that Tom Law & Sons, the building contractors?'

'That's us, sir. How can I help?'

Billy looked again at the page, and couldn't keep the smile from blossoming on his face. If there was still some distance to go, he'd already come far enough to begin. 'Sirs, I have a job for you. I need you to start straight away.' He paused, the smile still flourishing on his face. 'No, no credit needed, sir,' he went on. 'No banker's draft at all. Sir, I can pay you up front.'

The last diners did not leave the Queen Mary restaurant until the hour before midnight, which meant one day had turned into the next by the time the last kitchen hands had finished scrubbing the work surfaces down, scouring the grills and scalding every pan.

By day, the heat in the kitchens was nearly unbearable. By night, the residual heat left a thick, syrupy humidity in the air. Annie hadn't quite appreciated how cloying the atmosphere in the kitchen might feel. She'd been quite prepared to feel like an intruder, to perhaps feel a frisson of fear as Victor led her past the shadowy ranges and countertops, but she hadn't thought she'd feel as *sticky* as she did. 'I'll fetch you some water,' Victor said, and drew a cup from the tap. 'You get used to it when you're here. It's welcome in winter, but in summer there's more than one kitchen hand known to faint clean away.'

The plan, such as it was, was simple. The morning delivery would arrive at 5.30 a.m., at which hour Lionel – one of the morning porters – would open the kitchens for morning prep. By 6 a.m., this place would be a hive of activity again. M. Laurent wasn't due until the lunchtime service, but his sous-chef would be marshalling the kitchen to griddle three hundred fat pork sausages and poach a half thousand eggs. If Victor was right, that meant that, some time in the next five hours, a stranger would be visiting these kitchens. Some time before dawn, the larder would be being emptied – perfectly timed so that, a few short hours later, the new delivery would refill its shelves.

Annie followed him to the larders. At least, here, the air was several shades cooler than in the heart of the kitchen. By the light of a roving electric torch beam, he revealed the shelving. 'All of these kippers,' he said, drawing back the doors of the great refrigerated cabinet. 'These birds,' he remarked, lifting the torch beam to the rafters from which braces of pheasant and partridge hung. 'There'll be half this butter here by morning, you mark my words. We've pounds of lard will be shaved and gone. He'll have these sausages too – there's enough coming in by morning that it will replenish all we've lost.'

Annie was still. Something had robbed her of her voice, until at last she said, 'Have you thought what we'll do, when we catch him?'

Victor closed the larder doors, then steered Annie to a place where two tall cabinets stood on either side of a chimneybreast. Here, between the cabinet and chimney, three mops and their buckets were crammed into a narrow alcove. Victor levered them out, then made a little bow as if to invite his good lady across the threshold.

It was tight in the alcove, too tight to prevent Annie's body from pressing up against Victor's as they crouched down. 'I haven't thought about it,' said Victor, but Annie could spot a lie when she heard one. She supposed they'd just have to judge how brave they were when the blackguard appeared.

Annie was about to say as much when the sound of some clattering pan rang out across the kitchen. The unfamiliar dark could play tricks on a girl's mind, but there was no doubt about this: her eyes darted in the direction of the sound, she stifled a breath, she found that she was suddenly gripping Victor by the hand…

'Something sprang one of the traps. Oh, Annie, you're *shaking!*' Victor's voice hovered on the edge of laughter, but Annie noticed that he was still holding her hand. Part of her wanted to tear it away (how *dare* he laugh!) but another part enjoyed the feeling of her palm being caressed. 'You can't tell me you've never seen a Buckingham rat? As fat and well-fed as the lords up there.'

Secretly, Annie thought: *well, maybe the kitchen* needs *a thief or two if even the rats are well-fed.*

'You can't keep rats out,' said Victor, 'all you can do is catch 'em. It's been worse since the Housekeeping wing was destroyed. More routes in, they reckon. Mr Laurent's become quite chummy with the ratcatcher and his son. By all accounts, the ratcatchers in London are having a good war.'

Not for the first time, Annie thought, '*Well,* somebody's *got to.*'

Victor's hand had loosened on hers. It would be foolish, she thought, to keep clinging on, so instead she let it slide out of her grasp. Yet, even as the next hour passed, she found she could feel his impression upon her. Perhaps it was just the stickiness of the air, but somehow she felt the ghost of his hand in hers.

Her eyes flicked around the kitchen. 'Which direction do you think he'll come from? The back doors?'

'Not the restaurant floor,' said Victor. 'He'd be too conspicu- ous. But—'

Another sound rang out across the barren kitchen floor – not a rat trap being sprung this time, nor the unexpected clatter of pans, but a softer, scratchier sound: the sound of a key being turned in a lock.

Victor's hand was suddenly back in Annie's own. The sound of the key had been joined by the low, mournful creak of a door being opened, the gentle pad of footsteps on the tiled floor. It was at the sound of the door falling shut again reached them that they whispered, in concert, 'The shelter door!', for it was from here that the interloper approached.

There was something about those footsteps, thought Annie: something not quite measured, something not quite right. Here he came, in stutters and starts – an old man, perhaps, picking his way carefully across the kitchen floor.

'He's coming this way,' Annie whispered.

Then Victor's finger was upon her lips, urging her to silence.

By what pale light remained, Annie could see Victor's flared eyes and their look of startled panic. Gently, he drew his finger from her lips. His eyes remained locked with hers. In another corner, in another moment in time, they might have been two young lovers on the edge of sharing their first kiss. Indeed, for a mad, fleeting moment, Annie wondered if they might.

Then, just as her curiosity turned to expectation, another sound filled the kitchen air: not the stuttering footfall of whatever shadowy creature was coming their way, but the distant drone of sirens in the city beyond; the low, mournful wail which told them there was disaster to come.

Victor had started, but out in the kitchen the shadow man had started too. There came another clatter as, reeling round, his shoulder crashed into some hanging pans. His muted curse told Annie that one of the falling implements had caught him; one of his shadowy hands clutched the opposite arm, and for a moment he stood there, frozen in pain. Then he seemed to hear the sirens for a second time. He turned on his heel, started staggering back across the kitchen, the larders abandoned as he went back the way he had come.

In the alcove, Annie just gasped, 'It was him. Victor, we nearly had him ...'

Victor was gasping too. 'I would have confronted him, Annie. Honest I would. If he'd gone one more step towards those larders, I'd have ...'

For the first time, Annie truly understood that Victor was afraid. His panting protestations only made that fear more vivid. She took his hand. 'It's OK, Victor. There didn't have to be a fight. Don't you see? We *know* it now. We *know* when he comes. So we'll just wait another few days and here we'll be, ready to catch him in the act. Nobody needs to wrestle the sausages out of his arms. We'll have caught him with ... with egg all over his face!'

There was something so wild and wonderful about Annie's turn of phrase that the fear bled out of Victor. 'I always knew I wasn't a hero,' he whispered, wryly. 'I'll have to shape up, I suppose, when my call-up comes.'

'War might be over by then,' said Annie, and squeezed his hand in support.

Victor looked upwards. 'It doesn't sound like the war's going to be over,' he said. 'Come on, Annie. We'd better start helping guests.'

Out in the reception hall, the first guests were starting to appear. Bleary-eyed, dressed hurriedly – and, in one or two cases, only in pyjamas and robes – they poured out of the elevators and from the bottom of the guest stairs, there to be met by an army of night managers, concierges and hotel pages. The night manager on shift was already barking orders at the staff.

'We'd better muck in,' said Annie. She darted towards the chaos but, after three faltering strides, looked back. 'I'll see you soon, won't I, Victor? I – I don't mean for a hide-out in the kitchens. I mean...' What a strange feeling – but, somehow, after the torments of the night, Annie had found her courage. 'For a walk in the park? Or to a teashop, perhaps.'

Victor thought he had been afraid in the kitchens, but it was nothing compared to the trepidation he felt now. At last, just when Annie's face was about to turn crestfallen, he blurted out, 'Yes!', and hurried on his way.

Annie hurried on her way too. There were more than enough guests to help – and helping was what Annie did best, even when the guests instructed her, in no uncertain terms, that no help was required.

She was hurrying one of the waiters along, telling him she had a guest who was just *starving*, when she turned and saw Billy coming into the shelter through the main doors, shepherding an elderly lady on his arm. She hurried over to him. 'No rest for the wicked, eh, Bill?' she grinned. 'I've just brought a real fuss-pot down – couldn't wait to get a snack in his hands! I don't know how they do it. When those sirens start, the last thing I fancy is a...'

She'd been about to say 'snack', when her eyes were drawn to Billy's arm. There, just above his elbow, there was a distinct tear in his sleeve. She recognised it at once, for whatever tore the fabric had torn at his skin too. Blood had not poured from the wound but a little had seeped out, to form a crust around the tear.

Her eyes lingered on it.

She heard not a word that Billy said.

'Annie?' Billy's voice came to her out of the fuzz of her

thoughts. 'We'd better get back above. There'll be more guests. Annie? Annie, are you OK?'

No, she thought. She wasn't OK at all. She was a fool – a bloody fool! – because the truth had been staring her in the face all along. Ever since that brandy bottle. Ever since that sack full of produce Billy had brought home for their parents.

There wouldn't be any shadowy confrontation in the larders, because the truth was here, right now, and she was looking straight at it.

Looking at her brother, beaming back down.

Looking at Billy Brogan, the filthy profiteer.

September 1941

Chapter Twenty

'A problem, Mr Allgood?' Mr Knave looked at him owlishly through his spectacles, like a schoolmaster considering some particularly truculent child. 'In the *Orchestra?*'

Lucille sat on the floor in front of Mr Knave's desk. Max caressed her case for good luck before he reached into his jacket pocket and pulled out the flyers Daisy had been assembling: every bill or advertisement for 'Harry Dudgeon and the Moonlighters' she'd been able to find. The band, it seemed, were the hot ticket in London this summer.

Max spread the flyers across the desk and waited as Mr Knave considered them.

Some time later, the Hotel Director looked up with a befuddled expression. 'I was under the impression, Mr Allgood, that our appointment today was to discuss the outcome of the Summer Ball, and to look forward to this Christmas's extravaganza. Indeed, Messrs Arbuthnot and Lavigne are to join us at any moment – I'm told they have a vision to present.'

'Now Mr Knave, I'm not one for trouble. I just want music, pure and simple. But, if you wanted to discuss the *outcome* of the ball, well, here is it, in black and white. *Harry Dudgeon and the Moonlighters.*'

Mr Knave had reached into the desk drawer and produced a

bundle of his own: newspaper pages, one or two printed magazines, and a good number of envelopes. 'This was the kind of outcome I had in mind, Mr Allgood. The Society Pages. Letters from patrons. A mention of your climactic final song in the *Sunday Times.*'

It was this last remark that smarted the most – because that *hadn't* been Max's song.

And that was his point.

'I believe moonlighting is against the terms of my musicians' contract with the Grand Ballroom, Mr Knave – and, if you'll pardon my pedantry, it's rightly so. A place like the Grand is supposed to be exclusive. That's what draws people into a club. It's the point of a residency, just like when I was with the Creole Jazz. You can't see this group anywhere else, so you go to the club where they're playing. You come to the Grand. Now, this summer, Harry, Gus and Fred are touting their own show around town. It won't wash with me.'

Mr Knave was still fingering his way through the flyers. 'I'll admit it's quite a conundrum. And you say you had no idea? You hadn't granted them special dispensation?'

'My understanding is that Mr Adams rather tolerated this kind of thing – but I don't believe it's ever been quite as brazen. To form their *own* orchestra? To start calling it after their own name? To even call themselves *Moonlighters?* Mr Knave, this can't be right.'

By the silence in the office, Max was quite certain he'd made his point clear. Mr Knave seemed to be ruminating further. Then he said, 'You're right, of course, that the Max Allgood Orchestra is under contract with this hotel. I'd have to defer to the paperwork, but I believe that's the way your residency is structured. Do you see what I'm getting at, Mr Allgood? It's the *Orchestra* that's contracted to us, and your individual musicians are contracted to *it*. Ergo, the Max Allgood Orchestra couldn't take itself off for a night at the Savoy. But, as to its constituent parts…'

Mr Knave seemed to enjoy a problem of contractual logic like this. In a moment, he was on his feet and shuffling to the filing cabinet in the corner.

While his head was buried in the drawers, Max said, 'So you're saying it's perfectly permissible to go off gallivanting around town? Mr Knave, they're trading on the Buckingham's reputation.'

'It feels that way, Mr Allgood, but I don't see a place where they're advertised as coming from the Buckingham Hotel. That is, perhaps, very clever of them…'

Mr Knave was still ferreting through the files, working through the rudiments of this particular problem, when a knock came at the door and Marcus Arbuthnot presented himself. At his side, walking in his characteristic, elegant prowl, came Hugo.

'Mr Knave?' Marcus began. 'Are you quite ready for our appointment?'

Walter Knave looked up. 'Take a seat, gentlemen. Yes, yes, I should like to gather Mr Allgood's opinion on this matter too. I'm afraid he has come to me with a rather thorny problem of his own. Mr Lavigne, close the door if you might.' Hugo did as he was bade. Only then did the Hotel Director feel confident enough to say, 'It's this small matter of Harry Dudgeon's activities beyond the Buckingham. Gentlemen, I daresay you are familiar with the matter?'

Both Marcus and Hugo gave Max a vaguely sorrowful look. The dancers had been careful not to intervene in the conflagration around the Summer Ball, grateful that – after that single incendiary moment – Max had shaken Harry's hand. As far as they were concerned, the enmity had been put to bed. Since then, there'd been Saturday nights where Max and Harry had come together on trombone and piano and summoned a storm. Until this moment, they hadn't understood that the bad feeling went on.

Soon, Marcus and Hugo were considering the advertising bills. 'I must say, it's a tricksome one,' Marcus mused. 'It's this damn war, gentlemen. It makes a man want to *live*. And perhaps that's what's in Harry's heart too – this need to play, while he still can. And yet...'

'He's a fine musician,' Walter said, still at the cabinets. 'Read the Society Pages. They speak of our new pianist as though he's a revelation. That's not to say they don't have their eyes trained very clearly upon you, Mr Allgood – but your supporting cast has not gone unnoticed. Here, see.'

It was a piece by Jackson Ford, syndicated from the *New York Times*, that Walter picked up. Max tried not to let that little fact disrupt his sense of purpose, but it was hard not to be unnerved by the persistent appearances of that snake. 'Harry Dudgeon, formerly a percussionist under Archie Adams, reveals himself tonight as the beating heart of this new Orchestra. This is an act of reinvention rarely seen on the stage.'

'Now, look here,' Max began. For the first time he'd been unable to mask his mounting anger. 'Mr Knave, I need to know my Orchestra is committed. That we're all for the Grand. If Harry wants his own orchestra, well—'

Walter had found the old contracts at last. In this, he seemed in his element. His eyes roamed the reams of tiny writing until, like a swimmer too long under water, he came up for air. 'Well, you might be right after all, Mr Allgood. *Musicians are permitted to contract their services to other parties only by express permission of the bandleader.* That's you, of course. Now, you say Archie used to be flexible about this sort of thing. And, in a time of war...'

Walter let the thought dangle.

'I wouldn't be against my dancers taking part in competition,' Marcus intervened, as reasonably as he might, 'or taking private students. Now, if they were off dancing at the Savoy on a Saturday night...' He shrugged. 'But this is hardly the same thing.'

Walter closed the file. 'The discretion is yours, Mr Allgood, but I ask you to bear in mind the smooth running of our Orchestra – and Harry's vital place within it. He's prized, I'm afraid. Do you know, there were certain voices on the Board who believed he should lead the Orchestra in Archie's stead.'

Max tried not to be too disgruntled – because *of course* he knew this. 'My discretion, huh?' he said. Well, there was a weapon here, at least. Something to work with.

He was about to get to his feet when Walter declared, 'Mr Arbuthnot, Mr Lavigne. I believe you have a proposition for us. Are our eyes turning already towards the Christmas festivities?'

'The proposition comes from Hugo alone,' Marcus began, though it seemed he too was bursting in pride at the idea. 'I believe it's right that he explains.'

Hugo was grateful for the introduction, though his confidence was such that he needed none. 'Mr Knave, I'm given to understand the Buckingham has a reputation for styling its most recent balls in support of this war. They still speak so highly of the ball held in honour of those returning from Dunkirk. And of last Christmas, too: ONE GRAND NIGHT.' It had been an auction in support of the war relief fund, dances sold in support of the city. 'Monsieur, I suggest we follow this grand tradition with a ball that celebrates this bastion the Buckingham has become: a ball which venerates those world leaders who still serve their countries in exile. CHRISTMAS IN EXILE, it shall be called. A spectacular to show our solidarity with the Free

French, with the Pierlot government, with the Dutch London Cabinet and the new Greek office.'

Mr Knave weighed the consideration carefully. Evidently, he liked it, for he started nodding and repeating the words under his breath. '"Christmas in Exile". It has a rather nice ring to it – the Buckingham Hotel, conjuring Christmas, for those who can't spend it at home. You're right, of course, Mr Lavigne; these proud folks are ones who deserve a celebration. But there may be security concerns, in bringing so many prominent men together at once. It will have to be carefully thought through.'

'The Buckingham is already a melting pot of those with influence. We host them every day.' Hugo paused. 'Imagine, Mr Knave – Charles de Gaulle himself, dancing with Karina Kainz, while Mr Allgood's Orchestra plays.'

'Well, I like the sound of *that*,' Max chipped in.

'Mr Churchill,' Hugo declared, 'holding court by the cocktail bar!'

Walter Knave was not a man given to smiling, but he smiled now. 'And make us a target for every bomber in the sky. No, gentlemen, the Buckingham is a bastion – but we are not yet a fortress. I cannot promise these luminaries – but *Christmas in Exile*? Yes, I think the Board might just like the sound of that.' Once again, he stood, and extended his hand. 'Very well, gentlemen. I shall put it to the Board. Expect word before the month is out.'

The three men left Mr Knave's office with light in their hearts. Even Max, emboldened by what Mr Knave had discovered, felt some stirring of purpose again. 'You know, Mr Lavigne,' he said, as they reached the reception hall, 'I admire you. It's quite a thing to not be able to go back home, ain't it? And yet, here you are, figuring out ways to support your own.'

'You ever regret leaving the Americas, Mr Allgood?'

There'd been a tone of regret in how Max spoke, but now he shook his head. 'Some men can't look back,' he answered. 'Sometimes, there ain't any new frontier. You've got make it where you are.'

The two dancers were about to depart for the Grand, but now Marcus laid a hand on Max's shoulder. 'You don't mean to … fire Harry?'

'I mean for him to make a choice,' said Max, boldly. 'Either he's for the Grand, or he's not. He's with us, or he ain't. If he's chasing his own glory out in the clubs, well, he's poisoning the ballroom. I'm sorry, boys. It's time.'

There was no show tonight, but Max had it on good authority that Harry and the rest of the band had stayed on after the afternoon demonstrations to take drinks together in the back booth of the Candlelight Club. By evening, there was a strict policy in the club: no hotel staff, no matter how esteemed, were to be seen fraternising with guests. By day, however, the bar manager Ramon was happy to relax the rules. And here they were: Harry, Gus, Frank and a group of the rest, their table littered with Martini glasses, ashtrays overfilling with the stumps of cigars.

Max's first thought was how much he would have enjoyed sitting down with them. He missed the conviviality of musicians. Sometimes, being a leader wasn't all it was cracked up to be.

What a shame it was that he'd come here with confrontation in mind. He ought to have brought Daisy along – she'd have given him strength – but he supposed that would only make him seem weak.

Max barely had to announce his appearance. He simply hovered near the table and their eyes revolved to meet him. Never in all of his life had he felt more like a ghost at a feast – and these, the boys of his own Orchestra.

'I don't mean to interrupt you boys jawing,' he said, 'but Harry, I think we might have a few words.'

Harry looked up, wearing that same feigned smile he'd worn in the dressing rooms. 'Go ahead, Mr Allgood, I'm all ears. Pull up a pew, I'll get you a drink.'

Max had to hold his nerve. 'A private word, Harry, if you don't mind. I'll let you get back to your cocktails in five short minutes.'

At this point, Max turned away, levering his way to a booth a little closer to the terrace, and just praying Harry would follow.

'You don't have a drink, Mr Allgood.'

'I don't need one.' That was a lie; Max was longing for three neat shots of bourbon, each one taken directly after the other. 'Because this won't take long. Harry, we've got off on the wrong foot, you and I. We ought to have become brothers-in-arms, but instead...'

Harry was stock-still. 'Where's this going, Mr Allgood?'

'Harry, you're contracted to the Max Allgood Orchestra. Any work you take outside of that is directly at my discretion – that's by the word of the Hotel Board, by the way, not me. Now, I don't mind you filling in here and there. But what I do mind is when a musician in my Orchestra sets out on his own, to deliberately undermine what I'm trying to do here. So I'm telling you now: there's to be no more moonlighting, not if you value your place in the Grand. There's to be no more shows played while we're meant to be rehearsing. No more nights double-booked.'

Only now did Harry blink.

'I don't think so, Mr Allgood.'

Max stalled.

'Listen to me, Max.' It was the first time he'd called him by his Christian name; surely there was some flagrant insubordination in this. 'You don't get to come into my Orchestra and start throwing your weight around. Respect's earned, not given. Treat me like dirt, and I'll do the same to you. Here's how it's going to be. I'll give up my Moonlighters, but only when it's my name leading the Orchestra in the Grand. How does that sound?'

Max had started shaking. Now he really did need that bourbon.

'I'll fire you, Harry, if I have to. There are other pianists. You can have your Moonlighters for now and ever more. Then where will your family be? Without the security of the Grand, what then?'

But Harry just started laughing. 'Have you heard of Mr Jackson Ford, Max?'

Max stared dumbly, for suddenly he could summon no words.

'He's a New Yorker, a war reporter stationed here in the hotel. Now, what if I told you that this Mr Ford paid me a visit the other week? What if I told you we got chatting – and he started telling me all about his time in New York. Now, Mr Ford, *there's* a music lover. Wow, he had some stories to tell! Those clubs in Manhattan. Those clubs in Harlem. He spent a whole summer in and out of them – not just for the love of the music, of course, but because he was working on a big story. A story that very nearly cost him his life, actually. Well, you know this already, don't you, Max? But the scene in New York, that's run by some pretty shady characters. Italians, most of them. *Mafiosi*, I think you might call them. Cosa Nostra. The Black Hand. This ringing any bells, Max?'

Jackson Ford. Max had been trying to sideline that viper in his thoughts ever since that first night in the Grand. He'd almost managed it as well, for there'd been so much else to dominate his thoughts. But now his chest was tightening, his knuckles whitening as he gripped the edge of the table. 'It's no secret who runs the clubs in New York, Harry. It's the same in Chicago, Boston, Philadelphia. Louis Armstrong, Bing Crosby, all the greats back home – they all had some guy from the mob representing them. There isn't any secret that I did too. Joe Glaser, now there was a tough nut to crack.' Max had talked himself back into some confidence. 'But a man can't live like that forever. I got out, you see. I came to Europe, started building something new, somewhere the mob weren't shadowing my every move. And here I am, *your* bandleader, and—'

'You're full of horse-shit, Max.'

Max almost cried out.

'It took me a little while to get the real story out of Mr Ford. Well, everyone's out for what they can get – me included – and he wanted paying. I had to play a few shows with the Moonlighters to rustle up that kind of money. But tell me, Max, what would the Hotel Board do if they knew the *real* reason you left New York? What would they do if they... knew about *Nelson*?'

'Now, listen here, you dog. You speak that name again and I'll...'

'What would they do,' Harry smirked, 'if they knew that the woman you've brought here, the woman you're sharing your quarters with, isn't actually your wife at all?'

All of the indignation bled out of Max. He'd been right, all along. Jackson Ford really had recognised him that day in the ballroom – and Max really had been right about where he'd seen that face before: the townhouse, up by St Nicholas Park.

'What do you want?' Max whispered. He'd come here to settle this once and for all, but now he was hanging from a cliff-edge, his fingers being prised up one by one.

'You know what I want,' said Harry. '*I* was Archie's heir. I have been for years. I want what's rightly mine.'

'What do you expect me to do, Harry? The Board picked me. I don't control the Board.'

'Well, what do you think the Board might do if they knew the true story of Mr Max Allgood? If they knew they'd hired a scoundrel to their Orchestra?' Harry paused. 'Here's what's going to happen. From this day forth, *I'm* the one in charge of the musical direction of the Orchestra. Oh, there'll be a place for you, Max. I know talent when I see it. But *I'll* be the one setting the agenda. *I'll* be the one driving the songs. And, on the night of the Christmas Ball, you'll be fading into the background so that, by New Year, it's *my* name in the Society Pages. And, once it is, you'll be going to see Mr Knave and explaining: orchestras change; orchestras develop; orchestras have lives and personalities of their own. You didn't see it coming, but the Christmas Ball has proven it – it's Harry Dudgeon that society loves, not Max Allgood. After that, Max, you'll be just another trombonist in my Orchestra. Stay or go, it's up to you.'

'You bastard, Dudgeon. This is blackmail.'

But Harry just said: 'I'll keep your dirty little secrets, Max – but I'll take what's mine in return.'

Harry was whistling as he sauntered away, but Max just sat there, still plunging into that deep ravine that had opened inside of him. Half a world, he'd travelled. There were three thousand miles between Mayfair and Manhattan – and yet trouble always followed.

He was still sitting there, shaking, when he heard the laughter resume at the booth where the musicians were gathered.

'Everything all right, Harry?' one of the trumpeters was saying.

'Oh, everything's lovely,' Harry replied. 'Me and Mr Allgood, we're going to be the best of friends from now on. You see, we've come to an … *understanding*.'

Chapter Twenty-One

In the midst of all the heartache, the panic and moral conflict, there was yet pride.

Billy had been bursting with it yesterday evening when he met with the Ankers on the edge of Regent's Park. Here, he helped transfer the crates from the back of the laundry van to the Ankers' own truck, and accepted his payment in return. 'It feels a little light tonight, boys,' Billy said, filtering through the envelope they'd given him in the dim light of the laundry van. 'Are you sure I'm not being short-changed?'

The Ankers boys shared a swift look. 'We wouldn't think of it, Bill. You know how to keep us sweet.'

There was a bottle of Moët in the van for exactly this purpose. A basket of soaps and lotions, to please the Ankers' old mum. Billy handed them over and made certain to shake their hands. He was quite certain the payments they'd just handed over wouldn't match the tally he was keeping in his ledger, but he'd learnt across the last few weeks what a 'good loss' was; a little lost income was worth some peace of mind – and, besides, the last weeks had been the most bountiful of his enterprise. The Ankers were worth the price they exacted from him – and the extra they'd been able to provide, bringing down spare ribs and game birds to the shops, had been enough to maintain their interest in the whole affair. Perhaps there'd come a day when they wanted too much, but that hardly mattered to Billy, not anymore.

The end was already in sight.

The Ankers boys were repairing to a Camden hostel for the night – 'They'll keep serving behind the blackout, down at the canalside,' Dirk grinned – so left, swiftly, to make the deliveries. After they were gone, Billy had to hustle to make it across London before the blackout truly came down.

His parents were spending the evening in the blacked-out sitting room, among several of Eliza Hatchet's other halfway house guests. Billy's father was the first to rise, for his mother was swamped by the sewing she'd been taking in; there was much work for a seamstress, if you had the right connections, and Orla Brogan's workload had been steadily increasing. Even so, she set it down and rushed to Billy's side. 'There's tea in the pot, Billy,' she declared. 'I'll have a drop too.'

'There'll be no time for that,' Billy grinned. 'Fancy a stroll, Ma?'

Billy's father looked at him oddly. 'You're up to something, Bill.'

'That I am, but you'll have to see it to believe it. Come on, you don't need your coats. It's mild out there. And there's no siren yet.'

They seemed ready to resist – for who wanted to venture out into the blackout for a leisurely stroll? – when the sitting room door opened, and there stood Annie. By the look of her (tangled hair, ruddy-cheeked), she'd spent some time in the outside water closet.

Billy beamed. 'Well, there we are – the whole family! It's good we should do this together.'

'It's after dark now, Bill. Can't it wait until morning?'

'Come on, Annie, I've come all this way. Look,' he said, still beaming, 'if we get there and it isn't worth your while, I'll—'

'Can't you just tell us, Bill?' asked his mother.

'Yeah, *Billy*,' interjected Annie, in quite the most waspish tone Billy had ever heard, 'if you've got a *secret*, why not just *spill* it?'

'Because it's a *surprise*,' he insisted, wilfully ignoring Annie's tone (just *what* was her problem?). 'Come on, you'll hardly even have to walk. I've got one of the laundry vans outside.'

Billy made sure there was space for his parents in the cab – and this was cramped enough – but this meant Annie had to ride in the back, where formerly the crates of Buckingham produce had been, and the disgruntled look on her face as she slid into the darkness made Billy forget how cold and stand-offish she'd been inside the house. Now, he was certain, her sour look was because she'd been relegated to a piece of produce. 'I'm sorry, Annie,' he told her, earnestly, 'it really isn't far. And you're going to be so thrilled. You're going to be pleased as punch with your big brother.'

There were still roadblocks around one entrance to Albert Yard, so in the end he had to take a circuitous route – so circuitous in fact that, at first, his parents had no idea where they were heading. It was his father, who'd walked these routes with the ARP, who realised first. 'What's the meaning of this, Bill? You know it cuts your mother up, seeing the old house.'

'I don't want her to see the old house,' said Billy, driving past the various scaffolds and hoardings now erected around the bombed-out buildings. Then he ground the van to a halt and declared, 'I want her to see the new.'

A few moments later, he'd levered himself out of the van and hobbled round to release Annie from the rear. When she emerged, she looked even more disgruntled than ever. 'Billy

Brogan,' she said, 'you rotten scoundrel, you, I've been being bashed around in there like a ... like a common piglet!' But, by the time she'd marched round the side of the van to join their parents, just emerged from the cab, she too had fallen silent.

'See, Ma?' Billy thrilled. 'See, Pa? See, *Annie*? I told you I'd find a way. I made you a promise, and I wasn't going to break it.'

In front of them stood not the devastation that had been wrought on No 62 Albert Yard, but a fresh set of hoardings surrounding the construction site beyond. On those hoardings a sign had been erected: THOMAS LAW & SONS, BUILDING CONTRACTORS, and the address of an office in Bayswater. Behind, scaffolds rose like a fresh steel skeleton around what had once been the Brogans' beloved home.

'Billy, son, what in God's name is this?'

'It's home, Pa,' Billy replied. 'Or it will be. Well, what do you think?'

'I – I can't believe it,' Billy's mother stuttered. 'Billy, never in my wildest dreams ...'

'But *how*, son? *How*?'

'I told you,' Billy said, puffing out his breast, 'I've been doing errands for management.' He was still explaining, giving voice to every imaginary deed that rushed through his head, when his eyes fell on Annie. There she stood on the side of the road, not gazing at their old home like their parents, but gazing at Billy, her jaw open wide, her eyes – wide as they were – darting with disquiet. 'Well, little sister? I told you I'd get us home, and I have!'

Mrs Brogan had burst into floods of disbelieving tears. Her husband wrapped his arms around her as he too stared at the construction works. 'Billy, son, I don't know what to say.'

It wasn't done yet, thought Billy. He'd been able to make the down-payment to Thomas Law & Sons a few days ago, but he'd have to keep up with the payments if they were to complete the task on time. They were a professional outfit, builders and carpenters to the gentry – it was only by dint of his Buckingham connections that he'd convinced them to take this job at all.

'Well go on, Annie!' Mr Brogan beamed. 'Say something! She can't believe it, Bill. Can't believe what you've done. I told you, Annie – your brother might have been a rapscallion in his boyhood, but this here's a true hero. Off he goes soldiering, and he comes back a bona fide *hero*.' He stopped. 'Billy, how much did this cost? I'll pay you back, son. As soon as I'm on my feet, I'll—'

'You'll do nothing of the sort,' Billy replied.

Somewhere over the city, the sirens had started. As one, the Brogans looked to the skies. Moments later, Billy said, 'Come on, I'll get you back. But … I wanted you to see it with your own two eyes. So you'd know: this isn't bluster; this is real. We're all going back home.'

Annie looked reluctant to get back in the van. 'I'll walk,' she muttered.

'Don't be so soft,' Billy said. 'You can ride up front after we drop Ma and Pa off.'

'She can ride up front now,' declared Mr Brogan. 'I feel fit as a fiddle, Bill. I feel ten years younger. Annie, you jump up front with your mother. I don't mind rattling about for a few minutes yet.'

The silence, as they rode back to Eliza Hatchet's house, was so different to the silence of before. Billy could feel the disbelief and pride still radiating off his mother. When, halfway there, she reached out and squeezed his hand, he felt filled up.

'I love you, Bill,' said his mother, as the van ground to a halt. 'Because you've got the best heart, Billy Brogan. The very best.'

Billy was close to tears as well as he led her, by the hand, to the kerb and embraced her there. 'Give me a couple more months, Ma, and you'll be back home. They can't keep us Brogans down. And there's families like us all over this country. That's why . . .' He thought, fleetingly, of that mad dash across the French countryside, the Nazi army on their heels. 'That's why we're going to win.'

His father had been battered around more than he'd let on, thought Billy, as he watched him limp back through Eliza Hatchet's front door. But a few bumps and bruises quickly faded away; Billy knew that better than anybody. All it needed was a little good news, a healthy dose of hope, and the body quickly healed.

Annie was still ice cold when Billy slid into the driver's seat and brought the engine back to life. 'Next stop, Buckingham Hotel!' he declared, cheery as a cab driver ensnaring a particularly large fare.

He'd reached the second junction, the river hoving into view between the terraces, when he sensed that something still wasn't right. Annie hadn't breathed a word. 'Annie, what is it?'

'You know damn well what it is, Billy Brogan.'

There was a gap in the traffic. Billy might have pulled out and made for the bridge at Westminster, but instead he sat there, the engine idling. 'Annie, aren't you happy? We're going back home, Annie. Ma and Pa can pick up where they—'

'But I know how you've been doing it, Billy!' she shrieked, and turned to glare at him for the first time. 'I know exactly what you've done!'

'Annie, whatever you think you know—'

'I was there in the kitchens,' she snapped, and couldn't look him in the eye a second longer. She just reached for his sleeve, touching the spot beneath his shoulder where the shirt had torn. 'Victor worked out how someone was robbing from the larders – just before delivery, so nobody would ever know. We were waiting to see who – but, Billy, I needn't have bothered. I could have worked it out. That brandy bottle, Billy. And all these bits you've been taking Ma and Pa – more than just a bit of salvage. I just didn't know *why*. Not until… not until tonight.'

Her anger petered out into wretched silence. 'You've been stealing from Housekeeping too. You've been robbing from Mrs de Guise.'

Strangely, this seemed the greatest sacrilege of all. Annie wiped away a tear. 'Just start driving, Bill. I want to go back to my room. I can't… I can't think out here.'

Billy blurted out, 'But now you know *why*, Annie. Now you know *why*. I'm not some filthy profiteer, feathering his own nest. It's for Ma and Pa. It's for all the rest. Annie, it's for *you*.'

Her eyes flared. 'Don't you DARE, Billy Brogan. DON'T YOU DARE. We're meant to be *good*, us Brogans. We're meant to be… honourable.'

'Is it honourable, how much those lords have at the Buckingham Hotel?' Billy snapped. 'Look at me, Annie. LOOK AT ME!' She did, driven to do it by the sheer power of his voice. 'I couldn't leave Ma and Pa destitute. I couldn't do that to them.'

'I don't care,' Annie sobbed. 'I don't care. It's… it's wrong, Bill. You'll hang for it!'

'Hang?' This time, though he did not mean to, Billy had to stifle a laugh. 'Hang me, for a few rashers of bacon? Speak sense, Annie.' He started the engine again, if only for something to do with his hands. 'Nothing's going to happen to me, because nobody knows.' He fell silent, for another, more startling, thought had occurred. 'Do they, Annie? Does anybody know?'

Annie shook her head. She hadn't even found the courage to tell Victor; shame had driven her to silence.

'Then it's settled,' Billy said, trying to contain the hammering of his heart. 'It's all good. Nothing's changed. Nothing except—'

'*I* know,' said Annie.

'Well, it'll be over soon. As soon as I've made the next payments, it's over.'

'It's the others who'll pay for it,' said Annie, as the laundry van hurtled up Regent Street. 'That's what I'm worried about. Mrs de Guise, Billy – what happens when somebody notices how much has gone? It's Mrs de Guise who'll have to answer for it – and her with a baby not yet six months old. And…' Annie shook her head; these thoughts were just too fierce; she could hardly bear them. 'And Victor, down in the kitchens. M. Laurent's already on the warpath. He thinks they're wasting food. Damaging his kitchen. Sooner or later, he'll blame one of them and off they'll go. Victor's got *his* mother to think about too, Bill! His father's in a camp!'

They had reached Berkeley Square. This was no place for a laundry van to be seen, but Billy stopped in the shadows and fixed Annie with a suddenly baleful stare. '*Victor*,' he said. 'This is about Victor, is it? You've got a sweet spot for him. That's right, isn't it, Annie?'

'Did Frank say?' Annie whispered.

'Oh, Frank Nettleton said nothing. Frank keeps secrets like it's gold in a vault. No, it's obvious, Annie. But… these are our *parents*, Annie. You can't go worrying about a boy from the kitchens when our *parents* haven't got a roof to call their own. Good God, Annie – it's Ma, it's Pa!'

'No,' said Annie, ferociously – and, leaping out of the van, screamed, 'It's WRONG and RIGHT!'

She was halfway across Berkeley Square when Billy, realising suddenly that he couldn't let her go, leapt out of the van and stumbled after. His leg screamed in agony as he tried to follow, but still he heaved himself on. 'Annie,' he called out. 'Annie, wait!'

She stopped dead.

'Billy, *I* almost caught you! *Me*, Annie Brogan – and ... and I can't even put on a pillowcase properly!' She shook her head. 'And if you don't get caught, Bill, someone else is going to take the blame. It's been noticed. And ... and I won't lie for you, Billy. I won't, I won't, I won't ... I don't want Victor to be fired. Or Mrs de Guise to be blamed. Billy, I want you to stop.' She took a breath, wrapping her arms tightly around herself. 'And ... and if you don't, I'll *tell*.'

Billy took a step back. 'You'll ... *tell?*' he whispered, disbelieving.

'I don't want to, Bill. But it's other people's lives. And ... you're not a profiteer,' she sobbed. 'You're my big brother. You're a hero from Dunkirk. You're the best Brogan, Billy, you always have been. And ... and I don't want to be ashamed of you.'

The words echoed in Billy as he watched her take off, again, across the grass. 'Annie!' he called after her.

But if Annie heard at all, she paid it no mind. Soon, she had been enveloped by the shadows of Michaelmas Mews. Off she went, back to the Buckingham Hotel, carrying Billy's darkest secret in her heart.

His heart in wild tumult, Billy loped back to the laundry van and, slipping behind the steering wheel, coaxed the engine back to life.

What was wrong with her? Why couldn't she *see*?

I want you to stop ...

But how could he stop? He'd set it all in motion. He'd made the down-payment. By God, he'd *shown* his parents what he was doing for them.

I'll tell ...

In that moment, he understood that Annie didn't just mean she'd tell the hotel; she meant she'd tell their parents as well. It was the plaintive cry of every younger sister: *I'll tell*.

She'd left him with an impossible conundrum. His enterprise could not end; not yet, not when he wasn't finished; not when his family was still in such need.

He was still sitting there, slumped over the steering wheel, wondering what wrong step he'd taken to lead him here, when he was suddenly reminded of lying spreadeagled in the gutter, Mr Stockdale's henchmen kicking him fiercely in the ribs. The despair of that moment had been as nothing compared to this – and yet, just as back then, there was some twinkling of hope. A solution had presented itself to the problem of Mr Stockdale. It occurred to Billy, in a sudden flash, that the same solution presented itself now; that there was yet a way his enterprise could continue undetected.

The fire of this new idea propelled him. Soon, though the blackout was in full force – and the distant report of the ack-ack guns could be heard in the east – he was ploughing the dark roads towards Camden. The city had not yet been lit up in oranges and reds – perhaps it would be a light one tonight – but the streets were yet crawling with ARP wardens and fire patrols. In the end, he ditched the laundry van on a barren side-street and dodged the patrols until he stood in front of the St Christopher's Hostelry above the canal. With the sirens wailing as they were, it did not take long to find the Ankers brothers. Three Anderson shelters were dug into the yard out back, and in the second of them they slept sound as babies, bellies heavy with ale from the hours before.

'Listen,' Billy told them, having pleaded shelter alongside the other hostelry guests. 'Things changed tonight, and … And I need your help. There'll be more in it for you – a cut in the takings, whatever we get. But … Supply's going to be quieter from the Buckingham, at least for a time. But there's still hungry people. There are still shopkeepers in need. We can't let them down. So I need more from you. More from the farms. More from the villages. More from wherever you were getting it for Ken. Bring it to me, boys, and I'll make it worth your while. Money, Moët, whatever I can get my hands on …' Inwardly, Billy thought: *if I can't plunder the larders, perhaps there are still a few luxuries I can dredge up from the hotel, a few prized pieces that Annie needn't ever know about.* 'Just a little longer, boys. One last push.'

Rod Ankers shook him by the hand, while Dirk clapped him around the shoulder.

'We'll do what we can, boss,' they told him, gleefully. 'Brogan, you can count on us.'

October 1941

Chapter Twenty-Two

Lieutenant Raymond de Guise stepped into the welcome shade of the hospital outbuilding and doused himself in water from the pump. Two of his men, laid up with sandfly fever, were to be released from the hospital ward today, and just in time – for he'd heard whisper, this week, from up the chain of command: forces were being massed to cross the border back into Libya. Tobruk had been cut off since the spring, its garrison kept alive only by the bravado of the RAF and the courage of the fleet taking supplies – and rescuing injured defenders – from the besieged port city. But Erwin Rommel and his Afrika Korps would not be in the ascendant forever. Rumour had it that men from all over the Commonwealth, and beyond – for the Free French were in Africa now, the resurgent Hellenic army had joined them after the fall of Greece, and the Poles and Czechs were already bolstering the campaign – were to come together and cross the border.

And about time, thought Raymond. They'd been losing too long.

'The mail truck got through,' called one of his sergeants, appearing in the outbuilding door. 'Post's coming out now, Lieutenant. It's been beached on the front, but now it's here.'

A bundle of letters was waiting for him in the post room. He recognised his wife's handwriting at once. The invisible thread that tied him to her grew suddenly taut. He tore open the first envelope, devouring its contents: the story of his son Arthur's first night on this earth, a promise from his wife for the future they would share.

Frank on the sitting room sofa; Vivienne moving in, at last; Billy's family bombed-out and living on the charity of Lambeth...

A knock at the door, *'and, Raymond, a familiar face from the days before we met...'*

Raymond looked up. His eyes, which had seen so much horror across the long summer months, looked more horrified still. It took him some moments to go back to the letters. There and then, he read the story of how Hugo Lavigne had stayed the night with Nancy, Vivienne and Frank; how, some time later – having luxuriated under Raymond's roof all the while – he was appointed as ballroom dancer with the Buckingham Hotel; how he had been spinning them the story of that half-forgotten summer in Paris, the Hotel Acacias and the Casino de Paris.

The final envelope tore as it opened.

Inside lay Nancy's last letter, but on top of that a folded ivory page bearing the insignia of the Buckingham Hotel.

This is what it read:

YOU ARE CORDIALLY INVITED TO

CHRISTMAS IN EXILE

The Buckingham Hotel Christmas Ball

Saturday 6th December 1941

In Celebration of Friends from Near and Afar, In Brotherhood with Fallen Nations

Featuring:

THE MAX ALLGOOD ORCHESTRA!

and

The Buckingham Dancers

'*Raymond*,' Nancy had written, '*I send you this copy of the invitation now flying out across London, because I have a fantasy that you will be there in spirit, that if – on the night of the 6th December, you hold the Grand in your mind, some flutter of you might be caught there, dancing between the stars. So many are to come. They say that, among the officials of the Free French already attending, M. de Gaulle may make an appearance. And one thing is for certain: it will make dear Hugo as proud as any man alive, to think that he brings his countrymen some fleeting joy in this, their darkest hour...*'

As Raymond had been reading, his knuckles whitened and strained at the paper. Now, suddenly, he swung round. One of his subordinates was still sifting through the mail sacks, evidently searching for some communication of his own. 'Private,' he said, 'a paper. A pen.' Moments later, appropriately provisioned, he began writing a letter of his own.

It took him but two minutes to compose his missive. A further minute later, it was crammed into the envelope and Raymond was darting to the barracks back office, where one of his lance corporals was waiting.

'Woods,' he began, 'I need this on the next mail truck – do you understand?'

The lance corporal, a rangy figure with a fuzz of auburn hair, said, 'At once, Lieutenant – but it may take some time before it gets shipped out.'

'It's imperative, Lance Corporal.'

Ever since he began his tenure in the Grand, Raymond de Guise had been able to win men over with the look in his eyes. But what worked in the ballroom did not always work in a theatre of war. Now, Lance Corporal Woods just breathed heavily and said, 'Next mail shipment isn't for two weeks, Lieutenant. And even then, it has to go through normal process – you know that.' He paused. 'Look, between you and me, the Greek Cairos might be able to help. Their London office is operational now. They may have a mail supply.'

This time, Raymond's look worked wonders. Lance Corporal Woods took his letter and clung on tight. 'I'll see what I can do, Lieutenant – but there are only so many rules to bend. What's so crucial, in any case? Is it that son of yours? Lieutenant de Guise, is everything all right?'

Raymond drew the back of his hand across his brow, leaving dirty trails in his sweat.

'No, Lance Corporal. Everything's far from all right. I believe there's a plot unfolding, right now, under the noses of my family and friends – and here I am, two thousand miles away, powerless to stop it…'

'Girls, you've performed admirably today,' Nancy declared. 'Off to your rest now. You've earned it.'

They really had. Since her return, Nancy hadn't noted more than two or three days when the girls were running behind schedule, and that only because of unavoidable delays. Nor, in the last weeks, had she been able to detect any unusual discrepancies in the store cupboards; whoever had been damaging stock, or covering up their own mistakes, had obviously shaped up, because the last time Nancy had taken an inventory, not one item was out of place.

It was almost time to set aside the hotel and return to Arthur, but when Nancy returned to the Housekeeping Office, meaning to set her desk in order before locking up, she realised that not all the girls had left. There was Annie Brogan, lingering by the door of the lounge, her face set in some inscrutable expression. She'd been quieter of late – more studious, Nancy had thought, as if she was knuckling down, determined to play her part. Not for the first time, Nancy thought of her own first year at the Buckingham Hotel. Perhaps she expected too much of Annie. 'Annie, dear, you're looking a little peaky. Is everything all right?'

By her reaction, it was exactly the question Annie had needed to hear. She stuttered forward saying, 'Well, *actually*, Mrs de Guise, there is *something* I'd quite like to ask – that is, if you've got time?' Annie looked her up and down. 'I know it's time for you to be knocking off and all. I wouldn't want to hold you up, not when little Arthur's waiting at...'

Nancy rolled her eyes, though not unkindly. 'Come through, Annie. There's still tea in the pot. What's troubling you?'

'Probably this is a question for a priest, Mrs de Guise, only there isn't a priest here at the hotel, so I thought you were the nearest thing.'

Nancy screwed up her eyes and tried to suppress a grin. 'Not quite, Annie, but I'll do my best.'

'What should a person do, Mrs de Guise, if they think they've seen something *wrong*? Say, right here in the hotel, for instance? If you saw something that oughtn't have happened, what would you do?'

'Well, Annie,' said Nancy, guardedly, 'that's quite a broad question. What might you mean by... *wrong*?'

'I'm not talking about murder, Mrs de Guise.'

Nancy blinked, hard. 'I rather thought not, Annie.'

'Just something *wrong*, you know?'

'Well,' Nancy said, sensing that Annie's ambiguity was deliberate, 'there are all sorts of different wrongs in the world. If it's something you've dropped or spilled, there's really no need to worry. To be *wrong*, well, I suppose it has to be deliberate.' Nancy paused. 'We all make mistakes, Annie. We all do things other people might frown on, from time to time. To my mind, it's only ever truly *wrong* when it goes against the common good, the spirit of things. Do you see?'

Annie mused on this for a time. 'It's not that simple though, is it, Nance? I mean, Mrs de Guise. See, I was thinking about a starving man who steals a loaf of bread. The police might put him in cuffs, but it can hardly be *wrong*, can it, now? Not if he's got bairns to feed – like, like your Arthur!'

'That much is true, Annie. It isn't always as black and white as we see.'

'But then imagine a man who's stealing bread from someone who doesn't have much of his own. That *would* be wrong, wouldn't it, Mrs de Guise?'

Nancy reached out and put her hand over Annie's. 'Is there something you want to tell me, Annie?'

Annie reeled back. 'No, Mrs de Guise! No, it's only … Well, say a man was stealing bread – even though he didn't need any – and then he was giving it to those that *did* need it. If he was chomping on it hisself, that'd be wrong. But if he was handing it out to starving bairns – like your Arthur! – well …'

'You mean like a Robin Hood, Annie?'

'But now, say, Robin Hood's stealing and he's giving bread to all these hungry wretches. But he keeps a bit for himself, and sells it, so he can have a nice new cap. Would *that* be wrong?'

This time, there was no masking it; Nancy really was bemused. 'A nice new cap?'

'Or it could be anything. A nice pair of boots, to go off robbing more bread in. Or maybe a bigger basket, so he can rob even more bread.' Annie slumped back in her seat. The only thing that could help was another barley sugar, so she stuffed one in her lips and started sucking. 'It's hard to know where one thing ends and another begins.'

'Life can be a bit like that, dear.' The clock on the wall was inching towards two. Somewhere outside, Nancy's taxicab would be waiting. It wasn't just Arthur she wanted to be back for; she and Vivienne had a dinner planned, Hugo coming to see the baby – and perhaps even finish that story about the Exhibition Paris. At last, she said, 'The world tests us in lots of different ways, Annie. I've put my foot wrong too many times. Have I ever told you about my first season here? All I wanted was to see the ballroom, so I put on a gown I'd brought and in I went, one night ...' Annie's face opened up in horror; the thought of Mrs de Guise doing anything as unconscionable made her blood run cold. 'I could have lost my job. Now, to me – little Nancy Nettleton, just down from the north country – it wasn't such a terrible thing. And was anybody hurt? Well, not in any ordinary sense. But there was wrong in that too – because I was breaking rules that had been clearly laid out for me, rules I'd agreed to by coming here.' Once more, she paused. 'I suppose what I'm trying to say is – it isn't always easy to know what's right and wrong. What you've got to do is work out who's being harmed, and find your way from there. Does that make sense?'

Nancy didn't know why, but at this last sentiment, Annie suddenly picked herself up, her eyes aflame. 'It does, Nance! It does!'

'It's *Mrs de* ...' Nancy was about to admonish her, but caught herself at last; where was the harm, she thought, in letting one little formality slip, when no one else was here to notice. 'Off with you, Annie. You've got a whole afternoon to yourself. Stay out of mischief, won't you?'

'Oh I will, Nance,' grinned Annie as she scuttled off. 'I'll be quiet as a mouse, you can count on it.'

In the Grand Ballroom, the sounds of a raucous fast waltz reached fever pitch. On the dance floor, Hugo – dancing for the first time with Karina in his arms – pitched one way, then the next. In concert with the swooping trombone, he lifted Karina in the air, presenting her to the audience above.

That audience was comprised not of the lords and ladies, but Marcus Arbuthnot, Frank Nettleton and the other dancers in the Buckingham troupe – for this afternoon marked the first stage in preparations for the winter ball to come.

'Say, how did *that* feel?' grinned Max Allgood, now that the song was over. He called this one 'Somebody's Secret' and he'd opened his residency at the Edison Ballroom in New York with this every Saturday night for a year. It sure got those rich New York folks dancing, and – by the breathlessness of Hugo and Karina – he was sure it could get the upper-crust folk coming to the ball dancing too. By the time they'd got through the first three numbers Max had planned, they'd have shed a smidgeon of their elegance and embraced a little bit of the devil-may-care frenzy Max luxuriated in back in New York. 'We'll show those lords how to have a good time yet!'

'It's a fine balance, Mr Allgood,' Marcus announced, sashaying down to the dance floor himself, then inviting Mathilde and Frank to join him. 'But frenzy must be refined in a place like the Grand. We must retrain our grandeur.'

'Quite,' Max chipped in, still hopping from foot to foot with

Lucille – as if, in his mind, the music still went on. 'We just need to give 'em a nudge.' He grinned, but was hardly chastened, when he saw Marcus arching an eyebrow in response. 'Let's just see where the music takes them,' he went on. 'So are we agreed? "Somebody's Secret" opens the show. Then there's a medley – "Born to Dance", and "Winter Weather"…' The last was a Benny Goodman record, Max's favourite of the year. 'That's when the show really begins, and the dance floor opens up.'

Marcus took in the expectant faces of his troupe and announced, 'I think we're all in agreement, Max. Three numbers as fierce as these, and the dance floor will be more than ready to accept our guests. Shall we, perhaps, take it from the top? String them together?'

Among the dancers, Frank Nettleton certainly looked keen. He had already taken Mathilde by the hand. But, as Max turned back to his Orchestra, summoning them back to the music, he caught the eye of Harry, hunkering over the piano. 'A quick word, Max?' Harry piped up.

'Let's run this through first, Harry?' Max ventured, running a finger around his collar – for already he sensed something was wrong.

Pointedly, Harry closed the piano lid and said, 'Just two moments, Max. You can spare that, can't you?'

By the dazzling look in Harry's eyes, Max knew that he would brook no other answer than the 'Sure, Harry! Sure sounds important!' he managed to utter.

'It's that opening number,' Harry began, with a look of focus and concentration that Max knew was feigned. 'It isn't quite working, is it now?'

'"Somebody's Secret"?' he mouthed.

Immediately, he understood. '*Somebody's Secret*'. He'd written it, thinking of an old friend caught in the midst of a torrid love affair – but now, by the light in Harry's eye, it had taken on some darker meaning.

'I just don't think it's quite the kind of statement we're looking for, is it? An opening number sets the scene for a night. It's a summons. It's a call to the dance. "*Somebody's Secret*" – I don't think the Orchestra were quite feeling it like they should. As for the dancers…'

Max said, 'Seemed they were dancing perfectly well to me.'

'Yes!' Harry enthused. 'That's just the diagnosis. *Perfectly well*, when what you really want is *drama*.'

'I've been opening sets with "Somebody's Secret" for ten years.'

Harry shook his head ruefully. 'That's probably the problem. It's a bit… old, perhaps? A bit worn out? You want a song of the moment. That's the thing.'

Max's look darkened. 'I suppose *you've* got something that might fit the bill, have you?'

'Oh, plenty,' Harry said, his tone barely changing. Perhaps that was the thing that disgusted Max most of all – how naturally this all came to Harry, how comfortable he was with the duplicitousness. 'But there's one in particular that springs to mind. "Never the Lonely". It's a bit of a clarion call to arms – finding joy in times of disaster. It's got a great trombone part, Max. You and Lucille could really dive into a song like that.'

Max had hardened. 'What do you expect of me, Harry? What exactly do you want?'

Harry laid his hand on Max's shoulder. 'Just a little cooperation, Mr Allgood, like we agreed.' Harry's act of respectability faded for the briefest flicker; he sneered at Max and added, 'Let's give it a run-through, Max.'

Max tried not to look hang-dog as he returned to the front of the stage. At least it felt better, now he had Lucille back in his hands. He'd known that something like this was coming ever since that moment in the Candlelight Club. He hadn't yet told a soul; hadn't yet breathed of it to Daisy, for fear of what she might say. He was, he realised, as afraid of telling Daisy as he was of Harry unveiling the truth – so instead he'd buried his head in the music, just hoping for the promise of another day.

'Marcus, Hugo,' Max called out. 'We're going to try a different number, if that sounds good to you?' His eyes roamed over Harry. 'Harry's going to lead on this one – just to get the feel of it. It's a ... a waltz, Harry?'

'A quickstep,' Harry pronounced, 'but you'll feel it down there.' His eyes lit up. 'I promise you that.'

Then his fingers started rolling across the keys.

It was a bouncy rhythm, that was for certain. When Gus and Fred leapt in with their trumpets, the song came alive. The other musicians were slower to rise to the challenge – indeed, it was Max who was the last to find his place in the song – for it seemed, somehow, that Lucille put up a protest. But by the time Harry drove the song to its conclusion, in his trademark riot of piano, there was a sense of unparalleled delight on the dance floor beneath them. To Max's chagrin, it seemed to rival anything they had accomplished in the session so far.

Silence returned, and the dancers came apart. There was a certain breathlessness in the air. All eyes had turned to Max. 'So,' he stammered, 'how did that feel?'

'It's an uproarious number!' Marcus declared, full to the brim with his theatrical pomp. 'Something to get the blood flowing, the heart thundering along.' Then he stopped. 'But one wonders, perhaps, if it's more suited as a closing number? Something, perhaps, to top off the first act?'

To Max, it was the lifeline he needed: solidarity, though none knew it, from the dance troupe. He saw the looks the other dancers shared, slowly convinced himself that they too shared the sentiment. When Hugo chimed in, 'Who wouldn't be desperate to return to the floor, after a moment like this?', he felt certain he had the right of it.

He turned to Harry and said, 'Sounds like there's a lot of love for the song, old boy!' but then his heart skipped a beat. He had noticed the way Harry's expression was pitched perfectly between respectability and menace; the way he beamed broadly, while his eyes still glowered.

He'd been about to say, 'But let's keep it in reserve, shall we? Something to hit them with at the close of the act,' but the gravity of that stare was pulling him in.

Instead, he turned to the assembled crowd.

'Let's try it again,' he said, 'and roll it into the other two numbers. Ladies and gentlemen, I think we've got ourselves a new opening number!'

By the time the afternoon session was over, Harry's song was set in stone. As the dancers returned backstage, and Frank changed hurriedly out of his dancing clothes, he noted Max trailing after the rest of the Orchestra as they returned from the Grand. He was cradling Lucille to him as if he needed some comfort.

'Do you think everything's all right with him, Mr Lavigne?'

Hugo had been watching too. He hung there, elegant even in his shirtsleeves, until he said, 'Sometimes, a musician wears his heart on his sleeve. Max's is hanging there this evening.'

Hugo hurried after Max, catching him in the hallway without. By the expression on his face, Hugo knew something was wrong. 'Monsieur,' he ventured, 'it's the song, is it not? You know it to be wrong?'

Max seemed desperate not to be cornered. He took a faltering step backwards, 'It feel right to you, Mr Lavigne? To you and the rest of the troupe? Well, that's what matters...'

Max had taken another stride when Hugo said, '*Something* doesn't feel right, this is for sure.'

At this, Max stopped. 'You know, I envy you, Mr Lavigne. You've slipped inside the dance troupe as if you've been a part of the fixtures since ... since the days of Raymond de Guise. Me? I don't know if I'll ever fit. But ...' He shook himself. 'Hey, forget about it. We've got our opening numbers. Christmas in Exile – we're going to make your countrymen proud, Mr Lavigne. The Free French! They'll never have partied like it.'

A smile twitched in the corner of Hugo's lips. 'Let us hope so,' he said, with the merest hint of a bow, and watched Max on his way.

Frank was in his street shoes and itching to be off by the time Hugo returned. 'No taxicab for us, I'm afraid, Hugo,' Frank grinned, 'but it isn't far by bus. Or we can walk it, see a little of London too.'

There was yet light enough to walk by – for, though the autumnal nights were drawing in, the blackout had not yet come. It was only as Hugo and Frank came past the bombed-out railway yards outside Paddington Station that the darkness truly grew deep. 'You forget how badly London's been hit,' Hugo mused, 'when you spend all your days on Berkeley Square.'

He said it so sadly that it made Frank think he was, perhaps, dreaming of a different city altogether. 'And Paris?' Frank asked. 'Is it bad there too?'

'A different kind of wickedness,' Hugo ventured, and Frank fancied he could hear some venom in the Frenchman's voice for the very first time.

'I read about the Vichy government,' said Frank, who made it his business to read the newspapers the guests left behind. 'Marshal Pétain and ... I read he was a hero in the Great War, but now ...'

Hugo clapped Frank on the back. 'Men change across their lifetimes, *mon frère*. So shall you and I. Let us only hope we are on the right side of things, from now until the day we die.'

It seemed an unusually sombre thing for Hugo to say, but Frank supposed the spectre of his home country, overrun and collaborating with the Nazis, was enough to darken anyone's mood. There were millions of young Frenchmen in camps run by the Nazis; a whole generation of boys, like Frank, condemned to hard labour and prison cells. There was, Frank supposed, every chance Hugo's relatives were trapped in that system – and it occurred to him, now, that Hugo never spoke of his life as it had been immediately before he escaped Paris; all he spoke of were the older times, times of beauty and dance – Raymond and the Exhibition Paris, the joy of the java. Perhaps the present was so full of horror that all he held dear was buried in the past.

'But there'll be casserole tonight,' Frank grinned. 'I happen to know Vivienne got a nice piece of lamb from the butcher. Three ration-books, and coupons for the little ones, isn't too bad, especially when we get to graze at the Buckingham Hotel.'

At No 18 Blomfield Road, the smells of Vivienne's lamb casserole were so rich and enticing that it was driving even Arthur – who was yet to taste a thing but mother's milk – wild with pleasure. As Vivienne hovered over each pot, Nancy tried to marshal the children – but that was easier said than done, for Stan was reaching that level of tiredness where he might either fall flat on his face with exhaustion, or start bawling uncontrollably for hours to come.

Vivienne was a wonder: she barely looked harassed as she leapt from pot to pot.

'Perhaps we should feed him,' Nancy said, wincing as Stan

raced around the kitchen table. 'Satisfy the little soul first, before Frank and Hugo come.'

They were late already, Nancy thought, with a glance at the clock on the wall. 'Vivienne,' she ventured, 'about Hugo...'

She'd been about to broach the delicate subject of Vivienne's affection for the Frenchman – for Nancy had not yet forgotten the look they'd shared, nor Hugo's enigmatic words about falling in love time and again – but almost immediately she regretted it. Let Vivienne come to it in her own time, she thought, if she's to come to it at all.

Vivienne looked at her through the steam in the kitchen, inviting her to go on, but Nancy was saved from the moment by a sudden clattering at the front door. 'They're here,' she said, grateful for the distraction. 'I'll bring them through. Dinner time, Stan!' she announced, and swept him up as she hurried into the hall.

But neither Frank nor Hugo stood on the doorstep. All that she saw through the frosted window glass was the figure of the postman retreating down the garden path.

On the step was a single letter.

Nancy's heart stilled.

She hadn't known it would be like this; she hadn't known she would be both thrilling and yet filled with fear.

It was just as she suspected: an envelope of egg-shell blue, a litany of military stamps across its surface, her dear husband's penmanship, spelling out her name.

This, at least, answered one question in her heart – for, if he had written, he was yet alive.

Time lost all meaning. She scooped the letter up, ran a finger under its lip and unfolded the page from inside.

'Vivienne!' she called out. 'Vivienne...' In that same moment, she heard voices from without – the unmistakable sound of her brother's laughter. She spun on the spot, still treasuring the unread letter in her hands. 'They're here,' she called out. 'Vivienne, they're coming.'

Hugo was with him. Nancy could hear that familiar baritone, syrupy and warm. A hope surged up inside her – that, tonight, he and Vivienne might share a little more intimacy, just a few quiet words, perhaps, something to pry open her heart just a little further. She deserved it. After everything she'd been through, she had earned a little hope.

The door opened up. There was Frank, urging Hugo to slip through. 'Got to preserve the blackout, Mr Lavigne!' he grinned, tearing off his coat and boots. 'Nance, it smells amazing!' And soon he was on his knees, scooping up Stan, who had rampaged back towards them.

'Go on through, Hugo,' Nancy beamed, rising on tiptoes to kiss him on the cheek. 'I'll be through presently.'

Frank and Hugo vanished up the hall, and soon Nancy heard the first flurries of conversation, Vivienne coming to life as she led them through the menu she'd spent all afternoon preparing. 'Not quite like the Queen Mary,' Nancy heard her say. And, 'Oh, I rather think you might give them a run for their money,' Hugo said in return.

But all of that could wait.

With her heart beating wild in anticipation, Nancy slipped into the sitting room.

'*Dear Nancy...*'

Those words, those simple words, meant everything to her.

'*You must forgive my tardiness in writing. I am safe and well and stationed in* ▮▮▮ *...*'

Her eyes roamed over the sentences, so quickly that she hardly took them in. It was enough to just *see* his handwriting.

Then her eyes lit upon the centre of the letter, and everything changed.

'*Nancy, you must trust to me now. Remember who I am, and that I have only your best interests at heart.*'

She narrowed her eyes. She held her breath. She heard Vivienne, Frank and Hugo laughing from the kitchen, but suddenly it all felt so far away.

Vivienne was calling her name – 'I'm dishing up, Nancy!' – but, right now, she did not listen.

All that mattered were the words on the page:

'*Nancy, on no account trust Hugo Lavigne. Whoever he says he is, it isn't true. Whatever he says he's in London for, it can't be so. Do not, under any circumstances, let the man into our home. Do not, under any circumstances, permit him to be near our child. And whatever you do, Nancy, do not permit him into the Grand Ballroom. Believe nothing the man tells you – neither about me, nor about himself.*'

There was more, but now Nancy's eyes glazed over. Her name was being called out once more: Vivienne, summoning her to the party.

Nancy ghosted towards them, out of the sitting room, up the hall, the letter still clutched in her hands.

And there was Hugo, sitting at the head of the table, wearing the same dazzling smile that, only moments ago, had seemed so warm and enchanting.

In his arms was Nancy's son Arthur, gurgling with happiness to be seeing his dark-haired uncle once again.

'Hugo is going to finish telling us about the Exhibition Paris,' Frank beamed, buzzing with excitement as he heaped potatoes onto the plates. 'Well, come on, Nance! It's about time we heard the end of this one. I've been waiting for it all summer long…'

Chapter Twenty-Three

The Casino de Paris had come to life.

Thursday night in Paris: lights glittered across the peaks of the city, Notre Dame ringed in gas-lamps like stars brought to earth. Paris was still this evening, and as Ray followed the Seine by foot – just a few brief moments before the dancing began – he wondered, for the very first time, if this really *was* a life he could cast himself into, if the ballrooms and palaces of Europe was where he would build his life, so far from the terraces and railway yards of Whitechapel.

Until Georges had watched Ray and Hannah dance, then given them his blessing, he'd been quite certain this was just a strange detour in the story of his life. Now, somehow, it felt right. The idea he'd be able to relax into the dance, to let it flow naturally, to just be *him* on the dance floor – paying attention to poise and elegance, of course, but never so focused on technique that he forsook the feeling of a song – had transformed the world.

The Casino de Paris was no longer a place he feared.

Now it was a place he was eager to compete in.

The cascade of stars was wheeling above as Ray hurried back

to his digs, changed into the midnight-blue suit Georges had given him, and ran pomade through his voluminous black hair. The feeling of it, he decided, was not so unlike getting ready for a night at the Brancroft Social – but that feeling changed beyond recognition when, at last, he met with Georges in the lobby of the Hotel Acacias, and together they made their way to the Casino. 'You have the look, my boy,' Georges congratulated him. 'Now you need to take it to the dance floor. How do you feel?'

'Like I'm ready, Georges.' Ray didn't know how else to put it, but by some combination of the java and the freeing partnership of Hannah Lindt, he truly knew it to be so.

Dancers and their families were milling in the reception hall of the Casino de Paris, while a phalanx of spectators made their way into the stands. The moment he stepped through the doors, feeling the rush of voices, a wave of heat crashing over him, Ray felt the pull of the dance floor. And what a beauteous feeling this was – to be energised, excited, filled with courage for the fight ahead, instead of allowing all those niggling fears to overcome him.

There was the reason for it all, now: Hugo, a vision in black, approaching him out of the parting crowd.

In the time since Ray had last seen him, he'd trimmed and neatened his beard – but there'd really been no need; even unkempt, as he'd been dancing the java the other night, Hugo retained some old-world elegance. The tuxedo was debonair, but it was the way he was wearing it, unbuttoned and with one hand firmly tucked inside his pocket, that really stood out. He seemed so calm, so nonchalant, even in the frenzy around him.

'You're looking the part, Raymond de Guise,' Hugo grinned as he grew near. 'Feeling it too?'

'Georges, meet Hugo,' Ray smiled, and took him by the hand.

Georges extended his own hand, with just a little more hesitancy than Ray had done. 'You're the young squire who took my charge out dancing, then?' There was admonishment in Georges's tone, but there was curiosity too – for something in Georges seemed to like the cut of Hugo Lavigne. 'And competing against him, no less?'

'Like a hundred others,' Hugo declared, whirling round to show the dancers flocking into the Casino. 'Well, Raymond, I shall see you out there, with the music at its height. *Bon chance, mon frère.*'

Even Ray, with his rudimentary French, understood what this meant. '*Bon chance,*' he replied, and watched as Hugo returned to the crowd.

When he looked up, Georges was wearing an inscrutable expression. 'Remember, my boy, that your fellow dancers – brothers-in-arms as we are – are also your rivals. You must be gentlemanly in rivalry, but you are rivals nonetheless. This competition might make a name for you, or it might make a name for young Hugo – but there can be but one crown. Do you see?'

'Hugo is the one who helped me, Georges. I wouldn't be as confident right now if it wasn't for ...'

Ray had turned round, meaning to wave after Hugo in the crowd – but as soon as he saw him, his words petered into silence. There, among all the other milling dancers, Hugo Lavigne had just taken into his arms his partner for the Exhibition. A dark-eyed angel with a single tight braid of golden hair, small yet statuesque with lips full and red – there stood Ophelia Chalfont.

Ray couldn't help it. In the corner of his eye, he could see that Hannah had arrived at the Casino – and was, even now, searching for him in the crowd – but his feet were already taking him towards Hugo. The Parisian was too enchanted by whatever Ophelia was saying to notice until Ray was already upon them. Indeed, it was Ophelia who saw him first. The serrated look she gave him was one of a woman scorned, but the look Hugo wore was more astonishing still. Only moments ago, Ray had marvelled at how debonair Hugo could seem, even with his dinner jacket slung over his shoulder; he had never imagined that somebody as effortlessly elegant as Hugo could look like a startled rabbit.

'This is your … your partner, Hugo?'

Another unexpected look from Hugo: he sheepishly shrugged. 'I've known Ophelia since we were small. Old family friends, you see – well, everyone knows everyone in the ballrooms of Paris. Our fathers soldiered together.' Hugo paused. 'You don't mind, do you, Ray? It's just that – well, when you chose another, Ophelia was looking for a partner. She didn't want to miss the competition. And when she asked me … well,' and he twirled Ophelia around, 'some girls have a little more about them than others.' Somewhere along the way, Hugo had lost his sheepishness. More boldly at last, he said, 'I know I must seem a little ruthless, but it's ruthlessness you need in the ballroom, Ray. You jettisoned Ophelia, just like I did Cossette. We're all a little bit ruthless when we want to win.'

Ophelia was looking over Ray's shoulder. 'Off with you now, Raymond. Your club girl's waiting.'

Raymond turned. There was Hannah, standing at Georges's side. *Club girl*, he thought. What kind of an insult was that? He was bristling with the injustice of it as he returned to Georges's side – but there was never any chance to give voice to it, for very quickly Hannah had reached for his hand and said, 'Look, Ray. Look what Georges has gifted us.'

In Georges's hands was a silken bag, emblazoned with the embroidered legend of one of the finest tailors on the Rue Saint-Honoré. Delicately, he placed it in Hannah's arms – and, upon unfurling the silk, she revealed a hint of scarlet satin.

'Red and blue, to dance between the white pillars of the Casino de Paris,' Georges intoned, with a smile. 'The Tricolore itself, come to life when the music begins ... Well, my boy,' Georges went on, when he saw Ray's perplexed expression. 'When you don your midnight blue, you become something greater than you once were. So shall it be for Miss Lindt, today.' He smiled. 'My friends, it is time.'

In the kitchen at Blomfield Road, Frank had been gasping and booing as if at some pantomime villain. Nancy remembered taking him to see the village show when he was only a few years older than Arthur; back then, he had cooed and called out in much the same tone of voice as he did now.

Hugo did not seem to mind. He was still mopping up the remnants of Vivienne's lamb casserole with a heel of bread, grinning as he spun the story. 'Georges wondered if I'd been conning Ray all along, of course – if I'd had my sights set on Ophelia, and pushed him towards Hannah Lindt so I could have my wicked way. The truth is, I know that was what Raymond was feeling as well. He walked away from me with such an injured look in his eyes. But ...' He looked up, fixing Nancy with his eyes. 'Nothing could have been further from the truth. We each entered the Exhibition Paris with the partners we were fated for. Fate led us into that competition. I was but its instrument.'

'Rivals, just like Georges said!' Frank thrilled.

'And the competition was almost ready to begin...'

Hugo began to tell them: the open entry, lower championship at the Exhibition Paris would dominate the first two days of the competition, whittling a hundred dancers down to a victorious three couples. It wasn't until the third night that the seasoned professionals, Georges and Antoinette among them, were to take to the stage. 'Ray and I knew – by the following night, we'd either be victorious, or we'd be back in the clubs, dancing the java. But all of that was for the future – because, right now, the couples were flocking into the backstage dressing rooms at the Casino de Paris, the orchestra was marching out, and the first number was about to begin...'

Hugo's words faded in and out. Alone among them, Nancy was not being wrenched back in time, planted among the spectators at the Casino de Paris and hearing the band strike up – for her eyes had been drawn back to the letter in her hands.

The fateful words from Raymond.

On no account trust Hugo Lavigne...

'It was going to be a waltz,' Hugo was saying. 'We'd been forewarned of course – but quite what the music might be, we would have to find out. Now, in this, Ophelia and I were at something of an advantage. The orchestra playing that night was led by a Frenchman named Hubert Bain. I'd danced to his music so many times before – and it just so happened that the Chalfonts, of whom Ophelia was heiress, owned one of the very clubs where Hubert had grown up. In fact, the Orchestre De Hubert Bain had played at Ophelia's elder sister's wedding party. So we fancied ourselves a shoo-in, for the first round at least. And, as for Ray...'

Believe nothing the man tells you – neither about me, nor about himself...

Nancy was still staring at the letter when she sensed Vivienne's eyes upon her. Startled, she pushed the page under the table – for, if Vivienne had seen how fixedly she stared at it, there was every chance Hugo would too.

Frank sat rapt. In the story Hugo was spinning, the music had struck up. Out fanned the couples, all hundred of them, onto the Casino dance floor. The Exhibition Paris was about to begin.

'And there was Raymond,' Hugo beamed, his eyes lifting from Frank and dazzling the other diners. 'He and Hannah, in the very centre of the dance floor. By the heavens, they drew the eye – in midnight blue and startling scarlet, a couple with destiny wreathed around them. And there were we, Ophelia and I, only a stone's throw away…'

Nancy's attention had been momentarily dragged back into the story, Hugo's eyes landing upon her as he led his listeners into the heart of the tale. And perhaps it was because her concentration had lapsed, for just that split second, that she didn't notice Stan's curious fingers darting forward, from across the table where he was sitting on Vivienne's lap. Perhaps it was because she was too consumed with those words – *on no account trust Hugo Lavigne* – that she didn't see him grasping for the paper in her hand.

Too late, Nancy realised where Stan's curiosity had led him. In a moment, he yanked the letter out of her hand. The discarded envelope fluttered to the ground at her feet, but off went Raymond's letter, off across the empty bowls and silver platter, off across the gravy and water jugs, off to the other side of the table – and out of Nancy's grasp.

'Mama!' Stan was shouting, waving it triumphantly in the air. 'Mama! Look!'

Almost a hundred dancers had entered the Exhibition Paris.

In the end, only one couple would win.

Raymond de Guise – for so he was listed on the judges' score sheets – could hardly keep his eyes off Hugo and Ophelia as he and Hannah spun out onto the dance floor. The band, he knew, were just warming up; there would yet be some time before the first song truly began – and just as well, for the sense of composure he'd had when he slid into the Casino de Paris had been suddenly shattered by the sight of Hugo and Ophelia. Hannah could sense it too. 'You've tightened up. Raymond, what's wrong?'

But Ray could hardly give it voice.

His eyes scoured the crowd. Before he saw Hugo, he saw Cossette – the girl Hugo had been turning about the dance floor with when first they'd met. She, too, must have been feeling some hint of betrayal, thought Raymond. She, too, must have been hurting. By the looks of things, she'd found another partner – a beanpole of a Frenchman, with locks of russet gold – so at least she could still compete. Momentarily, Ray found himself churning with bitterness, convinced Hugo had been treating him just as he'd treated Cossette, a commodity to be used and traded around, anything to gain him an advantage in the dance. Then his eyes lit upon Ophelia, just as she slipped into Hugo's arms, and he thought: we've all been a little bit ruthless, to get where we are.

Was that what it took to succeed in the ballroom world?

If he was to truly take flight, did he have to play by these rules?

'Raymond?' Hannah whispered, leaning close to his ear.

Ray had watched her transform backstage, slipping into one of the dressing rooms in her simple day clothes, then emerging from them resplendent in a flowing, elegant gown that shimmered where the dangling Casino lights lit upon it. If Hannah had looked eye-catching in the clubs of Pigalle, now she looked like somebody born to the dance floor: a rush of such vivid colour that everyone else in the Casino seemed grey by comparison.

Yes, bedecked in scarlet red, she was the most striking of all the dancers in the Casino de Paris – but, somehow, Ray still seemed far away.

'*Ray?*' she went on. 'You're not focusing. Raymond, they're about to begin ...'

The band struck up.

The Viennese waltz – a dance from a bygone time, a dance which had thrived across the centuries for the sheer beauty and simplicity of its form. A classic like this had often opened the competitions Ray had taken part in, for it was the best sort of dance to sort the amateur from the professional. By the time this dance was complete, half of the couples who now took their first steps into the music would be jettisoned from the competition. Then, through three further rounds, the victors would be found. *Bon chance*, Hugo had said. Well, Ray needed all the *chance* in the world now. His heart was refusing to beat in time with the music.

'It doesn't matter,' Hannah insisted as they took off. 'Even if Hugo did all this to steal Ophelia – *I'm* here, aren't I? It's me, Ray. *Hannah*. And even Georges agreed, we *fit* ...'

Yes, thought Raymond, this partnership had been blessed by Georges.

And, *yes*, Hannah was here – his Hannah, who he'd chosen himself.

What did it matter if Hugo was manipulating him?

What did it matter if he'd been conned?

He'd got what he wanted, in the end.

Got what he needed to dance at his best.

'Hannah,' he whispered, 'dance on.'

They turned left. They turned right. Each turn and reverse rolled smoothly into the next: heads held high, backs arched back, Raymond and Hannah spun from one side of the dance floor to the other, weaving their way effortlessly among the other competitors. 'Don't look at him,' Hannah said, through closed lips, as they sailed past Hugo and Ophelia. 'Keep it tight now, Raymond. The song's nearly at its end…'

The orchestra brought the number to a close in an elegant swoon of saxophone and horn. Then, each pair of dancers came apart, turning – with hands still clasped – to face the front of the Casino. On a stage at the very head of the hall, a collection of six weathered judges had been carefully considering proceedings. Now, they rose to their feet, joining in the applause which reverberated from the spectators, and gathered over their notes.

'We've done enough,' Hannah said. 'Haven't we, Ray? We *have* done enough?'

'More than enough,' he said. 'It felt good, didn't it? I don't think we slipped up at all.'

'And first rounds, they're about the silly mistakes, the lack of technique.'

Ray nodded, distinctly aware that he was trying to convince himself. 'We'll know in but moments.'

In the end, it took a little longer than that – for the judges seemed to be engaged in some bitter rivalry over their last choices in the competition. The crowd of dancers watched with mounting anticipation as one judge broke away from the rest, muttered animatedly to himself, then rejoined the group in a flourish of passion. 'No!' he seemed to be saying. '*These two!*' Round and round it went, scoreboards being checked, impassioned declarations made, until finally the head judge – a Frenchman of Georges's vintage, with thick charcoal-coloured hair, wisps of white beard, and the look of nobility about him – stood on the edge of the stage and began, 'Number 8, Number 17, Number 6. You will be leaving the competition…'

By the time the judges had done, only half of the dancers remained. Here stood the remaining twenty-four couples, Raymond and Hannah among them.

'Ladies and gentlemen, we reconvene on the hour for our quarter-final quickstep, music – as ever – courtesy of Hubert Bain.'

Raymond looked to Hannah. Her hand was still in his; she squeezed it tight. 'Are you feeling good now? Feeling calmer?'

'I don't know if we ought to be calm or not,' Raymond said. 'But Hannah, it feels *incredible.*'

Backstage, Raymond saw Cossette swallowing her tears as she threw her dancing shoes back in her bag and took off. Hugo and Ophelia, who had also made it through the round, were so engaged in their own conversation that neither of them noticed as Cossette limped past, to disappear from the Casino forever. 'My heart just breaks for her,' Raymond said. 'If she'd been dancing with Hugo…'

'But she's *not*,' Hannah said, clasping his hand. If her eyes had been filled with sympathy for Cosette too, she had found a way to corral it, found a way to cast it aside. 'We've another round to go yet, Ray. The quarter-final to get through. Twenty-four couples, sliced down to twelve. Twelve to six. Six to…'

It was Hannah's fire that brought Ray back to the moment.

'Hannah,' he declared, 'let's go see.'

The dance floor had been opened to the Casino's spectators between rounds, and soon Ray and Hannah were watching from the stands as amateurs turned and pivoted to the storm conjured up by Hubert Bain. The joy out there was enough to make Ray forget that kernel of worry that had been hardening in his stomach. The next round was the foxtrot, a slow one if the rumours he'd heard circulating among the other competitors were correct. Well, he'd danced a formidable foxtrot in Brighton. He'd been given a commendation for his efforts in Hackney. He was just imagining what his first steps here might feel like when he felt a finger tapping on his shoulder – and, upon turning, was confronted with Hugo's dashing good looks.

While Ray had been lost in his dreaming, Hannah had stepped aside. Now, it was only Hugo who dominated his vision. In his hands was a small silver hip flask, its stopper already unscrewed. Hugo was offering it up as he said, 'A peace offering, Mr de Guise.'

Ray's eyes flashed between Hannah and Hugo. Upon seeing him, he'd been suddenly full of fire – but, now that their eyes met, all the enmity and wonder at betrayal seemed to melt away. Ray took the hip flask, but did not put it to his lips. Instead, he screwed the cap back into place and tossed it through the air, so that Hugo had to scramble to catch it. 'You tempted me with enough last night,' he grinned.

'It helped loosen the soul a little, did it not?'

Ray rolled his eyes. 'I'm going to let the music loosen the soul this day,' he declared. 'But I'll let you raise a glass with me when I beat you in this competition.'

At last, Hugo returned Ray's look with a broad grin of his own. 'This is the fighting spirit I see before me.' The thought had pleased him greatly. 'To the victors!' he declared, and took a swig from the hip flask himself. Then his eyes landed on Hannah. 'You two are the perfect fit, of course. Me, I am finding Ophelia altogether too *proper* – a little too stiff, a little too tutored. It is this, perhaps, that your body responded to, Raymond.' His mask fell away for a second and, with a sincerity that took Ray by surprise, he said, 'Please don't think me a scoundrel, Ray. I really do think Miss Lindt is the better partner for you. Indeed,' and in his voice was a certain wistfulness Ray had not encountered before, 'I rather think she might be the better partner for *me* as well.'

'I'm afraid I'm spoken for,' Hannah declared – and her hand was just snaking out to take Ray's own, when out on the dance floor three shrill blasts of a whistle rang out.

'The quarter-final,' Ray marvelled. 'Well, Hugo, may the best man win!'

Ray was feeling buoyant this time, feeling like he *belonged*. It was this feeling, he was certain, that would carry him through. In the heart of the dance floor, he took Hannah in hold – and this time, his eyes didn't flit around the Casino, seeking out Hugo and Ophelia, for his heart was bent on one thing alone: casting itself into the music, and riding its waves until the song reached its end.

This was *his* dance. He knew it as the piano and trumpets took up, as the percussionists drove the music onward, as he and Hannah pitched into the foxtrot's first step. The rumours backstage had been way off the mark: this was no slow foxtrot, but almost a quickstep, a song whose intensity only grew with every passing bar. Yes, Ray *liked* this. At moments, he closed his eyes, the better to feel the music he was exploring. Hannah turned with him. 'More gently now,' she whispered at one point – but Ray knew this music instinctively, felt like it was pouring out of his very heart. He danced on.

Then, the music stopped.

'I think we did it,' he whispered, brimming with confidence. 'I think we did enough.'

Even so, it was an agonising wait as, up on stage, the judges congregated, remonstrated with one another, started assembling their little slips of cards and finally – after all the false starts, the serrated looks, the dramatic rolls of the eye and the stately denouncements – began to recite the names and numbers of every entrant.

'Couple 23,' the weathered elder judge declared. 'M. Hugo Lavigne and Mme Ophelia Chalfont.' He paused, if only for dramatic effect. 'Congratulations, you will remain in the Exhibition.'

Some distance from Ray and Hannah, Hugo swept Ophelia into his arms and spun her around.

Ray squeezed Hannah's hand. 'Us next,' he said. He could feel the absolute certainty of it.

One after another, couples left the dance floor. A seventh couple pranced into the stands, eager for whatever refreshments their tutors had provided backstage. An eighth keenly followed, then a ninth and a tenth. By the time the judges gathered to announce the eleventh, and penultimate, couple to succeed, Ray's confidence had turned to doubt. Now, though he still clung to Hannah's hand, he dared not breathe a word, nor look her in the eye.

'Couple Number Ten,' the judge finally breathed out, with what Ray was certain was a reticent look over his shoulder. 'M. Raymond de Guise and Mme Hannah Lindt – you will be the final couple to join us in the next round of the Exhibition. To all our other competitors, I thank you for your passion and spirit this day.'

The other dancers were fanning out, either disconsolate or

contented with their lot, but Ray and Hannah stood marooned in the middle of the dance floor. Ray's heart, which had been keeping such a tumultuous rhythm, was suddenly stilled. 'We're through,' Hannah finally said, and only then did Ray turn to look at her. 'It's OK, Ray. We did it. We did it…'

The spectators were returning to the dance floor, eager to embrace the music of the intermission, and Ray and Hannah had to weave their way between them to disappear back through the stands. There, in the dressing rooms backstage, Hugo and Ophelia were still dancing, giddy with the drama of the moment. Ray was drifting towards them when, suddenly, another figure dominated his eyeline: Georges, that titan of a dancer, striding between the amateurs to reach Ray first.

'How's your heart faring, young Mr de Guise?'

Ray said, 'Beating its own quickstep, I think, but I'm calmer now.'

'A quickstep, when it ought to have been a foxtrot,' Georges smiled, ruefully. 'Raymond, do you understand what became of you out there? Do you know why you gave the judges such pause?' Georges's eyes took in Hannah. 'You, Miss Lindt? I hazard that you see what my ward does not?'

'We were ahead of the music,' Hannah whispered.

Ray looked at her severely.

'I'm afraid Miss Lindt has the right of it, Raymond. You were anticipating too much, a tiny fraction of a beat ahead of Mr Bain and his musicians. The judges could perceive it. Raymond, you had about you the air of a horse champing at the bit.' He smiled. 'They'll be watching you keenly from this moment on – more keenly than ever. You survive this round by the skin of your teeth, but you won't have such forgiveness again.' Georges rubbed his chin, thoughtfully, as he brooded on the matter. 'It's the club dancing,' he finally declared. 'Yes, it's loosened the soul – but this isn't a club. It's a competition – and *craft* counts. Unbridled passions are one thing, young man, but you must master those passions to succeed in the ballroom.' Georges stepped back. He was about to turn away when he looked at Hannah and said, 'You danced beautifully, my dear. I was wrong to doubt this partnership – but, between you, you will need to master the maelstrom, if you're to have any hope of reaching the final.'

In the kitchen at Blomfield Road, Nancy's heart was beating as wildly as her husband's had been back in 1926. No longer was there any hiding it. On the other side of the table, Stan waved Raymond's letter furiously back and forth.

'The semi-final,' Hugo was saying, holding Frank rapt even while Stan set up his hullabaloo. 'Only one dance stood between us and the final of the Exhibition Paris. One quickstep to show the judges what magic we could weave.'

Stan's shrill cry silenced Hugo. As one, he and Frank turned along the long barrel of the table, to find Vivienne wrestling with her son.

'My friends,' Hugo ventured, 'is the young man, perhaps, *bored* of my tale?' His lips curled upwards in a smile that Nancy thought looked suddenly supercilious, as if all the charm of old had been but an act, another of the disguises that dancing men wore.

'No, no, nothing like that,' Vivienne returned.

'One of these boys needs changing,' Nancy declared, lifting Arthur to her nose, 'and Vivienne, I'm afraid my son is not to blame. But look, I'll help. You must stay, listen to the end of the story, and …'

Suddenly, Vivienne too was on her feet. At last, she seemed to have understood the peculiarity of the situation, the way Nancy's sudden nerves had set everything on edge. 'Nonsense! Frank's the only audience Mr Lavigne needs. Nancy, we'll go together.'

Moments later, Vivienne was marching after Nancy, leaving the kitchen – and its duo of confused voices – behind. It wasn't until Nancy had taken her first step on the stairs that she looked back and, exhaling in relief, plucked the letter from Stan's grasping hands.

'What is it?' Vivienne breathed.

'Not here,' said Nancy. Then she beckoned Vivienne to follow – and together they hurried to the nursery at the top of the stairs.

She pressed Raymond's letter into Vivienne's hands. 'Read it.'

Stan was still making shrill cries, leaping up to try and seize the letter once more, while Vivienne marched through Raymond's words. Nancy had to wrestle him away, Arthur now lying on the mat as if about to be changed, so that Vivienne could finish.

'But Nancy,' she ventured, 'what does it *mean?* What can it possibly mean?' Vivienne sidled past, opening the door just a crack and listening out, as if to make doubly certain Frank and Hugo remained at the dining table below. 'They're *friends*, aren't they? What's Hugo doing here if they're not friends?'

'All I know is what's in that letter,' Nancy returned, trying to make some sense of all her jumbled thoughts. '*Whoever he says he is, it isn't true. Whatever he says he's in London for, it can't be so.*'

Here, Vivienne picked up the telling. '*Do not, under any circumstances, permit him to be near our child. Do not permit him into the Grand Ballroom …*' Vivienne shook herself. 'He's wrong though, isn't he? He's made some mistake. He's thinking of somebody different, somebody scurrilous from their past. Not Hugo…' Vivienne stopped. 'Hugo dances with Stan. He's cradled Arthur. Nancy, you got him a job in the Grand Ballroom – and he's…'

'He's been charm personified,' Nancy concluded.

'And don't they love him there?'

'If it wasn't for Marcus, he'd be leading the troupe. He won their confidence in but moments.'

'Then there's some mistake, Nancy. There has to be. What possible reason would there be for Hugo to arrive on our doorstep with a story like this?' Vivienne pressed the letter back into Nancy's hands, then scooped up Stan.

'I don't know,' Nancy admitted. 'But doesn't it come down to this? Who do we trust more, Vivienne? Hugo… or Raymond?'

Somewhere beyond the blackout blinds, somewhere far across the city, the low moan of the sirens started to sound.

'He's already in our house,' breathed Nancy, clinging to the letter.

'He's already in the Grand Ballroom,' said Vivienne, 'and…'

There came the clatter of footsteps on the stairs. A hand hovered over the nursery-door handle. Fingers rapped on the other side of the wood. 'Nancy?' Frank ventured, from the hallway. 'Vivienne?'

Nancy opened the door. There hung her brother, his eager eyes now radiating concern. 'We'll be down presently, Frank. Take…' she shared a secret look with Vivienne, then surreptitiously folded the letter into the folds of her dress; it would not do to involve Frank in this, not yet, '…Mr Lavigne down to the shelter. We're on our way.'

Frank gave his sister a regimental salute, then turned to gallop down the stairs.

At the top of the landing, Nancy took Vivienne's hand. 'Not a word,' she counselled.

Down through the house they came, through the kitchen and out into the dark garden beyond. The door to the Anderson shelter was already falling shut, so Nancy hurried across the dell, Arthur in her arms, and rapped at the corrugated door. Soon, Frank was pushing it back open – and Nancy and Vivienne were sliding within.

There was Hugo, standing hunched against the curved roof at the foot of the shelter. 'The young gentlemen,' he smiled, inclining his head towards the children, 'they are well? Fit and strong – and clean enough – to face the night?'

Nancy could hear the distant report of the ack-ack guns in the east. Holding Arthur more tightly to her breast, she found herself picturing Raymond in the heat of Cairo, burnished by the desert sun, carrying every scar of the battles he'd fought, his mind turning to desperation when he heard tell of Hugo Lavigne in his ballroom.

His hand feverishly writing out the letter she'd just received, wondering if it was already too late.

'Mrs de Guise,' Hugo ventured, more cautiously now, 'you are white as a ghost. The bombers, they are not so very near?'

Frank had scurried to the shelter door. Opening it but a crack, he peered into the night. 'Not yet, Hugo. We should be safe here.' He paused. 'Safe enough, perhaps, for you to finish your story?'

At once, Nancy marched to the bedstead dominating the shelter's far corner, and settled upon the old mattress and blankets piled there. 'Another night, Frank,' she said, severely.

'Another night, Nance? But we might be here until—'

'Not now,' Nancy insisted, her eyes brimming with some dark authority Frank recognised only from the days when he was young, and Nancy had to admonish him not to stray too far from her side. Then she caught herself, took in the bank of faces staring at her and added, 'Nights like these still fill me with horrors, I'm afraid. It's worse since Arthur came.' She stared into her baby's eyes; he stared back at her, with the eyes of his father. What was it Raymond was trying to say? What dark history was invoked in that letter? Was it a personal enmity, a friendship turned to bitterness and rivalry – or was it something altogether more troubling still?

She trusted her husband with her life.

His word was his bond, his promise, his honour.

He might have written anything.

And yet he had written of Hugo Lavigne, sent a warning halfway across the world.

Believe nothing the man tells you – neither about me, nor about himself…

'Perhaps something lighter, for tonight,' she said, suddenly aware how they were still gazing upon her. 'Something to keep the spirits up.'

'Then let's speak of Christmas,' Frank said. It was almost on the horizon. In a few short weeks, Nancy would be rallying the Housekeeping girls to decorate the great Norwegian fir that always stood proudly in the Buckingham reception. 'Christmas in Exile, the grandest night of the year. It's coming together, isn't it, Hugo? The dances are almost ready. Mr Allgood's putting together a set they'll still be talking about by spring – and Mr Dudgeon, too, he seems to be as much a part of it as Max! Maybe you'll get to sneak a look this year, Nance. Then you'd see … all the free governments of the world, dancing the foxtrot!'

Hugo beamed. 'All my countrymen, the brave Free French. As I understand it, two dozen are already in attendance. This is my chance to give them my gratitude for all they are doing.

To look them in the eye and tell them: we stand together. One hopes that M. de Gaulle himself will…'

A quake shook the city. Every voice in the shelter died. Moments later, Stan started crying. His fear was echoed in Arthur; on Nancy's shoulder, the baby started crying too.

Christmas is coming, thought Nancy, but we have to get there first.

And as that thought loomed in her head, her eyes returned to Hugo Lavigne, and the letter whose words were still seared upon her thoughts.

Believe nothing the man tells you – neither about me, nor about himself…

If Raymond was right, if nothing Hugo said could be trusted, if every word the man spoke was a lie, then what exactly was he doing here? What had really brought him to their door?

What did the debonair Frenchman really want?

November 1941

Chapter Twenty-Four

DISPATCHES FROM THE BUCKINGHAM HOTEL!
NEW YORK TIMES, NOVEMBER 11, 1941

By Jackson Ford, your man in LONDON

Armistice Day at the Buckingham Hotel and while talk of the United States returning to the fray, just as they did in 1917, proliferates around the Buckingham Hotel, its place as the single topic of conversation is quickly being snuffed out by the announcement of CHRISTMAS IN EXILE, the Buckingham's celebration of the defiant fallen governments who make their home in this rich, vibrant city: London, the last stand for the conquered dynasties of Europe. Rumour says that the ball will be attended by some very special guests – and it is no secret to say that security arrangements are more visible in these hallowed Buckingham halls than they have ever been. In an age like this, the gentleman nursing his Martini in the Candlelight Club might either be a ballroom dancer or an agent of the Crown, tasked with keeping this hotel's guests safe from harm. After all, the Buckingham Hotel has long been the playground of princes. But this week, as I waltz from ballroom to Queen Mary and back again, the feeling in the air is of something very special to come. In a few short weeks, the world will gather in the Grand Ballroom: an act of defiance, an act of joy, an act of celebration in life.

Who among us can ever say we are truly in exile, when we have found such a bounteous second home as this?

A good day was when only one or two minor (and easily disguisable) mistakes were made – and that made this a magnificent, superlative, *unheralded* day, because Annie Brogan had just finished polishing the armoire in the final suite of her shift and returned to the service elevator proud in the knowledge that today had been *flawless*.

It was all the birthday present she needed as well, because on this chill November day, Annie Brogan turned sixteen years old.

By the time she returned to the Housekeeping hall, she was having to tell herself to contain that pride. The moment Annie appeared, they broke out in song.

'Happy birthday to YOU!
Happy BIRTHDAY to ... YOU!
HAPPY BIRTHDAY DEAR ANNIE!
Happy! Birthday! To! YOU!'

Annie had heard the vicious crack of the ack-ack guns sounding with less volume than this, but at least the girls were tuneful. As they broke into cheers and applause, Annie fancied they had even been working on their harmonies.

They'd been working on more than that. One moment, Annie was being mobbed by the Housekeeping girls, bounced up and down as if she was a toddler receiving the birthday bumps; the next, the girls were fanning apart to reveal a mountainous, teetering Victoria sponge standing pride of place in the middle of the lounge table.

'What do you think?' Rosa declared, seizing the cake knife

and preparing to do battle with the sponge. 'I know it ain't got the smooth edges of them dainty things they make for afternoon tea in the Queen Mary – but, well, it's got charm, ain't it?' She carved the first piece, a thick wedge oozing fresh cream and raspberry preserve. 'It's us that made it. Mrs de Guise let Mary-Louise off shift specially. But it's that boy down in the restaurant you ought to thank.'

As she handed Annie the plate, then wrestled her down into Mrs de Guise's seat at the head of the table – Nancy, Annie noticed, was nowhere to be found – Annie stammered, 'Victor?'

'That's the one,' said Rosa, and proceeded to pour Annie her tea. There was cream for this too, a jug filled with thick, heavenly white, the like of which hadn't been seen in the Housekeeping Lounge since before the rationing began. The best was always kept for guests; cream could hardly be wasted on a chambermaid. 'When we said it was for you, there wasn't a thing he wouldn't do to help. Well, it's only a few eggs, a jug of cream, some jams. Nothing that would go missing in a place like those kitchens.'

'You'll have spilt more since Christmas, Annie!' one of the other girls hooted.

Any other day, Annie might have taken umbrage at that – especially on a day when she'd proven, without doubt, that flawlessness was possible – but the mere mention of Victor had set up a tumult in her heart. She'd been wanting to go to him for countless nights – wanting to ask him about that stroll they might take, the tea they might share, the afternoon they might potter together up and down the Regent Street arcades – but every time her courage had deserted her, for the secret she'd been carrying had grown more heavy by the day. If she saw Victor, if she looked into his eyes, she was quite certain she'd spill it all: 'It was Billy in the kitchens that night. My *brother* helping himself to your larders. *My* Billy, risking it all ...' And then what

325

would happen? Recriminations, no doubt. Billy, cast out of the Buckingham Hotel. Billy, out on the streets – or worse, locked up in some cell – so that her family was in even worse tatters than it was before.

Tonight was going to be even worse, because surely he'd be there, at their parents' lodgings, before the fall of the deep November dark. Surely he'd have been invited to take tea with them too. Billy Brogan: their hero, who'd spirited something out of nothing, who'd promised to put them back in their home by Christmas night; who'd break their hearts if ever they found out exactly what he was doing in their name.

'Annie, are you all right?'

It was Mary-Louise's voice. Annie looked up to find the older chambermaid studying her closely. Of course, Mary-Louise had been Billy's sweetheart for a little time, after he'd come back from Dunkirk. Probably she would think him a blackguard, too, if she knew what her war hero was doing, now that he'd been sent home.

'Oh I'm – I'm fine,' Annie stammered, but her sudden change in demeanour hadn't gone unnoticed by the other girls. 'It's Victor!' they had started cooing. 'Oh, lor', the mere mention of his name!'

'We'll go get him, shall we, girls?'

'Drag him off shift!'

'Make him a nice plate up, girls. Then him and Annie can have a get-to-know-you kind of chat.'

Only then did she say, 'I was just thinking – well, I should take some cake home for my parents. They'll love it. And ... and it's *lovely*, girls, that's what it is. Lovely that you all remembered. And ...' She looked around, desperate for some other distraction. 'We should leave a piece for Mrs de Guise too.'

'Oh, she's off with Mr Knave,' one of the other girls chimed in. 'She looked grave too, when she trotted off to see him. She could probably do with a big slice, lots of cream, when she gets back.'

'Exactly!' exclaimed Annie. 'And a half pot of tea too.'

It gave her just the distraction she needed. Moments later, she was arranging the impromptu afternoon tea on Nancy's desk, just inside the office at the back of the lounge, then scurrying back to the gathering of girls. 'My ma's going to love your cake, Mary-Louise. Rosa, she'll want you baking for *her* birthday next. It's only next month. The day after Christmas.'

Evidently the girls had wanted the party to go on and on, but all those thoughts of Billy and Victor had sent Annie's heart racing in two completely different directions.

It's going to be OK, she told herself. It's just a birthday night. And if Billy's there – why, there's no reason to even mention it. It can wait for another day. Whatever happens next doesn't have to happen right now. There's still time. Time to work out what's for the best. Time to find the path between right and wrong, before the truth worked its way free – and turned every last corner of Annie's world to ruin.

Only a short distance away, Nancy faced Walter Knave across the Hotel Director's desk while he studied the letter she'd just handed over.

'So you see, sir,' she went on, after allowing the silence to linger, 'I thought it appropriate to bring you into my husband's confidences. I know you spent only a little time with him, sir, that your tenures at the hotel did not overlap for long – but I hope you know, by reputation perhaps, that he is not a man given to histrionics. He is a fine, dependable, honest man...' At this, Walter Knave furrowed his brow; he had, of course, heard the story of Raymond's background – the East End roustabout who had adopted airs and graces when he entered the ballroom world. There'd been plenty of dishonesty in this, once upon a time, for he'd been hired to the hotel on the assumption he came from aristocratic stock, a notion that Raymond had worked hard to perpetuate. 'I think it would be wise to take what he says in the sombre tone it was intended.'

Mr Knave looked up. 'What do you think is the *specific* accusation Raymond is levelling?'

Nancy replied, 'There's much a man can't say in his correspondence. Letters get censored. Whole passages blacked out…'

Walter nodded. 'That's true, Mrs de Guise, but what I'm trying to get at is…' He waved the letter, airily. 'I'm given to understand – not being of the ballroom world myself, of course – that theirs is a world of deeply held rivalries. What I'm trying to say is that, when *I* read this letter, that's what *I* see. One dancer scorning another; some old bitterness, some old enmity, coming to the surface again. We all loathe it when worlds collide – and, forgive me for saying it, but your husband is no stranger to that particular feeling. As you know, he allowed the hotel management to believe he was born of good stock for many years before it was revealed that his origin was, shall we say, a little more rough around the edges than that…'

Nancy bristled.

'I hardly think my husband would write this letter, in a time of war, over some petty argument from fifteen years ago…' Nancy thought, suddenly, of Raymond watching Hugo dance with Ophelia, back at the Casino de Paris. Of course, some little piece of her wondered if it had all been a fiction, if Hugo had been making everything up all along – but to what end? *Why?* And besides, even if he *was* telling the truth, was that an argument that could have prompted such panic and concern so many years later?

'Men can harbour long grudges, if their pride is injured. I've lived a long life, Mrs de Guise. I've seen men resort to all manner of peculiar behaviours,' he coughed gently. 'Also, it *is* possible that Raymond is simply untrusting of another champion dancer in the ballroom where they once called him *King*. The war took that away from your husband—'

'He was proud to sign up,' Nancy interjected, sensing some element of disrespect in the Hotel Director's tone, then quickly remembering her place.

'But the ballroom is his home, Mrs de Guise, not the battle-front. So, when he heard about a debonair dancer from the old times who had come to stake a claim to the Grand, mightn't it be possible ...'

Nancy prepared to stand, then took a breath and simply straightened herself instead. 'I hardly think my husband is a petty man, Mr Knave.'

'But these are not petty things. And ...' There was something else Mr Knave wanted to say; he seemed to be dancing around it, as awkwardly as a novice in the ballroom. 'There's no right way to say this, Mrs de Guise, so you'll forgive me for being plain. But Hugo hasn't only placed himself at the centre of Raymond's old ballroom; as I understand it, he's placed himself at the centre of Raymond's family home as well. Mightn't it be that Raymond distrusts Hugo, simply for his proximity to *you?*'

Nancy just stared, dumbfounded.

'Do you understand my meaning?'

'I do,' said Nancy, severely. 'But Raymond is not a jealous man.'

'Perhaps not, but these are not ordinary times.'

Nancy reached for the letter. 'My husband has nothing to fear,' she said, 'but I believe we might, Mr Knave.'

'I should like to retain Raymond's letter, for a little time,'

Mr Knave said. 'With your permission,' he added hastily, upon recognising the disconcerted look on Nancy's face. 'I'll be honest, Mrs de Guise – I am hopeful this amounts to nothing more than I've said: a professional jealousy, a worry for the honour of the wife he misses so much. But it would be wise for me to brood on this matter, and perhaps defer to Mr Hastings and the Board.' He stopped. 'Are we in agreement?'

Nancy knew her cue when it came. In moments, she was on her feet, nodding her assent and retreating to the doorway. 'Mr Knave,' she said, before she left him to his thoughts, 'I hope you take what my husband has to say in the same serious spirit he sent it.'

She was still trying to shake off the feeling of Mr Knave's dismissiveness when she reached the Housekeeping hall – and, as she reached the door to the lounge, a sudden pang moved through her. If Mrs Moffatt had still been here, Nancy might have had somebody to turn to; if Mrs Moffatt had been on the other side of this door, cleaning up the mess the girls had left in their wake, Nancy might have been able to sink into the armchair in the office, unwrap one of the older lady's barley sugars, and pour out every niggle and fear in her heart.

But Mrs Moffatt was gone. It was Nancy, now, who had to sit in the office, listen to the girls and their problems, raise up a family around her and protect it from all ills.

She opened the door.

At least the girls had left the lounge in good order. She pottered past the long breakfasting table and through into the dark alcove of her office, lighting the lamp as she came.

There, on the table, was a fat slice of Victoria sponge, oozing out raspberry preserve and fresh cream.

*

It was six months since Albert Yard had been destroyed, but now it was being remade.

Billy had come at intervals over the last weeks, sometimes to chinwag with the construction workers (he had found it geed them along if he brought them a few odds and ends from the Buckingham as well), and sometimes just to gawk at this thing he had set in motion. Number 62 was not the only house along the row being hauled back into existence – and, indeed, the lights were already on behind the blackout blinds of the less-devastated houses at either end of the row – but, to Billy, it was the most magnificent. It was like watching the devastation in reverse. Very soon, there would be windows, and shutters, and blackout blinds of their own. Behind those blinds, they'd string up Christmas lights and roast a turkey. Then, at last, he could set this thing behind him. 'Saying goodbye to Camden Town' – that's how he'd come to think of it. He'd doff his cap to Mr Sellers, give the Ankers a fat bonus comprising a nice bottle from the store at the Candlelight Club, and then sink back into his duties in the post room.

One thing was for certain: he didn't mean to dip his toes in these particular waters again. It wasn't only that dirty look Annie had given him, though of course that rankled, it was the feeling of being *watched* all of the time. Billy wasn't sure how those secret service agents did it, always trading in secrets and lies, always pretending to be people they weren't. There were plenty of that sort flitting about the Buckingham Hotel – he'd become quite sure of it, over the years. But carrying a secret meant always looking over your shoulder. It meant never being *calm*.

He was standing by the place the old gate used to be when one of the construction workers, a burly man with his grey overalls rolled up to his elbows, ambled out of the scaffold and approached. 'Now, young Billy,' he remarked, removing his cap as he drew near. 'She's looking fine, ain't she?'

'She certainly is, Mr Law.'

Thomas Law was, as he was often keen to point out, an expatriated Yorkshireman who'd settled in London some time after the Great War. In 1919, the company he'd founded had been but him and a couple of the lads he'd fought with in Flanders; now it numbered fifty men, and together they had brought devastated roads back to life all across the savaged city. There was money to be made in disaster, as Billy had spent the last months proving.

'The problem's going to be getting that roof on before these first snows roll in,' said Thomas, one eye on the heavens. 'If it ain't the Luftwaffe, it's the blizzards that'll stop us. That sky looks swollen.'

'Does it make a difference, Mr Law?'

Thomas beamed. He was, Billy had observed, the sort of man who liked a bit of deference, who liked to lord it over those outside of his profession who didn't quite have the same skills. Billy was fine with that; he'd been letting the good lords of the Buckingham Hotel speak down to him for years. 'Oh, it's been the bane of builders since long before there was a city on this river, Mr Brogan. When the wind and the rain blow through, it's a devil to be putting up windows and walls – and a roof's the worst of the lot.'

Billy bristled. He'd been adamant about Christmas. That was the image he'd kept in mind since he'd made that first foray to Camden Town, the pact he'd made with himself on the night the bombs came down. His family were going to celebrate Christmas around the hearth in their own home. 'Will you get it done, Mr Law?'

'Well, that's where we get to the sticky part of this conversation, boy. Because you're a week in arrears already, aren't you? My lads are working every last hour of daylight to get this done, racing against the turn of the season – and I've been paying them out of my own pocket, the very same place where *you're burning a hole.*'

Billy screwed up his eyes.

'Come on, young man, out with it. I can't go on paying these boys on promises. I'm going to need to see something soon. Preferably, lad, by fall of night.'

Billy's first thought was that it was already growing dark. His second was that legitimate businessmen could be equally as intimidating as those who worked in the city's shadows. Thomas Law had always come across as a magnanimous, generous man – but so, he supposed, was Mr Stockdale when he spoke to his customers; last year, Ken had been the kindest of souls – until, suddenly, he wasn't.

'I've got it, Mr Law,' said Billy. It was only the whitest of lies; the money was almost within his grasp, but things had inevitably slowed down since Annie's ultimatum. He hadn't been able to make a proper delivery in weeks; a house could not be built on scraps from the trolleys and what plunder the Ankers brought in. 'I haven't let you down before, have I? I've been a good customer. I've just ... hit upon a couple of snags.' Billy's face had turned pale as the clouds above. 'Two more days. Can you cope with it for two more days?'

Thomas Law's face darkened. Then, after a pregnant pause, he said, 'The lads are already paid up until then, so I suppose there's no more harm in it. But I'll be moving them on to another site if there isn't payment by then. I can't say fairer than that, Bill. If you want your folks back home for Christmas, you'll meet me here with this last payment in full in two nights' time – and I'll shake your hand like a man.'

Billy could feel the knots tightening further in his stomach as he returned to the old laundry van and set off across the river.

He didn't want to be such a disappointment to Annie.

But he didn't want to let his parents down either.

It was like two people were fighting inside him, two boxers descending to a brawl.

He reached the north side of the river and pushed the van through the encroaching darkness until he had reached Camden Town.

It was going to be all right, because there were the Ankers boys, waiting in the rubble like they always did. He could tell they were there by their silhouettes in the darkness, his two loyal hands waiting in the ruins of an old haberdashers, their own van at an incline on the kerb.

They knew he was there as well. He only hoped he hadn't kept them waiting, for there was a long, lonely drive ahead of them – and, no doubt, they'd end up sleeping in some hedgeback rather than risk the blacked out roads. He hailed them once, then hurried round to the back of the van and drew out the battered leather suitcase he'd once salvaged from the hotel: left behind by some travelling businessman, no doubt, somebody so grand he might hardly have noticed. Inside it lay the two bottles of G&J Greenall he'd rescued from the Candlelight Club – the Ankers were partial to a rich man's liquor, and this brandy was from 1893, a perfect vintage – and a selection of perfumes and lotions he'd lifted from one of the suites when he'd been asked to attend a guest and take down a message. The Ankers needed their little boons to keep going; just like Thomas Law & Sons, they could not keep going on promises alone.

'Here you go, boys,' Billy began, forcing himself to grin – anything that he might seem breezy and unconcerned as he approached. Then he handed over the case. 'There's a pair of crystal glasses in there, some silver teaspoons too. They ought to fetch a few bob at a pawnbroker's – just keep it out of London, there's the Buckingham crest on those spoons.'

The Ankers boys were but hulks in the darkness, but somehow Billy sensed something was wrong. Ordinarily, when he brought them their payment, they couldn't be more eager in taking it into their hands.

'Boys?' Billy began.

'I'm sorry, Bill, old mucker,' Rod Ankers began, in his dull, bovine voice, 'it's nothing personal, you know, and we're good lads at heart, so we don't want to diddle you. So you hang on to those silver teaspoons. Maybe take them down some pawn-breaker's of your own.'

'We can't take payment off of you,' Dirk chipped in, with a voice just as bovine, 'it wouldn't be right.'

'Well, none of it's *right*,' Rod went on, 'but this would be wronger than most.'

'We can't take payment, Bill, because we don't work for you anymore.'

It took Billy a moment for the words to properly sink in. The Ankers boys were not short of intellect – it took a keen mind to work bees – but something was often lost in translation between them and their rustic, country ways, and Billy's city smarts. He stammered, 'Wh-what are you talking about?' but the Ankers boys were already plodding back to their van.

Billy hurried to keep up. 'I've got the contractors waiting,' he called after them. 'You know what I'm trying to do. The snows are coming in. There's a roof to be...'

Rod Ankers turned swiftly round and, upon seeing Billy careering towards him, clapped a hand on the younger man's shoulder.

The force of it stopped Billy dead in his tracks.

'I'm sorry, Bill. I truly am. But, look, it's like this: for these last weeks, it's like we've been running this ourselves. Now, we're loyal lads – and God knows we're sympathetic for your lot – but, well, what are you *doing* now, Bill? A few silver teaspoons to pay us for what we bring in off the farms – well, that's very welcome, and thank you *awfully* – but it's been us doing the deliveries and, lately, it's been us sourcing *all* the goods too.'

By this point, Dirk Ankers had already slipped behind the wheel of their van, and now the engine choked into life. 'Used to be you could get almost anything from the Buckingham, Bill. The bits we brought in were just the cream on the cake. Quite literally!' he laughed. 'There's plenty of thick cream flowing out of Forsyth's farm. But, look, if you're not keeping up your side of things, you can hardly expect us to—'

'*You're* taking over?' Billy snapped. Never before in his life had his demeanour changed so swiftly. A moment ago, he'd been bewildered; now, some incandescent fury rose up in him. The feeling was so unusual, it shook him to his core. '*You're* pushing me out?'

'We got another offer,' said Rod.

Billy's anger faded into understanding. He stood there, dumb-founded, while the Ankers turned the van round. Then, before they wheeled off, he cried out, 'Stockdale?'

Through the idling van's window, Rod and Dirk shrugged. 'It just makes sense,' Rod shrugged. 'Mr Stockdale's a rum chap. He'll pay us a steady wage – just to source stuff off the farms, you know, like we used to do for Ken. None of this playing delivery boys.'

'Well, what about *my* enterprise? What about *that*? Listen to me, boys – Stockdale's lining his own pockets, just like Ken was! I'm doing this for my family.'

Rod Ankers seemed to hesitate at that, for the notion had

clearly been preying on him – but Dirk had no such compunctions. 'That's your problem, Billy, not ours. We got families too.'

There was no time to say more, for the Ankers were already driving away, their van juddering over the rubble-strewn road as it disappeared into the blackness over Gladstone Park.

Billy's heart was hammering as he tumbled back to his own van, then sat slumped over the steering wheel trying to make sense of the last half hour of his life. It was some time before his hands stopped shaking.

It should have been so different. Right now, he ought to have been driving back into Lambeth, safe in the knowledge that, by tomorrow night, he could run a round of the shops, collecting up his takings – and then delivering them to Thomas Law. He ought to have been sashaying into his parents' lodging, toasting Annie's birthday and telling them all that the moment was nigh, the Brogans would be going home. Perhaps even Annie would have congratulated him, then. Perhaps all the horror and judgement in her eyes would have melted away, once she knew the end was near.

But *now*…

It would all have been different, if it wasn't for that night in the kitchens. If Annie hadn't realised it was him. If Annie hadn't made that ultimatum…

Annie, he thought.

He picked himself up.

Because he knew exactly where Annie was tonight. He knew that, even now, she was with their parents in the lodgings, celebrating her birthday with tea and cake and cards.

And if Annie was there, then it meant there was no chance of bumping into her at the Buckingham Hotel.

All it would take was one more foray into those larders. A few crates loaded up – and it would be done.

*

One by one, the waiters took off by the rear restaurant door.

One by one, the kitchen porters hurried off into the night, faces red and ruddy from their day's toil.

By now, Billy's presence was surely being missed in Lambeth – but that would be quickly forgotten if he walked through the doors, declaring they were all going home. Even so, as the hour tipped towards midnight – and Lambeth still a half-hour's forced march away – his heart started to quiver once more. It was only when he was certain Henri Laurent had himself vacated the Queen Mary that he stole onto the ill-lit restaurant floor, wove his way between the tables already decked out for breakfast, and past the wine-cellar stairs.

He was reaching for his ring of keys, about to slide into the kitchens, when he realised the kitchen was not as empty as he thought. Through the service area, he could see a coterie of kitchen hands still scrubbing down the surfaces.

And there, among them, stood Victor.

Billy froze. Of course, Victor had been there that night too; Victor, huddled up with Annie, keeping a lookout for whoever was plundering the larders. Billy beat his way back into shadow, keeping watch from the pools of darkness on the other side of the restaurant floor. Moments later, when one of the kitchen hands emerged to scuttle off home, he slunk back further. Perhaps, he thought, he ought to hide out in the private dining room – that place where the Free French, and Charles de Gaulle himself, tried to plot the fate of the free world – but he was still considering the matter when the kitchen door opened once again, disgorging Victor to the night.

The boy was on his way home, then.

Good riddance, thought Billy – for, though he was quite certain Victor was a very fine chap, and though he was quite certain he would make a fine suitor for Annie, he was also certain that the time was right, that the boy had been the last thing standing between Billy and his family's good fortune.

He waited until Victor was gone.

Billy stopped at the kitchen doors.

One more time, he thought. Just one …

Then a hand clapped on his shoulder.

'Brogan?'

Billy looked up. There hung the dark figure of Henri Laurent.

'M-Mr Laurent,' he stammered. He'd thought his heart was in turmoil earlier today, but it was nothing to the feeling of plummeting freefall in his breast right now. 'I was just—'

'That's *Monsieur* Laurent to you, and don't forget it. What are you looking for, Mr Brogan?'

'I was …' Billy had felt his heart in freefall, but now it took flight; he'd always had a silver tongue, 'the gift of the gab' as his mother called it, and soon an explanation was tumbling from his lips, as if of its own volition. 'This old war wound of mine's been playing up,' he said, hefting his leg. 'I thought – some ice, from the iceboxes, just something to pack against it. You don't mind, do you? I know I should have asked, but I've been bedding down in the post room ever since our house was hit, and …'

The chef's gruff demeanour seemed to have melted the moment Billy mentioned his war wound. Henri Laurent was reputed to be a dictatorial old brute, but there were two things he had respect for in this world: good cooking, and a good soldier.

He reached out and opened the door. 'Come with me, Brogan. I'll sort you out.'

'Oh, Monsieur Laurent, that's not necessary. I know the iceboxes, and …'

The chef looked at him curiously. 'Well, go on then, Brogan.

But mind you don't take the lot. Iceman isn't here for another couple of days, and we'll be taking it from the rooftops if we run out again.'

Henri Laurent lingered only to collect his great woollen coat from the rack just inside the doorway, then left Billy to the darkness beyond.

The vast, open kitchen, with all of its bounty.

One last time…

The Brogans had long since given up on Billy when the knock came at the door. 'Bill, you've missed the whole evening. By God, son, it's not even Annie's birthday anymore.'

'No, Pa,' grinned Billy, 'but I've got the best birthday present a girl could ever want.'

Soon, Billy was rushing through, rousing his mother and hoisting her to her feet.

'Annie, I didn't know what to get you for your big day,' he declared, forcing himself not to think about the last time they'd conversed, 'and the little book of verse I picked up for you – well, it didn't seem enough. So I'm here to tell you, Annie – and you too, Ma and Pa, that it's finished. I've done it. Thomas Law & Sons are working against the clock to get the job finished before the snows come, but by tomorrow evening, I'll be visiting him with the last payment. It might only be a couple of weeks, Ma. They'll be hobnobbing in the Grand, and we'll be waltzing ourselves back through the doors of No 62 Albert Yard.' He turned his eyes on Annie, begging her to be pleased. 'Annie, we're going home for Christmas.'

'Well, that deserves something,' Mr Brogan exclaimed, 'but I'm afraid we're right out of cake.'

'That doesn't matter,' said Billy, who was suddenly producing a small cardboard carton from his satchel, 'because I picked up these on the way.'

It was as Annie took in the collection of *petit fours* Billy had produced that her eyes darkened. Billy knew what that meant – she recognised them as the dainty pastries they served in the Queen Mary, with every afternoon tea – but he threw her a wink and whispered, 'It's all OK, Annie. It's all done.'

His mother was clucking about with the plates, finding something clean, while his father tidied away the draughts (Annie was winning; he was happy to call it a day) and cleared a space at the table. 'One last indulgence won't hurt,' he said, as he set everything in order. 'Not on an occasion like this, at any rate.'

'Billy, don't tell me you—'

'These were just off a trolley, Annie. Annie, I *promise*. And …' He dared to smile, cross the room and lay a hand on her shoulder. 'You were right, Annie. You always are. But it's finished now. It's part of the past.' He looked back, at his mother and father standing in front of the fire, and all the hope resurgent in their eyes. 'They been looking after us all our lives. I just wanted to look after them.'

Annie was silent – until, at last, she said, 'You promise me, Billy Brogan. You promise me you didn't go stealing again – because, if Victor's in trouble, if it falls on him, if he loses his job …'

'Oh, *Annie!*' Billy scoffed. 'I promise you. Annie, I *promise*. I just had to wait on some old money coming through. Payments I'd let slide. Jobs I'd done and not been paid for and we'll start the year afresh. A new year, and a new beginning. What do you say?'

The *petit fours* were already on a plate, and now Mrs Brogan was handing them round.

Annie took hold of one and, unable to resist the temptation, took a deep bite.

'A new beginning,' she said to Billy; then, taking in her parents' expectant eyes, 'The Brogans are going back to Albert Yard!'

Chapter Twenty-Five

London was not yet draped in white, but the flatlands of Norfolk had been wreathed in snow since the first bonfires were lit two weeks before.

It was no ordinary sight for a black man to be disembarking at Thetford, and less ordinary still for a middle-aged black man, wreathed in lambswool and swinging a trombone by his case, to be making his way along the platform – so, when the station guard saw Max Allgood emerging from the station front and considering the hastily scrawled directions in his hand, he knew something strange was happening in his little village today.

It wasn't only the onlookers who felt as if Max Allgood was out of place; Max himself knew it, the moment he left London behind and watched England's villages and downs rushing by. Now, as he exited Thetford station, following the other travellers towards the middle of town, he felt it most vividly of all. Max had spent the entirety of his life in cities; his years had been spent between the flophouses and clubs, the dance halls and speakeasies where he used to play. But here was England – beyond London, a different country altogether. Neither the map he'd jotted down, nor the directions he'd been given over the phone, seemed to make any sense, now that he was here, with the snowscape all around.

In the end, he stopped into a local post office to take directions – and, though even these were insufficient (all of the street signs of Thetford had long ago been taken down, the better to befuddle the invaders when they came), some time later he was standing outside a little cottage on the outskirts of town, its thatch capped in white, plumes of white-grey smoke trailing from the chimneystack on top.

He knocked on the wood.

The door, when it drew back, did not reveal a familiar face. The doughy lady with curls of white hair and warm, butterscotch eyes had once been part of the fixtures and fittings at the Buckingham Hotel, but had vacated that particular berth before Max himself had set foot on Berkeley Square. 'Mr Allgood,' she beamed, and stepped back. 'Come in, do. Archie's in the sitting room. He's been waiting.'

'Mrs Moffatt, ma'am?' Max ventured.

The white-haired lady smiled. 'Oh, I *was*. But you may call me Mrs Adams now. Well, call me *Emmeline*. Follow me, Mr Allgood. I've got tea in the pot already.'

Music wafted along the hallway: somewhere, Archie was hunkered over his piano, conjuring up some new creation. Max had known it would be so; a man might retire from a job, but he never retired from the vocation of his life. By the time Mrs Moffatt led him to the threshold, he hardly wanted to go in – just to hover there and listen.

It stilled his heart.

Archie knew Max had arrived; he sensed it on the edges of his vision. All the same, he continued to play – until, with a strange succession of chords Max was certain belonged more to a Chicago jazz section, he brought the piece to its end. Then he turned on the piano stool, took in Max and said, 'You found us,' with a grin.

'It took me a little while, Mr Adams. It isn't so far from London as the crow flies, but there's a world between us. Why, you'd hardly figure there was a war at all out here.'

'Don't be so sure,' Mrs Moffatt smiled, 'Archie here's a lance corporal with the Home Guard.'

Archie stood. 'A man needs more than music alone.' Then, ushering Max into the second room, while Mrs Moffatt went off to bring through the teas, he added, 'Not much more, but one can make exceptions.'

The front sitting room was as cosy as the Housekeeping Lounge at the Buckingham Hotel. The alcoves around the hearth, where a low fire flickered in the grate, were filled with all the books of their lifetimes; in the corner, a gramophone sat atop a cabinet that proudly housed a corner of Archie's collection – for the rest of the collection was so vast it had to be archived in the guest bedroom above. That was a library to make any musician envious, but right now Max's envy extended further.

In the Americas his name was known far and wide. But never, in all of that success, had music provided him with a *home* like this. Something in the permanence of it, the feeling of a rich, old world, filled him with yearning. It had been so long since he'd felt at home anywhere. The flight from New York, all the chaos he'd left in his wake – the years flitting back and forth across the Continent, trying to find a place to fit in; Paris, Milan, Vienna; the mad dash across France with the desperate idea they might make it across the Channel before the war caught up with them. Throughout all of it, it had been the hope of a place like this that had kept him sustained. Daisy, whispering in his ear: *We'll get there, Max. One day, we'll have a home that will last.*

And now it was slipping through his fingers.

That was why he was here, so far from the rubble of London.

If there was one person who might help, surely it was the man who had crowned him leader of the Orchestra.

If only he could find a way to say it.

Max was rescued from the tangle of thoughts in his mind when Mrs Moffatt returned to the room, bringing with her a tray full of teas and the little rock cakes she'd spent the morning baking. 'They're not quite of the Buckingham standard,' she said, 'but they work for us. And here, look, some barley sugars from my personal collection.' She set about pouring the teas, settling Archie in the chair by the fire and Max in the one opposite, and went on, 'Now, I imagine there's much to talk about. The Christmas Ball, it must be just weeks away? The first one, you know, since Archie and I were...' Mrs Moffatt's voice trailed off, as an old memory took over; it had only been a year since the sirens had sounded during the middle of last Christmas's ball, and both Emmeline and Archie were buried in the landslide that devastated the Housekeeping wing. 'But I've got to ask: my girls, how are they, Max? Now, of course, Nancy's written – and tells me everything goes well, that she's juggling everything like the star of the circus – but I sometimes wonder...'

Max grinned. 'It must be a hell of a thing, ma'am, to leave a place you've run half your life. But, as far as I see it, Mrs de Guise has got those girls whipped into shape. I don't know if they've missed a beat, since you left.' He caught himself, for suddenly he feared he'd caused some offence. 'That is to say, there's a hole there, no doubt about it. But as for beds being changed and brass being polished...'

'They'll be decorating the Christmas tree soon,' Mrs Moffatt said, wistfully. 'It was the treat of the year. Either take the girls into the Grand to bring down those chandeliers and get polishing, or have them scaling ladders, stringing up tinsels and lights. I'll miss that most of all.' She paused. 'But you haven't come to talk about chambermaids, have you, Mr Allgood? It's music you'll want to be talking about.'

'Indeed,' smiled Archie, 'you're always welcome here, of course. I should enjoy your company, for a few hours. And yet, even in your letter, you had the sound of a harried man.'

Max reached into a pocket and drew out a handful of paper flyers, each one emblazoned with the words HARRY DUDGEON AND THE MOONLIGHTERS.

Without words, he waddled across the room and placed them on the little hearthside table where Archie sat. Then he retreated back to Lucille, and let Archie browse through them.

There was a moment in which Max wasn't sure what the silence meant. Perhaps the elder bandleader thought Max was here to make some drama of his own. But then his eyes furrowed, he passed the flyers over his shoulder so that Emmeline could peruse them too, and he said, 'I always tolerated a little out-of-hours in my orchestra. It wasn't strictly within the terms of our contracts of course, but I took the view that it rather *helped* my orchestra get along. If you button a man down, sometimes he starts to feel ... in chains, somehow. He decides he needs to break free. Yet, if you let him go off and dance to his own tune here and there ...'

'It's like my girls,' Emmeline chipped in. 'I used to say: don't spend all your time up there in that kitchenette, chinwagging all night long. You get like a caged animal.'

'A little moonlighting can energise things, even. Music stagnates if it only ever listens to itself. But if one or two of your players are out there, listening to new sounds, experiencing new things – and they bring that excitement back to your orchestra? Well, you've little chance of festering then ...'

The silence returned. It seemed to Max that Archie hadn't been admonishing him, merely working through the thoughts of his own mind, and now he said, 'But this is more than just moonlighting. That's what's preying on you.'

'They're playing all over town, Archie. Look at that flyer – that's the night of the Summer Ball. They took off out of the Grand soon as the last note was played, headed right down to the Ambergris to meet the revellers. I let it go. I'm a good man,' and he crossed his heart, praying it was so, trying not to think of Chicago and New York, Daisy and all they'd left behind, 'and there's a war on. But... Harry, Gus and Fred – their eye isn't on the Max Allgood Orchestra, it's on the Moonlighters. I'm trying to drive the Orchestra one way, and they're wrenching it another.'

Archie lost himself in contemplation for a beat before he said, 'Orchestras are often challenged by the spirits of their players. But I have to say,' and here he paused, trying to divine the right words, 'I always found Harry to be a loyal, devoted player. A family man at heart – and we, the Orchestra, his family, just as much as his wife and children back home. Why, for years and years, he put the group before himself.'

Archie was circling the point, thought Max – reluctant, perhaps, to cast any aspersions on a man who'd, for so long, been a loyal lieutenant. But he hadn't come here to make excuses for the man; Max knew the true colour of Harry's greedy, self-serving heart. 'He respected you, Archie. He'd have followed you over the top. You're the man who brought him in.' He paused. 'But now he's there in *spite* of me. Don't you see? It isn't the same thing. He owes me nothing – and that's the result.' He flicked his hand at the flyers more pointedly than he'd meant to; his fingers had started twitching, as they did every time things got heated, as if they were playing up and down Lucille's imaginary keys. 'He's out there making a name for himself, and it's at the Buckingham's expense.'

Here came that silence again. By God, Max sometimes wished he could embrace the kind of thoughtful, contemplative silence that characterised a man like Archie's conversations. That kind of peace was hard to come by; it certainly wasn't found on the streets of New Orleans, or in the cells of the juvenile detention centre where he'd first learned to play.

'This is a complicated affair, Max,' Archie said, at last.

'I'll say.'

'And not a challenge I ever faced, I'm afraid.' The silence momentarily returned, Archie's face lined in rumination. 'The world's in flux, but the Grand has always remained. It was a constant in my life, and I'll hazard to say it was the one, shining constant in Harry's life as well. But it's been upended for him. He'll feel – cautious, nervous, afraid for the future for the first time in an age. Yes, couple that with the war and all the uncertainty it breeds, and I can quite see how my departure might make a man take stock of things, might drive him to big decisions of his own.'

'People do find opportunity in times of crisis,' Emmeline added, while Archie took stock of his own thoughts. 'There's a few making a fair wage out there on the black markets. Plenty of profiteers and pillagers in London, almost as soon as the bombs started coming down. It might be Mr Dudgeon's seen some *opportunity* of his own.'

Max bristled: yes, he knew exactly what kind of opportunity Harry had spied – but he wasn't ready to spill it yet, not unless it was absolutely necessary.

'Now, I wouldn't quite call Harry a *profiteer*,' Archie said, daring a wry smile, as if to test the atmosphere in the room, 'but I have an inkling he has his eye on a bigger prize. It seems to me that he's started chasing reputation – hoping, perhaps, to fill some vacancy at the Imperial, perhaps even the Savoy, when one comes along. He'd need to be a renowned bandleader in his own right to inherit a stage like that. Most likely, he'd need to have cut records. In another time, he'd be expected to have toured the world – but, without that accolade, he'd certainly need to be spoken of as a rising star.' Archie shook his head, thoughtfully. 'Is this what you're afraid of, Max? That you lose your star pianist, and gain a rival instead?'

'Gain a rival?' Max stuttered. It was the sheer innocence of the idea that had provoked such surprise in him. He breathed, sombrely, and said, 'I've already got a rival, Mr Adams. It isn't a post at the Savoy ol' Harry's after. It's *my* job he wants. By Christmas night, he means to be in charge of the Grand.'

This time, the silence in the sitting room had an altogether different quality. At least Emmeline had the decency to be aghast, thought Max; Archie himself was still looking at him inscrutably, as if he'd never heard anything as preposterous in his life.

'It's what I came here for help with, Mr Adams,' Max fretted, suddenly cradling Lucille into his lap and playing with the clasp on her case; something, *anything*, to take away the fire he was feeling. 'We're on course for Christmas in Exile now. The whole world's coming to see us. They're dragging ministers from war work to waltz to our music. Charles de Gaulle himself – if you listen to the tittle-tattle – is going to show his face. It ought to be *our* time. The spotlight on us, for the whole damn world!' There was some joyful frenzy in the way Max was speaking, but there was terror too. 'Well, ever since we started preparing, Harry's wanted control of the show. I was opening with "Someone's Secret". It's a hell of a number, Archie. But Harry's already had the Orchestra switch things around – now we'll open with one of his numbers, "Never the Lonely", instead. Now, it's a great little tune – don't get me wrong. It's got *spirit*. But it ain't mine. And that ain't all. The song we ought to have closed the first act with? Sent 'em off into intermission with some fire in their hearts? Well, now *that's* Harry's too – and, listen to this, there ain't even a trombone part in it, 'least not one to speak of. I've ended up hopping through and jamming along, carving out my own little hole in it – for a show that's supposed to be *mine*!'

Max had to take breath. It occurred to him, now, that to an outsider's ear he must have seemed crazed. To Archie's credit, he had kept an implacable expression throughout.

'He wants me driven out. By the New Year, he means to inherit the Grand. And... that's why I'm here. Now, I know it ain't the done thing. I know I'm a grown man – but I'm not a leader like you were, Mr Adams. I'm a musician, it's in my blood, but I don't command them like you do. And I wondered...'

'You want me to speak with Harry.'

It was the only thing Max had been able to think of. The last gambit of a despairing man.

'Just a quiet word, Mr Adams. Just to remind Harry that I was chosen to lead the Grand for a reason – that I deserve the same respect he used to give you.'

Archie had been silenced – Max had so little idea what thoughts were percolating, even now, behind the whites of his eyes – but, at this juncture, Emmeline Adams, nee Moffatt, did the thing she always thought best, back in her Buckingham days, whenever one of her girls was in need.

She shuffled over, filled up the teacups, and handed the biscuits around.

'Now, I don't know about orchestras,' she ventured, 'but it seems to me that *respect* is the same the whole world over. My Nancy might know a thing or two about that. If she's running the Housekeeping department as seamlessly as you say, well, it isn't because anyone *told* those girls to respect her – it's because she earned their respect. Now, it wasn't plain sailing along the way – there was a touch of resentment, even from those who loved her, when she took up as floor mistress last year. It isn't easy suddenly being the boss of girls you've grown up with in the department. And that's the thing, Mr Allgood – it just takes *time*. If Harry's a thorn in your side, now, you've got to work that thorn out yourself. You can't go asking someone else to do it for you – because, if you do, soon you'll have a half dozen other thorns. If Archie was to fight this fight for you, it would diminish you, sir. So ...'

Emmeline Moffatt had run her department for as long as Archie had worked in orchestras; she might not have known music as he did, but she did know *people*.

'You must face this decisively, Mr Allgood. Be kind, but be plain and firm – and, above all, be *honest*. Tell Harry that, if he wants to be a bandleader, he may do it somewhere else. You don't make those decisions, Max. The Buckingham Board made the decision to hire you, and it won't be undone just because Harry Dudgeon demands it.'

Max squirmed. He'd been hoping he wouldn't have to do this, but it dawned on him that only the full truth would do. 'See, that's the second problem I got, Mrs Adams.' He ran a finger around his necktie, closed his eyes, and told himself there was no more running: he was here, and he would have to fight. 'There's some ... *stuff* that's been dogging me from my days back home. New York, I mean. Well, Mr Adams, you must know what the clubs are like out there. Every dance hall's some sort of a racket. I'm talking about the *mafiosi*, Mr Adams. Mobsters. They got different rackets going all over town, and music's about the only legitimate business they have. But the way they run it – well, it's dirty, is what it is. Now, it's ... well, I don't like to say it in front of your good lady wife, Mr Adams, but there's worse than liquor being traded. There's…' At least Max had the decency to look ashamed when he said, 'There's girls. Yes, there, I said it. Music's tied up with all kinds of activities you wouldn't talk about in polite society back home – and, in my days, I been managed by one or two less than gentle men.' Perhaps that was enough; Max took a breath and, careful not to look Archie's wife in the eye, said, 'So you might say there are one or two things I'd rather got left in New York. Things I been careful not to mention to management. Except, it just so happens that Harry found out about one or two of these things and…'

Archie's face darkened, for the very first time. It was a strange, otherworldly thing to see such a genteel man turn suddenly severe. 'Do you mean to tell me that Harry is holding you to ransom?'

It was Emmeline who intervened, while Archie still looked on – his expression teetering on the edge of disbelief. 'Mr Allgood, the past never stays buried. Please trust me on that. We have, all of us, tried to bury things we've been ashamed of.' A wistful expression crossed her face, as if she was speaking of some buried secret of her own, later unearthed. 'You won't know this, Mr Allgood, but for years I couldn't speak of my son. Gone off to new parents, the moment he was born, and me just a girl, and… They drill the shame into you, until it's a part of who you are. But do you know the best thing that ever happened to me? Do you know the moment I truly stepped out of the shadows and learned to live in the light?' She paused. 'It was the moment I spoke the truth. The moment my son came back into my life, and I could stop pretending. So I suppose what I'm trying to say is…'

'We can't do this for you, Max,' said Archie, with some air of sadness, 'but *you* can.'

'My son's a big part of my life now. He was married this year.

And… you need to unburden yourself of secrets, Mr Allgood. You need to live free and clear. And if someone's holding a secret against you? Well, it seems to me there are two choices: you can keep that secret between you, and pay the price of it – your soul being chipped away, bit by bit. Or you can…'

'Let go of the secret,' breathed Max.

Emmeline reached over and topped up his tea. 'Well, then,' she smiled, 'it wouldn't be a secret anymore, would it? And maybe, then, its blade wouldn't be quite as sharp.'

Daisy wasn't sleeping when Max came through the door of their suite. Evidently, she'd been waiting up, staring out of the window in the gable and expecting his return. A social visit, he'd told her. 'Mr Adams invited me for high tea – that's what they do in good Olde England, don't ya know?' But of course she knew he was lying. Daisy had an uncanny ability to perceive deception. When he came through the door, she looked at him as if she knew he was about to come clean.

By the time he'd told her everything – of how Jackson Ford had sold their secret to Harry, how Harry was holding the Orchestra to ransom, of the pact he'd made to be pushed out of his own orchestra, just to save them from being exposed – her face had turned rigid. When he dared look in her eyes, he saw them full of fire.

'You damn fool, Max. *You damn fool*. It's your silence that's cost us. If you'd told me, I could have—'

Max silenced her with his words: 'I'm going to go to Mr Knave. I'm going to throw myself on their mercy.'

Daisy's eyes opened even wider, brimming with disbelief. 'What kind of a solution is this?' she snapped. 'Max Allgood, you've had some naïve notions in your life, but this one belittles them all.'

Max yelled, 'It's the only way. They might yet understand. If we leave it alone, we're finished. We'll be back to singing for our supper in the lowliest hovel. But if I come clean, isn't there a *hope*? And, by God, we *need* a hope.' Max's anger ebbed away. 'Give me this chance. You're the one got us out of New York. Well, let me repay the favour.'

'You can play a trombone like God gave you a gift, Max – but you don't have the words for something like this. You can't tell a lie.'

'I been telling lies all year, haven't I? I was telling lies all across the Continent. I was telling them all you're my wife, for a start. I haven't told a soul who you really are, or what you've done. I haven't told anyone you're my cousin. Or that Daisy isn't even your real—'

She shot him a look, as if to speak the truth even in the confines of this small room was a sacrilege.

'I won't let you do this, Max. There's too much riding on it. This is our home. This is our *future*. It's Nelson's future too.'

'There ain't no future,' Max snapped back, 'not for you or me, and not for Nelson either, if I lose the Orchestra. And unless I come clean, it's already gone.'

Daisy could not bear to look him in the face.

'You're acting like it's *my* doing,' Max gasped. 'I'm trying to fix it. I didn't let it slide. It's down to Jackson Ford. If he hadn't shown up here, why, we'd be—'

She turned on him, with a viper's tongue. 'If Ford wanted a little side hustle, why not just come to us? Why Dudgeon? We'd have paid him off, just the same.'

'Well,' Max slurred, 'that might have made sense – except, of course, that he recognised *you* from the townhouse up by St Nicholas Park. So we know *his* dirty little secret as well. You can't blackmail someone who's got the dirt on you as well. How many times did he come to see your girls up there? Every month, by your account.' Max stopped. 'You can't leave the past where it belongs in this world, can you? Someone's always there to dig it right back up. But what happened in New York wasn't our fault. It's just the world we was in. We did our best to break free – and look at us now, here we are! And there's only one shot at saving it...'

'You're a fool. You've been listening to your own music too long, Max. There's not a chance they'd keep us, not once they knew. You're forgetting – these are Englishmen, and they don't give a damn about the truth. All they care about is their *reputation*.'

Max stood. The fact that Lucille was in his arms was the thing that told Daisy he was about to leave the room again. He had taken three great strides towards the door when she called out, 'Stop, Max. Stop right there!'

'*Ava*,' he said, with his head in his hands, 'there's no other way. I won't walk blindly into it. If we're going to lose everything again, let's at least do it on our own terms.'

He set off for the door again, but this time Daisy was too swift. In seconds she had put herself between him and the door. 'Listen to me,' she told him, the panic rising in her voice. 'Listen to me, now. I got us out of New York, didn't I? I was the one who dragged both of you – you *and* Nelson! – out of that dirty, dirty world. I *saved* you, didn't I? I'm the one who got my hands dirty for it. I'm the one whose fingers ran with blood. If it wasn't for me, Nelson would be six feet under the earth – or else tossed in the Hudson and forgotten forever. And *you*? You'd still be Johnny Glaser's pet – a bonded man, every bit as much of a slave as our fathers used to be. He'd be getting fat off your blood and sweat, rich off your talent, while you went round begging for scraps. *I* put a stop to all that, didn't I? And I can put a stop to this as well.' Daisy paused. By now she had reached up, taken Lucille out of Max's hands and placed her by his side. Then, with both hands, she took hold of Max's cheeks and directed his eyes so that he was staring straight into hers. 'You just have to trust me again, Max. We can still have it all. This can still be a home.' A smile crept onto her face. 'You see that, don't you? It's not lost yet. Just have a little faith in me. You trusted me once. Just trust me again.'

For the longest time, Max was still. All the fire he'd built up, the engine driving him down towards the Hotel Director's office and everything that came after, seemed suddenly to have died away.

The truth, he thought. There'd been so much sense in what Emmeline and Archie had been saying – and yet the truth was such a dangerous thing.

How much easier was the comfort of lies?

'I don't want anyone to be hurt,' he stammered, still gazing into Daisy's fathomless eyes. 'This isn't the New York night. Those things don't go unnoticed here. They aren't so easily forgotten. This isn't Hell's Kitchen. It's Mayfair. And nobody...' Max gulped hard, unable to truly believe he was in this position again, that the world he'd escaped was manifesting right here, all around him, as he overlooked the beauty of Berkeley Square. 'Nobody has to die.'

December 1941

Chapter Twenty-Six

The Buckingham's reception hall was never barren – for the hotel's famous revolving doors were never closed to visitors and guests – but, at midnight, it was ordinarily at its most peaceful. Tonight, however, everything had changed. In the heart of the hall, a towering Norwegian fir tree had been hauled into place. The workmen who'd hoisted it upward were still tidying away the ropes and pulleys with which they'd positioned the tree, but as soon as the Housekeeping girls arrived, fanning out in awe around its magnificent branches, they stopped to watch this spectacle instead. Nancy had already asked them to bring up the great chests, brimming with baubles and tinsels, from their resting place in the basement. Now, she marched towards them, opened the first chest – and took out both the crystalline star and cloth angel that would take pride of place on the tree's uppermost bough.

It had been a year of firsts. In a few short weeks, Arthur would celebrate his first Christmas on Earth – and Nancy would spend her first Christmas as a mother. The magic of that would surely eclipse the thrill she felt now, but there was no denying the wonder in the girls' eyes – and Nancy would well remember the feeling she'd had that first year in the Buckingham, when Mrs Moffatt had brought her here to take part in decorating the tree. She had never seen a sight more wonderful – and what a joy it was to see that same emotion mirrored in her girls right now.

'Stateliness,' she grinned. 'Elegance. Majesty. And just a little bit of … flair. Here in the Buckingham, we have to be *perfect*. So your instructions are thus: you are to have fun tonight, but Mr Knave will need to see perfect balance in how we decorate this tree. And with that in mind …' Nancy marched to the tree and hung a single crystal orb from one of the lowermost boughs. 'I think we should begin.'

She was mindful that she ought to stay, for the thought of hotel management discovering a lopsided Christmas tree by morning was too terrible to risk, but to their credit the girls took to their task with aplomb. Some had been here to see it done before, and their instincts about elegance and majesty were soon filtering down to the other girls. By the time the scaling ladders were brought into place – the workmen enjoying the chance of mingling with the chambermaids – Nancy could envisage what the complete picture might look like, the cloth angel perched proudly atop a glittering cascade of ruby red and snow white. Yes, Mr Knave and his colleagues on the Board could be quite pleased with the transformation their reception hall was going through this midnight.

Annie Brogan had been one of the girls tasked with decorating last year's tree – but, to her eye, it was all a little bit *stuffy*. The Brogan family tree was a much more joyful affair than this.

And there'd be a tree this year, wouldn't there? A Brogan tree, back in the Brogan house, just like every year. Billy had taken his opportunities, chanced his luck, bent every rule and code of conduct – but he'd given Christmas back to their family.

If only she could get rid of the unnerved, conflicted feeling in her belly. It would be a good thing to share in the joys of the season.

She was handing baubles up a chain the other girls had made – Rosa now on the scaling ladder halfway up the tree – when she caught sight of Victor emerging from the darkened Queen Mary corridor. It must have been a riotous dinner service, for the last orders had been taken more than two hours ago – and, ever since then, kitchen hands had been scrubbing the place down in anticipation of breakfast. To Annie's eye, Victor looked exhausted, his features bunched and red. His satchel was slung over his shoulder, still trailing his standard issue gas mask – Annie had given up carrying hers months ago – and his head was hanging in exhaustion. Yet, when he saw the majesty of the tree, his gaze was drawn upwards. He'd been marvelling at it for a few moments – Victor had never experienced the wonder of a Buckingham Christmas – when Annie caught his eye.

The smile came suddenly to her face. Just as suddenly, it came to Victor's. Across the reception hall, through the outstretched arms of the tree, they each lifted a hand to wave to the other.

Then Victor hurried on.

'Just go and talk to him,' Rosa called out, holding court from halfway up the tree. 'Go on – at least say thank you for sorting out those ingredients for your cake. That boy deserves a peck on the cheek for that.'

Victor was already picking his way through the store rooms on the approach to the tradesman's exit when Annie caught up with him, quite out of breath, she couldn't even call out his name – so he had almost stepped into the snow gently tumbling down across Michaelmas Mews when he realised she was there. 'Annie,' he gasped, 'are you all right? Has something happened?'

She must have looked a sorry state – doubled over, heaving for breath, bracing herself on the storage shelving as she was.

In a desperate attempt to seem nonchalant, she waved her hand airily and spluttered out the words, 'Oh – no – *nothing* – that is to say, nothing *bad* – I ... I wanted to say ... *hello.*'

By the end of the sentence (if 'sentence' it truly was), she had at least regained some composure. She smiled wanly at Victor and added, 'Hello.'

'Hello, Annie ...'

The boy looked so confused. His face was still ruddy from the heat of the kitchens, even though the snow whirled across the open doorway behind him, and Annie had the sudden feeling that she was making a fool of herself – that, very soon, she'd have to tramp back to the Christmas tree and all the girls would be asking her how it had gone.

'Victor,' she ventured, 'do you want to go for a walk?'

There – she'd said it. She'd spent so long wondering if Victor might ever ask her that she'd tangled herself in knots.

Victor flashed a look around. '*Now?*' he asked, bewildered. He glanced over his shoulder, at the strafing snow over Michaelmas Mews. 'Annie, it's after midnight. And it's ...' He wrapped his arms around himself, as if to pantomime how frigid the night truly was.

'Not – not now,' Annie stammered. 'But I was thinking ... soon. Before the ball? And, if it's too cold, well, there's a café I like, down on Piccadilly. I say I like it, but – well, I've never been. But I've looked in at the window. They have hot currant buns. I should like a hot currant bun.'

For the first time since she'd caught up with him, Annie dared to meet Victor's eyes. She wasn't certain what he was feeling: there was confusion in those eyes, but she dared to hope there was anticipation, expectation, some sense of a thrill as well.

'A hot currant bun sounds very nice indeed.'

The words sent Annie's heart soaring. So rapidly did it take flight that it wasn't until a split second later that she realised it wasn't Victor who had spoken.

She turned over her shoulder. There stood Mrs de Guise, now dressed in her winter coat, ready to brave the cruel December night.

'Annie, you'll be missed in reception,' she said, with a flicker of a smile. 'You don't want Rosa claiming the angel for herself, do you?' Then her eyes turned on Victor. 'And you, young man – I should think you'd really enjoy a currant bun in the company of a fine, hard-working, good-natured member of my Housekeeping staff, wouldn't you?' When Victor was dumbfounded in response, Nancy added, '*Annie*,' and at this Victor suddenly came to life.

'Yes,' he said. 'Yes I would.'

Nancy slipped past them, into the rippling veil of snow. 'Goodnight, young love.'

As the snow swallowed her up, Annie and Victor looked nervously at each other. 'So,' Annie said at last, 'I'll find you, shall I? This week, when you're next off shift? We can go down through St James, stop for that tea along the way.'

Victor's eyes sparkled as he too stepped back, through the doorway and into the snow. 'And that currant bun,' he called back.

Annie meant to let him go, then – the moment seemed so perfect, she was happy to let it linger – but, as the first snowflakes wreathed around Victor, another thought exploded through her. 'Victor,' she called back, 'all of that business in the larders, all of those things going missing... it hasn't happened again, has it?'

Victor contemplated it, for just long enough that Annie was quite certain he was about to say 'Oh, Annie, it never stopped.' Her heart, which had just moments ago been turning somersaults of joy, suddenly tightened. She thought of Billy, and how on earth he'd scraped together the money to pay the builders their final fee. But then Victor's face lightened and, instead of confirming all her worst fears, he sheepishly said, 'Not once, not since that night we were ... in the kitchens. Together.'

Annie remembered that moment too. The recollection of it, the very idea that their lips were so close to touching, made her blush.

'I reckon we frightened him off, you and me,' grinned Victor, and stepped back along the mews. 'And if that doesn't earn us a currant bun, I don't know what will!'

While Annie and Victor were still limping awkwardly through a conversation about currant buns, Nancy reached the snowy expanse of Berkeley Square – and was more grateful than ever that the Board had signed off on the taxicabs to take her home. Here it came now, a black hulk sailing through the pristine white.

Her body was aching to see Arthur. Her heart was aching too. The day had been long, the night so vast; she was glad to slip inside the taxicab and take the weight off her feet.

Indeed, her eyes were growing heavy even before the cab had left Berkeley Square. The snow coursing past the windows gave the city a dreamlike quality, and this only pulled her further towards sleep. She was skirting its edges, thinking of Vivienne and the children – and trying not to think about Hugo Lavigne, nor the contents of that insidious letter – when she began to perceive that something was not altogether *right* in the journey. Perhaps there was some fresh devastation – or else some fresh construction site – that the taxicab had to work its way around; or perhaps it was only the onslaught of snow, changing the contours of the city she loved – but, somewhere along the way, she became quietly convinced that she was not being driven in the right direction.

The concern bubbled up in her, banishing any prospect of sleep, until at last she said, 'Sir, I don't mean to question you, but ... we are going to Maida Vale? Blomfield Road?' She could have sworn they'd just passed through the Marble Arch, then banked left to follow the fringes of Hyde Park, but the whirling snow occluded so much of the city without. 'Sir?' she repeated, when no immediate answer came.

'You're in good hands, ma'am,' the driver finally replied, half-turning over his shoulder as he banked into one of the side roads beyond the park. 'I'll have you there shortly.'

'You're going in the wrong direction,' Nancy insisted.

'I'm sorry, ma'am. It's the instructions I received. I'm sure it will make sense at the other end.'

Nancy reached for the door handle. 'You'll tell me what this is about right now or—'

'We're here, ma'am.'

Abruptly, the taxi came to a stop and the driver stepped out of his seat, hurrying round to open Nancy's door. There he stood on the snowbound street, offering Nancy an arm. 'I'll find my own way, sir,' she declared; to accept his help now would be to accept whatever was happening to her. Brushing him aside, she emerged onto a street of tall townhouses crowned in white, somewhere – she judged – in the vicinity of Eaton Square; but there was no chance of simply slipping away. Before she had taken two steps, the driver had taken her arm, quite against her wishes. 'I'm sorry, Mrs de Guise. You'll simply have to trust in me for a few moments and all will be revealed.' Nancy drew back, but the man's grip was hard and fast. 'I'm under orders to bring you in, Mrs de Guise.'

'Bring me in where?' Nancy seethed.

The driver inclined his head along the row, where a black door had opened in the face of one of the townhouses. Though no light spilled from within, Nancy could clearly see that a figure had emerged. A small barrel of a man, with a rotund belly and a bowler hat perched upon his jowly face, stood in the darkened doorway. The shadows were too deep for her to make out the features of his face, but a strange frisson moved through Nancy, a flicker of recognition.

'Mrs de Guise,' came the man's rich baritone, 'I hope you'll forgive us this night.'

'Mr ... Mr *Charles*?'

How long had it been since Nancy set eyes upon Maynard Charles, former director of the Buckingham Hotel? He'd left the Buckingham on the eve of war, driven out of his post by secrecy and lies – and the sallow vindictiveness among former members of the Board – but every whisper she'd heard since suggested he was working somewhere in Westminster, dedicating his considerable talents to guiding Great Britain through the war. Yet to see him here, on the other side of the shifting curtain of snow, seemed scarcely believable. It wasn't until the taxi driver had brought her closer – Nancy no longer resisting his grasp – that she was certain it was him. Mr Charles looked a little leaner than in the days he had dined at the Queen Mary each evening, a little less jowly and a little more lined, but it was undoubtedly him. He inclined his head in greeting and said, 'I would have attended you myself, but it was decided it was not appropriate I be spotted by the Buckingham. I know you'll understand, Nancy. Tongues never stop wagging in that establishment. Loose talk costs lives.'

Nancy was dumbfounded. 'Mr Charles, I just don't understand. What am I doing here?'

'Follow me, Nancy. All shall be revealed.'

There had always been something warmly commanding about Maynard Charles. He'd ruled the Buckingham Hotel with an iron fist, yet had tender words for almost all of its underlings; he'd venerated those born on high, but had all the time in the world for those born low. If there had always seemed something severe about Maynard Charles, there seemed something just and *fair* about him as well.

It was this that drew her through the door.

'Mr Charles,' she ventured, following him to the foot of a dark stairwell, then up the crooked stairs, past offices where secretaries were still busily hammering away at their typewriters, and a lounge where two men in gabardine suits were sprawled on old sofas, sleeping off their day's work. 'It's been two years since I saw you, sir. A lot has changed. But...'

She was about to ask him why she was here, but at that moment Maynard brought her to the building's second landing, opened a narrow office door and beckoned her through. Inside, a younger man was sitting at a desk. He stood to attention the moment Mr Charles appeared, but Maynard waved him airily back to his seat, and ushered Nancy to a chair by the room's chimney breast. Here, another desk was cluttered with papers. Maynard reached into the tumult and came back with a letter Nancy had seen before.

Her heart stilled.

'Nancy, before I explain any further, I have to ask you: have you shown this letter to anyone else?'

The last time she'd seen this letter, it had been in the hands of Walter Knave, which could only mean that, by some circumstance, he'd delivered it here. Not for the first time, Nancy was hit with the inalienable feeling that there was much she didn't understand about the workings of the Buckingham Hotel.

'Mr Charles, why have you—'

'Come now, Nancy, you must have wondered what implications this letter might have. Why else take it to Walter Knave?

You must have wondered why he kept it in his possession? Not for those feeble minds on the Hotel Board...' Maynard must have been referring to the lesser Board members, for his relationship with and respect for John Hastings had always been of the highest ideal. 'Who else read this letter, Nancy?'

'I showed it to Vivienne.'

Nancy saw the sudden flash of concern in his eyes.

'She wouldn't tell a soul, Mr Charles. Vivienne isn't the woman you once knew. She's fine and loyal and... She's my very best friend.'

Maynard Charles nodded, betraying no further hint of surprise. Perhaps he too had been watching Vivienne from afar. 'And your brother, Frank?'

'No, sir, not yet. Frank is ... Frank's enamoured of Mr Lavigne, sir. I didn't want to draw him into it. Not yet.'

Maynard Charles nodded. 'You've a wise head, though it can't remain that way for long. Your brother will have to be brought in.'

'Brought in, Mr Charles? But, sir, what's this—'

'Mr Knave was concerned enough about this letter to pass it up the chain of command. Naturally, being a Buckingham-oriented issue, it has fallen to me to investigate the credentials of Mr Lavigne. Well, it may surprise you to learn that, in the same moment Lieutenant de Guise wrote to you, he sent another communiqué through the military channels from Cairo. That reached us some time prior to your receipt of this missive. It has actually caused some head-scratching here in the Office – because it would have been better if Raymond hadn't been quite as ... prolific, shall we say, in sharing his concerns. But he loves his family dearly, and wanted to warn you in person.'

Nancy was dumbfounded. 'But warn me about *what*?'

'I think, Nancy, it is time that you heard this from the horse's mouth.'

Nancy just stared, not daring to believe in the words she had heard. 'Raymond?' she breathed. 'Raymond's here?'

'I wish my powers stretched as far as plucking a man of his calibre directly from the theatre of war,' Maynard said, shaking his head ruefully, 'but if you follow my associate, Mrs de Guise, you might get the next best thing.'

In the military attaché's office, at the embassy in Cairo, Lieutenant Raymond de Guise heard his name called by one of the ambassador's manifold staff, then followed the dour-looking steward into a small communications room at the bottom of the corridor. Here, behind blacked-out windows, a single telephone sat upon a naked table. Its receiver was already in the hands of the staff colonel who'd organised the briefing. A beefy man of indomitable appearance, he invited Raymond to take the seat he had moments before vacated and said, 'I'm bound to remind you of your responsibilities, de Guise. Not a word of operational concern. No inkling of anything beyond your primary concern. This communication is being listened to by your superiors, but you're to act as if it's being listened to by your King's enemies as well. Do you understand? Any contravention of your orders can lead to an immediate court martial.'

'I've given my word, sir.'

Raymond took his seat at the table, brought the telephone receiver to his ear and said, 'Nancy?'

There was a brief pause before he heard her voice. How many months had it been? 'Raymond? R-Raymond, is that *you*?' It was clearer than ever that she was half a world away. Some piece of him tightened, while some other piece melted away; he might not have been able to touch her, but here was his Nancy. He'd rarely felt like he needed her as much as he did in this moment.

'Nancy, I'm not sure how much time we have, but you must forgive me – your letters have been following me around the desert. I came to them so late. And...' What use was the explanation? It all melted away and, instead, he simply said, 'By God, I've missed you, Nancy. And... how is my son?'

'He's well, Raymond. He's well.' Her tinny voice kept fading away, then exploding back into his ear. That voice, carried across continents and oceans. There was every chance, even on these secure lines, it was being eavesdropped on – but hang it, thought Raymond, let the Nazis listen to his love; they loved their wives and girls just the same in Berlin as they did in Mayfair, Maida Vale, Carlisle, Penrith. If they had one thing in common, one thing that could end this blasted war, perhaps it was that. 'But Raymond, listen – your letter, and Hugo, and—'

'It's why they've let me call,' Raymond interjected. There was so much he wanted to ask of her – to relive every second of his son's young life through her words – but the urgency of the matter weighed as heavily upon him as the staff colonel's eyes. 'Listen, we haven't got much time. It might be none of you do. Hugo Lavigne isn't a man to be trusted. Perhaps he was, once upon a time. Perhaps there was a good man there, long ago – but all that changed, after the Exhibition Paris. Listen, it's my resolute belief that he came to Blomfield Road that night, in full knowledge of the fact that I wasn't there – and that I was beyond everyday contact. He didn't come looking for me, Nancy. He came looking for my absence, so he could use you to get into the Grand.'

When Nancy next spoke, there was trepidation in her voice – but there was some stony defiance as well. That was the Nancy he'd fallen in love with: dependable, unwavering, even in the face of catastrophe. 'Raymond, *why*?'

'It all goes back to that final day of the Exhibition Paris,' Raymond went on. 'Lord knows why he's been telling it – spinning his own legend, it seems, but leaving out the incriminating parts. The Hugo Lavigne I knew back then thought about nothing but the ballroom. A dancer extraordinaire. The world was opening up for him back then, just like it did for me. And then…'

'Then what, Raymond?'

'Well, then he fell in love with—'

'With Hannah Lindt,' Nancy whispered. 'Yes, he told me.'

'Well, there's two things love can do to a man,' said Raymond sombrely. 'It can lift him up and make him set sail for the stars. Or it can … corrupt him. Oh, Nancy! None of us knew the way the world was about to turn. Back then, we thought the great wars of the world were over – that now there'd be a lasting peace, and men like us wouldn't have to be soldiers. We could be ballroom dancers instead. And maybe – maybe he'd have stayed a good man, if only there'd been peace. Maybe Hugo would have stayed the best of men, if only he hadn't fallen in love…'

'Couple Number Ten…'

Ray and Hannah held their breaths, clung on to each other, and closed their eyes in trepidation.

'Congratulations – you are joining us in the final round!'

Ray opened his eyes. He'd ended the quickstep, unfurling Hannah out of his hold, not knowing where the time had gone, nor with any real instinct about how well he'd danced. Only six couples were to dance in the final waltz, and four of them had now been called. Now, he and Hannah had become the fifth. He hadn't realised his legs were trembling quite as fiercely as they were until Hannah teased on his arm, trying to lead him away to the other victorious couples. Somewhere along the way, the Exhibition Paris had started to mean the world to him. He'd had the thirst to win before, but now the feeling was transcendent.

As he and Hannah sashayed off the dance floor, their heads held high, Ray caught sight of Georges de la Motte at the forefront of the spectators crowding the Casino's edge. The elder statesman of dance looked as proud as Ray himself felt. Georges nodded, sagely, and it felt like all the congratulations in the world to Ray: something – whether it was magic, or purely momentum – was lifting him up. If he and Hannah could ride that feeling through the final round, they would be crowned champions, perhaps even make the news sections of the *Dancing Times* – and how Ray longed to be something more than a footnote in that esteemed publication!

When Georges broke his gaze, Ray was finally able to look around at the other competitors still holding each other – trying their best to look dignified, even while the nerves gnawed away inside them – across the dance floor. Hugo himself had his eyes wide open, staring defiantly ahead – but he did not notice Ray and Hannah as they passed; he seemed focused only on surviving the tension of the moment, Ophelia's head buried in his shoulder, not daring to look up.

'Couple Number ... Eighteen,' announced the head judge. 'Congratulations, you are our finalists.'

Ray darted a look back. Couple Number Eighteen, a long willowy Parisian girl and her raffish partner, were embracing in the heart of the dance floor – but Hugo had finally let his emotion show. His hopes dashed, he hung his head – and, unable to extricate himself from Ophelia's anguished embrace, remained beached at the front of the dance floor while the other couples left and the spectators rushed out for the intermission's wild tango.

Ray was still in a whirl of disbelief when Hugo and Ophelia appeared, hustled off stage by the euphoric dancing around them. Out there, Hubert Bain and his orchestra were stirring up a song of such triumphalism that the amateurs' dancing was almost as frenetic as it had been in the clubs of the night before. Part of Ray was desperate to go and watch – was it hubris, or just self-belief that made him certain he could win this now? – but the draw of Hugo was too much. He clung to Hannah's hand and said, 'They should have made it. They should have made it. We've got to go to them, Hannah.'

Hugo was leading Ophelia through the dressing rooms, as if already making an escape from the Casino de Paris, but Ray wove his way through the other dancers until at last their paths joined. When their eyes met, the debonair Frenchman gave a wan, accepting smile. 'I shall be licking my wounds in the clubs tonight, Raymond de Guise. Perhaps I shall see you there?' And he lifted his arms, as if about to whisk Ray into a hold, perhaps to dance the java with him there and then. Ray stepped back in surprise, but Hugo was beaming. 'It does not pay to be bereft for too long, *mon frère*. The dance must go on.'

It seemed there was something egregious in what Hugo had said, because no sooner had the words left his lips, than Ophelia ripped her arm out of his and simply clung to herself instead. Hugo wheeled towards her, ready to console, but very quickly Ray realised her pain was not to do with what Hugo had said; it was to do with Ray – and, more particularly, it was to do with Hannah, who suddenly loomed on Ray's shoulder.

'I'm sorry, Ophelia,' Ray ventured. 'I felt certain you'd sail through. The two of you together, you dance like you're on …'

Ray was about to say 'the clouds', but brusquely, Ophelia cut him off, 'It's a disgrace. A disgrace of the highest order. That somebody like *her*,' and she thrust an accusing finger past Ray, directly at a flabbergasted Hannah, 'should be in this competition at all. That those judges should see fit to put a German *bitch* through instead of a true Parisian. By God, it's only a few years since they were killing us. Lining us up and *killing us!*'

Hannah stumbled back, as if she might flee. Indeed, when Ray reached for her hand, she shook it off, as if she couldn't bear to be touched. Perhaps it wasn't the first time she'd heard such accusations. Ray had heard enough of it, even back in Whitechapel: the German butchers' shop, standing on the corner, with its windows smashed in; the old man in the pub one evening, covered in venom and scorn from some of the younger men just come back from France.

'My father died fighting these bastards,' Ophelia seethed, 'and now here they are, just waltzing around Paris, like they're not the sons of killers. Like they're not the daughters of devils!'

Hannah reeled backwards, the tears already filling her eyes. Ray reached for her again – 'Hannah, don't listen,' he breathed, brimming with feeling, 'she's just upset, she's angry with the judges, not with you …' but Hannah herself cried out: 'You're not the only one who lost in that bloody war!'

Every eye backstage had turned upon them. Even those couples ejected by the competition had stopped drifting away; now they stared at a very different kind of spectacle.

'I'm sorry for your father,' Hannah blurted out. 'I'm sorry for everyone's father. But I wasn't holding a gun, and … and my brother died in that war. Cut down, somewhere near Verdun – him and all the boys he was leading. So don't for a second think *you* have it worse. Don't for a second think I'm not grieving too. And ... I've just as much right to dance as any!'

'Right to dance?' Ophelia snarled. 'You've the right to rot, and that's all – you and all your sorry kind! – you're animals, the lot of you, all animals! I wouldn't just ban you from dance. I'd – I'd ban you from Paris. I'd ban you from the Earth. Look at you, standing there as if you belong – but everyone knows what you are, Hannah *Lindt*. Everybody knows you're rotten to the core.'

How had the atmosphere changed so suddenly?

He ought to say something. He knew he ought to stop this thing before it grew even wilder, even more bitter, than it had. 'Hannah, let's go,' he said – but it wasn't what she needed to hear. Her feet were planted solid, the tears were streaming unchecked down her beautiful cheeks, all the pent-up emotion of her life – that buried memory of her brother, the cruelty and shame of her countrymen – pouring out of her.

Then Hugo declared, 'It's *you* who's the disgrace,' and turned defiantly towards Ophelia.

Ophelia cringed back; very evidently it had not been what she expected.

'You've no right to say such things. We came here to *dance*. If there's one thing that can bring us together, it's *that*. They danced in Berlin, didn't they? They danced in Vienna, just the same as they danced in Paris and London and Rome. It's meant to be joyful in here – and *you*, you have to bring down *hate*.' Hugo stepped backwards. His arm wrapped, suddenly, around Hannah – so that even Ray had to slide out of the way. 'Do you know what I think, Ophelia?' he concluded, with a second blaze of fire coursing out of him. 'I think I'm *glad* we didn't make it to the finals. I don't want to win a thing, not if it means dancing with someone like *you*.'

The effect could not have been starker if Hugo had lifted a hand and struck Ophelia flat across the face. Even some of the onlookers felt it. They winced and looked away, no longer willing to even spectate on the devastation in the room.

Ophelia turned and fled.

The intermission was almost over. Out there, the judges were reassembling. Ray ventured close and said, 'Hannah, can you dance?'

She looked so shaken she could hardly walk, but she picked herself from Hugo's arms and said, 'I'll try.' Then she hurried to one of the alcoves, straightening her gown, dabbing powder back onto her face to mask the channels her tears had cut.

While she was gone, Ray said, 'Hugo, you shouldn't have …'

Hugo just shrugged. 'Ophelia can go to hell.' Then he paused. 'I meant what I said, Ray. It's meant to be about dance in here. All the problems of the world, they're for out *there*. In here, we're meant to cultivate joy. What else is there?' He looked beyond Ray's shoulder, to where Hannah was re-emerging from the alcove. 'She's shaken up. You'll have to calm her down, Ray. Lead her in it, until she gets the feeling again. I just pray it isn't too late. You could really win this, you know.'

The call had come: out in the Casino de Paris, the judges had taken up their stations at the head of the dance floor.

Ray turned to face Hannah. He took her hand, tenderly, and drew her near. 'We can still do this. We'll dance away from it all. Just follow the music. I'll be following it with you.'

Hannah nodded, though there was such uncertainty in her that it was difficult to know if she believed.

'I'll be watching from the stands,' said Hugo, with a devilish wink. 'Hannah, take flight. You're one dance away from the glory.'

Ray could tell she was still shaking as they reached the dance floor. Even as the band struck up and Ray took her in hold, she did not feel as light in his arms as she had in the previous round. Nor, Ray had to admit, did the dance feel as effortless to him.

By the time the waltz reached its conclusion, Ray thought he could feel something of the old magic in him. Looking at Hannah, now, it was difficult to believe she'd been distraught only a short time ago; somewhere in the joy of the dance, the hatred had sloughed off her. She was shining again.

But it was too late. The judges wasted little time in deliberating the first act to leave this final round. 'Couple Number Ten,' the head judge announced, 'please leave the dance floor.'

After that, the announcement faded into a fugue. Ray and Hannah stood, in a haze, at the edge of the dance floor while the rosettes were awarded. By rote, they joined in the applause as the victorious couple were crowned. And it wasn't until later that night, back in the clubs of Pigalle, that Ray could take stock and appreciate how close he'd come to something very special, how much he had to be proud of in this trip to Paris which had given him such brio, such confidence – and a new name that he would wear, like a costume, throughout the rest of his days.

It wasn't until that club in Pigalle that he saw the lightness return to Hannah either; not until she was dancing the java that he saw the colour return to her face, a smile lighting up her delicate, beautiful features once again.

But by that time, she wasn't dancing with Raymond at all.

That night, and for every night thereafter, she danced in the arms of Monsieur Hugo Lavigne.

In the little room off Eaton Square, Nancy clung to the telephone receiver, still feeling the very last vibrations of Raymond's voice as the tale finally came to its end.

She looked up. There was Maynard Charles, propped against the blackouts, a White Owl cigar trailing from his lips. He'd smoked those all throughout his tenure at the Buckingham; something in the familiarity of it brought her comfort, even while Raymond's story hung in the air.

'But I still don't understand,' she went on. 'What does Hugo want? What if he did fall for Hannah Lindt? What if, in the end, she fell for him too?' *It's years ago*, she wanted to say. *How does it change what's happening right now, in the city we love?*

'Remember where Hannah came from,' Raymond implored.

The word 'Berlin' came to Nancy's lips. 'But how does it…'

'All I knew, at the start, was that Hannah came from Berlin. It wasn't until our tour continued, and Georges took us to Berlin and Munich, Vienna and Prague, that I really knew the world was as big as it is. And… Hannah wasn't just a club dancer. She was an heiress. The daughter of a prominent German socialite, a man who'd been decorated in the Great War, a man moving among the corridors of power in the new Weimar Republic. And…' Raymond's voice started to crackle down the phone; Nancy held it tighter, desperate for him not to fade away. 'By the time we reached Berlin, Hugo and Hannah were deep into their romance. They were married the year after. For years I lost touch with Hugo, but sometimes – just sometimes – we'd find ourselves together, thrown into the same competition, dancing in the same ballroom, the same palace. And Hannah…' Raymond swallowed, as if the thing he was about to say was too horrible to contemplate. 'Hannah died, giving birth to their child. The child perished too. But Hugo stayed close to Hannah's father. He stayed bound to them, by blood. And…'

There was another crackling on the line, and Nancy heard her husband's voice suddenly muffled. It seemed, suddenly, that there was another voice, similarly muffled, coming down the line. No doubt her husband was sharing some hurried exchange with whoever was overseeing him in the room.

'What Lieutenant de Guise is being cautioned he cannot say across the line is nothing other than this,' Maynard interjected. 'Hannah Lindt's father was second cousin by marriage to a man named Joseph Goebbels. In 1927, the year Hugo first met him at a Lindt family summer party, Mr Goebbels was a talented writer and polemicist, employed as district leader for the young Nazi party in Berlin. Now, he is one of Mr Hitler's chief strategists, dictating policy and controlling the flow of information across the Reich.'

Nancy felt a cold chill. Her body was heavy as lead. Raymond's voice had returned to the line, but she could hardly hear him for, in her mind, she was so far away; though her eyes remained open, all she could see was Hugo Lavigne cradling her infant son in his arms.

'Hugo's associations don't end there,' Raymond's voice finally broke through. 'His great uncle is a man named Laval. Pierre Laval, a diplomat after the war. These days he reports directly to Marshal Pétain.'

'Phillipe Pétain,' mused Maynard Charles, 'the Lion of Verdun.'

Nancy knew that name well enough. Pétain was the man they named prime minister in France – but his government was but a puppet of the Nazis; the Free French recognised not a soul within it.

'Nancy,' Raymond said, 'I need you to be strong, now. I need you to protect yourself, and to protect our son – because I can't be there. I can't do it for you. And I love you, Nancy. You're too precious to risk a hair on your head. And...' Raymond's voice reached a new fever pitch. 'They're going to ask you to help, Nancy. But Nancy, take for the hills before you put yourself in harm's way. Run back to Lancashire, as far as you can from the Buckingham Hotel, before...'

Raymond's voice died again. Again, there were but muffled voices – and Nancy knew, in that moment, that her husband was being admonished, that somehow he'd broken rank, that he'd done one of the very things he'd been instructed not to do: implored her to abandon her post, and by doing so give Hugo a clue that his secrets were slowly being unfurled.

'Nancy,' Raymond's voice returned, 'they're going to ask for your help.'

Her eyes flashed around the room, taking in the stony mask of Maynard Charles's face. So, now it became clear: she hadn't been spirited here, under cover of darkness, for a long overdue tête-à-tête with her beloved. She was being enlisted. She herself was being sent to the war.

'My help?' she stuttered.

'Keep our son safe, my darling.' Raymond's voice caught in his throat. He paused, before he brokenly said, 'And keep yourself safe too. I'm coming home. And... let there be a home to come back to.'

The line went dead.

She looked up, through shimmering eyes, at the kindly, lined face of the former Hotel Director – and, for a reason she could not immediately fathom, felt suddenly as if she was a pig being fattened up for market, that Maynard Charles was the one feeding her tasty treats until, at last, he came with the butcher's knife. 'You must understand the game we are playing now, Nancy. It is our steadfast belief that Hugo Lavigne is no mere ballroom dancer. Rather, he is a man of military intelligence, dispatched by his paymasters – perhaps in Vichy, perhaps Berlin – to infiltrate the Buckingham Hotel. The seat of exiled governments. A place where drinks flow fast and lips are often loose. We believe he has been reporting back on gossip overheard ever since he stepped into the ballroom.'

'Then stop it,' Nancy said, her eyes shining and bright. 'You plucked me off the streets tonight. Send a car and pluck him off Berkeley Square.'

Maynard Charles shook his head. 'Lavigne is not the only servant of foreign governments at large in London today. Nor, I am afraid to tell you, is he the only one known to fraternise at the Buckingham Hotel – though I will admit that his cover has been less permeable than most. Nancy, I don't expect you to understand this at first, but I would like you to take this on trust: sometimes it is better that we leave these characters at large than that we incarcerate them. A man left to do his master's bidding can often lead us back to that master. He can unwittingly expose his associates in crime. He can, if we are clever about it, receive false information, which he feeds back as true to his masters – and, by doing so, helps us to advance our own causes without quite knowing that's what he's doing. These are shadow wars, Nancy. Lies and counter-lies, spun in a web. So Hugo will not be arrested. He will be,' and here Maynard paused, lending the word a strange emphasis, '*observed*.'

Nancy understood that emphasis only too well. 'Observed … by me?'

'I must ask you to perpetuate your relationship with Hugo Lavigne, and report back to me in person. I will not ask you to lead him into any trap, nor to pump him for information that might incriminate him – not yet. But I will ask you to be observant, to be open to conversation, to …'

'To *spy*,' she said.

'We must beat him at his own game.'

A sudden thought had occurred to Nancy. She lifted herself from her seat, so alarming was the idea. 'Sir, it was Hugo who conceived of the idea of Christmas in Exile. He and Mr Allgood went to see Mr Knave. They persuaded him that this should be the ball – that we should spend Christmas celebrating the exiled governments. The Buckingham, as a bastion of the free world…'

Maynard Charles nodded. 'We are already apprised of this situation. A brazen ploy by an enemy agent, but one suspects that Mr Lavigne has made brazenness part of his *modus operandi*. You can rest assured, Mrs de Guise, that the Buckingham Hotel has already been elevated to a new level of threat, according to our protocols. Does it surprise you to discover that we have always, since even before the war, had security agents stationed at the hotel?' Nancy tried not to betray her surprise, though by the look on Maynard's face she could tell she'd done a rotten job of disguising it. 'The ballroom will be a swarm of security staff on the night of Christmas in Exile. Our agents will shadow Mr Lavigne's every move. But this brings me to the final matter of the evening, and one I am grateful your husband is not here to overhear. Nancy, there is one part of the hotel to which our agents cannot easily gain access. One part of the hotel it is more difficult to infiltrate than the rest. I am speaking, of course, of what happens behind the ballroom doors. Of those private spaces where the dance troupe and musicians hold sway.' Maynard paused. 'We need a man on the inside of the troupe. A man who might want to do his bit for the war. A young man who, perhaps, was not permitted by some quirk of his medical history to sign up. A young man eager to do his bit…'

Nancy had thought her blood was already running cold, but now it felt as if her heart had suddenly stopped beating. 'Mr Charles, he's just a boy. My Frank already does his bit. He works the telephone exchanges. He takes shifts on the observation post, up on the hotel roof. He—'

'He can do more.'

For the first time, she stood. The blood had started pounding in her again. In a frenzy, she said, 'He's just a boy.'

'He was a brave young man when he accompanied the fishermen out to Dunkirk. He's proven his steadfastness time and again. It is time he rose to another challenge.' Maynard looked across Nancy's head and nodded at his subordinate, who reached out, as if to take Nancy's arm once again. 'Breathe not a word of this, neither to Frank nor Vivienne. One of my agents will attend you soon, to take Frank into our confidence. I'm afraid I must insist on this, Nancy. It brings me no pleasure to put those I value highly at risk, and rest assured I am not asking either of you to wade into this mire alone – but I'm afraid I *must* ask. I'll send word soon. Right now, I'm told your taxicab is awaiting.'

Nancy bristled with anger, though she knew not where to direct it: at the men in front of her, at Hugo Lavigne, or at the very engine of war itself?

'If anything happens to my brother, I'll not forgive you,' she said as she took her leave.

The night was still thick when the cab dropped Nancy off at Blomfield Road, and Nancy's heart still beating a wild percussion as she fumbled a key in the lock and came through the doors. All was still in the house; the wintry silence of a night without bombs was upon them. Nancy crept, carefully, up the staircase, then ventured into the nursery where Arthur lay asleep. She was still standing over him, drying her eyes, telling herself that *this* was what mattered, that *this* was what they were fighting for, when she heard footsteps – and turned to see a weary Vivienne approaching her through the dark.

'I thought I heard you, Nance.' Vivienne stopped dead. 'Something's wrong, isn't it?'

Nancy reached out and took her hand.

'It's just ... the war,' she whispered, brokenly. 'And Christmas coming, without Raymond, without ...' She was going to say 'hope', but caught herself at last. 'Do you ever think the world isn't quite what you thought it would be? That you've been blind, but suddenly your eyes are being opened?'

Vivienne said, 'Oh, *all* the time. And then ...'

'Then you put on the kettle,' sighed Nancy, 'and you make the toast, and you keep putting one foot in front of the other until you *know* the world again.'

And even though it was almost three o'clock in the morning, that was exactly what they did.

Chapter Twenty-Seven

In the first hour of blackout, on a still, siren-less night, a dark silhouette lifted itself from the Underground at Baron's Court and bowed into the darkness of the cemetery on St Dunstan's Road.

He passed three ARP wardens making their rounds before he reached the nondescript little townhouse on Humboldt Road. Hubris took hold of him, and he even doffed his cap to the third man – a portly little fellow, proud to be doing his bit for the city he loved – and wished him a good night. A common pleasantry like that might have drawn attention, but it was less suspicious than silence.

This man had not lived in silence, never in his life.

This man had lived in music and song.

The music had been different, of late. The song he'd been singing had taken on a different beat. There'd been a time when the music of his life was the joyous, lively music of the ballroom. Now, it was the rhythm of the marching band.

He slipped into the townhouse – there was no need to knock to announce his appearance – and followed the darkened hall to the back of the building, where his associate was.

The door clicked shut behind him.

'Things have changed,' his associate began, without the need for any preamble – for this was no common meeting of friends. 'An opportunity presents itself. Your ploy has been more success-ful than we could ever have dreamed, Mr Lavigne. The English are so very predictable. Not only must they be defiant against unimaginable odds. They must be *seen* to be defiant. They must *celebrate* this defiance. The Englishman is not as humble as he likes to think. He enjoys the glory he so despises in others. And here we are …'

'Christmas in Exile,' purred Hugo Lavigne.

'Our sources are confirmed. *He* shall be in attendance.'

'Every chambermaid in the Buckingham Hotel knows this.'

'No,' replied Hugo's associate, 'every chambermaid at that lousy hotel *thinks* they know it. But I am confirming to you here, tonight, that M. de Gaulle will spend an hour at the Buckingham's Christmas Ball, to take in toasts with his Free French generals, and raise a glass with the other runaways of Europe.' He stopped, made a steeple of his fingers, and peered at Hugo across the ill-lit shadows of the room. 'The moment has changed, and therefore so has your purpose.' He reached beneath his seat and drew out a coal black revolver, which he handed by the barrel to his subordinate. 'A Webley Mk IV. A Britisher's design, of course, and easily disposable for that.'

Hugo shuddered as he accepted it. In moments, it had vanished into the folds of his overcoat. 'Sir, I was sent to the Buckingham Hotel to listen. I wasn't sent to—'

'You were sent there as an agent of this war, as part of our attempts to secure a lasting peace. A lasting peace that can only come with our total domination of Europe. The information you have filtered back has, so far, been … *disappointing*, Mr Lavigne. And so … you may consider this a field promotion. No longer are you our eyes and ears in the Buckingham Hotel. Now, you are …'

Hugo could feel the Webley pressing against his hip. 'I know what I am.'

The superior officer had another gift for Hugo: a small, brown envelope, unmarked by any hand. 'Absorb these instructions; then destroy what you have read. It's all in there. Your means of escape, should you be able to leave the ballroom in the confusion, and ...' One final gift: a paper parcel, no bigger than the nail of his thumb – and, inside it, a small, chalk-coloured lozenge, dusty to the touch. 'A means of last resort, M. Lavigne – should you succeed in your mission, but be captured in the event. You must not – I repeat *you must not* – be taken alive. There is too much information swirling in the backwaters of your brain. So instead: one final dance ...'

The dance we all come to at the end of the show, thought Hugo. *The dance with Death.*

The other man smiled. 'I never realised my career would embrace its commission, but these are not ordinary times.' There was a decanter of brandy on the table between them. The man poured two stiff measures. 'A drink with me, Hugo. A toast to the coming end. We are but months away from overrunning this little island. We are but a shade from showing Mr Churchill his defiance has all been for show. These are a people who turn retreat into victory. Let us put one more nail in their coffin by tomorrow evening. Let the Free French fall, just as their brothers did in Paris and Lille. And by midnight tomorrow, my friend, you will be returning to your homeland a hero of the war.' He put the brandy to his lips and swallowed it whole. 'That is, of course, if you do the job that you must. If you kill M. Charles de Gaulle, in full sight of all those who matter in London Society, at the Buckingham ball.'

*

'I can't … I don't believe it,' said Frank.

The midnight hour was almost upon them – and, as the front door closed in the little house on Blomfield Road, it seemed as if the world had shifted on its axis once again. Frank picked himself up, shook off the numb feeling, and hurried to the window in the sitting room – where, upon peeling back the blackout blinds, he looked out upon the pristine snow. Two sets of heavy boot-prints snaked away along the garden path. The engine of the retreating charcoal grey Ford Anglia was already fading as his visitors returned to the night.

He turned to Nancy, who stood with her arms wrapped around herself in the doorway. The children were restless upstairs, but Vivienne was fussing around them; Vivienne was always fussing around them, for such was her way. This was how she fought through all the calamities of the past: in muslin cloths and bottles of milk.

'It isn't right, is it, Nance? There's some mistake. Some catastrophic mistake. Hugo can't be—'

They hadn't permitted her to keep hold of the letter Raymond had sent – for paranoia told them that Hugo might stumble across it, and in doing so suspect his fiction had been exposed – so all Nancy had to convince Frank was a solemn promise. 'Raymond knew his associations. He knew he'd fallen in love with the daughter of a Nazi general. He knew Hugo remained loyal to the family, even after her death. And—'

'It doesn't mean he's a villain. A man who dances like that can't be filled with hatred, Nancy. He just can't. It wouldn't work. He wouldn't *fly*.'

'The intelligence service has done its homework, Frank. Raymond's fears – they're not without merit. That Hugo just turned up on our doorstep, that he used us to gain entry to the

Buckingham Hotel, that he's becoming the star of the Grand, fraternising with every member of the Free French...'

'He's a proud Parisian.' The panic, the disbelief, was mounting in Frank's voice. 'When we came back from the Buckingham that summer night, he was talking about Paris, how much he hated its fall. You should have heard him talk about Vichy. Then you wouldn't believe.'

Nancy crossed the room to wrap her arms around her little brother. There was such goodness in Frank. Thank heavens he hadn't been sucked into the infantry like all of the others; going to war changed a man irrevocably. There were some things that, once you saw them, you could never unsee. If only that goodness could persist in him until the end of his days – but, in moments like these, as Frank's eyes opened to the reality of the world, Nancy could see it being chipped slowly away. 'I think he lied to us, little brother.' Frank stiffened in her arms. 'I think he used us to plant himself in the Grand. And I think he did it for the express purpose of getting close to the Free French.'

'But what now?' he whispered. 'What now, Nance?'

'Well, Frank, you heard them.'

Two of Maynard Charles's security operatives had arrived after the blackout, entering Nancy's home without knocking, just as had been agreed. Nancy had been asked not to brief Frank on their arrival, but she had spent her whole life caring for her brother and in the end, defying their instructions, had told him that they were to be visited by security agents wanting to discuss a very particular matter. Even so, the way the colour had drained from Frank's face as the officials described the true story of Hugo Lavigne had been terrible to behold. The protestations he'd put up, met only with the blunt certainties of Maynard Charles's men, had made her yearn for simpler times.

And then: the fear she'd been nursing across the last two days, ever since she met with Maynard Charles. 'Frank,' one of the agents had asked, with a syrupy voice designed to charm, 'do you want to do your bit for your country?'

Of course he did. It was what he'd wanted ever since the war's declaration, ever since he'd marched down to the War Office, expecting to take the king's shilling, only to be declined on medical grounds. It was what had driven him down to Rye, where he'd joined a fisherman on his odyssey to Dunkirk. It was what sparkled in him even now, despite his disbelief, despite the uncertainty surrounding them.

'They told you not to be a hero, Frank. You do remember that, don't you?'

It had all been a blur, but Frank could at least remember this.

It was the elder of the two security agents who'd outlined their proposal. '*Ears*, young man. That's all a job like this requires. *Eyes and ears.*' Frank had already been asked to swear his fealty to the Crown, to place his hand across a leatherbound Bible and make an oath of secrecy, 'and treachery if you break it, young man'. Now, as the agent spoke, it felt like the old, familiar world of the Buckingham was being remodelled. 'The Buckingham Hotel is already under close surveillance, Mr Nettleton. We have eyes and ears across the establishment – but what we have never had, nor ever had cause to need, are eyes and ears backstage at the ballroom. But now... The situation has developed. The moment has come. You will never be asked to *act*, Mr Nettleton, but you will be asked to report back on everything, however banal it might seem, that you hear. Sedition and treachery are commonplace now. We must root it out.'

Nancy released her hold of him and said, 'No heroics, little man. Just listen and observe, and ... and don't let him know you for what you are now, Frank. Don't let him take you for a spy.'

'But if they're right about him, if everything they're saying is true, then they're just letting him dance on. Tomorrow night, there he'll be, with some diplomat's wife in his arms. I've …' The agents had already acquired the ball's guest list, along with each dance a particular guest had reserved with every member of the troupe.

Nancy seized his shoulders. '*No*, Frank. *No*. If you want to be a hero in this, you do as they say. You listen and you watch, and you don't let on, even for a second, that that's what you're doing.' She let go of him, watched as he drifted to the hearth and slumped down in the armchair by the fire – the same armchair where Raymond always used to sit. 'Frank, this is a deeper game than either of us know. If they wanted to arrest Hugo, they'd have done it already. But …' She tried to remember the way Maynard Charles had explained it. 'He's of more value to them with his secrets intact. They'll use him, just like he's been using *us*. And we have to let them, Frank. This is their world, not ours.'

'I knew the Buckingham was the home of exiled governments,' said Frank. 'I just never understood it was a battlefield for foreign spies. Because … that's what they're doing, isn't it? They're going to spy on the spy, and we're going to help them.'

Nancy smiled, weakly. Her brother hadn't been a baby for a long time, but it was sometimes so hard to think of him in the cruel, adult world.

'Hugo Lavigne isn't dancing the java anymore, Frank. If Raymond's right, he left that joyfulness behind long ago. Now, he's dancing in a different world altogether. A darker dance, Frank. A more dangerous dance.'

'The dance of spies.'

'The Grand Ballroom might be filled with the most precious, garlanded guests the Buckingham has ever received – but tomorrow night, it's going to be teeming with others as well.

Undercover agents. Spies from both sides of the war. The Buckingham isn't only hosting a Christmas ball, Frank. It's hosting a battleground.'

Every other soul in the Buckingham Hotel was anticipating the beauty and magnificence of Christmas in Exile, but to Annie Brogan all that paled in comparison to the moment she'd been anticipating since that last November night: her stroll through the snowy pastures of Mayfair with Victor.

She was waiting for him by the tradesman's entrance as soon as her shift ended – and, though he kept her waiting, the hour she spent idling there had quickly flurried by. By the time he arrived, her anticipation had reached a new pitch – so intense, it seemed, that she garbled saying hello, repeated herself three times, and had already rattled off a list of everything that had gone wrong in her shift (she'd accidentally polished the Continental Suite, which had been turned over by Rosa only half an hour before) by the time Victor offered to take her bag. She flushed crimson red as she handed it over.

'It's very light,' said Victor as they tramped through the frozen slush along Michaelmas Mews.

'Oh, that's because there's nothing in it.'

Victor looked at her curiously as they came to Berkeley Square.

'I just think it's smart to carry it. I wanted to look like a proper lady this afternoon. Well…' Annie stopped on the edge of the square. When she looked up at the townhouses, she thought: *these are the places* real *ladies live, but I could at least feel like a real lady today, couldn't I*? 'A currant bun,' she shrugged. 'A currant bun would do nicely.'

The war had a different feeling about it this year. As last Christmas approached, the bombs came down every single night – and the good old boys of the RAF were duelling with the Luftwaffe, giving their lives so that the likes of Annie could sleep soundly in their beds (or else in the shelters). Though there seemed no end in sight, a kind of lasting, grim defiance had settled over London. The barrage balloons hanging above the rooftops seemed perfectly normal. Annie knew that plenty of the chambermaids no longer cared to carry their gas masks. 'Just another day,' Mary-Louise so often said; she didn't even go to the staff shelters if the sirens sounded anymore.

There was still danger, thought Annie, but we know how to cope with it. Besides, it was difficult to feel that peril right now. Difficult to feel anything but *hope*. Part of that was to do with the idea that she might really be spending Christmas back at Albert Yard – but mostly it was because she'd dared to thread her arm into Victor's, and together they were walking to her favourite café in all of the world.

'I've tasted a lot of currant buns,' said Victor, once he'd devoured his and attended to a face covered in jammy smears, 'but not one like this. Thank you, Annie.'

Annie was scattering pennies on the table, as if she might pay.

'I won't hear of it!' Victor declared.

'Oh, but I want to,' Annie returned. 'It's good for a girl to pay her ...'

But Victor looked set for a fight. 'You might be the one who suggested it, Annie, but I'll be damned if any girl is paying for *my* currant bun. It's my treat. You ... you can get it the next time.' The promise implied in this seemed to occur to Victor a moment too late, for suddenly he stalled. 'That is, if you want there to be a next time,' he declared.

'I needed that,' he finally said, having finished the pot of tea and returned to the snowy boulevard without. 'The dinner service is going to be the biggest we've ever had. The *biggest*. Mr Laurent would have us all flogged if we didn't turn up, fighting fit for a battle. Every private dining room's been filled. They won't say it out loud, but... *Mr de Gaulle*,' he whispered. 'They're serving up roast beef, but some of the lads reckoned we should be serving up frogs and snails. They really do eat them, you know. A Frenchman enjoys a buttery snail.'

'I'll stick with currant buns,' grinned Annie.

'Me too,' Victor returned. 'But you've got to give it to these French folk – they know how to keep a tradition alive. Just like my pa used to...' Victor's voice trailed off, as it always did when he brought his father – locked up in some internment camp – to mind. 'Sorry, Annie. I didn't mean to bring things down. It's just...'

'It's Christmas,' Annie said, recognising the feeling. 'Nice as it is, I reckon it makes you think of what you've lost. I'd give anything to have all my brothers and sisters back for the season.' *But at least we'll be in the old house*, she thought. Now, if only she could break free of that sickening feeling that the only reason they were going back there at all was because of Billy and all his dark deeds.

'You've just got to look after what you have got,' said Victor. He had hold of her hand.

'Do you want to... go to the arcade? Up on Regent Street?' he said. 'All this talk of Christmas, and I haven't bought a single present.'

'Regent Street?' Annie baulked. '*Regent Street?* I've been getting all my presents from the covered market, down in Lambeth. You can pick up all sorts if you have a sniff about.'

'Oh come on, Annie. You've got a lady's satchel on your shoulder – and very nice it is indeed. Don't you want to go looking round some ladies' shops?'

Annie had to admit that there was something tantalising about entering the grand arcades that bordered Regent Street, stepping through the golden arches and gazing through windows at shops that sold pocket-watches worth more than her yearly salary, gentleman's tailors who counted Royalty among their clientele, shoemakers afforded the Royal warrant – but there was something unnerving about it too. The deeper Victor led her along one particular arcade, the more convinced she became that they were being *watched* – as a passing policeman might watch out for pickpockets.

'There's no law against looking through windows,' said Victor. 'Come on, Annie, just one more gander…'

She hadn't expected a potter through these gilded arcades to energise Victor so much, but his curiosity quickly became infectious. Soon, they were standing in front of a shop that sold leather goods. Purses, handbags and other satchels were mounted in a grand display in the windows. The name of the shopkeeper, BICKERDYKE, LEATHERSMITHS SINCE 1848, was stencilled in gold above the glass.

'What do you think, Annie?' Victor said, marvelling at one particular clutch bag. 'That's craftsmanship, that is. I reckon that would make someone the best Christmas present.'

'Oh, give over!' Annie suddenly laughed, unable to control the squall that burst out of her lips. 'We can't go gallivanting around shops like these. Victor, they'd hardly let us through the door. For a start, you've still got jam on your whiskers!'

Whiskers was a generous description of the downy fluff Victor had started growing on his jaw, but he quickly reached up to wipe away the sticky raspberry preserve. Then he turned back to the window. In the reflection, he could suddenly see the drab clothes he was wearing – the starkest of contrasts to the fine woollen suits of the gentlemen perusing the exhibits in the store.

He reached for the door handle.

'Victor!' Annie gasped.

'I just want to see that clutch bag,' he grinned. 'My ma would like something like that. It's been so hard on her, Annie, ever since my father was locked up. Wouldn't it be nice if she was to open something like that on Christmas morning?'

'Well, it'd be nice if Mr Knave gave us each a thousand pounds but…'

Annie stalled.

Impossible things did sometimes happen, didn't they? Like the Brogans returning to Albert Yard, and all in time for Christmas.

'I think I could afford it,' said Victor, quietly. Was Annie wrong, or did she detect some modicum of embarrassment, perhaps even *shame*, in his voice? 'I've been doing a few extra jobs around the hotel. Working extra shifts in the kitchen. I've been squirrelling it away – and maybe, just *maybe*…'

There was something frighteningly familiar about this line of thinking, thought Annie. Something in the words that brought her brother Billy to mind.

She took a step backwards.

She opened the distance between herself and Victor.

She furrowed her eyes, wondering, *just wondering*…

Then Victor looked up. 'I'll have to come back in something smarter, of course. They'll think me a pickpocket and sweep me out before I've crossed the threshold. And…' He seemed to have seen the unnerved look on Annie's face, for something changed in his own countenance. 'Annie, are you all right? I… I'd like to get you something special too. Something for Christmas.'

Annie's other thoughts seemed suddenly to be chased away. 'Oh Victor, I wouldn't want anything from these shops even *if* you could afford it!' she exclaimed. 'Listen, next time we go for a currant bun, we'll go down to the covered market afterwards.

You can… you can get me a ribbon. For my hair. Yes,' Annie grinned, warming at last to the idea, 'a ribbon for my hair and I'll wear it on Christmas night.'

In two short hours, the Grand ballroom would open its doors – and Christmas in Exile would begin.

As Frank opened the door to the backstage, it was already a hubbub. Marcus liked to gather his dancers some hours before an event as prestigious as this – not only to help limber up their bodies, but also to limber up their minds: their spirits, their passion, their imagination. Karina and Mathilde were already wearing the gowns in which they would glide out when the band struck up. One or two of the musicians were sharing a quiet tête-à-tête with Marcus, no doubt running through the finer points of the set they'd been practising all season.

And there was Hugo, preening in one of the mirrors, bedecked in a suit of midnight blue.

Midnight blue.

Why was that the detail that lodged so suddenly, so bitterly, in Frank's mind? It took him a moment to recollect: it was midnight blue with which Raymond had been presented, that evening in Paris; a suit of midnight blue that he'd danced in throughout his ballroom life. There was every chance Hugo had found it in the wardrobes here: Hugo Lavigne, wearing the clothes of Raymond de Guise as he prepared to dance in the ballroom of which, had it not been for this war, Raymond would have been king.

Hugo turned to him and smiled.

There was nothing different about that smile, thought Frank. Hugo had given the same twinkling, irrepressible grin before. He'd used it to charm Nancy. He'd used it to sidle into Vivienne's thoughts. He'd been using it all year to build his reputation in the Grand. And now…

'No java tonight, young Frank,' Hugo beamed, and the echo of what Nancy had said was so strong it took Frank by surprise. 'How are your nerves holding up, *mon frère*? You do not seem ... impassioned, perhaps?'

Frank summoned up what courage he had and smiled in return. 'It wouldn't be a Buckingham ball if it didn't inspire nerves, Mr L-Lavigne.' He managed to control his stuttering; Frank had suffered, once, with a stammer that blighted his days. The confidence the ballroom had instilled in him had gone some way to alleviating that affliction – but nerves always brought it back, and never in his life had he felt these kinds of nerves before. There, in front of him, stood a servant of the enemy.

'I am quite certain you will do the ballroom proud, young sir,' Hugo said, casually returning to the mirror, carefully running pomade through his lustrous black hair. 'Just remember all of which we have spoken: *music*, Frank.' Their eyes met through the mirror into which Hugo was staring. 'Lean into the music, let it inhabit you – and forget all else. Shut your eyes to everything around you. Everything but the dance ...'

Frank hardened. He felt his legs turn suddenly heavy. What advice was this, from the mouth of a liar? Hugo had been espousing the same thing all year: lose yourself in the music, shut yourself off from the world around you; but what else was he in the ballroom for, but to keep his eyes and ears peeled, to absorb every last little thing, to make mental notes of it all and report back to his masters?

Frank started to back away.

How on earth was he to dance tonight, with all these thoughts pounding through him?

'Are you – are you well, *mon frère*?'

'Oh, I'm – I'm f-fine, Mr Lavigne. I'll be fine, as soon as there's m-music ...'

There was no use loitering here until the dance-floor doors opened up. In moments, Frank had reeled backwards, out of the dressing rooms and towards the little dance studio behind. Perhaps, here, he could find some strength. Perhaps, here, he might summon some resolve.

But of course he wasn't alone – because there sat Mr Allgood, hunched over the baby white practice piano, running his fingers up and down the keys, one chord running into another as he sought to lose himself in the music.

Quite why Mr Allgood might be devoting these hours to the piano, Frank had no idea. There was Lucille, untouched in her case by his feet. He looked up when Frank appeared, but did not break from the music. 'Sometimes it just calls to you,' he remarked, as some minor key melody rolled out of him. 'You never know when you might be called on. A bandleader's gotta be ready for anything. You look a little distracted, Mr Nettleton. Is anything wrong?'

Funny, because Frank had been thinking the very same thing about Max. Those words of his – *'ready for anything'* – could they have meant that Max somehow *knew*? That Max, too, had been tasked with seeking out anything untoward in the ballroom, looking out for sedition among his ranks?

Not for the first time, Frank could feel himself shaking.

'Mr Allgood,' he ventured, inching nearer, wondering exactly what he could say, 'when you said *ready for anything* ...' He glanced backwards, fearful Hugo might have followed him here. 'Do you know if something ... *bad* is going to happen tonight, Mr Allgood? Do you know if someone's going to ...'

Max had still been tinkling at the keys, but now the music stopped.

Now there was only silence between them.

So, thought Frank, *he must know*. By the startled look in Max's eyes, the sudden shock and fear of it, there was no doubt about it. 'I don't want anything bad to happen tonight, Mr Allgood,' he breathed.

'No, kid,' Max said, and made an ungainly leap from his seat, snatching up Lucille as he rose. 'Me neither.' Then he bouldered past Frank, nearly tumbling over his own feet as he hurried for the back exit. 'I'm sorry, young man. I gotta go!'

The first guests of the evening passed beneath the boughs of the resplendent Norwegian fir, then through the ornate, sculpted arch that led down to the Grand. The first eyes to take it in belonged to King Zog of Albania and his retinue; the second, to a detachment of officials from Hubert Pierlot's Belgian office. Among the third group of guests who marched into the ballroom's extravagant environs were two men who appeared on the guest list as ministers of the Crown – but who, in truth, took their orders from men deep in the government's shadowy employ, men as far removed from the King as paupers from princes. Soon, the ballroom was filling up around them. Soon, members of the Free French, the Hotel Board, the extended Royal family of Norway – who had called the Buckingham their second home since long before hostilities began – were taking cocktails around the empty dance floor, awaiting the spectacle to come.

And in the Hotel Director's office, tucked away behind the reception hall, Walter Knave knew the time was nigh.

A knock came at his door. Moments later, one of the hotel secretaries had delivered John Hastings, head of the Hotel Board, to the office. 'Are you ready, Mr Hastings?' Walter began.

The portly American man nodded, stiffly. 'It isn't just our dancers and orchestra who must put on a show, Mr Knave. Please – lead on.'

Walter Knave led the way across the bustling reception hall, through the prized guests now flocking towards the ballroom, and across the busy restaurant floor. The Queen Mary was a hive of activity tonight, but soon that would be over – for every guest taking dinner here was about to be summoned by the music.

So were the guests who now dined in the six private dining rooms that flanked the restaurant floor. Mr Knave and Mr Hastings made haste for the greatest among them, slipping past the two doormen – one in the hotel's employ, one dispatched by the Crown – who stood sentry there.

Inside, twelve men were dining on M. Laurent's finest roast beef. Glasses had already been raised, then emptied. In here, the red wine flowed.

At the head of the table, a lean, moustachioed man with an intense expression lifted his eyes. Here was a man sentenced to death by the country that had been stolen from him; a man who had not blinked in the face of catastrophe; a man who still dreamed of a world set to rights, a war worth winning.

'General de Gaulle,' Walter began, once the dining room had fallen silent. 'May I introduce Mr John Hastings, the head of our Board. Mr Hastings, please meet General de Gaulle, our most prized guest.'

'General,' said John Hastings, his voice brimming with the utmost respect. 'I am proud and delighted to host you this evening. I do hope our restaurant's service has been to your liking. And, whenever you are ready, I would like to accompany you personally to our Grand Ballroom – and a night, I hope, that will honour everything you and your people are fighting for. A night that will honour the free world…'

In the Candlelight Club, the clock inched towards 6 p.m. In one hour's time, the band would strike up.

It would, Harry Dudgeon was evidently thinking, be the last time the Max Allgood Orchestra ever played.

From the shadows in the corner of the crowded cocktail lounge, Daisy watched Harry holding court with a host of the Orchestra's other musicians. He was a talented pianist, that was for sure – and, by the looks on the faces of the musicians, he was a talented raconteur as well. In another world, he would have made a talented bandleader. But the one thing he most certainly was not – at least, not in Daisy's book – was a talented liar, a talented cheat, a talented manipulator. Daisy knew this for a fact, because she was all three.

If he thought tonight was the night he took control of the Orchestra, he was wrong.

Tonight was the night all his ambition came to an end.

Daisy was not proud of the woman she'd become, but it was some significant time since she had felt any guilt or shame in it. She looked around her now, at the lords hobnobbing with the city industrialists; at the diplomats taking cocktails; at the stars of stage and screen. None of them had grown up like she and Max. None of them had *ever* gone hungry, nor had to steal to keep a roof above their head. Just to protect their families. That was why they'd never learned the hard lessons Daisy and Max had long ago incorporated into their souls. They didn't have the rougher edges it took to win a battle like this.

Daisy had made a promise: she was going to get out of New York, find a new home, protect it at all costs.

If Max had given up, she would just fight harder.

She had been keeping an eye on the musicians for an hour already, but there was no more time to wait. The hour of the ball was drawing near; every minute, a chance that slipped through her fingers. She watched, now, as the musicians took their last round of drinks. It was then that she made her approach. Sashaying across the bustling club – where the guests, too, had sensed the hour, and begun taking their leave so that they could claim the best tables in the Grand – she reached the booth just as Harry Dudgeon was rising. The story he'd been telling must have been uproarious, for several members of the Orchestra were cackling with mirth. Harry, too, had been cackling – but when he turned and saw Daisy looming there, it quickly wiped the grin off his face.

'Harry, I wondered if we might have a quiet talk together – just the two of us.'

Harry seemed to take this in with a level of incredulity that gave him great joy. Evidently, he still felt as if he was holding court with the Orchestra, for he was still playing to them as he said, 'Mrs Allgood, haven't you heard? There's a bit of a shindig tonight. Has it passed you by?'

He was shaking his head sardonically, adding, 'Come on, boys – we've a show to put on!' when Daisy said, 'It mustn't wait, Mr Dudgeon. I'll only keep you five minutes. It concerns...' She hadn't taken her eyes off him; her gaze was penetrating. 'It concerns Max.'

At last, her gaze really did penetrate Harry.

Harry looked around and, gathering his composure, whisked the other musicians along. 'Two minutes, boys. I'll join you by the Grand. This won't take long.'

By the way they all nodded and hurried on, Daisy wondered if they'd already sworn some fealty to him – or whether it was just Harry's natural charm, geeing them along. Well, that would have to end too.

'I'll walk with you, Harry,' said Daisy. 'No sense lingering.'

Feigning that she didn't want them to be overheard ('This hotel's full of gossips and spies, Harry, *you know that*'), Daisy steered Harry towards one of the lesser halls, the service elevators tucked round the corner and the crooked service stairs just up ahead.

'Let's cut to the chase, Harry,' Daisy said, her words bitter, but her tone full of charm. 'I know you know about New York. I know Jackson Ford sold you our story. And there's no use in lying about it: it's all true, every last bit.'

Harry nodded, stoutly; it seemed he enjoyed the straight-forwardness of this exchange, if nothing else. 'So might I start calling you by your real name? The name your mother gave you?' He took a breath before saying it, as if – in spite of his bravado – he needed to steel himself. '*Ava.*'

'That won't be necessary. I'm Daisy now, and Daisy I'll be staying. You see, Harry,' and they passed by the service elevators to the darker hallway beyond, 'we both have a vested interest in keeping certain things secret. The way I see it, the moment you go shouting all that from the rooftops, you lose your power over my dear Max – and, well, I'm quite *sure* you want to hold on to your power over him, don't you? I'm quite *sure* it's giving you a little thrill, on top of everything else.'

'This is just business, Daisy. Your cousin Max has something I want. I have something he wants. It's a simple trade. My secrecy, for the Orchestra. Max has been understanding of it, so what are *you* here for? Why *you* and why *now?*'

Daisy draped an arm around him. She felt his body tense, though he had the self-control not to try and cast her off. 'I have a different deal in mind, Harry.'

With those words, Harry lost what self-control he'd had. He stepped out of her arm and strode ferociously away. 'I'm a married man,' he snapped, 'and I know your old profession, remember? So I'll keep myself clean. Touch me again and you'll be—'

'Oh, Harry, you flatter yourself. I'm not offering you *me*. I'm offering you money.'

'Money?' Harry recoiled.

'Just keep walking with me, Harry. Keep walking. I'll make you see.'

Harry followed her, round the last bend in the hallway. 'I haven't got much time...'

'You see, Harry, when Max first explained the agreement you'd made, it struck me there were much better ways of getting what you wanted. Money, Harry. It makes the world go round. You've been moonlighting with your band all year long, looking for a little something to line your nest. A bit of reputation, and a bit of a treasure hoard – that's what you've been after. Well, couldn't we come to a better arrangement?' Daisy had drifted ahead of Harry now; she beckoned him to hurry on. 'You already know the reason we left New York. What you don't know is that there was plenty left over from the money I stole. We needed that mobster's ill-gotten gains to get us to Europe, but there was plenty left over. So what I'm saying is—'

'I don't need your money,' Harry laughed. 'It's the Orchestra I want.'

'With enough money, you could have both. Think about it: enough money to hire the best musicians; enough money to take Harry Dudgeon and the Moonlighters out of the Grand forever; to tour, and build that reputation you're after – and who knows, one day, to end up in residence at the Imperial. The Savoy.'

Harry was still. 'Why would I do that?' he finally whispered. 'I have everything I want right here.'

'Oh, Harry, but every man has his price. Come here,' she smiled, 'let me whisper it to you. Let me make you an offer you can't refuse.'

Harry darted a look around. 'How much?' he ventured.

Yes, thought Daisy, she'd hooked him in now. 'Come here,' she said, 'I don't want anyone to hear this,' and when he stepped closer, she bent to his ear. 'I had to do some rather unsavoury things to get us out of New York.'

'How much, Daisy?' Harry snapped. 'I haven't time to play games...'

'Jackson Ford told you what I did, didn't he? But did he tell you exactly *how*?'

Daisy clutched Harry's wrist, as fiercely as she could.

Harry recoiled, but it was too late; Daisy was holding him fast. His eyes flashed around. Quite without knowing it, he was standing at the very top of the service stairs. The steps plunged into shadow beneath, the stairwell echoing and empty.

His blood ran cold.

The surprise on his face was a delight to Daisy. 'You *do* know,' she smiled.

Harry was grappling, but Daisy was bigger; she planted her feet rigidly, so that she loomed above him, and Harry was on the very precipice of the first step. 'The last man who tried to *own* Max was a man not unlike you, Harry. A man of greed. A man of scorn. A man out for himself and himself alone. Do you know what happened to Johnny Glaser? Music manager. Mobster. Racketeer.'

'Let go of me,' Harry seethed. 'Let go of me, you—'

'He was found dead, Harry. Dead after a drunken stumble down the stairs at St Nicholas Park. He'd been running us girls for twelve hard years. Oh yes, he didn't just manage musicians – not good ol' Johnny Glaser. If there was a way of leeching money from a soul, he found it. But then ... well, then, he sunk his claws into my son as well.'

'N-Nelson,' Harry stammered, still reeling. 'I'll take you with me, you bitch. You push and I won't let go. We'll go down together ...'

'Nelson was a shy boy. A better pianist than you, Harry, but he didn't have the guts he needed to live in a world like ours. So he did some time. He fell in with the wrong crowd. And Johnny Glaser promised him ... well, you know the rest. A way out of the slums. He had the talent for it. But first he'd have to be one of Johnny's enforcers. If he wanted his chance at a big break, he'd have to break some bones, bury some bodies for Glaser first.' Daisy paused. 'And I couldn't let that happen. Just like I can't let *this*.'

'You're mad! Stark, raving mad!'

'I'm not mad. I'm a mother. I fought back against the mob, Harry. I can fight back against a *musician* ... It's just a shame your fingers aren't wearing the same jewels and rings Johnny was. Just a shame that wristwatch on your arm isn't worth a small fortune. That's what got us all out of New York. That's what set us up in Europe. And I'll be damned if we're losing it, all because of *you*.' Daisy shook her head. 'Goodbye, Harry.'

The terror opened Harry's eyes so wide they seemed unreal.

Then, from the shadows below, there came a voice: 'Daisy, *no!*'

It was, perhaps, the only voice that could have saved Harry's life. Moments later, in an ungainly tumbling of footsteps, Max himself had appeared from below. There he stood – and, it seemed to Daisy, then, that he was poised to catch Harry as he fell.

'It ain't worth it, cous',' said Max. 'Glaser was scum. He spent his years ruining lives. He'd been ruining ours for years. He'd have destroyed Nelson. But Harry? Just look at him. He's just some club pianist, and he's about to be out of a job.' Max drew nearer. 'Let him back up, Daisy. Do it for me. Do it for Nelson, if you must. But let him back up.'

Harry sensed a moment's hesitation in Daisy. In a second, he'd gained a foothold. In the next, he'd shifted his weight so that he could tumble against her. Extricating his hand, he wrenched round, staggering back across the landing at the top of the stairs. 'You'll pay for this, you brutes. Attempted murder, that's what this is, and ...' A thought penetrated his fury. He turned his eyes on Max, who slowly advanced up the stairs, finally reaching the point where Harry had been braced. 'Out of a job?' he seethed. 'Just some club pianist? It's my goddamn Orchestra. You're finished! The pair of you are finished.'

Max reached the top of the stairs. By now, he was quite breathless. Funny how somebody famed for the power of his lungs could be defeated by a simple staircase. 'I'm afraid not.' He took the last step. 'Harry, you're fired.'

There was a pregnant pause before Harry started laughing. '*Fired? Fired?* On whose authority?'

'My own, Harry. Mr Knave has been very clear with me: manning the Orchestra is my responsibility, and I'm exercising it tonight. I'm telling you to leave.'

Harry shrugged. 'You know the rules of our agreement, Max. I'll blow your whole charade wide open. One little word, that's all it will take. You're not a travelling musician. You, and your cousin here, are runaways of the law. Grand larceny – and ... and *murder*. So you've got two choices.' Harry stopped. 'No, actually – you've got *one* choice. Walk away from here right now, and I'll keep your secret. Me? I'm going to go down there and lead my Orchestra out – by God, you see if I don't.'

But Max was unmoved. 'I'm not standing trial in your court anymore, Mr Dudgeon. You won't be taking to the stage tonight. I'll be playing the piano in your stead – and, if it isn't quite the spectacle we'd imagined, well, at least it'll be *me* at the front of *my* Orchestra.'

'You're not listening to me. There might be a war on, but you can't pretend those things didn't happen ...'

The smile that flourished on Max's face caught Daisy

completely off-guard. Every ounce of panic had left him. Somehow, for the very first time, he seemed in control.

'I'm not going to,' Max said, simply. 'I'm going to tell them it all.'

Frank was still sitting in the rehearsal studio. Mathilde had come to sit with him, for a time. He'd tried to tell her that everything was well, that he was just picking his way through the nerves that had beset him, but surely even she could see something was wrong. It was the thought of being found out that needled at him. He wondered how men like Hugo did it: how could you sit inside a lie every single hour of your life? How could you spin those stories around you, so that nobody saw the real you? Sometimes it seemed as if he, Frank Nettleton, was the only one in the Buckingham Hotel not harbouring some terrible secret.

The door opened up. In waddled Max Allgood, with the pianist Harry Dudgeon chasing soon after. Daisy was somewhere behind them, the look on her face as stony as the grave.

Max barely gave Frank a second look as he walked past. He was almost at the second door, about to enter the dressing rooms, when Harry snarled, 'Think about this, Max. You've been hoodwinking the Hotel Board. You'll be out on your ear anyway – but you could still have your dignity.'

Harry snatched Max's arm and Frank watched as Max found himself wheeled round. Fleetingly, it looked as if the two men might come to blows – what this could possibly be about, Frank had no idea – but Max simply picked himself free and said, 'I went to see Archie a while ago. I thought he might be able to help me. A wise bandleader like that, one you'd known all those years – he must have something wise to say. But in the end, it wasn't *Archie* who helped. It was that good lady wife of his, the one who used to run Housekeeping here. And do you know what she said?' Max smiled. '*The truth will set you free*. I might lose my Orchestra, Harry, but once the Board find out what you've been trying to do, it won't fall to you. No, if I die, let me die by my own sword. You'll hold no knife to my throat anymore.'

Max vanished through the dressing-room doors.

Frank watched as Harry followed, Daisy tramping after. By the time he heard, 'Roll up, roll up!' thundering from Max's lips, he too had been drawn to the dressing-room doors. Inside, the Orchestra were suddenly standing to attention. The dance troupe had rallied as well, drawn into the sudden fray.

There, among them, stood the dashing figure of Hugo Lavigne. He looked so striking, thought Frank, in Raymond's suit of midnight blue, his black mane of hair perfectly sculpted, his dazzling eyes certain to captivate the hearts of every soul in the ballroom tonight.

Those dazzling eyes found Frank and rooted him to the spot.

'Come, *mon frère*,' he seemed to be saying, 'Mr Allgood has something to say.'

But when Frank didn't move, a glimmer of something different entered those eyes: something puzzling, something questioning, the sensation that all was, perhaps, not right; that something was eating Frank away from his very insides.

Courage, Frank told himself. *Don't let him know.*

And: remember the lesson of Raymond and Ophelia as well; for how could Frank even contemplate dancing, when he felt this knotted inside?

In but ten minutes' time, the doors would open up.

Frank lurched through the dressing-room doors.

'*Do you know the moment I truly stepped out of the shadows and learned to live in the light?*' Mrs Moffatt had said. '*It was the moment I spoke the truth.*'

412

Max was clinging to those words as the musicians and dancers all turned towards him. He tried not to look at Gus and Fred, for by now they had surely realised something was wrong in the plot to which they'd been party. Instead, he hoisted Lucille aloft – she'd have to help him with this; he couldn't do it alone – and began.

'Ten minutes, folks. Ten minutes until we mosey on out there and put on a *show*. It ain't long, is it? It sure ain't long enough to tell the story of my life, but that's what I'm gonna do. I hadn't been here long before it caught up with me. The past. Well, most of you know how I got my start. Petty larceny, juvenile detention – those things weren't so unusual for a boy like me. But I got lucky. While I was inside, I found music. I got playing on the cornet – and, from that day on, everything changed for me.' Max paused. 'Of course, just because I found music, it didn't mean I'd left that world behind. What most of you *don't* know, what most of you can't appreciate, is that the New York night ain't like it is, here in Mayfair. Most of you got your start in the clubs, and I'm damn sure you saw some shadowy things if you stuck around in those Soho clubs long enough, but you didn't do what we did. You didn't fraternise with mobsters, racketeers, pimps when you played. You didn't owe your livelihoods to 'em. But that's the price I paid for my music. I had a talent, a God-given *talent*, and if I was going to use it to lift myself up, well, I'd have to do some time among the lowlifes …

'I thought I'd left all that behind when I got to the Continent. And here – the Buckingham Hotel! The seat of princes. Boy, I could make something of myself here. I'd never have to look over my shoulder again.' But that was exactly what Max now did, and by doing so directed the gaze of every musician and dancer to Harry Dudgeon, standing behind him. 'Until Mr Dudgeon here came into contact with a certain war reporter, a man named

Jackson Ford who sold him certain secrets I thought I'd left, buried back home.' Max was still for a moment. 'Gentlemen, Harry has been blackmailing me since summer. Threatening to expose my past, if I don't give up the Orchestra. Sirs, I've been a fool. The world is on fire, I have no home but the one this hotel has given me – and I have family, yes, *family*, who are depending on me for their new beginning. So I have spent long months rolling with Harry's demands. I gave in to every one of his *suggestions*, I've allowed myself to be sidelined in my own Orchestra. I planned to slide quietly away, while Harry took centre stage. But...'

The whispers had started among the musicians. They shuffled closer together, muttering darkly as their eyes flashed between Max and Harry.

'A wise woman told me that the truth will set you free. Well, I'd rather die by the truth than give in to lies. I'm sorry, but if this is to be the last show I put on, I'll do it with my head held high. So here it is...

'I'd been stumbling, from debt to bad debt, before I met him. Johnny Glaser: a man who knew the New York night like the back of his hand. He'd already got rich off his other business interests. The bordello he was running, at a place up on St Nicholas Park. The rackets he ran. But time had run out on his major interests – Prohibition was long gone, and all the money from bootlegging liquor and moonshine was dried up. So he turned his hand to the club scene. Other mobsters did it. Why not Glaser? Boy, he had some charm. Boy, did he swagger! And, fool that I was, I believed it when he told me he was on his way to being a legitimate businessman. I believed it when he told me he could make me rich. So Johnny Glaser became my manager.

'Glaser treated me right, for a while. There was a roof over my head, plenty of work – and, boy, plenty of liquor to keep me in place too. Matter of fact, he treated all those he owned nicely... for a time. That bordello up on St Nicholas Park? Well, it just so happened an old cousin of mine was working there and—' The door slammed behind Max; when he looked round, he became suddenly aware that Daisy had taken her leave. Perhaps he ought to have left this part out of it – but how else to make them see all that they'd been through? How else to make them understand?

'He'd started out treating those girls nicely, as well. But they were slaves too, slaves just like me. And my cousin – well, she had a secret of her own. A son she'd had to keep quiet, a son she'd hidden away. A son named Nelson. Now, Nelson was a rum little chap. The apple of his mother's eye – and very quickly mine as well. He had the family gift, you see. A gut feel for the music. Set him at a piano and the blues that rolled out of him – boy, you haven't heard a thing like it! It was like magic to me. And that's when I made my first mistake. I thought I could help Nelson along, help him make something out of the gift God gave him. Only, as soon as I introduced him to the clubs – well, I was introducing him to the *night* as well. Pretty soon, I wasn't the only musician in the family yoked to Johnny Glaser.

'Glaser knew talent when he saw it. Nelson was a shy kid. Daisy had kept him sheltered from the world, like only the best mothers can. A sweet, unsuspecting soul, that was Nelson – but that had its dark side too. Because Nelson didn't know, until it was too late, how Glaser was sinking his claws into him. *I'll get you on stage at the Cotton Club, if you do me a few little favours.* Seemed like a good deal to Nelson – but those favours soon put him on the wrong side of the law. And being on the wrong side of the law – well, that made him a pawn in Glaser's pocket. Leave aside the drink and the dope he was drawn into – Nelson became Glaser's *man*. And we could all see how that would end: Glaser fat off Nelson's spoils, and Nelson just another sacrifice, another boy sitting on Death Row, paying with his life so some other man could get rich and fat.

'So me and Daisy, we figured out a way to get Nelson out. If it just so happened it made clear our own getaways – well, so much the better...'

When Max paused to take breath, Harry's voice suddenly filled the silence. 'So now we come to it, Max. Don't go sugar-coating it. Tell them what you did. Tell them you're a thief. Tell them how you *killed*...'

In the dressing rooms, there was a collective intake of breath.

'Stealing from men who make their living from the suffering of others – well, Harry, I'd hardly call it theft. And as for kill-ing...' Max's eyes roamed across the Orchestra, trying to judge their horror by the way their faces had variously contorted in surprise, dismay, disbelief. 'It was a simple plan. Getting out of New York needed one thing, and one thing only: money. I didn't know how to get it – but, boy, Daisy did.

'You see, the kind of men who frequented that townhouse up on St Nicholas Park were men of means. Glaser knew how to rope them in. He knew how to make them pay. And Daisy, well, she knew her way around a man like that. And she knew exactly the man to go after. A man who flaunted his wealth. A man who wore it on gold chains around his neck, diamond watch at his wrist. And a man who, though he looked a respectable sort to the world, enjoyed a bit of debauchery at night...'

'So you stole from him,' Harry snorted. 'You stand there and you talk about theft like you're a damn hero – not just some lousy crook, a lousy crook with a *whore* for a cousin...'

Max might have dropped Lucille then. He wanted to bring his hand back and slap Harry squarely across the jaw. But he'd renounced violence a long time ago. The city streets had beaten it out of him, and for three decades he'd known that it was only music, not violence, that could pay his way.

'You stole from him, and when your manager found out what you'd done – you killed him to keep him quiet...'

Max shook his head, stoutly. 'You won't fill my head with lies, Harry, not this time. We did steal. We did what we had to survive. And yes, Johnny Glaser did find out. Yes, he did go to St Nicholas Park to confront Daisy, to castigate her, to punish her in front of all those other girls. But it was Johnny who started the fight. It might seem unconscionable, here in Mayfair, that a man could treat a woman like that. But if any one of you ever saw the same bruises, the same bloodied abrasions, on the faces of someone you loved – well, you'd want to kill as well.

'Johnny was dragging her, dragging her by the hair, dragging her out of the townhouse, dragging her off – off to be taught a lesson, he said, but everybody knew what that meant. Daisy did the only thing she could...'

Max could barely bring himself to describe it. The way Daisy had sunk her teeth into Johnny's arm, the precious few moments of release it had brought her while Johnny reeled back; the way he'd teetered at the top of the stairs, clawing out for Daisy yet again – until, in the last moment, she'd slapped him with all her might, slapped him so hard he tumbled backwards, head over heels, and lay in a crumpled heap at the bottom of the bordello stairs, his skeleton twisted in sickening, unnatural ways.

'Daisy stripped Glaser of his rings, his wristwatch, the cash in the billfold in his back pocket. Enough to get us on that ocean liner. Enough to see us safely to Paris, to hire a few musicians, to put together an orchestra of our own. We'd have made a success of it, if the war hadn't come. And all that was past would have remained buried, unless...' Max's implacable gaze levelled upon

Harry once again. 'Ford knew it all because he was a regular visitor to St Nicholas Park. Of course, he said it was an undercover investigation – but a man like that, taking on the mob? No, he was in their pay as well – just like every last one of us. It's safer for Ford that he's here, selling secrets at the Buckingham Hotel, than back home in Harlem. Telling his little stories about life in wartime, but really he's just another runaway himself, another man spending Christmas in exile . . .'

With those words, Max straightened himself. Opening his arms, still bearing Lucille aloft, he turned to take in the Orchestra as one. 'Harry's out of the Orchestra. He'll not play a note tonight. Now, it might be that tomorrow I'll be dragged into Mr Knave's office. It might be that all his fears about me and my kind have been proven true – that I'll be booted outta the Buckingham like a bankrupted guest. But tonight I'm the bandleader. Tonight, by the power vested in me by the Board, Harry's *out*. But we've still got a show to put on. We've still got the whole damn *world* to entertain! And I mean to do it. I mean to do it with every ounce of my being . . .' He saw their horrified eyes, sensed Harry shifting behind him, about to put up some protest, about to try and rally his supporters in the ranks.

There was a moment of fractured silence. Every musician before him seemed to be teetering, uncertain what to make of the story Max had just spun. Were they confounded by the real history of the man who led them? Or was it Harry's scheming, his exploitation, that had given them pause?

'Now hang on, Max,' Gus Black trumpeted, 'Harry's hardly had a hearing here. You can't just . . .'

'I don't know about this, Max,' came another dissenting voice. 'It's minutes away from the first number. How are we to—'

Harry strode forward. 'Boys, we're being led by a *fool*. Damn it, I knew he was a charlatan – I knew he was a crook – but

I didn't take him for a fool until this very second. We'll settle this later, Max,' he snarled, and pushed past, as if to join the Orchestra's ranks. 'This is *my* ballroom, and has been since you were slumming it in Hell's Kitchen, hanging with racketeers and whores. So I'm playing tonight.'

Max closed his fingers over Harry's arm and held him fast. 'I'll be damned before you disrespect me again. Boys, I'll go out there and play alone if I have to. I'll live or die by Mr Knave's call, when it comes. But there'll be no mutiny in my Orchestra – not tonight, not *any* night.' He took a breath. 'None of you can judge. None of you were born to the same world as me. Music's the thing that rescued me. We talk a great game in the Buckingham Hotel – that music's what we live for, that music's the reason we were sent down to Earth. But it's *real* for me. There's beauty and grace here in Mayfair, there's elegance enough for kings, but where I come from, music was the very difference between life and death. That's *me*. That's how *I* was made.'

Max heaved Harry backwards and pushed bodily through the musicians, until he was standing at the doors. 'I don't care how we do it out there, but we're putting on a show. Maybe it's my last ever, maybe I'm a stain on this hotel and its blessed *reputation* – but tonight there's gonna be music. Tonight there's gonna be drama and passion and romance. Tonight they'll be dancing like they've never danced before. So you can follow me out there, or you can follow Harry into disgrace. Either way,' and a wild, unbidden grin burst onto his face, where previously there had just been panic, outrage, determination, 'it's time we faced the music.'

Chapter Twenty-Eight

In the kitchens of the Queen Mary restaurant, Victor peeped out of the serving hatch. The security agents standing outside had quickly come to attention, but it wasn't on behalf of Mr Knave and Mr Hastings. Some moments later, Victor's shoulders were suddenly being crowded with half a dozen other kitchen hands all eager to see the door as it disgorged Charles de Gaulle and his lieutenants.

There came a cavalcade of voices: M. Laurent was batting the kitchen hands away, dispatching them back to their work. 'One table's cleared, but we've three dozen more waiting service. On with you, now! There's scrubbing to get going. There's a pot wash stacked high. And you, boy, I need you in the larders.' He pressed a leaf of paper, covered with his own scrawl, so hard at Victor that he rocked on his heels. 'There's more prep yet, boy. I'll need it all fetching out. And … those larders, they're still full, are they? What are the stocks looking like?'

Victor ran a finger under his collar; it was blisteringly hot in the kitchens. 'They're full, chef. The orders are coming in like clockwork. All that business before, it's … it's over, chef.'

Henri Laurent nodded stiffly, then propelled Victor on his way with a sudden thrust between his shoulders. 'See to it that it stays that way, boy.'

Victor had already started hurrying away, tumbling over his own feet as he picked his way to the larders – so nobody saw the way his face had flushed suddenly crimson; nobody saw the breath of relief he took at turning away from M. Laurent; nobody saw the way his eyes lit up when he opened up the larder doors and, plunging into their frigid interior, started scouring the shelves for the items on the chef's list.

The doors had opened. Across the Grand ballroom, the applause rose up, a tumultuous tidal wave that crashed over them all.

From the backstage doors, Max Allgood emerged, striding – in that strange, bow-legged way of his – across the sprung dance floor and rising to the stage.

One after another, the Orchestra followed.

Backstage, Harry Dudgeon stood stock-still. 'You know he's finished, don't you?' he hissed, as one after another the musicians marched out to their glory. 'You know they can't keep him here, with a history like that? Who do you *think* they're going to come to, once they get rid of Max? Who's next in line, you bastards? He's signed his own death warrant! He's thrown in the towel! He's—'

'He's going to *stun* them,' announced David Brody, almost on the threshold itself.

Harry rocked back. 'It's just talk,' he spat. 'Just bluster. *Stun* them? He's half the piano player I am. This ball's going to be a disaster.'

David Brody vanished, until at last all that was left of the Orchestra was Gus Black and Fred Wright, twin trumpets in hand.

'Come on,' Harry frothed, 'let's get out of here. Let him hang himself, up on stage. By New Year's night, it'll be us up there. Harry Dudgeon and the Moonlighters, back where we belong.

This is *our* ballroom. *Our* fate. The Americans haven't seen fit to join this war, and we won't have one leading the Orchestra for long.' Harry turned on his heel, ready to lead his bandmates away – but, by the time he had reached the rear dressing-room doors, he realised he was alone. When he looked back, he could see that neither Gus nor Fred had moved. 'Boys,' he said, with a military sternness in his voice, 'don't you know which side your bread's buttered?'

'That's the problem, Harry,' Gus shrugged. 'It's the biggest night of the year.'

'You know the kind of crowd waiting out there,' said Fred.

'Biggest night of our careers,' Gus said, unable to meet Harry's eye.

Harry lurched back towards them. 'You don't want to wake up tomorrow, knowing you made a mistake …'

At last, Gus looked up. 'No, but I'd like to wake up tomorrow, knowing I played at Christmas in Exile. I'd like to wake up, still hearing the applause.'

Fred and Gus – former trumpeters with Harry Dudgeon and the Moonlighters – marched out to meet their crowd.

Darkness over Lambeth, the sky curdled with clouds.

Thomas Law was waiting with his wagon outside the freshly planted gates of Number 62. The gruff Yorkshireman looked unusual, swaddled in a black winter coat as he was, his ARP helmet planted squarely on his head. 'I'm off out on patrols,' he said to Billy Brogan as the younger man tumbled from the truck, 'but I didn't want to miss you. Here, son, you take these.'

Thomas's hand was outstretched, and dangling from his fingers the keys to the new front door – but Billy declined to take them, grinned, and hurried round to open up the laundry van from the other side instead. Then, with all the decorum he'd learnt at the

Buckingham Hotel, he helped his mother and father out onto the street that had been theirs for so many years, the street that had been transformed.

'I wanted you to take them, Ma,' said Billy. 'It's your house. Yours too, Pa. I just … helped it along a little.'

Thomas Law didn't mind who he handed the keys to; the pride of a job well done was evident upon his face as well. He stayed only to see Mrs Brogan slipping the key into the new lock, the front door falling open at her touch, before he strolled off along the yard.

'I'm not sure I can carry you over the threshold, Orla, not this time,' smiled Mr Brogan. When he looked back and winked at Billy, it made the younger Brogan's heart surge. That was what he had wanted all year – indeed, what he had wanted all his life – the subtlest of 'well done's from the man he cared for most, in all of the world. 'But, look, maybe I can give it a go …'

Billy's voice echoed when he spoke, for every room in the house was empty. 'What do you think, Ma?'

'Billy,' and her voice echoed too, 'you've worked a miracle.'

A miracle, he thought, as she put her arms around him. Well, much work went into miracles. He'd seen that at the Buckingham: all the research, expense and meticulous planning that went into giving that establishment its sense of luxury and grandeur. Miracles weren't always ordained from above; oftentimes, they were ordained by ordinary men and women, with grit, determination, and a lot of hard work.

Hard decisions as well.

Billy was glad he was leaving all that behind.

Mrs Brogan had danced on, into the kitchen. 'The old range survived,' she said, still feeling lighter than air.

'Aye,' said Mr Brogan, 'but there's plenty didn't. Billy, you've done a grand job. The grandest. But you can leave your old man to it now. I'll have a dining table back by Christmas, if I have to go out and chop the wood down myself.'

The truth was, there was plenty for sale in the markets, if you knew where to go. Another consequence of war: houses were being cleared all of the time, all their old items put up for sale.

'You're not going out chopping down trees, William,' Mrs Brogan laughed, admonishing him with a slap on the back of the hand. 'I'm sure our Billy can help us out with some furniture.'

Billy suddenly felt his mother's expectant eyes on him. God, but he loved her. It was the measure of a man, how well he treated his mother – and nothing made Billy happier than to see her standing here.

But then he thought of all the money he'd given to Thomas Law, the sudden emptiness of his pockets, the ledgers he was determined to burn in a hotel fireplace, burying the evidence of his every misdeed.

All the things he'd hoped to leave behind.

'Leave the boy alone, Orla. I'll get this house sorted,' said Mr Brogan. 'Beds for all the young'uns, when they come home. A dining table. Old cabinets and chairs by the fire. A little corner for Annie, all of her own. Yes, it can be *home* again.'

'Yes, and twice as fast if our Bill's got anything to do with it!' Mrs Brogan beamed.

It was the esteem in which she held him that moved Billy. He felt it filling him up, like a warm cup of cocoa on a chill winter's night. His lips came apart and, almost without knowing it, he said, 'I'm sure I could get *some* bits, Ma. A settee for the sitting room, that might be easy enough. Some chairs for the fire.'

'We'll need beds again, beds in every room,' repeated Mr Brogan, and Billy thought he had never seen his father as brimming with life, so filled with hope for the future, since before the war.

Why, then, the strange sadness creeping back into his heart? All of those things needed *money*, thought Billy.

A voice echoed in him, words a friend had spoken long months ago. It took Billy some time to remember who had given voice to these particular words – but at last the image of Mr Sellers popped into his mind, the back room of his shop in Camden Town, the old man's voice heavy and low:

'I'd be a bad friend if I didn't tell you, Bill: it's easier to walk into this world than it'll ever be to get back out.'

The band struck up.

'Gather!' Marcus Arbuthnot declared, sweeping his troupe together as he sashayed to the dance-floor doors. 'Make no mistakes, my loves – the night is about to begin, and all your passion, your talent, your imagination must be called upon, if Christmas in Exile is to be the triumph it must…'

Marcus went on, but Frank heard only snatches of whatever he said next. It was those words that were giving him trouble: *all of your passion, your talent, your imagination, must be called upon.* Something in it brought to mind that story of the Exhibition Paris in 1926, and how the feeling of the dance seemed to desert Raymond when he held Ophelia in his arms. Only the java had woken him up. Frank tried to shake the ill feelings away; if only *he* might have thrown his body into a java right now, perhaps then he might stop thinking about Hugo Lavigne, and all Frank had been asked to do.

Don't be a hero.

There was little chance of that. Right now, Frank wasn't even sure if he could be a dancer.

The couples were forming. Out in the ballroom, Max's first grand number was reaching its height. In only a few short bars, the dancers would have to flurry out, Marcus leading the troupe like the general he was.

Mathilde sidled close to Frank's side. They were to be the third couple out of the doors, following Hugo and his partner, who themselves danced in Marcus and Karina's wake. 'Don't let me down, Frank Nettleton,' Mathilde smiled as she took his arm.

'W-what?'

Mathilde faltered as she said, 'Are you nervous?'

Frank faltered too. 'Y-yes,' he stammered. 'Th-that's it. It's a big night. The biggest of them all.'

'The music will look after you, young sir. You may have absolute faith in that.'

Hugo's voice – it seemed to be chiming directly into Frank's brain. He looked round, and there was the raven-haired Frenchman, looming above. 'I've never known you nervous, *mon frère*, but nerves can be a fine thing. A truly fine thing! Just…' Hugo touched Frank's shoulder, oblivious to the way the younger man tensed, '…don't let them conquer you. Let them melt away.'

'Now we dance,' Marcus beamed, with one last look back at the troupe.

'*Bon chance, mon frère,*' Hugo added, and gave Frank a long, slow wink.

The dance-floor doors opened up.

Across the Grand Ballroom, the chatter died away. Lords and ladies, exiled ministers, dethroned kings and the retinues of fallen queens, all turned as one to watch as the fabled dance troupe of the Buckingham Hotel emerged.

Here came the russet-gold champion, Marcus Arbuthnot, with Karina Kainz, the radiant star of Vienna, in his arms. After them came the Grand's new champion: the exiled Parisian, the runaway dancer, the ballroom's beating dark heart. In his arms hung a beauty as raven-haired as he was; together, as they launched into the quickstep, they were light as shadows, as spirited as the air.

Behind them appeared two of the troupe's slighter dancers: the young buck Frank Nettleton, and in his arms the elfin princess, Mathilde Bourchier. There was no stopping them then. Into the tempest they danced, the three star couples forming a constantly shifting constellation across the dance floor.

Then the rest of the troupe rushed in, and the night came alive…

'You're tense, Frank,' Mathilde whispered, as they pivoted in perfect synchronicity with the other couples of the dance floor, inverting the constellation, just as Marcus had planned. Seen from above, the scene was one of almost mathematical beauty. 'Frank, loosen up; you're holding me too tight…'

It took a beat before the words penetrated Frank, for the truth was he'd lost the rhythm of the music and had simply been gliding onward, letting his body remember the choreography his heart and mind could not. 'I'm sorry,' he whispered, barely moving his lips. 'I'm…' His eyes ought to have been on Mathilde, the perfect image of a couple in love – every show dance was a story of romance, Marcus often said – but instead they kept being drawn to the guests crowding the balustrade at the dance floor's edge. There were faces here he recognised, but they milled among a sea of faces he did not. The clientele of the Grand had changed this year. Where once, English lords and their acolytes used to fill this hall, now he saw huddles of ministers, the wide-eyed faces of lost Continentals; where once there were crown princes, now there were diplomats, ambassadors, generals and colonels come straight from the war. Tonight, it seemed that guests had been drawn from every far-flung corner of the Earth.

And behind them flitted other figures: lowly figures, concealed figures, unremarkable men in black dinner jackets and charcoal ties, men nursing their Martinis by the bars; men tapping their feet metronomically to the beat, even while the Orchestra reached a feverish pitch.

Once you knew the hotel was crawling with security agents, you could never forget it.

Was the silver-haired old man taking cocktails with his wife by the dance floor's furthest edge really working for the Crown?

Was the cocktail waiter, who lingered too long beside Mr Knave, Mr Hastings and all of the Board, really in the King's employ, here to guarantee the safety of the guests?

Were the two brothers marvelling at Max Allgood really listening to the music, or was it all a well-rehearsed act?

Frank and Mathilde pivoted past Hugo and his partner, and Frank could not contain the shudder that ran through him. On it went, coursing into Mathilde – who worked hard to maintain her footing. Sometimes, it felt like *she* was the one leading Frank. He seemed so wooden, perhaps even leaden, tonight.

The song reached its stormy climax. Twin trumpets joined the cavalcade of Max's piano. Then, in a final flurry of horns, it was over. Max Allgood stood up, turned to his appreciative crowd, and bowed.

On the dance floor below, Marcus and Karina spun out of hold. Hugo released his partner and swept heroically up the steps that led to the balustrade. It took Frank a moment longer to disentangle himself from Mathilde; only now did he see that her reproachful eyes were suddenly full of confusion, suddenly brimming with concern.

'I'm OK,' he told her, when he sensed her questioning eyes. Then, if only to dispel the moment, he gazed around. 'Who's your first tonight?' The guests were crowding the balustrade. Marcus had already found his first reservation, a middle-aged dowager in a gown of florid rayon and silk.

And there was Hugo. He had reached the balustrade at the head of the dance floor, and there was guiding a willowy blonde Parisienne, the wife of some diplomat by the looks of her, down the glistening mahogany steps. Yes, it made sense that dances with Hugo should have been reserved by the French contingent in the Grand; and yes, it made sense that they were drawn to him as a symbol of their fallen world. In the end, he had to will himself to turn his eyes away.

What sweet things might Hugo be planning on whispering in her ear as she danced?

What if, by the height of the evening – with the Moët et Chandon flowing through her veins, a third cocktail raised high in a toast – she was the one whispering into *his* ear?

What secrets did she carry?

The band was almost ready. There stood Frank, all at sea. Frank's eyes darted around, until at last he saw the young lady with auburn hair in a striking scarlet gown waiting, with folded hands, at the dance floor's edge. 'Mr Nettleton,' she said.

Lillian Tanner was a peer's daughter, a keen student of the ballroom. Her father was a regular benefactor of the Buckingham's balls, and Frank had already danced with her on several occasions. That, at least, made this a little easier.

Frank took a breath. Somehow, he would have to shed himself of this ugly, tense feeling.

Not for the first time, he thought of Raymond: Ray Cohen, donning a suit of midnight blue, slicking back his hair with liberal amounts of pomade, and becoming Raymond de Guise.

So, Frank decided, he would simply have to *perform* – and, in the performance, forget the fear that dogged him.

'Miss Tanner,' he declared, allowing her to take his arm. 'Shall we?'

The band struck up.

The dance began.

He met Miss Tanner's eyes as they danced, and allowed himself to smile. Yes, there was something about smiling – even if you didn't feel it – that changed everything. For the first time, he eased into the dance. Suddenly, he was lighter; suddenly, more willing.

Some songs later, Frank was dancing with the daughter of one of the Greek ministers-in-exile when Max set down Lucille, returned to the piano keys, and brought his rambunctious number, 'Say Something Softly', to its preposterous, overblown conclusion. When the song ended, in a sudden burst of trumpets and piano keys, there was such breathlessness on the dance floor that the couples who'd been caught up in the dance promptly fell apart, gasping for breath. Then, amidst the laughter and applause, Max Allgood picked his way to the front of the stage, lifted Lucille aloft and declared, 'Ladies and Gentlemen, a song like that ought to be a good send-off into intermission …' He looked over his shoulder, taking in the entirety of the Orchestra, marvelling that only an hour ago all had been lost – and now here he stood, victorious upon the stage. 'But we've got something special, before we come to that. Take your partners, please. This one's a little number I call "I'll Never Dance Again".'

Frank watched as Max's face broke into a wild, triumphant grin.

'But let's dance to it all the same!'

The dance floor was shifting. Partners were coming apart, the dance troupe gravitating towards the balustrade where their next charges were waiting. Frank's final reservation of the first act belonged to one of the London debutantes of last season. As she took Frank's arm, his eyes fell – quite by accident – upon Hugo. It had been some songs, now, since Frank had let the idea of Hugo's ulterior motives in the ballroom invade his thoughts.

But now those thoughts rampaged back into him.

Now, the music faded away.

He watched as Hugo reached the head of the dance floor, where his charge for the act's final dance was waiting. Another of the Free French ministers' wives, this lady was some years older than Hugo – but, as Hugo introduced himself, she stepped aside and, through the hubbub on the dance floor, Frank heard her say, 'I'm afraid I've been asked to step aside, but perhaps I might dance with you later in the evening? I should like that very much.'

'Step aside, *madame*?'

Frank ought to have been taking his own partner in hold; she clung on to his arm with an inexperienced dancer's neediness, asking him for support. Yet he shuffled three steps closer, drawn into Hugo's conversation.

'Mrs de Gaulle should like this dance.'

Hugo's intended partner stepped aside, revealing a lady only a few years older than Hugo, with short dark hair and pearls around her neck.

'M. Lavigne, may I introduce Madame Yvonne de Gaulle.'

Frank had frozen, though the rest of the dance floor continued to buzz. For Hugo's part, he looked dignified, honoured as he greeted the General's wife. He took her hand, bowed as one might to a queen – and how strange that was, how unlike a true-blooded Frenchman to genuflect before royalty – before he rose again and invited her to the dance floor. Soon, Frank could see Walter Knave and John Hastings of the Hotel Board joining Yvonne as she prepared to take Hugo's arm. 'Our star of the night, Madame de Gaulle,' John Hastings was saying. 'Mr Lavigne has made the ballroom his own. Let him show you how...'

'The honour is mine,' said Hugo, and moments later he was turning Madame de Gaulle onto the dance floor, just in time for the band to strike up.

You're being a fool, Frank, he told himself. *You're not the only one in this ballroom...* He had to tell himself that there were security officers everywhere – not just the ones M. de Gaulle and his retinue had brought with them, but the secret ones, the ones hidden in plain sight, the ones that not even Mr Hastings and Mr Knave knew about.

Dance was a performance, he reminded himself. Well, so too was espionage.

There was a different dance going on in the ballroom tonight. It was clouding his every thought.

Mme de Gaulle was no natural dancer, but within moments Hugo was making it seem like she could glide across the dance floor tiles. Such was the skill of the hotel dancer. Yvonne turned at his direction, pivoted and switched her weight, adjusting her balance at the tiniest inflection from Hugo – and the true magic of it was that she was conscious of none of it, completely at Hugo's command as they danced.

Frank told himself: it's just dancing.

They're not sharing secrets yet.

But as the dance came to its close, as the Grand filled with applause, as Max Allgood and his Orchestra took their bows and Hugo – the black-hearted star of the show – led Yvonne de Gaulle back to the balustrade and the ranks of the Free French who had been gazing upon her as she danced, he knew that something was wrong, all the same.

Hugo Lavigne wasn't just dancing among the exiles of the Buckingham Hotel.

He was ingratiating himself with men of power.

'Ladies and Gentlemen, that's only half your show. Knock back a cocktail to set the heart aflame, and we'll be back in thirty minutes.' Max bowed. The applause was about to begin again – but then, suddenly, he added, 'I promise you, this ball hasn't even begun!'

Some of the guests in the ballroom shared strange looks. The manner of this new bandleader was certainly *different* from the dignified, composed air of Archie Adams – but there was no denying the passion in the ballroom tonight.

The dancers ought to have left too – and, indeed, most of the troupe were already relishing the applause as they soared after the musicians – but Frank Nettleton stood beached in the middle of the dance floor, for he hadn't been able to take his eyes off Hugo Lavigne. The terrible thing was that Yvonne de Gaulle still had her arm threaded through his. More terrible yet was the gathering of Free French officials who opened up to welcome Hugo and the General's wife back to the group.

Hands were being shaken.

Hugo, slapped heartily on the shoulder, like a long-lost friend returning from war.

Frank had seen folks greeting the soldiers returning from Dunkirk like that: survivors of a fallen world; somehow it bound them together.

He flashed his eyes around.

None of it made sense. How could they let him get so close, when they *knew* what he was?

Did General de Gaulle already know?

Was it all just a game to them, this dance of secrets and lies?

Frank's eyes flashed around the room. Who was *watching* him? Who was *listening*?

'It is always a pleasure to meet a countryman of such standing,' General de Gaulle seemed to be saying. 'M. Lavigne, once the dancing is done, I should be honoured if you were to join us for a drink. I am told a corner is to be made available, at the Candlelight Club.'

'Sirs, I would be honoured to raise a toast with you tonight. To freedom. To honour. To the Free French!'

And, with that falsity on his tongue, Hugo turned back to the dance floor – only to find Frank Nettleton standing alone there, his big eyes staring, his feet rooted to the spot, his mind racing with a thousand tortured thoughts as he struggled to believe how easy it was for a man of such treacherous character to slide into the company of the leaders of the free world.

Far above the Grand Ballroom, Daisy Allgood swept the last of her possessions into the green leather suitcase.

What was this salty discharge running down her face? Why were her cheeks so raw and wet?

Daisy reached up and dabbed at her eyes. What a fool she was – she hadn't cried since she was a young woman, first waking up to the fact that she was trapped in that bordello, indentured just the same as her grandmothers had once been, the property of some sadistic man.

She wasn't sure what was making her fingers shake. Part of her thought it was just the indignity of Max spilling her life story. Part of it was the gaping disappointment of knowing, once and for all, that her dream of escape was over.

But another part of her, a part she was working so hard to deny, couldn't let go of that memory of St Nicholas Park. The way Johnny Glaser had tumbled backwards. The sting of the slap as she'd brought her hand across his face.

The *pleasure* she'd felt when she watched him plunging to his death.

Yes, that was the hardest part: to admit to the pleasure.

The tears were a release, she realised – for, by good fortune and the better nature of her cousin Max, she hadn't turned murderess after all. Johnny Glaser could rot in hell, but Daisy wouldn't join him there. She'd been saved from it by the smallest of slivers.

Even so, the world was crumbling around her. She'd been so close. Riding the tails of Max's talent, right to the top. There could have been a home here. She might have brought her son.

But now she'd have to go.

Leave Max to his last desperate bid at glory; now they knew what she was, she'd have to vanish.

The hotel was barren as she dropped through its layers. The sounds coming from the ballroom were more magnificent, more boisterous than Daisy had ever known in the clubs back home – quite what the guests here would be making of Max and his raucous set, she didn't know – but at least it gave her cover to hurry out of the hotel through the tradesman's entrance.

She had reached the snowy environs of Berkeley Square when she saw him. There was Harry Dudgeon, face lit up – in contravention of the blackout – by the flare of the cigarillo that trailed from his lips.

He had already hailed the taxicab on the other side of the square.

'Yes, yes, *Ava* Allgood,' he smirked, taking a long luxurious pull on his cigarillo. 'Time to be off, now the truth catches up with you. You know, I knew there was something rotten about the pair of you from the moment they showed you into the Grand.'

What tears there had still been in Daisy's eyes were now frozen to her cheeks, but she rather liked the feeling of that: it was as if her emotion was frozen too.

She took a stride towards Harry. 'You always had it easy, didn't you? Spoilt little rich boy of London? Taken under Archie Adams' wing? Nice, safe job in the Grand.'

'Get off with you, Ava,' Harry spat, for the taxicab was drawing close to the colonnade. 'Your reprobate cousin's playing his last show, I swear it. He might have won the rest of the band over with that little speech of his, but it won't do for management. They haven't any time for *your sort*.'

It was those last two words that made up Daisy's mind. How often had she heard those words before? *Your sort*. Somewhere in the deepest recesses of her brain, something snapped.

'There's good folks and bad in the world. Some of the good are rich and some of the bad are poor. But there's just as many the other way round. You'll never understand, Harry. You've had it too easy for too long.'

This time, it wasn't the flat of her hand that connected with her tormentor's face. Daisy had learnt something along the way, and her fist was clenched as it connected with Harry's jaw.

Harry reeled backwards. The most delightful thing was to watch the cigarillo fly out of his mouth.

Harry crashed down beside it. His eyes, when he looked up, were not just full of rage – they were full of humiliation as well. He scrabbled to pick himself up, but by then it was already too late. Daisy had no interest in him any longer; she simply wheeled round, opened up the door of the taxicab that had now ground to a halt, and slipped inside.

By the time Harry was on his feet, remonstrating that the

taxicab was meant for him, she had already given the driver the address of a little hostelry she knew down on Brixton Hill.

She nursed her sore fist.

What goes up, always comes down.

This was *why*, thought Frank. This was the whole reason for Christmas in Exile.

He had hurried through the dance-floor doors with the feeling of Hugo's eyes all over him, and now – while the rest of the dance troupe straightened their evening wear, or powdered their faces in the dressing-room mirrors – he couldn't stop the roiling feeling in his gut.

It was just like they'd said: Christmas in Exile itself was contrived for the moment he'd witnessed, out there in the Grand. A means of introducing Hugo to the highest, most important people among the Free French. His hand clasping General de Gaulle's own – Frank thought he would never forget it. And now, they were to take cocktails together after the show.

Then he remembered what Nancy had said: why the security agents left Hugo a free man at all. So that they could use him, just like he thought *he* was using *them*. Feed him lies, instead of secrets. Follow the trail of lies back to whoever he worked with. Exploit Hugo as a weapon in the war…

His heart was beating too fast – Frank was an honest man, and it hadn't occurred to him until these last days that there might have been different *kinds* of honesty in the world – but at least these last thoughts calmed him down. It was good to know there was purpose in what was happening in the Grand. It was good to know that greater minds than his were in charge.

A shadow fell across him.

He looked up, into Hugo Lavigne's beaming face.

'Young sir, you looked like you'd seen a ghost, out there on the dance floor.' He bowed down, his hand hovering over Frank's shoulder. 'A stiff drink of brandy, perhaps. When one cannot java, one might find comfort in a drink. Here, allow me.'

There was a decanter of brandy on one of the counters. In moments, Hugo had poured two small measures. He handed one to Frank.

Frank had never enjoyed the taste of liquor. Hugo had swallowed his in one, but Frank had to move through it in stately sips.

'Has it warmed your heart?' Hugo asked, before he drifted off to join Marcus and the rest of the troupe.

'It h-has,' Frank lied; all it had really done was unsettle his stomach, and he'd already been unsettled all night. 'I'll dance better in the next half, Mr Lavigne, you can count on it.'

'Oh, *mon frère*, you were already *magnifique*.'

Frank couldn't look at him after that. It was only in looking away that he could compose his thoughts. 'It's OK,' he kept telling himself, a petition and a prayer. 'He doesn't know you know. It's all part of the game. You've just got to get used to the game…'

By the time he dared look up, Hugo was nowhere to be found.

Frank lifted himself from the seat where he'd slumped. 'Mr Lavigne?' he ventured – but, of course, there was no reply: only the rear door clicking shut in the corner of his vision; only Hugo's ghostly absence, and the sound of retreating steps.

'D-do you know where Mr Lavigne went?' Frank asked, with his eyes fixed on the door.

'A gentleman's intermission,' Marcus announced, with his usual pomp, separating himself momentarily from his tête-à-tête with Mathilde. 'He'll be back momentarily, young Nettleton – rest assured of that. Hugo wouldn't miss our second act for a king's ransom.'

At least this was true, thought Frank. There was nothing on God's green Earth that would separate a man like Hugo Lavigne from the opportunity to inveigle his way further into General de Gaulle's circle.

And yet...

There were still twenty minutes to go before the band re-assembled – Frank wouldn't miss it for the world either, but nor could he deny the gravity pulling him towards that rear door.

He slipped out, only to find himself in an empty hallway. The door to the little rehearsal studio was itself falling shut, so he hurried that way and slipped inside – just in time to see a flash of midnight blue vanishing through the next door, out into the hotel.

Where Hugo was going, Frank could not say. And nor, perhaps, could the security agents stationed in the ballroom – for surely they were still gathered at the cocktail bar, the balustrade, the marble arch that led into the Grand. All of them, waiting for the dancers to re-emerge, waiting to see how skilfully Hugo Lavigne infiltrated General de Gaulle's entourage.

So *somebody* ought to follow.

By the time Frank reached the reception hall, Hugo was waiting at the golden guest elevator. Such was the privilege of such an esteemed ballroom dancer – most hotel staff were consigned to the service elevators and stairs, but men like Hugo, and Raymond before him, could freely fraternise among the guests.

The moment the doors opened and Hugo slipped into the elevator's interior, Frank darted across the reception hall, weaving along the Housekeeping hall until he reached the shadowy service stairs. He took three steps at a time, reaching each landing just in time to hear the ring of the elevator's bell. Then, checking first that Hugo remained within, he hurtled back to the service stairs and continued to climb.

Intuition told him Hugo was returning to his quarters.

Breathless, Frank reached the Buckingham's uppermost storey, directly beneath the attic eaves where the chambermaids made their home. Pausing only to gather his breath, he slipped through the doors at the top of the service stairs and stole along the hallway, past the Continental and Oceanic Suites, until he reached a conflux of hallways. From just round the corner, he heard the tell-tale ring of the elevator bell – and dared to peep round to watch as the doors of the golden cage rolled back, the elevator attendant emerging to shepherd Hugo onto the deep, burgundy carpets of the hall.

Hugo turned on his heel.

So did Frank.

Moments later, the Parisian had vanished round the next corner, marching with a dancer's elegant stride until he had reached the corridor tucked behind the palatial suites, and the bank of doors where the hotel's most prized employees were quartered.

Frank did not dare follow, not until he heard the sound of a key in a lock, a door falling closed. Only now that he was certain Hugo had vanished into his quarters did he turn the last corner, then steal – in his own soft, dancer's steps – to the closed door.

On any other night, there would be nothing untoward in this.

Hugo was just a dancer, returning to his quarters for rest and recuperation.

But Frank's heart was beating a different rhythm tonight; the music inside him was discordant, the dance lacking feeling, the whole piece in syncopated time.

He steadied himself with a breath; then ('Don't be a hero,' echoed Nancy's voice in his mind), crouching low, he pressed his eye to the keyhole in the door.

It was so hard to see within. By squinting, he could just about make out the old four-poster bed on which Hugo slept every night, the bedside cabinet and armoire against the furthest wall. It was a grander room than the chambermaids got, but – even as highly regarded as Hugo was – it paled in comparison to even the smallest guest suites.

A shadow moved across the keyhole, momentarily blinding Frank.

When it moved on, he saw Hugo for the first time. He had taken up a vantage on the edge of the bed, and in his hands was a small vanity mirror edged in silver. This he seemed to be holding to his open mouth, angling his head that he might peer within.

A stranger sight Frank had rarely seen. Mr Lavigne rolled his head first one way, then the next, craning at odd angles as if to inspect the very back of his throat. A toothache? Perhaps that might have made sense, if Hugo had shown hints of any grievance when they were down below – but a man suffering from some sudden pain in the mouth did not speak so eloquently as Hugo, and did not throw back a glass of brandy with the devil-may-care that he had.

'*Sacré bleu!*' Hugo cursed – and, by instinct, Frank rocked back on his heels.

By the time he pressed his eye back to the keyhole, the scene was stranger yet. Holding the mirror at arm's length, Hugo had taken his other hand and inserted it into his open jaws, as if to swallow his own fingers. Now, he twitched oddly. Now, he wrenched his jaw around. Before he choked, he removed his glistening hand; then, after composing himself with several breaths, he assumed the posture again, reached into the back of his throat – and, grunting oddly, brought his hand out with a single molar tooth between his thumb and forefinger.

Frank had never seen anything as preposterous in his life, but the look on Hugo's face seemed somehow victorious. His bottom lip was glistening red, a thin trail of blood and saliva connecting his fingers with the dark strands of his beard.

Carefully, he got to his feet. After that, Frank could see no more – for Hugo had moved beyond the range of the keyhole, evidently bowing over the dressing table and tidying up the grisliness around his lips.

Frank repositioned himself, desperate to see – but there was nothing. He repositioned himself again, but all he could see was the midnight blue outline of Hugo's back.

Then, suddenly, his sight of the room was completely obscured. In blind panic, he staggered backwards, desperate to scamper along the hall and out of sight before Hugo emerged.

The door opened up.

Frank was rooted to the spot.

'*Mon frère?*'

Even though December was deep and bitter, Frank had never felt as cold as he did in that instant. He had to force himself to turn round, but it was like dancing in treacle; it took every ounce of strength, just to pivot and turn.

There was Hugo, standing in the doorway at which Frank had, moments ago, been kneeling.

'M-Mr Lavigne,' Frank stammered. Then a miracle: somehow, his subconscious mind summoned up the solution his waking self had not been able to find. 'I-I was sent to find you, sir. It's Mr Arbuthnot. H-he's gathering all the dancers. He wants to rally everyone before the next dance.' Frank's heart was beating too fast: these were not nerves; this was terror. 'We'd better go, sir. The guests will be …'

'But of course,' Hugo declared, and something in his tone melted the outer crust of Frank's anxiety. 'I will be but one moment. Sometimes, a gentleman dancer needs to retire between acts – it is a restorative for the soul. To dance can take so much from you. Wait just a moment.'

Hugo turned on his heel, then disappeared into the room.

Part of Frank wanted to run. Moments later, he would think that he ought to have fled there and then. But, right now, it seemed that running would only provoke yet more suspicion.

Hugo reappeared in the doorway.

His face was set in a rigid mask.

His right hand, grasping a gun.

Frank had never seen a revolver before.

Now he was staring at one in the hand of the man he'd thought his mentor and friend.

And the gun was staring back.

Hugo hadn't even flinched as he raised it. Nor did he flinch as, taking three great strides, he closed the gap between himself and Frank, drove the barrel of the little revolver into Frank's ribs and said, 'I'm sorry, Nettleton, but you're a much better dancer than you are an actor.'

By instinct, Frank drew backwards – only to find that Hugo's other hand had closed around his collar, bracing him tight against the gun. Was it to muffle the shot? thought Frank. Was this the last second of his life?

'If you thought that little ruse would fool me, Frank, I'm afraid you haven't got the measure of me at all this year. But I suppose I should give you some credit.' Hugo brought the tip of the gun up, toying with Frank, pushing it into his chin so that Frank was compelled to look upwards, directly into Hugo's bitter blue eyes. 'How much do you know, Nettleton?'

'Know? Kn-know, sir? I don't—'

Hugo wrenched him round, heaving him bodily off his feet and casting him towards his bedroom door. For a moment, Frank scrambled for balance – but no amount of training in posture and poise could keep him from landing in the carpet's deep shag. At least, he supposed, the barrel of that gun wasn't touching him any longer. Not that it would save him, if Hugo pulled that trigger – but there was some hope in this. Surely there was *some* hope.

'You haven't called me *sir* all summer, Frank. *Mon frère*, you've been nervous all night. Your eyes all over me in the ballroom – and I have to assume that you haven't simply fallen in love. No, you *know*, Frank. Tell me what you know.'

Mon frère, thought Frank. 'You're not my brother,' he gasped, eyes darting left and right. 'You're not Raymond's brother. You're—'

'*Raymond*,' cursed Hugo, and shook his head in realisation. 'A letter reached you, did it not? Yes, yes, I told them they couldn't stop it forever – but my associates were better than I thought at keeping Raymond's letters from your door. Frank, how long have you known?'

An idea hit Frank. He cried out, 'I'm not the only one. It's no secret, Hugo. You're being watched. All the time, you're being…'

Hugo rushed forward – but it was not a bullet from a gun that silenced Frank; it was the hard cap of his dancing shoes, cutting an arc directly into Frank's face. For a moment, he saw stars. The whole world was spinning. By the time he came back to his senses, Hugo had taken him by the scruff of the neck, and was dragging him into the bedroom. 'I don't want to hurt you, Frank. I like you, boy.'

'Like me? Mr Lavigne – Mr Lavigne, you're a traitor!'

'*Traitor?*' he smirked. 'Don't tell me you still believe in such things as *traitors*. This is for my country, you fool. This is for the Paris I love.'

'Paris?' Frank gasped. 'No, no – you're lying. This is for Hannah Lindt.'

It was the first thing Frank had said that floored Hugo. Frank could see the shock, the horror, on Hugo's face. Yet, moments later, the gun was being raised again, levelled at Frank where he lay, still crumpled – the blood cutting a rivulet down his cheek – on the carpet of Hugo's room.

'What do you know of my wife?' he snarled.

'I know you lost her. And ... and I'm sorry, Hugo. I am! And I know who her father is, and what he does, and what he means to you. And ... I know you're *wrong*, Hugo. I know what you're doing is wrong.'

'*Traitors*,' laughed Hugo. '*Right* and *wrong*. You sorry fool, it's as if you never grew up. You still believe in *good* and *bad*. Well, welcome to the real world.'

'It won't work anyway, Mr Lavigne. They're *using* you. Whatever secrets you're stealing from them, they're ones you're being fed! You're just their plaything.' Somehow, the words had emboldened Frank. His eyes darted around. There was no way past Hugo and out into the corridor, but perhaps there was a way through – for Hugo was standing with his legs planted wide, and if Frank was sprightly, perhaps he could roll underneath him, stumble Hugo as he took flight and got far away.

The words had hit Hugo hard.

He seemed to linger over them.

But why, then, did he start to smile?

'Oh, Nettleton, you really think I'm here for ...'

Frank took his chance. In the same moment that Hugo started to smirk, he sprang forward, diving awkwardly through Hugo's legs, forcing them apart as he flew. Hugo stumbled, crashed against the armoire – and, though that was exactly what Frank needed, he did not look back. Instead, he dived out of the bedroom door, his feet windmilling underneath him, and ran.

'Help!' he screamed, as he crashed through the next doors

445

and reached the start of the suites. 'Somebody, *please*!' But, of course, there was no reply – for every soul who populated the Buckingham Hotel was now gathered in the Grand, waiting for the dancing to resume.

Frank could hear footsteps: desperate footsteps, clattering behind him. Something drove him right, through a nondescript narrow door and into the darkness beyond.

The rooftop above.

The observation post.

Yes, thought Frank, as he reached the scaling ladder and heaved himself, hand over hand, to the trapdoor above – this was the place to hide.

It was only as he burst through the trapdoor, to find one of the more elderly concierges half-sleeping in the observation post, that he realised his mistake. No sooner had he hoisted himself up, then slammed shut the trap, the concierge – a Mr Jacobson, if Frank remembered correctly – woke startled from sleep and said, 'Nettleton, what the devil are you doing up here?'

'Sir,' Frank panted, 'it's Mr Lavigne. He has a gun.'

'A gun, by God? Nettleton, a *gun*?'

The trapdoor beneath Frank started bucking; Hugo was forcing it from below.

'You've got to help me. Mr Jacobson, he's one of *them*. He's with the enemy and—'

'Nettleton, you've gone quite mad!'

The trapdoor opened.

Frank jumped onto it, forcing it shut with all of his weight. '*Please!*' he bellowed. 'He's a spy. Mr Lavigne, he's a—'

A gunshot from below splintered the wood directly beside Frank.

Frank leapt backwards. It was all the opening Hugo needed. Next instant, the trapdoor was being flung open. First came

446

Hugo's outstretched hand, still clutching the revolver tightly. Next, his perfectly sculpted black hair appeared. It took but seconds for the Parisian to leap through. Then, brandishing the revolver aloft, he said, 'Who knows, Frank?'

Frank staggered backwards, stumbling against the concrete frame of the observation post. 'They know, Mr Lavigne. The security service. They're all over the Grand. You're found out. All the information you're collecting, all the secrets and gossip, it's all at their command.'

Hugo seemed to take a second to process this information. 'They're arranging lies and counter-lies. They'll take me into the Candlelight Club later tonight and let some little pieces of information slip through. I'll leap upon them, feed it back, but it will all be lies. They'll try to butter me up, use me to trick my own masters. Yes, I can see that now. A clever ruse, but not uncommon.' He paused. 'Just a shame that—'

In that second, Mr Jacobson – who had been standing, in frozen horror, at Frank's side – threw himself forward. With outstretched hands, he leapt for Hugo's outstretched arm, the gun a black bulb at its end. 'For the King!' he cried out.

It occurred to Frank, then, that Mr Jacobson was of an age where he'd hoisted himself over the top and raced toward the guns once before.

This time, however, was different.

Hugo scarcely flinched as he pulled the trigger. The crack of the bullet split apart the night.

It split apart Mr Jacobson as well, opening his breast in a dark, scarlet bloom.

Frank watched, uncomprehending, as the old man crashed back against the observation post and fell there, his life's blood pumping out of the hole in his chest.

*

Somewhere beneath, in the chambermaids' kitchenette, a sudden sound of thunder interrupted the sounds of Cab Calloway playing on the gramophone in the corner.

Rosa looked up from her dancing. The Housekeeping girls liked to think they were part of the Buckingham balls – and, consequently, whenever the great and the good were foxtrotting through the Grand, a slightly less-polished, slightly more raucous, party was going on in the kitchenette. Tonight, there was even a bottle of sherry being handed round. 'Did you *hear* that?' said Rosa to the surrounding girls.

Mary-Louise had gravitated to the window. The blackouts were still up, but she was certain it had come from somewhere out there. 'But there's no sirens tonight,' she said, 'so it can't be …'

'That was the second time,' said Rosa. 'I swear it sounded like … gunshots.'

'Oh, give over, Rosa!' one of the other girls hooted. 'It's more likely something on that recording, isn't it?'

'Better turn it up anyway,' said Rosa. 'I was just getting into the swing of that one. I don't fancy being interrupted again. Now, *somebody*, pass me that bottle …'

'You couldn't have,' whispered Frank, throwing his arms around Mr Jacobson's fallen body, his hands suddenly scarlet with blood. 'Mr Lavigne, we need help. He's dying. Hugo, he's *dying*.'

'This is your doing, *mon frère*.'

Frank looked up. 'Never my doing,' he breathed, stoutly.

'People die in a war. There are always casualties.' Hugo had turned away, but at once he turned back. 'I shall need your belt, Frank.'

Of all the things Hugo might have said, this was perhaps the strangest. Frank could barely look at him. His hands scrabbled at the gaping wound in Mr Jacobson's chest, but there was no hope of stemming the blood flow.

'I don't want to leave you dead on this rooftop, *mon frère*. You are, after all, a decent man. It is unfortunate that we should meet in such circumstances. I should have liked to show you the clubs in Paris. I should have liked to take you to Montmartre and La Pigalle, and dance as Raymond and I once danced. But I cannot let you follow me, Frank. So I am left with two options: the gun, or...'

Frank was shaking as he lifted himself and unthreaded the belt from his trousers, his hands so slippery he could scarcely get any purchase as he drew it out.

Hugo snatched it from his hands. As he did so, a single snowflake drifted down and landed upon Frank's stained hands. There it sat, a perfect crystalline shard of bloody red.

Hugo had noticed it too. 'It is a cold night, Frank. Take shelter where you can.'

Before Frank knew what was happening, Hugo was retreating towards the trapdoor. The gun was still directed at him as Hugo took the first step below. It was directed at him every step Hugo took, as he sank back into the hotel. It wasn't until some time after the trapdoor was closed that Frank dared to leave Mr Jacobson's side. Only then did he understand Hugo's purpose in taking his belt: the trapdoor was tied fast from the other side. He heaved on it with all the might he could muster, but it wouldn't move more than an inch.

Frank was marooned on the rooftop of the Buckingham Hotel.

He rushed back to Mr Jacobson's side. There was still life left in the old man, though every ragged breath made blood bubble upon his lips. 'I'm here,' said Frank. 'I'm still here. Just hang on, Mr Jacobson. Hang on, please.'

There was strength enough that Mr Jacobson could take Frank's hand. Was this the last vestige of life, leaking out of him? Frank tried not to think those desperate thoughts. He looked into the old man's panicked eyes. 'What – d-did – he – want?' Mr Jacobson gasped. 'A man – like – that, in – *our* – hotel?'

'Secrets,' Frank whispered. 'He's spent all year trying to learn secrets. And now, tonight, he's to drink with General de Gaulle. He's dancing with the Free French...'

'Then – why...'

Mr Jacobson's voice was failing him. 'Save your strength,' Frank told him, but the old man was determined to go on:

'Why – the – gun?' he uttered. 'Secrets – don't – need... *guns.*'

Frank faltered. He screwed up his eyes.

Mr Jacobson was right. Hugo's purpose in the ballroom was meant to go unnoticed. Until but moments ago, he had thought his secret safe. Yet there had been a gun in his dresser, all along. He had wielded it without hesitation.

And no sooner had Frank thought of that, he was thinking of that other mysterious thing he'd seen: Hugo reaching into his mouth, wrenching out a – false? – tooth, tidying himself up before he returned to the ball.

'It isn't just secrets, Mr Jacobson,' he gasped. 'I think – I think it's... *murder.*' He looked down. Mr Jacobson's eyes were slowly closing.

'I watched him in his quarters, sir. He was...' Frank hardly knew how to describe it, '...reaching into his mouth. He pulled out a tooth, slipped it in his pocket.'

Mr Jacobson gave the last, grim laugh of his life. 'I'd – say – that's no ordinary – tooth, Frank.'

'Mr Jacobson?'

'A poison pill, Frank. You heard rumours of them in the Great War. Higher than... my station... of course...' He started spluttering. 'For agents … behind enemy … lines … in case they were taken … alive.'

'But, sir, if he's taken it out …' A hundred different scenarios cascaded through Frank's mind, but ultimately there was only one that made sense.

No, Frank thought, the poison pill meant to take Hugo's own life, in the event he was captured, was to be put to some other purpose.

Murder in the ballroom.

It couldn't be …

General de Gaulle?

'Mr Jacobson, we – we need to get off this roof.'

Frank lifted himself, picked his way across the observation post, through the girders, across the barnacled ridges at the heights of the Buckingham Hotel. Daring himself to its very edge, he clung on to the slates with one hand and looked down: a taxicab was wheeling away, vanishing into the dark towards Regent Street. In its wake, a man in a white dinner jacket loped, bellowing out some fury of his own.

At once, Frank knew who it was: Harry Dudgeon.

'Help!' Frank roared. 'Mr Dudgeon! Help!'

He wailed and wailed into the night.

The dressing-room doors opened, and in sashayed Hugo Lavigne.

'Monsieur!' Marcus exclaimed, with his usual pomp. 'We were beginning to fear. The Orchestra has already marched out.'

Marcus swept the dancers together, taking Karina by the arm. Soon, Hugo's own partner was standing at his shoulder; the rest of the troupe was lining up, and only Mathilde Bourchier left alone.

'But where *is* Frank?' she asked, with mounting despair.

'My young *frère* is most shaken,' said Hugo, with a rueful

shake of the head. At once, all of the dancers in the dressing room had turned to him. 'Mathilde, did you notice the nerves in Frank tonight?'

Mathilde had no need to dwell on it. 'I did,' she admitted. 'He wasn't himself.'

'It is the pressure of the occasion,' Hugo announced. 'I tried to talk the young man round, for he is *magnifique*, but I fear I have failed. He was backstage but a little while ago. I suggested a stiff drink. Perhaps... the Candlelight Club?'

Out in the Grand, the band had struck up.

'It is too late,' Marcus sighed, with enough melodrama to satisfy a discerning audience at the London Palladium. 'Mathilde, my dear, you will have to be excused from our introductory dance. Sally out and join us as soon as the guests are welcomed back to the floor.' He turned round, opening his arms to the troupe. 'One more time, ladies and gentlemen. The most important audience of our careers awaits...'

The most important audience.

Telling words.

The doors had already opened, so nobody saw the smirk that curled the corners of Hugo Lavigne's lips – for this was, indeed, the most important audience of his life.

It was, he knew, to be the very last one.

'There's somebody screaming out there,' said Rosa, more aggrieved than ever that she'd had to stop dancing. 'I just know that there is.'

The sherry had been half-drained, and this accounted for at least half of Rosa's sudden temper – to the constant amusement (and, one or two times, the horror) of the other chambermaids, she was partial to a drink, and very rarely just one. But as soon as she took the needle off the gramophone, planting her hands upon her hips in her best impression of a glowering floor mistress they'd all once known, the other girls knew she was right. It was dull, and seemed so far away, but there was definitely somebody screaming.

What's more, the voice was familiar.

'That's my Frankie,' Rosa declared. Moments later, she had hurtled to the windows and begun peeling back the blackout blinds. 'Something's going on out there, I'm sure of—'

'*Help!*'

Frank's voice again. It seemed certain, now, that Harry Dudgeon down below on the street had heard it too – but not even he knew where it was coming from; his head was diving left and right, searching the snowbound skies above.

'*Up here!*' came Frank's frantic tone. '*Mr Dudgeon, UP HERE!*'

'I know where that is.'

Rosa turned promptly round. There stood Annie Brogan. Instead of clamouring for a spot at the window like the rest, she was scampering towards the kitchenette doors, heading out into the chambermaids' hall beyond. 'It's the observation post!' she called. 'Come on, girls, something's wrong!'

It was no good. Mr Dudgeon was gazing into the sky, but by now the snow was growing thicker, and the veil it cast between them was too thick.

The cold had started to bite. Frank drew back from the gutters and picked his way back through the observation post. A faint, ragged breath played on Mr Jacobson's breath – but Frank was certain, now, that he was sliding out of the world.

A sudden banging came from the trapdoor, a thunder of fists sounding on the other side.

'Rosa?' he cried out. 'Rosa, is that you?'

'Frank Nettleton, what the devil are you doing up there?' came

Rosa's gently admonishing voice. Ever since they'd been stepping out, she'd enjoyed teasing him when she got the chance. 'Here, is this your belt, Frank?'

The trapdoor burst open, and through it Rosa appeared like a jack-in-a-box. From her hands, Frank's belt dangled loosely. 'Who's done this, Frank? Frank Nettleton, you're meant to be in the ballroom. Frankie, what on earth's …' It was then that her eyes landed on Mr Jacobson, lying wraithlike in the snow. Her mouth opened in a silent scream, but Frank was already reaching for her, hoisting her up through the trapdoor. He'd thought to force his way past, but behind her came Mary-Louise – then, at last, Annie Brogan, shivering into the night.

All of their faces were masks of disbelief as they took in the bloody scene.

'Frankie,' Rosa gasped, at last – and would have fallen into his arms, there and then, if only Frank hadn't been pushing wildly past them.

'Stay with him,' he yelled back; then, when Rosa put up a protest, he repeated the words with more force than he'd meant. 'STAY WITH HIM, girls. He's dying. He mustn't be alone. But Rosa, I – I've got to go …'

The ballroom was a blitz.

Up on stage, Max Allgood seemed possessed by the spirit of the music itself. He too seemed to be dancing, as he weaved through the front row of his orchestra, his neck thrown back and Lucille pointed skyward, letting out her song. There was beauty in this ballroom. Enough joy to propel the dancers into a different world. It was, Hugo reflected, rather a shame that other things were occupying his mind. He would have liked to have leant into the enchantment of this room.

But at least he was to leave it a free man. His paymasters had wanted spectacle. They'd wanted the eye of the world. 'That's what you performers are for, M. Lavigne. Your stars shine bright, and then shine no more.' It was true that, for the longest time – for many long years, in fact – his desire to sashay into the ever-after, to join Hannah in that great ballroom of the sky, had been growing. Yet, faced with the choice, he had discovered a sudden and inexplicable thirst to go on.

His paymasters would get what they wanted.

By the end of the night, Charles de Gaulle would be dead.

Only not in quite the way they had intended...

And, if the stars aligned – as they always did, for a man as debonair as Hugo – then he would be gone forever from the ballroom, his very best performance his last.

The music reached a pitch. So too did the fervour in Hugo's heart. He lifted his partner from the dance floor, and onward she sailed, on and ever on – until, at last, he brought her breathless back down to earth.

Breathless, just like that man he'd left on the hotel roof.

Just like General de Gaulle...

Frank reached the reception hall, his heart pounding the wildest rhythm of his life. His legs pounded madly underneath him as he tore across the black-and-white chequered tiles.

The music was sublime. It crashed over him, increasing in fervour with every step he took towards the ballroom doors.

His hands still left sticky impressions as he pushed open the doors and clattered into the ballroom's throng.

A cocktail waiter, bearing a tray of garish glasses, reeled round him as he ran. Some other guest cried out when Frank trod on the tails of her gown, heaving her backwards as he passed. Yet Frank heard nothing.

He had almost reached the dance floor's edge. The assault

on his senses was brutal and quick. There, between the other couples, Hugo had some elegant partner in hold; her eyes were closed as he carried her on some dreamlike journey through the song. Mathilde danced below him; it was she who caught his eye. Her fury was real – for Frank had abandoned her for the act's opening dance – but then she saw the bloody smears on his dinner jacket, the snowmelt in his hair, and in an instant she perceived something was wrong.

But Frank did not linger. He turned – and there, just beyond the dance floor's head, were the huddle of Free French, Mr Knave and Hastings at their side.

Frank crashed towards them.

It was possible, by now, that Hugo had seen – but the time for caution had long ago vanished. 'Mr Knave!' Frank cried out, clawing his way through the first of the Free French security guards. 'Mr—'

A fist connected with Frank's face. Before he knew what was going on, he was flying backwards, landing spreadeagled on the floor. 'Let me up!' he screamed, for now one of the Free French was bearing down upon him, pinioning him by arms and legs. 'Stop! Stop! Let me…'

The music went on. The joyful storm continued. But there, on the ballroom floor, Frank was held fast. The French security official was a burly figure, and too late Frank realised what he'd done: from their perspective, he was just some bloody marauder charging straight at their midst; as far as they were concerned, it was Frank who was the danger, not the hidden assailant still dancing below.

A hand was coming towards his mouth, ready to silence him, when Frank saw Mr Knave's hand land on the security official's arm. Some hurried words were exchanged in French – Frank had never appreciated that Mr Knave might be a talented linguist – and then he was being heaved back to his feet.

'What's the meaning of it, Frank?' Mr Knave demanded. Only then did he take in the state of Frank's clothes.

The young dancer was himself breathless, but he staggered forward, clutched on to Mr Knave and declared, 'We had it all wrong. *Everyone* had it all wrong. He isn't here to steal secrets at all. He isn't just a spy, sent into high society. He's a killer, Mr Knave. He's already killed. And he came here with a mission...' The words had emboldened Frank. At last, he found his breath – and, releasing his grasp upon Mr Knave, he turned to take in the stern face of General de Gaulle himself. 'He came to kill you, sir. By poison or bullet, he means to kill you tonight.'

On the dance floor, the slender waif whirling in Hugo Lavigne's arms felt the world suddenly change. Until this moment, her eyes had been closed as her partner led her on through the music – but, all at once, she felt his arms release her. The music buoyed her along for a fraction of a second. Then she felt a sudden absence – and, when she opened her eyes, it was to discover that Hugo had stepped suddenly out of hold, that even now he was backing away from her, his impenetrable gaze fixed on some point above her head.

'Sir?' she questioned. 'Sir?'

Hugo turned tail and started to run.

'Get him out of here!' snapped one of the security agents – and Frank, who was suddenly aware of a good number of discreetly dressed guests abandoning their positions and flocking to where he stood, watched as the Free French officials closed ranks around General de Gaulle, obscuring him from the rest of the Grand.

'Are you certain, Frank?' Mr Knave ventured. Then, as if only now realising the ragged state of the young dancer, he said, 'Frank, the blood…'

'It was Mr Jacobson, up on the observation post. He tried to stop him and…' The emotion flurried out of Frank for the first time. 'I'm sorry, Mr Knave. They told me not to be a hero. *Wait and listen and be patient and don't let him know*… but if I'd done that…'

Mr Hastings was at his side now. He braced Frank by the shoulder. 'You may have saved the General's life, young man. You may just have changed the fate of this war.' He bowed to Mr Knave, whispered urgently, and said, 'Follow me, boy. To the director's office.'

The ballroom was still a whirlwind. Frank glanced desperately around. On the dance floor, a woman stood alone, like a pillar of rock in an ever-shifting sea. Hugo Lavigne was gone, the dressing-room doors now flying open as a stream of cocktail waiters, unremarkable-looking guests and one particularly plump barman – security officials, every one – followed where he had gone. At the marble arch, the Free French had gathered. General de Gaulle was still masked behind a barricade of arms, but now two of his guards were scouting out the path to the reception hall ahead.

A weakness such as he had never known flooded through Frank.

'Mr Hastings,' he said, 'I'm afraid I feel rather faint.'

'A brandy will sort that, young man. Keep your chin up. You've done remarkably tonight.'

But Frank Nettleton was already fainting clean away.

The gun was back in Hugo Lavigne's hand. He'd hoped to get through this night without once using it, but that hope had already been proven useless on the rooftops above. Now, as he cantered along the Housekeeping hall, he felt its cold touch in his fist once again. He'd had to bury it in the dressing room – for this suit of midnight blue could not mask a revolver – but at least there'd been time to unearth it before they followed him through those doors.

Of all the things that might have happened, that it should have been Frank Nettleton to disrupt things. The boy was good for nothing – nothing but the ballroom, and at that he didn't truly have the elegance to thrive. But Hugo had always been a sentimental fool; to kill a man was one thing, but to kill a man of whom you were rather fond was a different thing altogether. If only he'd left him dead on the rooftop, tonight might have been so very different.

There would be hell to pay, in the end. His associates would forever look upon him with the purest distaste and displeasure. When word got back to his father-in-law that all their efforts had been in vain, he would not be able to show his face again. Well, he would have to cope with that. There had been other, darker devastations in his life.

First, though, he had to get out of this alive.

By good fortune, no lousy hotel page or concierge was loitering by the tradesman's exit, so Hugo was able to slip out. His dancing shoes left deep impressions in the snow that was gathering here, but at least the alley was criss-crossed by tracks already. That would make him more difficult to follow.

As he reached the edge of Berkeley Square, he stopped dead.

The security officials were already pouring out of the hotel's famous revolving bronze doors, spilling down the marble steps and to the colonnade. His associates had made it clear there would be a car waiting for him on one of the square's branching avenues – but, suddenly, there seemed a hundred miles between here and there.

He dared to peep out of the shadows of Michaelmas Mews. These were no mere waiters coursing through the colonnade in front of the hotel. Waiters of the Buckingham Hotel did not carry Webley revolvers.

Some mad, frenzied part of him felt laughter coming to his lips.

Then he heard the footsteps behind him.

There was no training in the world for a moment like this, but Hugo knew the power of a good feint – he'd long ago learnt that in dance – so bowed down to his instincts at last. At once, he took a great stride out of the mews, lifted the revolver and fired a single bullet high over Berkeley Square. It was only a show of strength – that was all – but it ought to be enough to give them pause.

As soon as he fired, he started to run.

In seconds, their eyes had found him. Seconds later, voices cried out. But the English were too genteel for their own good; the thought of somewhere as proudly palatial as Berkeley Square becoming the site of some battle offended their very senses, and Hugo had the chance to release one more shot behind him before he'd cantered halfway the length of the square.

Two more bullets in the revolver. As chance had it, he still had the tooth with its cyanide capsule in his pocket – so there was no need to save one. As he reached the first avenue branching off from the square, the Britishers now crying out like a hound pack as they gave chase, he reached over his shoulder and released another shot.

Somebody cried out.

Somebody plunged into the snow.

That ought to have given them yet more pause, thought Hugo. By now, the driver sent to fetch him must have picked up on the hullaballoo. By now, if the man had any courage, he would be wheeling round, his engine roaring and ready for the chase to come.

Hugo loosed the last shot of his revolver and dived into the blackness beyond Berkeley Square.

There was his car.

It was a black Rolls Royce, idling under one of the dead street lamps – and, as Hugo hurtled towards it, the door opened up. 'Get me out of here!' Hugo roared as he approached. 'They're coming! They're coming this—'

Out of the Rolls Royce emerged a portly man of shadow, his face lit up by the light of the White Owl cigar he was chewing.

As Hugo skidded to a halt, three black Bentleys came skidding out of the side streets. Each one of them opened its doors, disgorging more men dressed in black.

At the sight of their bowler hats, all the hope vanished from Hugo.

Only an Englishman would *ever* be seen in a black bowler hat.

He lifted the revolver, but of course there was no hope in this either – for every bullet was already spent.

The Englishmen started tightening their circle around him.

'Mr Lavigne,' came the voice of the first man, as he snuffed out his cigar in the snow. 'It seems that that particular dance is not to continue.' The portly man had reached Hugo's side now, loitering just far enough away that the Frenchman could not strike him round the face. 'Never mind, though,' he continued, 'because my colleagues and I have been preparing for this – and there are lots of different dances we can go on, once you're safely locked up. My name is Mr Maynard Charles, and from now on I am the only thing standing between you and a traitor's noose.' Maynard Charles gave a sharp whistle, two fingers pressed to his teeth, and promptly one of the Bentleys drew near. 'So come on, Mr Lavigne. Let's dance.'

Chapter Twenty-Nine

**DISPATCHES FROM THE BUCKINGHAM HOTEL!
NEW YORK TIMES, DECEMBER 8, 1941**

By Jackson Ford, your man in LONDON

'A day that shall live in infamy...'

Well, you said it, President Roosevelt. As the feuding Max Allgood Orchestra took to the stage on Saturday night, serenading an audience that comprised all the many stalwart faces charged with saving the free world, few guests of the Buckingham Hotel could have dreamt that, while they were still nursing the hangovers and exhaustion wrought by an evening's wild dancing, an event of immense global significance would be taking place on the other side of the world. Yes, the cowardly Japanese attack on the American naval base at Pearl Harbor has rendered obsolete all the gossip of Christmas in Exile: the oddity of an Orchestra whose bandleader appeared determined to play piano and trombone at one and the same time; the strange disappearance of the dance troupe's star performer in the middle of proceedings; the rumour of gunfire on the ordinarily serene Berkeley Square.

Set against the opening of fresh hostilities, the goings-on of 'Christmas in Exile' have largely been forgotten in the cocktail lounges and bistros of the Buckingham Hotel. Now, the talk is of the might of the New World coming to the Old World's defence; how quickly the Americans might have soldiers on the streets of London; what plans might be mounted to take the battle back into Continental Europe – and to wrest from Mr Hitler's hands all the countries he overran in the spring of last year. Mr Churchill, the English lords expound, has already declared war upon the Empire of Japan in solidarity with his American cousins; when, then, will President Roosevelt send his first soldiers across the oceans to enter the fray?

Yes, war is an ever-changing beast. It never stays the same for long.

And nor does the career of your roving reporter, for this column marks my last dispatch from the frontier of the Buckingham Hotel. But rest assured, my tenure in London is not yet over – and there will, no doubt, be many stories to report once our fine, upstanding countrymen arrive upon this embattled island . . .

War is an ever-changing beast. It never stays the same for long.

'Nothing does,' said Nancy, her voice trapped halfway between sadness and hope.

In the kitchen at Blomfield Road, Nancy and Vivienne fussed with pieces of hot buttered toast, a soft-boiled egg for Stan, and apple puree from the jars in the larder. The tea was brewing, thick and dark, and Vivienne had already scraped what honey there was from the bottom of the jar. There was milk in a jug, day-old pastries scavenged from the hotel, and a little pot of marmalade for spreading on top. All in all, this breakfast was a banquet – not quite fit for a king, but a banquet all the same.

A pity, then, that it couldn't be enjoyed – for the nerves in Blomfield Road, already fractured into a thousand tiny pieces by the treachery of Hugo Lavigne, had been shaken further by the BBC News. Late last night, Mr Churchill's sonorous voice had resounded across the airwaves. They were replaying it on the wireless right now: '*You will remember that a month ago, with the full approval of the nation and of the Empire, I pledged the word of Great Britain that, should the United States become involved in war with Japan, a British declaration would follow within the hour...*'

'Wars near and far, then,' said Vivienne. 'But perhaps... perhaps there's hope in it, this time. Perhaps it draws us closer to the end.' She had spoken the words with a shiver, no doubt harking back to all the friends and cousins she'd left behind in her native New York, wondering if they too were about to be summoned to war.

Nancy nodded, as she spooned apple puree into Arthur's waiting mouth. She'd thought the same, though dared not say it out loud. In the past, when Mr Churchill addressed the nation, there had been a grimness to his tone, a solemnity in keeping with the severity of each occasion – but, unless she was very much mistaken, she had sensed some hint of relief in him this time.

He'd been asking for it for so long.

At last, the New World was being summoned to the war.

'London's going to change,' said Vivienne.

'It hasn't stopped changing,' Nancy chipped in.

'Sometimes,' Vivienne sighed, 'all you want is... nothing to happen. Give me a year – boy, give me a *month*! – of nothing, and I could be a happy woman.' Their eyes met, and it was clear to Nancy what they were both thinking about. Neither had seen the events of Christmas in Exile first-hand, but the harrowed, haunted look on Frank's face when the security agents delivered him home that evening, the ghostly way he sat with his cocoa and told them all that had happened in the ballroom, would never leave Nancy's mind.

'I think we're a country mile away from *nothing*,' Nancy said, 'but... there might be brighter times yet. If the Americans come to London – well, you can't count on anything anymore, but you've got to hope the New World isn't filled with traitors.'

Vivienne shuddered. 'I still can't believe – a Frenchman, a Parisian no less, and... He had us dancing for him...' She couldn't finish the sentence; the silence was enough.

'There was a time when I thought...' Nancy faltered; she wasn't sure if she should go on, for right now it seemed such a facile feeling. 'I wondered if there might have been some tingle of romance between you and Hugo.'

Vivienne exhaled. 'Men tell you all sorts of lies, don't they? Sometimes, they don't even need words. Sometimes all it takes is a look. I... I'm not ready, Nancy – not even for a good man, the kind of man I thought Hugo really was. It's too soon.'

Nancy nodded. 'Well, let's thank the Heavens for that. Hugo Lavigne fooled us all. I should have hated it if you...' By God, why were words so difficult? There and then, Nancy decided to disregard her fears and simply say out loud what was on her mind. 'I'm glad you didn't get your heart broken again, Vivienne. Hugo Lavigne has already ruined too many lives.'

'How do you think it happens, Nancy? That a man like that – a good man, if Raymond's right – goes so horribly wrong? What happens to a man to turn him from ballroom dancer into...'

'An assassin.'

It was not Nancy who had spoken. The voice seemed small, overly cautious, strangely far away – and, when Vivienne and Nancy both looked round, it was to see Frank standing in the kitchen doorway, still dressed in his navy-blue pyjamas, an old dressing gown hanging open around his shoulders.

'Come here, Frankie,' said Nancy, and soon Frank was being whisked to the head of the table, plied with toast and marmalade, hot tea and butter. From now on, Nancy decided, she would save all her butter for Frank. There he sat: the hero among them. There was more courage in her little brother than in half the soldiers fighting this war – of this, Nancy was certain. 'Our mum would have been proud of you, Frankie. Our father too.'

Frank liked the sound of that, but what he liked even more was the pride, the relief, the love that was billowing out of Nancy.

'What do you think will happen to him?' Frank finally asked. A whole day and two nights separated Frank from that perilous escapade on the Buckingham's rooftops, the snowy silence punctured by gunshots right there in Berkeley Square – and only now that the shock was wearing off did he try and picture where Hugo Lavigne was right now, what might have been the debonair dancer's ultimate fate.

'Some things are better not thought about,' said Nancy, pouring more tea.

'But . . .' Frank shook his head sadly. His mind had been filled with images of Hugo in shackles, dark rooms and military men grilling him – grilling him and worse – for information. 'There's a part of me still wonders if there's goodness in him, somewhere. I know it sounds silly, but . . . It couldn't all be lies, could it? A man who could dance like that? A man who knew what *joy* felt like.'

Vivienne looked fondly at Stan and Arthur and said, 'We all start out like that. Little boys and girls. Some of us end up killers. Some of us end up saints. Most of us end up . . . in between, somewhere, just doing the best we can.'

'I think,' and Frank gulped back his tea, struggling with the words, 'I think we shouldn't trust an outsider again, Nancy.

Let's just keep it the five of us, right here, keeping each other safe. That's what I want.' He'd already decided: no matter what miracles Billy had performed for his family, he wasn't going to go back and live with the Brogans. They'd been such estimable hosts, Albert Yard the very best digs in London, but something had shifted in him now. 'I want to be with my family,' he said, and took in Vivienne as well – for they were, all five of them, bound up by blood. 'Even if it means sleeping in the sitting room, until war's at its end. Just the five of us, and never let another soul come near.'

Nancy's hand had closed over his. 'Hugo Lavigne fooled us,' she said, softly. 'But it doesn't mean the world's full of traitors. It doesn't mean everyone's corrupt. What's the point of winning, Frankie, if we just hide away? If we decide everything's already lost? The war's bad enough out there, Frank. We don't have to let it into our hearts.' She buttered him another piece of toast; that was the last of the butter gone, now. She topped it off with the last scrape of marmalade from the pot. 'There's treachery in the world, but there's so much goodness too. And you, Frank, *you* showed that to everyone, on the night of the ball.' Nancy had hold of Frank's hand again. Now, she reached back and took Vivienne's too. 'So let's just hold on, the five of us together. Our little family. Because things are changing now. We mightn't have to hold on for very much longer – and then ... then, when this war's over, when we finally come through – as I *know* we will – we can get on with living.'

The last time Max Allgood was brought to the Hotel Director's door, it was to be welcomed into the grand institution that was the Buckingham Hotel. Today, he stood here alone, knocked on the door, and readied himself to leave. Upstairs, his cases were already packed. Lucille, whose case dangled from his left hand, had been polished inside and out. It was a good thing to set your possessions in order before you left a place.

'Come in,' came the feathery voice of Walter Knave.

So Max opened the door.

From the threshold, he could see the diminutive Hotel Director standing behind his desk, a steaming teacup in his hand.

He noticed he and Mr Knave were not alone.

Perusing the bookshelves on the opposite wall was Mr John Hastings of the Hotel Board.

The plump American man turned to greet Max with a face much less rigid and pinched than Mr Knave's. Rebalancing his spectacles on the bridge of his nose, he invited Max to sit.

Max wasn't sure that he wanted to.

'Mr Knave. Mr Hastings. I got something to say before we start. Now, I know it's not *proper* and I know it ain't *orthodox*, and I know I'm lackin' in all sorts of manners and *et-i-quettes*,' he said the word like it was something from a strange, unknown language, 'but I gotta get it out. I'm sorry. I'm sorry for what I've brought on you, but I want to say this: it's been a *blast*. All those dukes and duchesses, ambassadors and ministers dancing to music *I* wrote? I've imagined my career going a whole load of different ways, sir, but I never imagined playing for kings. So, I'm sorry it had to end this way, but ... we made memories, didn't we? That ball, it won't be forgotten.

'Well, I suppose I'll spare us the heartache and take my leave, gentlemen. Daisy – well, *Ava*, if we're going to go by what's right – took some digs off the Brixton Road, and I reckon we're good there for a few nights. At least, until I figure on what's next.'

He turned on his heel, but at that moment, Mr Knave said, 'Sit down, Mr Allgood. In this present moment, I am still your employer – and I haven't yet instructed you to vacate this office.'

It was only now that Max felt the real tension in the room. The feeling that he was trapped again was growing tighter around him; he had no choice but to sink into the seat in front of Mr Knave's desk.

'Mr Allgood, it goes without saying that I am disappointed beyond measure,' Walter began. 'You must know what kind of risk we were taking in hiring a man of your background. The Buckingham Hotel is a place of old-world values. A place of glamour and grandeur. That we chose to appoint a man whose life has been spent in clubs and bars was risk enough. That we appointed an *American* to an establishment as proudly British as ours was seen, by some, to be an act of indecency. Yet I was convinced, in the end, that we should make our compromises. That we should be willing to come to an accommodation, in order to bring new life and feeling to our ballroom.' Walter shook his head. 'But you lied to us, Mr Allgood – and, by doing so, you put this hotel's most valued asset, its *reputation*, at formidable risk.'

Max gritted his teeth. 'Sir, if you'd give me a few moments, I can—'

'There's no explanation necessary, Max.' John Hastings had stepped away from the bookshelves, and now he too loomed over the table. 'I think we have the full story here.' And he brandished a leaf of paper, which he had just unfurled from the envelope in his hand. 'Harry Dudgeon delivered this to the hotel by hand this morning. He's insisted that we reinstate him as pianist in the Orchestra going forward, and laid out the full chronicle of the story you've been hiding all year.'

It was the first time Max had smarted. 'That's the way it is, then? Harry's to get his way, after all?'

At once, John Hastings tore the envelope in two. Then, he fed each half into the hearth fire flickering behind the grate. 'Mr Dudgeon was fired from his post at the Buckingham Hotel on the night of the Christmas Ball. That hasn't changed. And he is not to be reinstated. If there is one thing I abhor more than a liar, Mr Allgood, it is a blackmail artiste.' He stopped, promptly brushing his hands clean.

'But this still leaves us with a problem,' Walter intervened. 'You brought a woman of some disrepute into our hotel, a woman who is wanted by law enforcement in her own country, a woman who – with your help – assumed a false identity, posing *as your wife*, in order to hide in plain sight.'

'Now, Mr Knave,' Max said, wagging his finger, 'it's not quite true that Daisy's a wanted woman. Wanted by certain nefarious New York types, I'll admit – but I don't believe there's an active police investigation...'

For a moment, there was silence in the study. Max could tell, by the deepening lines on Walter Knave's face, how dearly the old Hotel Director wanted to dismiss him from his sight.

Probably it was a matter of decorum.

Max was learning something new all of the time:

You weren't supposed to talk about mobsters and contract killers in a world as refined as the Buckingham Hotel.

'There is another problem, Mr Allgood,' Walter announced, through gritted teeth.

Amidst the various items piled up on his desk lay a copy of that morning's the *New York Times* newspaper. This he suddenly picked up, then cast down in front of Max.

The headline was familiar. A different iteration of it had been splashed across every front page for the past two days:

JAPAN WARS ON U.S. AND BRITAIN; MAKES SUDDEN ATACK ON HAWAII; HEAVY FIGHTING AT SEA REPORTED

'Pearl Harbor?' Max began, screwing up his eyes in puzzlement. 'Now, Mr Knave, I hardly think you can lay that one at my door...'

'Decorum, Mr Allgood!' Walter suddenly snapped. 'Good God, man, this is no time for making light. This is the most significant moment in the war since France was lost. Everything changes now. The signals have changed. We're on a new track now, and we must get a grasp on it quickly, before our competitors.'

Max flashed a look between Mr Knave and Mr Hastings, uncomprehending. 'Sirs, I was under the impression you'd asked me here to formalise my departure. I'm quite happy to do it without all the *la-di-dah*, if it suits. You gentlemen sound like you've much to be getting on with.' He lifted himself up, loosened his collar in nervous anticipation, and then dared to say the thing he knew would cause them the most consternation: 'Of course, I *did* put on a good show, gentlemen. I *did* entertain them, down there in the Grand. So, if you could see fit to send me on my way with my last pay cheque, I'd be much obliged. Daisy and me, we're gonna need something to get us going...'

'Sit down, Mr Allgood.'

Max was already at the door.

'*Sit down!*' repeated Walter Knave, quite breathless with frustration.

In the end, it was John Hastings' calming eyes that led Max back to his seat. 'What Mr Knave is trying to say, Max, is that the Japanese bombing of Pearl Harbor has changed everything. The world is about to change, once again. There will, very soon, be a very different kind of clientele flocking to London – and our rivals, at the Imperial, the Ritz, the Savoy, will be clamouring to catch as much of it as they can.'

Walter Knave rolled his eyes dramatically. 'The *Americans* are coming.'

'Which means,' John Hastings went on, 'that American money is coming to London as well. And we should like to draw as much of that new business to the Buckingham as is possible, Max. We must not let it slip away.' He clicked his fingers. 'So now we come to it. This situation is not ideal – it presents us with some significant *challenges* – but having a fêted American musician at the head of our Orchestra may be advantageous in the year to come. As such...'

Max could hardly believe what he was hearing when John Hastings added, 'We would like to see if we can come to a new accommodation.'

'Why don't we keep it simple? Why don't you just say what you mean? Am I... am I being kicked outta the hotel, or not?'

Walter shook his head wearily once again. 'There is a world of nuance to attend to, Mr Allgood, but... The Hotel Board has decided that this is a situation that might be managed. A scandal that, with some deftness – and some hefty payments to certain newspapermen – might be tidied away.'

'It has been the subject of much debate at the Board,' John Hastings went on, 'but we think the advantages of retaining your services outweigh the costs incurred in keeping this secret. Of course, it helps that we had another eye-catching situation develop at Christmas in Exile.'

It helped, too, that the security services were instrumental in tidying away the drama of Hugo Lavigne, his purpose in the ballroom, and the narrow escape M. de Gaulle had, quite without knowing it, made on the night of the ball. A secret kept in the national interest also turned out, in that case, to be beneficial for the Buckingham Hotel as well.

'It has been decided,' said Mr Hastings, 'that your cousin must never show her face at the Buckingham Hotel again. It goes without saying, of course, that she is not welcome as a resident in these halls – and, regrettably, it has also been decided that, for reasons of decorum, it would be better if you yourself found alternative accommodation. Under the circumstances, no stipend will be made to your salary to help with new costs incurred – I hope that is understandable to you, Max.'

Max's eyes were as wide as saucers. 'Absolutely none of it's understandable, Mr Hastings. Absolutely none of it! I thought I was about to spend my own Christmas in exile. Now you're telling me ...'

'It comes with certain conditions, Max.'

'What conditions are they?'

'Your absolute silence,' said Mr Knave.

'And your absolute honesty, from this point on,' Mr Hastings went on.

'Unfortunately, you have unwittingly become this hotel's most prized asset. You may thank the Japanese for that. So let us draw a line now. Your next engagement comes on Saturday night. I expect your Orchestra to be on top form, Mr Allgood.' Walter Knave sat back at his desk and started shuffling papers. 'Oh, and one more thing, Mr Allgood, before you leave.'

Max was already on his feet, swinging Lucille as he beat a perplexed retreat the door.

'Yes, sir?'

Walter Knave fixed him with a knowing look. 'You may begin auditioning new pianists at your leisure.'

The news of the Japanese attack on Pearl Harbor was being gossiped about even in the chambermaids' kitchenette, but Annie Brogan wasn't sure what to make of any of it.

Whatever the future might bring, she was grateful for the

opportunity not to talk about it tonight. Leaving the kitchenette behind, the girls gathering around the wireless and the BBC news, she scurried down through the hotel's many layers until she found Victor waiting at the tradesman's entrance.

'Can you believe it?' he ventured, as they tramped along the snowbound mews. 'First, the ball and then...' There were whispers, all across the Buckingham Hotel, that something terrible had befallen the ball. The kitchen hands said they'd heard gunshots fired on Berkeley Square. One of the porters had been watching from the windows as a flotilla of black Bentleys screeched around the hotel's colonnade and the dashing French dancer was wrestled to the ground.

There was no need for gossip when it came to the news, though. The devastation of Pearl Harbor was no mere rumour. There it was, splashed across the pages of every newspaper in the hotel.

'Oh, I don't want to talk about that,' said Annie, shivering into the wind rolling up Regent Street. 'We can't help that, Victor. We can't change that. Let's just...' The omnibus was almost upon them; Annie put out a hand to hail it down. 'I'm more nervous about you meeting my ma and pa than about the Americans,' she said, with a crumpled grin.

In the old days, Annie wouldn't have knocked at her own front door – but today it seemed right.

She needn't have bothered; it took only seconds for the door to open up, revealing her big brother Billy standing on the step.

'Get yourself in here, Annie Brogan!' Billy beamed. 'Get on in. Wait until you see...'

A wave of good feeling crashed over Annie as she stepped through the doors. Suddenly, her mother and father had appeared from some inner room and, together, they helped her out of her coat. After a hurried introduction, she and Victor were being swept along the hallway, drawn to the sitting room by a combination of her parents' excited voices and a strange kind of gravity. Through these doors was the scene of every Brogan celebration, every family argument, every family renewal. Six months ago, she'd been certain it was gone forever.

Now, somehow, even the *smell* was the same.

It was this that made every doubt Annie had been harbouring fade suddenly away. This wasn't just a recreation of her home; this *was* her home.

'It's still a bit empty, of course,' Mrs Brogan began, 'but there's enough to be getting on with. We'll have a bedroom for you by Christmas night.'

'And … look!' declared Mr Brogan.

An old wooden trunk was open at his feet, and spilling from it all the paper chains, tinsels and baubles that decorated the Brogan house each Yuletide. There was yet more magic in seeing this; Annie had thought it lost to the fires – but evidently some things had been unearthed intact. She dropped to her knees, urging Victor to do the same, and trailed the old paper chains through her fingers.

She turned around the room, taking in the new picture rails, the hooks on the wall. Some of it was different from how it used to be, but only ever so slightly; Annie had never imagined that Billy's memory could be so precise. Tentative at first, she lifted one of the old wreaths from the wooden trunk and took it to the hook above the hearth. 'Shall I?' she said, grinning back at the rest of the family.

'One moment, Annie,' Mr Brogan grinned. Then, turning to Victor and Billy, he said, 'I'll need some help with this, gentlemen.'

Annie hadn't dared to imagine there might be a tree this year, but moments later it was being hauled into the room by the three men, its boughs still tied back in string so that it could slide, unmolested, through the doors. As Mr Brogan snipped each strand, the branches popped out. 'Well, go on, Annie,' Mrs Brogan beamed. 'You can get started now. We can *all* get started.'

'I think this calls for some music,' Mr Brogan declared.

From somewhere, there appeared a gramophone. From somewhere else, a record was drawn from its sleeve. Annie had little idea whether these were the genuine relics of their past, or just imitations brought in to replace what was lost – but, when she heard the first song begin, none of that seemed to matter.

'*Silent night, holy night!*'

Annie's heart was bursting with warmth.

'*All is calm, all is bright*'

She looked at Victor, busily dangling stars on strings from the picture rail above the hearth.

'*Round yon Virgin, Mother and Child.*
Holy infant so tender and mild
Sleep in heavenly peace,
Sleep in heavenly peace.'

She gazed at her brother. All of the things he'd done – the larders plundered, the Housekeeping stores pillaged, the countless little thefts that made up his enterprise – it had all been for this. And yet ... she knew it had ended some weeks ago. She knew he'd not been able to finish the way that he'd started. Her brother was, perhaps, the most resourceful man she'd ever known. 'Tell me, Billy,' she whispered, sidling close to him, the music drowning out her words. 'After all that unpleasantness, how *did* you find the money to finish it off?'

Billy looked her in the eye. 'Oh, just jobs around the hotel,' he said. 'Christmas tips from the guests. You'd be surprised how generous folks can be, if you help them with their letters. There's a lot of rich folks at the hotel. And ...'

Billy might have said more then – but, at that moment, Mrs Brogan reappeared from the kitchen, bringing with her a tray full of steaming mugs of cocoa. The first, she pressed upon Victor. 'That's for all your hard work, young man. And ... Annie's father and I have been thinking. We should very much like it if you and your mother might join us for Christmas Day. Now, we haven't actually consulted Annie on this,' and here she turned to her daughter, 'but I rather think it might be something *she'd* like too ...'

Annie felt the blood rushing to her cheeks.

'Oh, Mrs Brogan,' Victor said, with an air of exemplary politeness, 'that would have been just wonderful ... except, I'm just so sorry, but my mother's already made plans. Our cousins are coming. There'll be six of us, if I'm right. My mother's baking a chicken. Well, she's been so keen to use her new kitchen. We're to move into a new house too, you see. With luck, we'll get the keys the week before Christmas.'

Annie's face blanched. Her eyes furrowed. She fixed Victor with a questioning look, because until this moment she hadn't known that such change was afoot in Victor's life; he hadn't breathed a word of the change.

'New Year then,' Mrs Brogan declared. 'As soon as you're settled, young man, I'll expect you at our table.'

Mrs Brogan was beaming as she swept on to deliver the next mug of cocoa to her husband, but only confusion coloured Annie's face. 'You didn't say,' she ventured. 'A new house, Victor? But ... but where are you going?'

'Oh, it isn't far,' said Victor, and it seemed to Annie, then, that he was deliberately avoiding looking her in the eye. 'You must come, Annie. I should like that. Yes, and—'

'But h-how, Victor? I thought ...' *That times were tough*, she wanted to say. *That you were scraping pennies together, struggling with ration books, dependent on your pay each week from the Buckingham Hotel.* Then she remembered that afternoon they'd gone shopping along Regent Street; her purse had just about stretched to a currant bun, while Victor happily perused the displays at Bickerdyke's Leathersmiths in the arcade. 'Victor?'

At last, he looked up. At least he had the decency to look embarrassed. His face was suddenly flushed even redder than it was at the end of a long Queen Mary shift.

'I've been doing some extra shifts,' he mumbled. 'Extra jobs at the hotel. Running errands for Mr Laurent, you know...'

Annie felt the world falling away.

Her eyes darted sideways, where Billy was hanging sprigs of holly on the wall.

Extra jobs.

Running errands.

She'd heard those words before.

Sometimes, when you reach an understanding, it feels like the world has jolted on its axis. So it was for Annie Brogan. Everything felt suddenly wrong. Everything felt *dirty.* The lies were filling the air around her, choking her, making her gag. She'd been so full of joy only moments ago. Now she understood how blighted that joy truly was.

'Oh, Victor,' she gasped, with her eyes still fixed on Billy. 'You didn't...'

Annie didn't wait for a response. She could see it all now. The seams where the lies didn't quite fit together.

There was only one thing to dispel this feeling of sickness, so she clattered across the sitting room, down the long hall and straight out of the front door.

The blackout was not yet in effect, though the afternoon was hardening to night. She tumbled down the steps of Number 62

Albert Yard and reeled along the ravaged road, all the visions she'd had of her perfect Christmas disintegrating before her eyes.

Halfway along the road, she could hear Victor calling her name – but the footsteps that clattered behind her surely did not belong to him, because his voice faded the further she fled. She had almost reached the end of the road, coming past the hoardings that hid the devastated corner shop, when Billy's hand landed on her shoulder. She reeled round, if only to shake him off, and saw him standing there, panting for breath, pleading her with his eyes.

His injured leg was paining him. He clung to it tightly, and it was only this that kept Annie from shaking him off and fleeing again.

'Annie, it isn't what you think. Victor needed a little help, that's all. And ... well, so did I. People have got to help each other. You see that, don't you, Annie?'

Annie spat, 'Then it's exactly what I think. Oh Billy, you *promised*. You swore! And instead you ...'

Billy looked back. 'You saw the look on their faces, Annie. I couldn't leave it unfinished. It's Ma and Pa. They been through enough—'

'And *Victor*? My ... my Victor?'

At last, Victor had appeared behind Billy. Sheepishly, he looked at Annie. 'You're angry with me,' he said. 'Oh, Annie, I didn't want to make you angry. But ... you *knew* it was Billy, didn't you? You knew and you didn't tell me.'

'He *promised* he'd stopped,' Annie sobbed.

Billy went to hug her, but she staggered back.

'I *did* stop,' he said, 'but ... things got complicated again. I know you can't see it. I know you don't understand. But right and wrong, they're not always straightforward, and I ...'

'You *hired* Victor.'

The two boys drew alongside each other. Annie looked from one to the other, the two most important young men in her life, and wondered for the first time if she could tell the difference between the two.

'I'd gone to the kitchens,' Billy explained, 'thinking all I needed was one last trip into the larders ... and there he was, just setting off for home. And it got me thinking: well, our family's not the only one in need, is it? You said it yourself, Annie. You're the one who told me. Victor's father's in an internment camp. His mother can hardly make ends meet, even with all that Victor brings back from the hotel. Maybe there was a way I could help him. And if *I* could help him, well, maybe we could help each other.'

'It wasn't so dangerous, Annie,' Victor chipped in. 'It's easy to hide it, when you work in the kitchens. You know what's about to spoil. You know what's coming in on the orders. It's just a little dance around the edges. That's all it is. And ... nobody's getting hurt.' And at last Victor said the words Annie had heard so many times before. 'They don't ration the rich.'

Billy looked back along the devastated road. 'We don't have to go much longer, Annie. Really, we don't. But Ma and Pa need furniture to make that house a home. Pa still doesn't have work. And Victor's ma – well, she needs a helping hand too. Once it's sorted, we'll stop. I promise, Annie. I *promise*.'

Annie felt a burning in her gorge. Was it truly possible that a person might throw up from pure disgust? 'You said that once before ...'

There was silence.

Only silence, up and down Albert Yard.

Fat flakes of snow had started to fall in between them. To Annie, it made Billy and Victor seem even further away.

'*Walking in a winter wonderland ...*'

'It can be over even more quickly if – if you'd help us, Annie.' Billy took a step forward. 'A hand in Housekeeping, and we'd be finished so much sooner.'

'Billy Brogan, you're a fool. Lie to me as much as you want! Lie to the world, if you like! But don't you *dare* lie to yourself.' Annie pawed at her eyes, unable to stop the tears from falling. 'Look around you, Bill. Look at the ruined homes. There'll *always* be somebody else to help. There'll *always* be some reason not to stop. First it was the house – the roof and walls! Now, it's … Victor's house, and furniture for both, and, and …'

'The war keeps rolling, Annie. Don't you want to feel *safe?* Don't you want our parents to …'

Annie took a ragged breath. 'Of course I do.'

Billy took another step towards her, sliding through the veil of snow. 'It'll work out, Annie. It's worked out so far. And do you know why?' He flashed a nervous look at Victor. 'Because we're in it together. We've all got something to lose. Any one of us spills this secret, and we'd *all* be in trouble. *All* of us, Annie. Even you …'

'Me?' she gasped. '*Me?*'

'Oh, Annie, of course. You've known about it for months – and you didn't breathe a word. What do you think Mrs de Guise would make of that, if she ever found out? I'm sorry, Annie. I didn't want you mixed up in it all. I really tried to keep it to myself … but here we are.' At last, he was close enough that he could drape his arm around her shoulder. This time, Annie did not have the fury to cast him off, to stagger back. For the first time, Billy had the decency to look anguished at what he'd done. 'I'm sorry, Annie. You got to believe how sorry I am. But me, you and Victor – we're in this together now. And you can help. You *can*. With you, we could really make it work. I'm sorry,

Annie.' Billy looked wan, but at least he tried to smile. 'You're working with us now.'

Across London, the snow was tumbling down. In a house in Maida Vale, a patchwork family held their children up to the windows to watch the big fat flakes settling upon the Anderson shelter in the garden. In the ostentatious environs of Berkeley Square, the Buckingham Hotel swarmed with both diplomats and spies, while a reprieved trombonist walked bow-legged through the empty ballroom and marvelled that his countrymen were coming, that he'd been given a second chance to forge a home here among the great, the garlanded and good. And, on a street corner in devastated Lambeth, a young chambermaid saw her future unfolding before her – and wasn't sure what chilled her most, the ceaseless march of the war, the bitter touch of the coming winter night, or the way her black marketeer brother smiled at her as he welcomed her into his trade.

War marches on.

War changes everything.

From the city streets around us to the souls we carry within, not a thing remains unscathed.

Epilogue

British Military Barracks, Kasr-el-Nil, Cairo

10th December, 1941

The sun had been relentless over the barracks at Kasr-el-Nil, but as evening threw its cloak across Cairo, the ferociousness was slowly being sapped out of the heat.

When the telephone rang in the subalterns' office, the clerk who took the call was already prepared. 'Yes, sir,' he began, 'I can confirm it's secure, sir. All the checks have been certified. Yes, sir. He's waiting right here, sir.' Then he looked up at the dark-haired lieutenant waiting in the corner. 'It's all yours, de Guise. I'm under orders to leave this between you, but rest assured I'll be waiting outside. You're to report to the captain as soon as you're finished.'

As soon as the subalterns' office door closed, Lieutenant Raymond de Guise bent over the table and put the telephone receiver to his ear. 'Sir?'

The voice that came buzzing down the line was one that brought such rich, vivid memories back to Raymond. In the oppressive heat of Cairo, it was difficult to recall his days gracing the dance floor at the Buckingham Hotel – but the deep, dulcet tones of Maynard Charles brought its every detail back to mind.

'Lieutenant, there's much I'm not able to say of the events that have unfolded over the last few days, but I do have authority to tell you that, thanks to the information you relayed, arrests have been made – and that the dance troupe you once led now has a gaping hole in its heart.'

Raymond exhaled. So, then, Hugo Lavigne was no longer a problem. 'And my wife ...'

'She was kept at a distance from the action.' Maynard Charles paused. 'Alas, your brother-in-law was not so fortunate.'

Panic creased Raymond's features. Frank might have been a grown man, but in Raymond's heart he would always be a boy – and boys as innocent, as naïve, as Frank did not deserve to be dragged into this war. 'Sir, please tell me—'

'He lives, Lieutenant. He has been shaken up, but no more than that. And yet ... Mr Nettleton's condition prefigures the purpose of my call. You will be aware, by now, that this war of ours is about to take a most interesting turn. London is about to change again. So too the Buckingham Hotel. And our experience in the ballroom has prompted a certain panic in the Office – a panic that we have not, in fact, had eyes and ears where we must; a panic that we have been blind to certain goings-on at the Buckingham Hotel; panic that we have not been as in control of the situation in London as we had thought. The Buckingham is not just the home of displaced governments, Lieutenant. It has become a sorting house for enemy spies, and the last days have shown us how remiss we have been in overseeing the situation.

'Lieutenant, the hotel is about to be filled with our American friends. I need eyes on them – the eyes of someone I trust – and I am afraid my faith in Frank Nettleton has been tested. He is a brave young man, an impassioned young man – we have much to be grateful for in that – but as a trusted pair of eyes, a man capable of secrecy, lies, subterfuge? Well, doubts abound in the Office. He was foolhardy in the Grand; he was instrumental in the events of that night, but in being so he directly contravened his orders not to insert himself into the action. No, we shall not call on Mr Nettleton's services again.'

Raymond hesitated. Some inkling of what Maynard might have been asking had begun to stir, deep inside.

'Lieutenant, have you ever considered that there might be a future for you beyond the infantry? A way to serve your King and Country that does not involve your sacrifice in the desert?'

'Mr Charles, you might have to be more clear with me.'

'Oh, Lieutenant,' Maynard laughed, 'you'll have to learn to cope with a little lack of clarity. We are fighting the same war, Raymond, but not with the same weapons. Yours have been the tank and rifle. Mine are guile and secrets, misinformation and whispered words.' Maynard Charles stopped. 'Enough, Lieutenant. There is much business to attend to, before the Americans land on these shores. They are to be our allies, of course, but their presence here will present certain challenges and we are all eager to be ahead of the game. Raymond, I am in need of a certain kind of man. A man who has already proven how smoothly he can slip between different worlds. A man of self-assurance and charm; a man whom others might take into their confidence, even while the counsel he keeps is his own. A man who already knows his way around the Buckingham Hotel. My eyes and ears in the Grand...'

In the sweltering heat of the subaltern's office, Raymond closed his eyes. An image coursed across him: the Grand Ballroom at the height of summer, the hotel buzzing with its new American clientele, the new Orchestra in the ballroom swinging to the sounds he'd first heard in the Cotton Club, that season he'd been in the States.

His wife Nancy, standing framed in the ballroom doors.

His infant son, on whom he'd never yet laid eyes.

'What do you think then, Raymond? I have already been

granted the authority to make this happen. A change of pace, perhaps. A mission, for which you might be the only suitable candidate in all of the world.' Maynard paused before going on. 'Raymond, old friend, it should please me no end if you might agree to work for me again ...'

Acknowledgements

To my wife, Hannah, my children, George and Henrietta, and my family. Thank you for supporting me in everything I do. I love you!

To my manager and friend, Melissa Chappell, thank you for your loyalty and endeavour and for listening to all my ideas. I love that I can now say I'm a dancer, a judge and an author!

A huge thank you to Kerr MacRae, my literary agent. Thank you for always being there. Without your guidance and expertise none of this would have happened.

A big shout out also to my Orion publishing team: to Sam Eades and Snigdha Koirala for their editorial expertise, to Lynsey Sutherland and Yadira da Trindade for their marketing magic, and to Francesca Pearce and Frankie Banks for pulling together a brilliant PR campaign. Thank you also to the Sales team for promoting my books with such energy, and to Paul Stark and Jake Alderson for another stunning audiobook edition.

To Lou Plank and the team at Plank PR, thank you for your endless support and enthusiasm. To Yvonne Chappell, thank you for always picking up the phone and always knowing what I'm meant to be doing. And to Scott and David at Bungalow Industries, I appreciate all your hard work, support and positive feedback more than I can say.

Last but by no means least, the biggest thank you to book-sellers and my readers all over the world, for being such fantastic advocates for my books. I am so grateful for all your support, you are the reason I tell stories. I loved writing about Raymond's adventures as a young man in Paris, and hope you love this book too.

Much love,
Anton

Credits

Anton du Beke and Orion Fiction would like to thank everyone at Orion who worked on the publication of *The Paris Affair* in the UK.

Editorial
Sam Eades
Snigdha Koirala

Copy editor
Francine Brody

Proof reader
Liz Hatherell

Audio
Paul Stark
Jake Alderson

Design
Tomás Almeida
Joanna Ridley
Charlotte Abrams-Simpson

Editorial Management
Charlie Panayiotou
Jane Hughes
Bartley Shaw

Finance
Jasdip Nandra
Nick Gibson
Sue Baker

Marketing
Brittany Sankey

Production
Ameenah Khan

Publicity
Frankie Banks

Sales
Jen Wilson
Esther Waters
Victoria Laws
Toluwalope Ayo-Ajala
Rachael Hum
Ellie Kyrke-Smith
Sinead White
Georgina Cutler

Contracts
Dan Herron
Ellie Bowker

Operations
Jo Jacobs
Dan Stevens